IT TAKES ALL KINDS OF MEN
TO FIGHT A WAR

SERGEANT JACK KELLY
Man of the world, veteran of two wars, wooer
of women from Stuttgart to Seoul. His hustle—
trading weapons and supplies under the table
for any outfit with the cash to pay.

SERGEANT JIM ASPBY
Man on the run, uneasy lover and father, proud
member of the U.S. Army. His hope—that the
real heroism of GI's on the front lines might rub
off on him.

WARRANT OFFICER
PRUDHOMME
Man with a mission, a good military cop, a
close acquaintance of evil's true face. His oath:
to nail Harry Scheldt, a criminal and killer
with powerful connections to the Army's upper
ranks.

THE SOLDIER'S PRIZE

THE SOLDIER'S PRIZE

Dan Cragg

BALLANTINE BOOKS • NEW YORK

Grateful acknowledgment is made to the following for permission to reprint previously published material:

Arkham House Publishers, Inc.: excerpts from "The Whisperer in Darkness" by H.P. Lovecraft from *The Dunwich Horror and Others* (1963).

Yale University Press: excerpts from the Tale of Kieu by Nguyen Du; translated by Huynh Sanh Thong. Reprinted by permission of the publisher.

Library of Congress Catalog Card Number: 86-90948

ISBN 0-345-33526-0

Manufactured in the United States of America

First Edition: December 1986

Author's Note

Although this is a work of fiction, much of it is based on historical facts and I believe the reader should know where the story line departs from those facts.

The Eighteenth U.S. Infantry Division of this story is fictional but modeled on the organization and area of operations of the real Twenty-fifth Infantry Division in Vietnam. My description of the Eighteenth Division otherwise bears no resemblance to the real unit, its activities in the Vietnam War, or the men who served in it.

The Viet Cong Ninth Division did exist, but its strength and operations are inventions of my own. The South Vietnamese Fifth Division was also real and, during the time I was with it, based at Bien Hoa, South Vietnam. Likewise, the 199th Light Infantry Brigade was real, and the events described in the chapter titled "Mocking the Midnight Bell" are based on an actual operation that occurred in the general area described; the officers and men of the brigade, as they appear in this story, however, are purely fictional characters.

Fort Sherman, Missouri, is loosely based on Fort Leonard Wood, which is near Waynesville, in Pulaski County, Missouri. There all similarities end.

The events of Tet 1968 are composites of two real attacks on the city of Saigon. "Second Tet," as it is often called, occurred in June 1968. To the best of my knowledge, however, no enlisted billet in the city of Saigon was ever directly attacked or penetrated by the enemy during either offensive. The John Houston Bachelor Enlisted Quarters (BEQ) really existed, however, and in June 1968, some of the heaviest fighting occurred less than a thousand yards from there.

There really was a place called the Free World Military Assistance Office in Saigon, at number 12 Tran Quoc Toan Boulevard.

The Metropole BEQ was real, and it was bombed by

the Viet Cong on December 2, 1965. Other places are also real: the Plaza, the White, the International, the Fitzsimons, and the Town House BEQs. Streets, neighborhoods, cafes (particularly Le Cabanon and the Hien Doi), landmarks, sights, sounds, and ambience of the city of Saigon (she will *never* be Ho Chi Minh City to those who loved her) are as I remember them.

The quotes from Nguyen Du's epic poem, *Kim Van Kieu*, are from the magnificent bilingual edition translated by Huynh Sanh Thong and published by Yale University Press (New Haven: 1983), and appear here with the kind permission of the publisher.

I want to thank Owen Lock for making this book possible and Jeremiah Post, who, while he was never there, nonetheless lived through all of it.

For gold the merchant ploughs the main,
   The farmer ploughs the manor;
But glory is the sodger's prize,
   The sodger's wealth is honour!
               —Robert Burns

Prologue

From far away came the staccato rattle of machine-gun fire. It sounded eerie to Jim Aspby, like the memory of a war fought long ago, but it was only the Seventh Regiment hurrying to catch up with the main body of the division before darkness finally closed in. They were coming up a road from the west, and they were coming fast, just barreling along and blasting away at the countryside. "Reconnaissance by fire," an officer remarked dryly. The division had been out along the Cambodia-Vietnam border for two weeks now, chasing elusive Viet Cong guerrillas, and all Aspby could think about was getting back to the American advisers' compound at the base camp, where he could unpack his gear and sleep between sheets instead of on an air mattress. He shivered under his poncho.

"How far you suppose we are from Bien Hoa?" he asked Frank Symonds, the radioman.

"Doggone if Ah know," Symonds drawled.

The convoy had been on the road since dawn and had

only made thirty miles toward home. The rain, intermittent all day, was now a damp mist that covered everything with a shiny coat of wetness.

Nobody knew why they had stopped this time. All day long it had been start, roll a few miles, stop; start again, roll a few more miles, and stop again. Maybe they were waiting for the Seventh Regiment to join up; possibly the engineers had found booby traps up ahead. Vehicles were strung out along the narrow road as far as Aspby could see in either direction. Soldiers swarmed everywhere, stretching, urinating, horsing around, trying to work off their irritation at being cooped up in trucks and jeeps all day long.

A tall officer stepped up to Aspby's jeep. It was Lieutenant Colonel Hatcher, the division G-4 adviser, the detachment's logistics expert. Hatcher's black hair, mustache, and wrinkled, perpetually sun-browned face made him look like a Mexican. He claimed to own a ranch somewhere in the southwestern United States, and he was always saying how one day he would retire there and raise horses, but Aspby knew him for nothing but a big talker. The colonel was always giving Aspby long and complicated reports to type, and each time Hatcher promised him a bottle of bourbon in return. The whiskey had never been delivered, but the reports kept coming.

"Well, men," Hatcher drawled, "it's the beginnin' of the end for 'em." He meant the Communist guerrillas, but he nodded toward a grove of trees rising out of the mist about a hundred yards off the road. "I was up to Lai Cat in the old man's chopper yesterday, 'n' they was bombin' 'n' strafin' the poor bastards. They's livin' like rats out there in the jungles and I kinda feel sorry for 'em. I tell you, this war's just about over."

"Yes, sir," Aspby replied. "The only war we got, 'n' it's almost over."

Hatcher patted Aspby on the shoulder and sauntered on down the road.

The sound of machine-gun fire had grown louder in the past few minutes. The Seventh was closing. That might mean the convoy would be on its way shortly. Aspby shivered again, this time at an all-too-familiar weakness in his guts. Two months ago, during an operation in Phuoc Tuy Province, they'd had to call in a special chopper to take him back to Bien Hoa with a case of amoebic dysentery. I hope I'm not coming down with it again, he thought. It had been an ordeal: high fever alternating with chills, and his insides oozing out in a watery gruel.

The weakness passed, and he felt better. He breathed in the chill air deeply. It was clean and carried the smell of growing things, and somehow made everything seem more important than it had a few moments before. Suddenly he didn't want to go home, he didn't want to sleep in a real bed again, he didn't want to be dry and warm and drinking a cold beer. In fact, if it meant leaving Vietnam, Jim Aspby didn't want the war to end. But it was ending. Col. Hatcher was right. Everyone was saying the same thing. It was November 1962, Jim Aspby had been in South Vietnam just about a year, and the greatest event in his life was coming to an end. First thing Monday morning, he promised himself, he would go see Sergeant Major Oates at corps headquarters and extend his tour another six months. If I can't stay here for the rest of my army career, he told himself, at least I can be one of the last Americans to leave.

"Light's fading quick," Symonds muttered. "Hope the hell we get on before it gets dark. This is ambush country after dark."

Aspby sighed and fixed his attention on the palm grove just visible through the swirling mist. The handguard of his carbine was slick with moisture. This strip of road was almost painfully beautiful now even in the rain. What would it look like in good weather? he wondered. Suddenly he wanted the day to be warm and dry and bright, and he yearned to be alone in this spot with a picnic basket and Miss Hoa, a cheerful, full-breasted young clerk-typist back at division headquarters. Perhaps they could sit under those trees and eat and drink and tell each other all about themselves. After a while, lulled by the warm day, the wine, and her lilting accent, he would drop off into a light sleep. Later, he would gallantly offer to drive her into Saigon, to save her the long bus ride she took every day from the Bien Hoa station. She would accept gratefully and demurely, although she would be pleasantly embarrassed at the attention. Then, laughing and joking, they would enjoy a pleasant ride all the way to her home, which, he imagined, would be in one of Saigon's cool and quiet suburbs. There he would meet her family. He would sit stiffly and formally across the table from her older brother—no, her father—sip a lukewarm beer and exchange courtesies as she translated for them. Her parents would not be at all alarmed that their daughter had just spent the day out in the provinces with a foreigner because they would sense he was an upright and honorable man.

With the Vietnamese, Aspby always felt important, upright, and honorable. They were so polite and deferential toward American guests in their homes that it was impossible not to like them—even if, as he realized, many only wanted American friends for the cheap watches, radios, cosmetics, and detergents they could get at the post exchange. No matter. He still loved the attention. In fact, from the moment he had set foot on the ground at Tan Son Nhut Airport, everything about Vietnam had worked its magic on him—the people, the climate, the land itself.

"Goddamn, I love this place," he whispered to himself.

"What's that, Jim?" Symonds asked.

"Nothing, Frank," Aspby replied, embarrassed at his daydream, "nothing. Just nothing."

Thirty months later, after spending time at an army school for administrators at Fort Benjamin Harrison and in Germany, Aspby found himself on a long flight from Travis Air Force Base to Tan Son Nhut for the second time in his life. During those months, the

United States had decided to make a firm stand against communism in Vietnam, and Aspby saw his opportunity to help and support the two countries he loved. He volunteered for a second tour.

Just Behind the Battle, Mother

SERGEANT FIRST CLASS JACK KELLEY ALWAYS KNEW that sooner or later Sergeant Major Tom Riley would get even with him, and when Jack arrived at Fort Sherman and discovered that Riley was the post sergeant major there, he knew the accounting would come soon. Actually, it took Riley about six months.

Jack and Riley never had liked one another, but the feud had had its beginnings when they served together at Ferris Barracks in Erlangen, just outside Nürnberg, Germany, back in 1957. The occasion had been a troop information and education class (TI&E) one Saturday morning in the post theater. The subject was the recent report of the Cordiner Committee, a study group established by the secretary of defense in March 1956 and headed by Ralph J. Cordiner, president of General Electric, to study the enlisted grade structure of the army. The object of the study was to find out how the army and the other services could alter the grade structure in order to retain good men in the top enlisted ranks. Among other things, Cordiner had recommended establishing two new enlisted grades, E-8 and E-9 (sergeant major), in order to give long-service noncoms and noncoms on the rise someplace to go other than back into civilian life. In those days, top enlisted grades ended at E-7, master sergeant in the army.

During the question-and-answer period Riley had stood up and launched into a vigorous speech in praise of the recommendation. He was a master sergeant, at the top of the ladder, and every man in the audience knew his praise was motivated by pure self-interest. Many of them were draftees who cordially despised their senior NCOs, and they concluded on the spot that the Cordiner proposals were the most arrant nonsense anybody had ever heard of. Sergeants were an insufferable lot as they were; what would they be like if the army added two more grades to their ranks?

Despite the hooting and occasional catcalls that greeted Riley's remarks, things would have been all right if he had not made the disastrous mistake of referring to the new ranks by an expression that was only then becoming current: "supergrades."

Upon hearing this word, Jack jumped up and shouted, "Hey, Sarge, we'll call the E-nine 'Super Senior Sarge,' and he'll be issued a lined cape and two E-sevens just to keep it off the ground as he inspects the garbage cans behind the second platoon's barracks!"

A dead silence lasting all of three seconds followed this remark, and then pandemonium reigned as two hundred men laughed, shouted, screamed, and whistled their total approval of Jack's wit and courage for having shut up Master Sergeant Tom Riley once and for all.

The incident had become famous, and the nickname "Super Senior Sarge" stuck to Riley ever after. He had never forgiven Jack for that. Now, on a Friday in April, 1965, Riley was about to get his long awaited revenge.

The summons to report to the post sergeant major's office had come after reveille formation. Jack had just dismissed his platoon when the company first sergeant called him aside.

"Jack, Riley wants to see you up at post head-quarters."

"Well, shit! It's about time," Jack had said. That had been at six-thirty in the morning. First Jack had a leisurely breakfast, and then he returned to his room in the barracks and changed into his dress uniform. Then he visited his duty section for a while. It was past nine o'clock before he finally showed up in Riley's office.

The post sergeant major's secretary was at least sixty but always tried to make herself look younger by the lavish use of makeup. This morning she had failed again.

"I have an appointment with Sergeant Major Riley, Miss Gritz," Jack announced. He wrinkled his nose. Miss Gritz reeked of cheap perfume.

"What time?" she demanded. Her voice sounded like fingernails scraping across a blackboard.

"Ole Riley didn't say."

Miss Gritz bridled at the disrespectful remark. "Well, sit down over there, and he'll call for you when he wants you." She extended a bony forefinger in the direction of a straight-backed wooden chair against one wall.

Jack sat. The cloying scent of Miss Gritz's perfume was almost too much to endure at first, but as the minutes dragged by, Jack's sense of smell began to deaden. He fished a pack of cigarettes out of his left sock and lit one. Good NCOs never carried anything in the pockets of their uniform coats because the bulges made them look unmilitary.

"I would appreciate it if you didn't do that in here. The smoke gets in my hair," Miss Gritz explained. Jack wondered if her perfume would linger on his uniform.

"I'll finish it in the hallway, then."

"Better not do that, Sergeant. The sergeant major might call for you at any time, and you should be ready."

"I'll be in the hallway when he wants me," he said, stepping through the door.

He smoked slowly, taking in the tempo of the headquarters building. Riley's office was next to the commanding general's, where a constant stream of officers came and went. He knew staff work for what it was—stupidity. On the staff, men rushed around responding to artificial crises deliberately invented to keep them on their toes. No officer he had ever known *liked* duty on the staff, but they all *wanted* it because a successful assignment there looked good on an officer's record. As a matter of fact, it looked good on an enlisted man's record, too.

Yet there was something about an army staff that excited Jack: a feeling of importance at being an insider close to the center of power and decision. Jack thrived on being at the center of things. If his job at the post quartermaster depot had consisted only of running humdrum office operations, he would have stifled. But Jack had made of the job what he wanted.

When the first sergeant at the Fort Sherman replacement company had first wrangled Jack Kelley an assignment to the post ration breakdown point, he suspected that putting Jack in there was something like introducing a vampire into a bloodbank. But he never regretted it.

"Frankly, Top," Jack told him shortly after his arrival at the post, "I don't give a shit where you send me. I didn't want to come to this place to begin with, and I plan on staying here only as long as it takes to politic me another assignment."

"That ain't a very regular army gung-ho attitude, Kelley," the first sergeant replied, running a hand over his smooth, bullet-shaped head. All first sergeants, in Jack's experience, had smooth, bullet-shaped heads and the personalities to go with them.

" 'N' just where is it you want to go, Kelley?" the first sergeant asked amiably.

"Anyplace I can get rich without goin' to jail for it."

The first sergeant laughed in a deep basso. "Har, har, Kelley, you're a card! Wasn't you in Vietnam, with the old MAAG, a few years back? 'N' don't I 'member you from somewheres in Korea, back about ten years ago?"

"Right, Top. I was with headquarters command in the MAAG and Eighth Army HQ, fifty-four to fifty-five."

"Yeah." The first sergeant put his hands behind his neck and leaned back in his chair. "You got a reputation for takin' care of yer friends, Kelley. Right?"

"I never fucked anybody yet, Top."

"Well, buddy, I know you ain't no quartermaster man, but yer records show you're a damned good administrator. They need a guy who can handle the paperwork down at ration breakdown, 'n' that's where I'm recommendin' the personnel officer put you. Me and Mr. Fitzpatrick are like that." The first sergeant crossed his fingers.

"Is that really the way you are, or is that the way you hope to be?" Jack asked.

The first sergeant laughed. "Boy, Kelley, you sure are a cheeky bastard."

"You know me well enough to call me that, Top?" Jack laughed. "But I *do* take care o' my buddies, First Sergeant."

"'At's what I wanna hear, Kelley. 'At's just what I wanna hear."

And Jack did take care of the first sergeant, the personnel officer, everyone, even the civilian employees, and especially the post's mess sergeants. All of them were padding their headcounts so they could draw extra rations for their personal use. Some traded the rations among other NCOs at the post for things they needed in their own units; others sold cuts of meat and other foodstuffs to the local citizens; and some just fed their families and their friends' families on what they could steal from their messhalls.

Jack never took any direct payment for himself, but he did accept favors from grateful recipients of his managerial talents, and he was always careful to hold aside the best of everything for his best friends.

Before long Jack was on good terms with everyone at Fort Sherman. Everyone, that is, with the notable exception of the post sergeant major.

He strolled out to the front of the building to finish his smoke. The post headquarters sat on a high hill overlooking Fort Sherman. He drank in the scene spread out below: hundreds of two-story, buff-colored wooden buildings with green-shingled roofs lining neatly planned grid squares of roads and blocks. Here and there the spire of army chapels and water towers punctuated the skyline.

Jack recalled the day he had first come to Fort Sherman. It had been an early evening late in November, and a cold wind had been blowing down off the plains of Kansas. He remembered huddling inside his overcoat and shivering. It was a comfortable memory now, in the verdure of spring.

Jack had never been to Fort Sherman before that day in November, but now, as he looked out over the springtime gently enfolding the countryside, he was struck by how much the fort looked just like every other army post he'd ever seen: Fort Dix, Fort Bragg, Fort Sam Houston, Fort Benjamin Harrison, or Fort Sherman—they were all the same. In each barracks, at the end closest to the street, were the cadre rooms, small cubicles assigned to NCOs who had no families. At the rear end, on the ground floor, were the latrines. Upstairs, on that end, would be more cadre rooms. Between the private rooms for NCOs and the latrines, open "bays" slept twenty men to a floor—forty, double-bunked, if the barracks was crowded.

At either end of each building was a porch with dozens of initials carved into the wood. Mops, brooms, and buckets hung from racks fixed to the outside walls. During the week the barracks would be spotless, with every object in place, linoleum floors buffed shiny, and sinks and commodes in the latrines freshly scrubbed. Each man's wall locker and footlocker would be secured by hefty padlocks, and laundry bags would be neatly tied at the foot of each bed. Blankets would be pulled so tightly over mattresses that a quarter would easily bounce on any one of the twenty thousand beds made each morning at the post.

On Saturday morning between eleven-thirty and twelve, however, everything would suddenly go straight to hell as soldiers flew into the wild bacchanalia that is weekend on an army post. Some would scatter to the winds, running as far from the army as they could before dragging their weary bodies back in time for reveille on Monday. Those with no cars and little cash would stay on the post, drink cheap beer in the enlisted clubs, eat pizza and hamburgers in the barracks, and throw their trash everywhere. By Monday morning, the living areas would look and smell like garbage dumps.

Then would come reveille, when barracks sergeants would emerge yawning and cursing from their rooms and stomp through the bays; men would drag themselves bleary-eyed from between soggy sheets, stumble into the latrines, and the week would begin all over again. Magically, by work call at eight A.M., the barracks would be as spotless as they had been the previous Saturday morning.

And so this cycle, like nature's seasons, had gone on at Fort Sherman for years, as it had everywhere in the United States Army on every post Jack Kelley had ever known.

"The sergeant major will see you now," Miss Gritz shrieked, miffed that she had to come looking for Jack.

Riley loomed behind a huge desk. His perfectly bald, coconut-shaped head reflected the light streaming in the window behind him. He seemed a caricature of some god of war, with hairs bristling out of his enormous flaring nostrils and fingers thick as sausages. Jack had forgotten just how ugly Riley was.

"Well, well, well. We meet again, Kelley," Riley rumbled. He blew a thick cloud of cigar smoke across the desk. Jack just stood there. Riley did not offer him a chair.

"I know whatcha been doing," Riley thundred in his

most ominous voice. He squinted up at Jack, hoping for a reaction. Jack showed none. "I oughta put you outta business, young fella. How'd ya like that?"

Jack cleared his throat. "If you did that, Sergeant Major, you'd have all yer NCOs in open rebellion."

Riley considered his cigar. "Yeah, wise-mouth, I know it." He cocked his great head to one side, waving smoke away with a pudgy hand. "That's why I been layin' off on ya. Until now, that is."

Riley permitted a long silence to develop. The glorious morning sunlight streamed in at the window. Dust motes danced in a halo above Riley's head. Kelley was expected to sweat out the silence. Instead, he asked if he could smoke.

"No," Riley rumbled.

"Mind if I sit down, then?" Kelley gestured toward a leather couch in the center of the room.

"Yes. You won't be here much longer. I just called you to give you some news, Kelley. I'm leavin' Fort Sherman in a month. What do you think of that?"

"I think it's very *good* news, Top."

"I bet you do," Riley said sarcastically. "But it ain't, not fer you." Riley now permitted himself his nastiest grin.

Here it comes, Jack thought, and he braced himself.

"You got a good deal here, don'tcha, Kelley?" Riley said.

"Fucking-A I do, Sergeant Major."

"Kelley, you're as crooked as a broke-backed snake, do you know that?" Riley thundered.

"Riley, if you were as tall as you are ugly, you'd have to sleep in a fucking bowling alley, did you know *that*?" Antagonizing Riley was the wrong thing to do, Jack realized, but he could not resist.

Riley remained outwardly calm. He knew he had the upper hand. He took a moment to control his voice. "Well, Kelley," he said, "I'll tell you what I do know. Things aren't goin' so good for us over in Vietnam. By what I see on the TV and in the reports, they'll be need-in' quite a few good men over there pretty soon. No soldier worth his salt wants to sit out a war. I know you're a good soldier, so instead of makin' you hem and haw about volunteerin', I went and volunteered yer services through a friend of mine up at Department of the Army. Yer orders are on the way. What do you think of *that*?"

"Who's replacing you?" Jack asked. The question threw Riley. He had expected some sign of agitation.

"Billy Goats Oates," Riley answered in spite of himself.

"Where *you* goin'?"

The interview was not proceeding at all as planned. "Military district of Washington," Riley muttered quickly. Then in his booming voice: "Okay, Kelley, get lost!"

Jack walked to the door. As he was going out Riley shouted after him, "Enjoy yerself in Vietnam, boy! Har, har, har!"

Miss Gritz glared at Jack evilly as he walked past her desk. He realized she had been listening at the door. She probably always listened at the door.

"You're lookin' good today, Miz Gritz," he said cheerily. "Who's yer undertaker?"

Jack decided not to go to work that day. Instead, he visited the post personnel office. Sure enough, they'd had a message from the Pentagon ordering Jack to the Military Assistance Command in Vietnam. Somehow Riley had had Jack declared excess at the post and immediately available for reassignment, and had done it so quietly that Jack had never caught wind of it. He fumed inwardly. With all his contacts at Fort Sherman, this time they had failed him. Riley's revenge was complete. Jack realized his mistake too late. He had underestimated Riley's abilities.

Jack returned to the barracks to think, but as he lay on his bed, drinking cold beer from his tiny refrigerator, someone knocked on his door.

"C'mon in, it's open."

A heavyset, red-faced man in ill-fitting civilian clothing entered the room. Jack froze, smelling military police all over his visitor.

"Sergeant Kelley?"

Slowly, Jack set the beer on his night table and sat up on his bed. He nodded casually at the big man.

"I'm Special Agent Prudhomme, Fort Sherman criminal investigation detachment." He held out his credentials—a big badge glittering in a leather carrying case.

"Yeah." Jack sighed, staring at the badge. "Care for a beer?"

"Don't mind if I do," Prudhomme answered affably. This surprised Jack. "Sorry to bother you at home, Sarge," he said, taking in the tiny room at a glance, "but I had to see you right away, as much as you're leaving us pretty soon." He winked at Jack as he took the bottle of beer.

How the hell did he know I was leaving? Jack wondered. He was beginning to feel vulnerable, a sensation he did not like. First Riley and now this guy had managed to sneak up on him. And he should have anticipated this visit, because he knew precisely what Prudhomme was after.

"Sarge, I'm gonna come straight to the point," Prudhomme began, setting the bottle down. "I've been assigned to investigate a situation at the post quartermaster depot. We have reason to believe a ring of crooks is operating down there, diverting tens of thousands of dollars' worth of government equipment and supplies." Prudhomme paused. "I'm not here to fuck with you, and this visit is off the record, but I want to know what you know about these diversions. Take your time."

"What makes you think I know anything?"

"You know something," Prudhomme answered confidently. He took a book off the shelf beside the window and began leafing through it. "Word is, you know about everything on this post."

Jack stared at him without answering.

"*The Dunwich Horror and Others*," Prudhomme read the book's title. "*The Best of H. P. Lovecraft*. Arkham House. 1963. Six fifty in hardback. Hmmm. Is this a fuck book?"

"Ever see a fuck book with the word 'horror' in the title? I don't read 'em. Prefer the real thing."

Prudhomme selected a passage at random: "'I have read with great interest the *Brattleboro Reformer*'s reprint (April twenty-third, 1928) of your letter on the recent stories of strange bodies seen floating in our flooded streams last fall...' Sounds like something I might be interested in—professionally, that is." He chuckled.

"I don't have to tell you a thing," Jack said.

Prudhomme nodded, his nose buried in the book. "Sure. Want me to leave? If I do, I guarantee I'll look *very* closely at *you*, Jack, and then your name will appear, as if by magic, in the subject block of my report."

Jack decided to tell him what he wanted to know. Actually, Jack had no part in the massive diversion of supplies and equipment that had been going on. The small deals he had worked while at the depot had netted him only favors and goodwill among the post's military personnel.

"I know the mess sergeants inflate their headcounts so they can take the extra food home with 'em," Jack admitted, "and we all look the other way. All I do is arrange special rations for 'em sometimes. What the hell. Ever try to make it anywhere except the army with only a grammar school education? Half those mess sergeants have trouble reading the fucking master menu. Why, I know a Puerto Rican mess sergeant in one of the training brigades, a magician when it comes to dressing up the slop the army gives him to feed the troops, he's got to get a KP to read things for him."

"I'm not interested in guys like him. What about the really valuable stuff that's being covered up on the inventories?"

"The goddamn rednecks are responsible for that shit. I only do small stuff. I'll give you a 'for instance': sometimes I get nice pastries from the messhall and use 'em to grease the skids at places around the post. Then I can get stuff fixed for buddies. Over at the motor pool, I can get just about anything that goes into or onto a motor vehicle fixed for nothin'. Sergeant Baxter, over at the headquarters company mess, has this black first cook who makes the best tarts and turnovers you ever ate. The boys at the motor pool love 'em. And so if once in a while somebody gives me something I didn't ask for just 'cause he likes me, I should look the other way?" Jack grinned. "Actually, I *do*, if you get my drift."

"Kelley, I want names and specific incidents."

Jack hesitated but finally began to recite some names. After only a few seconds, Prudhomme stopped him.

"Jack, these names you've mentioned, they're all civilians. Aren't there any GIs involved?"

Jack remained completely silent. There were, of course, military personnel involved, but as far as Jack was concerned, Prudhomme would just have to ferret those people out on his own.

Prudhomme shrugged, finished his beer, and stood up. "Thanks for your help." He offered his hand. His grip was strong and warm. "We're gonna bust up that mess down there, but you're well out of it. Long as you just scrounge 'n' grease up your networks, Kelley, do favors for other people, and try to make life easier for folks, you'll be okay. But remember: where you're goin', the temptations to get into real trouble are greater than in a backwater like this place, so be careful over there, you hear?"

Jack nodded.

"So long, Sarge, and good luck. And Kelley, remember this, too: *never* underestimate your enemy." Prudhomme tossed the book he had taken off the shelf onto Jack's bunk and left.

A Letter to the World

Saigon, Vietnam
25 August 1965

Dear Jay [Aspby wrote]:

Sorry not to have written you before this, but I've really been busy since coming back here this time. And let me tell you, when I stepped off the plane at Tan Son Nhut last May, it was like coming home again.

I'm working now at the Free World Military Assistance Office, the liaison detachment between General Westmoreland's headquarters and the various Allied military contingents that are fighting with us here. Interesting work.

The old town has changed somewhat from the way I remember it back in '62. But the change is for the better, I think. You can't imagine the energy and optimism around here these days! Westy's inspired this whole command with his own personal magnetism. We're here to win this war now, Jay, and everyone senses and feels it. It's like the air is charged with pure oxygen and

18

everybody walks with spring in their step. You keep a watch on the papers, old friend, because big things are about to happen and this war will start shaking loose pretty soon now.

Do you remember me telling you about Jack Kelley, the wheeler-dealer from my days here with the old MAAG? Well, Jack's working for me now! I never thought I liked him very much because when I first knew him, back in '62, he was more interested in making business deals than attending to his military duties, or so it seemed to me at the time. But you only get to know a guy when you work with him. Old Jack's not such a bad sort after all, really a sharp cookie when it comes to managing the paperwork. And he plays a mean hand of cribbage!

Jay, I can't tell you how emotional my comeback was. I volunteered to come back from Germany, it's true, but that was more from a sense of boredom over there than anything else. I realized in coming back to this command how much the years in between these two tours seemed dull and unfulfilled to me.

Well, my heart's been here since I left the place in '63, and I realized this when the plane touched down at Tan Son Nhut last May and I got off and breathed the hot, humid air of Saigon once again. That very same night I was back at Le Cabanon, sucking down a cold "33," and there I had my first disappointment. The old Frenchman went and hired himself a bunch of bargirls! What a distraction! Used to be, you could go in there, enjoy a beer, have a sandwich, and just relax, but now these girls, speaking broken English, are all over you, begging Saigon tea and fumbling with your crotch.

Well, I succumbed after a while. I think I could get used to this particular woman, Lien's her name, but you know, most of these Vietnamese gals don't know how to make love properly. Most of 'em just lie there like pillows.

Oh, yeah, something about Kelley I forgot to tell you.

When I was here the first time, I loaned him a couple of hundred bucks. Well, when I got transferred up to the ole "Fighting Fifth," back in September '62, I lost touch with him, and when I went home I just wrote the money off. I figured circumstances had beaten me out of it, if Jack hadn't borrowed the money originally with no intention of ever repaying me.

Do you know what? The first thing Jack said to me when we met again was, "Jim, I know I owe you that $200 and I'll pay you back, every cent." I said sure, sure, take your time. I figured he was just saying that. Well, he did pay me back, every red cent, and the first payday after I got on the new job. I respect a guy like that.

A word about the Vietnamese we work with.

The Free World Military Assistance Working Committee, what this whole lash-up is called, is actually headed by a Vietnamese lieutenant general. He's quite an odd old sock but a real fighter who, because of his uncertain politics, has been relegated to this backwater assignment to keep him out of the playing. I understand he's pretty wealthy, too. But he is also a real war hero, and they say he was a very capable field commander of which the Arvin (army of Vietnam) could always use dozens more.

The general's chief executive officer is a Colonel Tang, who's quite a character in his own right. I deal with him every day, and we've become good friends. He jokingly calls me his "son," and I call him "Father." He likes Scotch and Salem cigarettes—the only two things about the Arvin soldier any American can be sure of. Well, we share the interest in Scotch and have had some fine hours, back in his office, all of us gorging and getting loaded. Boy, do these guys like to party!

But seriously, this Colonel Tang is a wise and experienced man, and I've taken him as my mentor. I never respected any Vietnamese officer like I do this guy, and I can't figure why, with a war on, they're wasting him down here. He should be on the general staff. No wonder they were losing this war before Westy came here.

Well, Jay, it's been a long time since we were boys together and went our separate ways, me to the army, you to the Free Library and your map collection. Next time I stop by Philly we'll have a few at the Cherry Tree Inn.

Until then, my best to Joyce and Jonathan,

Jim

Old Arizona Again

"**G**EORGE, I SEE BY THE *Army Times* THAT 'FOSSIL' Foster is getting a division command in Vietnam," Mary Oates commented at the dinner table one night.

"Ummm?" remarked her husband, Sergeant Major Billy George Oates. Mary called him by his middle name, but everyone else in the army knew him as "Billy Goats." She detested the nickname, but her husband did not seem to mind it.

Sergeant Major Oates was deeply absorbed reading the *Waynesville Gazette and Advertiser*. Reading the *Gazette* was the one way he kept in touch with what was going on in the community just outside Fort Sherman, and as the post sergeant major, he believed it was important for him to know these things.

"George, I said that 'Fossil' Foster is getting a division command in Vietnam, did you hear me?"

"Mary, if you keep reading that goddamn scandal sheet, you'll ruin your mind for anything worthwhile."

"I just thought you'd like to know, George. We've been so close to the Fosters all these years."

"The closest I ever got to old 'Fossil' was on Omaha Beach, and even then we were in different battalions," Oates snorted.

"You were his first sergeant, George!"

"Well, yeah, but that was much later, during the Bulge, and then the Germans split us up, after we got captured." Oates chuckled. "Otherwise they might've lost the war six months earlier."

Oates would never forget that morning. The Germans had swarmed over them so quickly that their unit had been taken completely by surprise, and almost before he knew it, the officers had been segregated from the enlisted men and were being marched off through the swirling snow. He could still see the little gaggle of his company officers, trudging off through the woods under guard.

"I just thought you'd like to know, is all, George." Mary sighed.

"I truly love that old bastard," Oates said as he put down the *Gazette*, "but so what if he's getting a division? You aren't saying I oughta volunteer to go back there to be with Foster again? Mary, I've been to Vietnam before, and I had two other wars before this one."

"I just thought you'd like to know, George," Mary repeated.

"Well, I already knew."

"And you didn't *say* anything?" Mary was shocked. "You let me find out about it through the *Army Times*?"

"Sorry, love, but it musta slipped my mind."

In reality Oates had been following events in Vietnam very closely since he had come to Fort Sherman. He read all the intelligence reports that came in to the post commander in his daily reading file, and he followed the news closely. So closely did he read the daily orders that he knew which of his old friends were serving there and what they were doing in the war zone.

The next morning there was a postcard waiting for him in his basket. Apparently it had arrived late the previous day, and his secretary had singled it out of the morning's distribution and put it on top of the other papers she had stacked on his desk for his official reading. It was from Jim Aspby, postmarked APO San Francisco 96243, and it said in a scrawl Oates only made out with difficulty, "Need a good cribbage partner. When are you coming over?"

Oates recalled that Aspby had gone back to Vietnam somtime in 1965 as a specialist fifth class. Now the return address read "SFC James Aspby, HQ USMACV, FWMAO." Aspby had gotten himself two promotions in a little over two years. Oates marveled at that and wondered what the acronym "FWMAO" might stand for. He put the card in his briefcase. He would show it to Mary that night.

He started in on the pile of official papers. On the very top was a copy of the military police blotter from the previous day. Oates read with a rising sense of dismay a litany of minor crimes and transgressions, all of which pointed to a breakdown in discipline among the soldiers at Fort Sherman. Incidents of drunkenness and widespread drug use—mostly marijuana—were bad enough in any command, but Oates was particularly depressed to see the names of three noncommissioned officers among those busted by army CID agents for dealing in drugs.

Next Oates opened a folder that contained letters to the post commander from private individuals concerning such matters as the indebtedness and malfeasance of enlisted personnel assigned to the command. The very first letter in the pile was from the ex-wife of a battalion sergeant major in one of the training brigades. She was complaining that she had not been paid child support in six months. Oates knew the family well. He knew this wife as a decent, uncomplaining woman who one day had just taken one beating too many from her drunken lout of a husband.

Oates dialed the sergeant major's office. A clerk answered. It seemed the sergeant major had not arrived at work yet. Oates glanced at his watch and, barely able to suppress his anger, said:

"Tell him I want to see him, Specialist. Tell him I want him up here at post headquarters and standing tall in my office at sixteen-thirty sharp."

Oates hung up. By four-thirty that afternoon he would have calmed down enough to talk to the man, otherwise he was not sure he could keep from punching him out. This letter had only brought matters to a head. For some time now Oates had been receiving reports that the man was a very poor troop leader. Normally the post commander let Oates handle NCO problems informally, through the noncommissioned officer chain. It was time now for the general to call the man's battalion commander. Oates put the letter into another folder, so he could take it into the general's office later that morning, when they would talk privately about enlisted affairs on the post.

How do men like him make rank in my army? Oates wondered. But he already knew the answer: officers and enlisted leaders who did not have the guts to come down on incompetents. Well, Oates promised himself, this particular sergeant major's military career was about to come to an end.

Oates also knew that the breakdown in discipline among the soldiers on the post was due to lack of leadership ability among the noncommissioned officers and was compounded by the fact that the army kept shifting its officers in and out of units so frequently that the sergeants and the lieutenants never got a chance to learn how to work together. This was all tied to the war in Vietnam, which these days took priority over everything else in the army. Fort Sherman had become nothing more than a staging area for troop movements into Vietnam, although the basic purpose of the post was supposedly to train soldiers for duty everywhere in the army. The best men, the best equipment, were all going to

Southeast Asia. Oates knew things were worse in other
commands, especially in Germany, but things were getting bad all over. Vietnam was sucking up the lifeblood
of the U.S. Army.

Sergeant Major Oates sighed. He would just have to
work longer hours, increase his visits to the units on
post, keep closer contact with his brigade sergeants
major, get out more among the troops, hold more meet-
ings and seminars on NCO leadership, and just plain
work harder. That things weren't far worse at Fort Sherman was really a tribute to Oates because he had been
doing all those things for two years.

Oates stood and stretched. It was nearly eight A.M.,
and he had been in his office since six. The light glinted
off the two silver stars mounted between the laurel
wreaths around his Combat Infantryman's Badge. That
meant one award of the badge for each war in which the
sergeant major had fought as a footslogger—three of
them now. The riot of color represented by the many
rows of decorations and campaign ribbons splashed all
over the left breast of his uniform jacket was topped by
the Distinguished Service Cross (the second-highest
award for heroism under fire), followed by a Silver Star
with three oak leaf clusters and a Bronze Star with five
oak leaf clusters for valor. The single silver oak leaf
cluster fixed to the center of his Purple Heart ribbon
meant that he had been wounded in action five separate
times—on one occasion, his body had been peppered
with more than fifteen fragments from a German antipersonnel mine in France, but still Oates had managed to
bounce back from a hospital in England in plenty of time
to get himself taken prisoner at the Battle of the Bulge in
December 1944.

He glanced again at his watch. It would be nine
o'clock back in Washington. "Fossil" Foster was the
head of some army staff agency at the Pentagon these
days. Getting ready to go over to Vietnam, Oates reflected as he dialed the general's office telephone
number from memory. Many times the general had told

him, "Goats, you want an assignment, especially in my command, you call me, anytime."

They called him "Fossil" because General Winfield Scott Foster was an amateur paleontologist of some renown. Once he had even discovered a new species of a type of long extinct bug, which the scientists had named after him, something-or-other *fosterii*. The general never tired of telling people about it, but Oates could never remember the Latin names, only that it was something like a crab or a centipede. General Foster was as proud of that little bug as he was of the Congressional Medal of Honor he'd won on the Normandy beachhead on June 6, 1944.

"Sergeant Major! Fancy you calling me at this hour," General Foster said when he came on the line.

"General, is it firm that you're getting a division in Vietnam?"

"Firm, Goats. It's 'Old Arizona Again' for me. Remember that old song from the Fourth Cavalry's frontier days?"

> Oh, it's old Arizona again,
> It's old Arizona again.
> It's a place where we all have been.
> We have all been there before,
> And we're going back once more,
> Back to old Arizona again.

"General I want to go back with you, as your division sergeant major."

"Yessir," the general agreed at once.

Within thirty days they were both there again.

Saigon Reveille

THE PASSENGER IN THE TINY CITRÖEN PANEL TRUCK
sat with a Thompson submachine gun clasped tightly between his knees. To anyone observing him from the sidewalk he appeared as harmless as any other bored
deliveryman at five o'clock in the morning.

The truck, showing no lights, turned left into Nguyen
Cu Trinh Street from Cong Quyen and proceeded slowly
toward the Metropole Bachelor Enlisted Quarters a
hundred yards away on the right. Dawn was creeping up
the eastern horizon, and the air was cool and fresh.

The driver squinted through the windshield. A lighted
cigarette dangled carelessly between his lips. Behind
him, in the cargo compartment, sat five hundred pounds
of plastic explosive. An inch of detonating cord stuck
through into the cab, just behind the driver.

The concrete guard kiosk on the sidewalk in front of
the Metropole was very close now.

"Remember," the passenger said slowly, "do not ignite the fuse until I have finished firing and am clear of the truck."

"Right," the driver muttered, and inhaled on the cigarette. They had been through this in dry runs countless times. It would take them fifteen seconds to run back to Cong Quyen and around the corner, where a car waited to speed them away. To be on the safe side, the fuse had been cut to burn for thirty seconds.

The Vietnamese policeman on duty inside the guardpost yawned and stretched. It had been a long night. Listlessly, he scratched a mosquito bite on the back of his neck as he watched the slowly approaching panel truck with little interest. His orders were to permit no vehicles to stop in front of the American quarters. Then he noticed that the truck was running without lights. That was strange.

The policeman's whistle was already piping shrilly, warning them away from the building, when the terrorists rolled to a stop directly in front of his guard station.

The machine gunner got out firing. Bullets thwacked and smacked all around the astonished policeman, but miraculously he was not hit.

The American military policeman on duty just inside the lobby ducked to the floor at the first shots. He lay there, heart pounding in his chest, as stray bullets caromed through the lobby from the street. The Vietnamese night clerk fled to the rear of the lobby and took the stairs to the second-floor landing two at a time.

The MP drew his automatic and, crouching, scuttled like a crab to the door. He saw a man running down the street and a Thompson gun in the gutter, its stubby butt pointing toward him. The door on the passenger's side of the small panel truck hung open, and through it he could make out another man in the driver's seat, fumbling with something. A white blur whizzed past him. It was the Vietnamese policeman retreating to the back of the lobby. Inside the kiosk the policeman's riot gun leaned uselessly against a support.

The MP began firing at the driver with his .45.

The second terrorist touched the lighted end of his cigarette to the detonating cord. It did not catch. Suddenly the cab seemed full of bees! One stung him sharply on the tip of his nose, so hard it made his teeth ache. Another flicked the cigarette out of his hand and into the gutter, where it fizzled out in a stagnant puddle. He tumbled into the street and crouched sweating beside his truck. Above him, back in the cab and seemingly a mile away, the fuse dangled harmlessly in the fine morning air.

"Never use a cigarette lighter on a fuse," he had been told many times by the Viet Cong demolitions expert who had trained him for this mission. "A match will do," the grizzled veteran had said, "but the glowing tip of a cigarette is always best."

"Bomb!" screamed the Vietnamese policeman as he flew up the lobby steps three at a time. The MP's automatic had jammed open on the empty clip, telling him it was time to abandon the heroics. He spun around and followed the two Vietnamese up the stairs.

Outside, the remaining terrorist uttered terrible oaths as desperately he fumbled a cigarette pack out of his shirt pocket, shook one loose, and stuck it between his trembling lips. He was forced to insert it at a very odd angle because blood still dripped from the tip of his nose where one of the MP's bullets had clipped off a quarter inch of flesh. He flicked his lighter once, twice, three times; it flashed each time, but the wick failed to ignite.

"Fuck your mother!" he whispered at the lighter, and shook it violently. He flicked the wheel a fourth time, and a tiny blue flame appeared around the base of the wick. Holding his breath, hoping a sudden breeze would not start up, he screwed his mouth awkwardly to one side, twisted his head grotesquely to keep the blood away from the glimmering flame, and sucked it into the end of the cigarette. He puffed one, two, three times and, when the tip was glowing redly, touched it to the fuse and waited until it began sputtering.

Arms and legs pumping furiously, Private Nguyen Van Binh, Sapper Company 45C, People's Liberation Army, darted back toward the Cong Quyen intersection and safety. He was aware of a high-pitched wailing sound, "Eeeeeeee!" following him down the street. It was only himself, screaming, expecting at any moment to be cut down in a hail of gunfire.

Aspby woke with a start. Shots echoed in the street below his window. His roommate, Jerry O'Neill, a navy yeoman at the Saigon headquaraters, was awake, too. "Shots?" he whispered. Their room was very small, their beds separated by only the width of a tiny night table.

"Yeah." Aspby slipped his feet into his shoes and walked toward the window.

"Goddammit, no!" Jerry hissed. "Stay away from the windows!" Aspby hesitated.

"I'm takin' cover out in the hallway," O'Neill announced, and that made up Aspby's mind. He followed O'Neill outside.

The hallway was crowded with other residents, rumpled and grumpy from their sudden awakening, but no one showing any signs of real concern or fear. The men milled about, talking in low voices. Someone flicked open a lighter with a tiny metallic clang and lit a cigarette. Suddenly someone down the hall laughed loudly.

"What's goin' on?" Aspby asked of his neighbor.

"Dunno," he replied, lighting a cigarette. Aspby's own smokes were back inside his room.

"Can I bum a smoke?" he asked the man.

"Aw, fuckit," O'Neill announced, "I'm goin' back to bed."

"No, Jerry, wait a sec," Aspby protested, his hand outstretched for the cigarette paused in midair.

A tremendous blue light filled their room at the same time the door flew from its hinges and into the hallway, slamming O'Neill into the opposite wall.

Aspby experienced a tremendous concussion to the side of his head that made him think the wall had jumped out and hit him; the air *whoosh*ed out of his lungs. An eerie quiet came over everything, as if he were on the bottom of a swimming pool watching a dozen divers trying to wade through the murky water. The air filled with dust, and men reeled like drunks; mouths worked silently, and it was several moments before Aspby realized a bomb had detonated and the concussion had deafened him. Panic seized him. He would have to spend the rest of his life deaf!

"Who the fuck turned the lights off?" O'Neill shouted from beneath the door.

"Oh, thank God!" Aspby breathed. His hearing had come back, and he was so relieved that at first he did not notice that the lights were still on.

O'Neill struggled to his feet and staggered into their room. He was a ghastly sight, covered with blood. Aspby followed him back into the room. The place was a shambles. The windows had blown inward, scattering glass all over; the air conditioner sat in the middle of Aspby's bed, where it had come to rest after caroming off the refrigerator, ripping the door from its hinges as it flew through the air.

Jerry had collapsed on his bed, unnoticed by Aspby, who walked to the windows and stared over the balcony outside. Nguyen Cu Trinh Street looked like a picture of some European city after a WWII bombing raid. All the storefronts along the street had been blown in by the blast, which had also ripped off the roofs so that Aspby could actually look between the rafters into the top floors of the buildings across the street. A deep hole gaped in the pavement where the Citröen had been sitting.

O'Neill lay gasping on the top of his bed, blood streaming from a deep cut in the top of his head. He was still stunned and muttered for Aspby to turn on the lights. Aspby leaned over and inspected his wounds. It was blood from the head wound that had blinded him, but Jerry had also sustained a bad blow to his right eye, which had already swelled shut.

"C'mon, Jerry, gotta get you out of here." Aspby managed to get one of O'Neill's arms around his neck and helped him to his feet. They shuffled into the hallway and toward the stairs. The stairwell was dark and littered with rubble, and men stumbled up and down, yelling and shouting. Some were assisted by others, and some were alone, moving down carefully step by step, bracing themselves against the walls. Still others headed for the upper floors, with the flashlights clutched in their hands cutting like searchlights through a hostile night sky. Aspby took the stairway to the Tran Hung Dao side of the building, and when they at last emerged onto the second-floor landing, he noticed for the first time that Jerry's bare feet had been cut to ribbons by glass and debris. Aspby, by that time, was covered with O'Neill's blood, and looked just as much a casualty.

The first-floor lobby was filled with medical personnel who had rushed across the street from the 218th Medical Dispensary. Two medics grabbed O'Neill at the bottom of the steps; two others, over his protests, placed Aspby on a stretcher and carried him across the street.

"Set me down! I'm okay! I'm not even scratched!" Aspby hollered as they carried him past the crowds of rescuers and onlookers thronging Tran Hung Dao Boulevard.

"Easy does it, ole buddy," said one of the medics. "You've lost a lot of blood, but you'll be okay."

They set him down in the lobby of the dispensary and ran back to the Metropole, leaving him on the floor with a dozen real stretcher cases. Aspby lay there and looked around. He recognized this place. Back in 1962 it had been known as the Fitzsimons Bachelor Enlisted Quarters, reserved for only senior noncoms. One of the men who had lived there in those days stuck in Aspby's memory. He had been the fattest soldier Aspby had ever seen, so big, it was rumored, that a carpenter had had to make a special addition to his chair so he could sit behind his desk in the office where he worked.

"Fuck this shit," Aspby muttered at last, and got up.

He walked through the bedlam to the men's room, where he washed off most of O'Neill's blood. Then he realized he was wearing only a pair of shorts and shoes. A passing medic showed him where the linen closet was, and he wrapped a blue cotton patient's robe around himself. He wore it the rest of that day, until the military police allowed the residents back into the Metropole to claim their personal belongings.

When finally he was allowed back into his room, he inspected the door lying in the hallway. He picked it up and propped it against the wall. A hole had been punched clean through the solid hardwood paneling, and the object that had made that hole had struck the top of O'Neill's head. Aspby measured himself against the hole and discovered that it came up to his Adam's apple. If it had hit him instead of the shorter O'Neill, the projectile would have crushed his windpipe.

After the Metropole bombing, Aspby was assigned temporary quarters elsewhere in the city. The place was the Town House, on Hai Ba Trung Street, in the heart of uptown Saigon and only a short walk from the best bars and nightclubs. But the Town House room was a terrible place to live. He had to share it with three other men, and the toilet always smelled vaguely of excrement, and it was this distasteful odor that always greeted Aspby when he came home at night.

He moved in with Lien, the bargirl he had met that first night back in Saigon when he had visited Le Cabanon, an old French colonial watering spot on the corner of Nguyen Van Thinh and Pham Van Dat streets. The place had changed with the times. Before, there had been the wrought-iron tables with marble tops on which he and Irv Gonsalves had played interminable cribbage games; now, there were plastic chairs and wooden coffee tables. Five Vietnamese hostesses were on him as soon as he walked through the door, all beseeching him to buy them drinks.

"Hello! Hello! Come siddown. You buy me one

dwink?" Aspby permitted himself to be led to the bar, where he ordered a bottle of "33" beer. The girls were not pros, Aspby realized, because they meekly sat down by themselves as soon as he indicated he would not buy. One, shorter than the others but well proportioned and with an unusually aquiline nose for a Vietnamese, caught his attention. Another, he noticed, had a beautiful body and lovely hair, but her face had been terribly scarred by smallpox.

He watched the straight-nosed one out of the corner of his eye. She partook little in the boisterous bargirl talk of the others, and once, Aspby caught her glancing back at him. She smiled and looked quickly away.

Aspby took his beer and sat down among the women. Eagerly, they made room for him.

"How long you Saigon?" one asked boldly. She was a heavy woman with long black hair bobbed in front. She had a smooth, round face.

"I come today. I come Tan Son Nhut from States this morning."

"Ohhh, you cherry boy!" the big one exclaimed, and they all laughed. Aspby ordered a round of drinks. It cost him five hundred piasters, less than five dollars, but the girls' compliments and caresses more than compensated for the money. He ordered more beer, and when the drinks came, the girls toasted him exuberantly. For each one-hundred-piaster glass of "Saigon tea"—real tea or colored water—the women received forty piasters as their share.

Aspby smiled at the long-nosed one. "What your name?" he asked in pidgin.

"My name Susy," she answered, embarrassed at the attention. Her reluctance impressed him. Usually a Saigon bargirl would be all over you if you gave her any kind of opening.

"No," Aspby said disdainfully, "what your Vietnamec name, *real* name?"

"Lien." She smiled.

"Miss Lien, I am very pleased to meet you," he said in Vietnamese.

"Oh, he speak Vietnamee!" the big girl shrieked.

"Only a little bit," Aspby protested, again in their own language.

"Good heavens, this American is handsome," one of them said just loud enough for everyone to hear.

"You are all beautiful," Aspby returned the compliment. "We all go home together, yes?"

"You take *five* girl one time?" the big one exclaimed in mock amazement, but her expression told Aspby that if he did, she wanted to be first.

"Sure! Maybe six, even seven! You have more friends?" The women erupted into raucous laughter. Aspby was having a good time. It had been so long since he had been among these people, he had forgotten how earthy and unaffected they could be.

Taking a Saigon barmaid home was a complicated operation requiring discretion. The girls did not want the world to see them bringing Americans into their homes, and the Americans did not want the local police to see them with a girl, because then they would be a target for a shakedown.

Lien passed Aspby her address. She lived on Tran Hung Dao Boulevard, "close Plaza Hotel," she told him. Aspby knew the Plaza, a large bachelor enlisted quarters—BEQ in military parlance—not far from the Saigon Central Market and the train station. The note was his invitation to follow her there. She did not mention price. That would come later and was negotiable.

Aspby hung around Le Cabanon until closing time. He knew if he did not do that, even though the assignation had been arranged, he might come back later to find no one waiting there for him. When the girls climbed noisily into a small blue-and-cream Renault taxi to go home, Aspby followed in his own cab.

Lien lived in a squalid, overcrowded tenement. Her tiny room had no water, no screens on the windows, no fan. A rickety bed sat in one corner. There was one chair, a stand-up, double-door wardrobe, some suit-cases, cardboard cartons, and a few personal possessions stacked in corners. The place made Aspby feel sad and guilty, but at least it wasn't a prostitute's crib. Lien actually lived there.

Lien stripped to her panties. Aspby undressed quickly and sat beside her on the bed. Except for prostitutes, Vietnamese women did not usually kiss on the lips; neither did they like prophylactics because they were a sign of mistrust, and no bargirl liked being put in the same category as a common whore.

Aspby kissed her in the Vietnamese fashion, gently nibbling and snuffling around her cheeks and neck. When he sensed she was ready, he removed her panties, but noises intruding from the street, and the sounds of voices and radios from elsewhere in the building interrupted his concentration. Under the circumstances, it was no surprise that neither of them became frenzied. Still, Aspby sensed that if they got to know each other better, that would happen in time. Perhaps Lien did too. At the last moment, she locked her legs around Aspby's waist.

Later, Lien prepared a delicious bowl of noodle soup from scratch. She cooked on a small kerosene stove in the middle of the floor. Aspby washed the soup down with a warm bottle of "33" beer. As he ate, Lien told him about herself.

She came from Nha Trang, a beautiful city on the South China Sea, in north-central South Vietnam. "I have babysan," she told him. The Vietnamese had picked up the American GI's slang and freely referred to "babysans," "mamasans," and "papasans." The child, a girl of about four, was living with Lien's parents in Nha Trang. The child's father had been a soldier. They were not married. Having a child out of wedlock, especially by a soldier, had ruined Lien's chances of ever making a match with a man from a proper Vietnamese family. So Lien had come to the big city to make her fortune.

Aspby was touched. Hers was so typical of the stories

one heard in this sad and lovely country. He impulsively
gave her a thousand piasters before he left. The surprise
and pleasure on her face made him feel good. "Buy more
beer," he told her. "I come back. I see you tomorrow
night, okay?"

Aspby began seeing Lien regularly, and their relationship settled into a routine, so it came as a surprise when
Aspby made his proposal one night in early January
1966.

"You, me, we live together, okay?" he told Lien.

"I rent apartment for us. You find nice one, okay?"

"Oh, yes!" Lien replied almost in a whisper. It was
too good to be true, she thought, but Aspby was serious.

They rented a place from a woman Lien knew. It was
just off Le Van Duyet Street, near Hong Thap Tu Boulevard. Lien hired a man with a pushcart to tote her wardrobe to the new place. The rest of her things she was
able to get into the back of a small Renault taxicab. Once
they were settled in, Aspby bought two nice fans and a
small icebox from the American military exchange. They
were luxuries Miss Lien had never had before, nor had
she ever dreamed of having such things.

Their relationship was a practical one. For his financial support, Lien provided Aspby with domesticity. Sex
was there, too, when he needed it, but as time went on,
sex became less important to Aspby than just having a
place to call his own, where someone would tend to his
needs.

Lien was a good cook, a shrewd businesswoman,
thrifty, and a good judge of character. She was always
there when Aspby needed her, but his demands were
never insistent, so she was free to indulge in an active
personal life.

As the months passed they developed mutual respect.
Lien came to appreciate Aspby's good points. He was
open-handed and faithful and never challenged her sway
over their domestic affairs. He paid her $250 a month
regularly, and from that money she paid all their bills;

other, smaller sums were always forthcoming when she asked for them. Lien had never before in her life known such security.

Then Lien began to put on weight.

The baby boy born to them complicated everything. The child came about the time Aspby was beginning to tire of Lien's company and was thinking of dumping her. Now he felt responsible for the boy and felt he could only discharge this responsibility through continued support of his mother.

By the time Tan was born, Aspby had been assigned permanent quarters at the John Houston BEQ, where there were more comforts than Lien's apartment afforded—a shower and Western-style bathroom. Besides, the Vietnamese police had begun shaking them down, coming into the apartment early in the morning or late at night and not departing until they had been sufficiently bribed.

Aspby began spending most of his nights at the John Houston.

"You no love me no more," Lien pouted one afternoon.

"No good stay here, honey. Police come, *beaucoup* trouble me," Aspby replied. Reluctantly he laid aside the paperback novel he had been reading, *The Spiral Road*, by Jan de Hartog, a fascinating story about the Dutch in Indonesia.

"Babysan, he cry, no have papa," Lien said.

"Bullshit," Aspby snorted. Then in Vietnamese: "Baby have mama, happy very much. Drink milk, fat very much."

Lien laughed at Aspby's execrable Vietnamese. She was only teasing him, anyway. She was mildly displeased with him this afternoon because apparently he preferred his book to her conversation about what she and her landlady had been up to that day. Tan slept peacefully suspended in a tiny hammock stretched between a portable frame. As Lien talked she rocked it gently with one foot. Her toes were stubby and spread wide apart, the result of never having worn anything except sandals until she had come to Saigon.

Aspby looked upon his son. He was a beautiful baby. The boy smiled in his sleep, and Aspby experienced a pang of love so desperately sweet it brought moisture to his eyes. In the boy's face he recognized the best features of his mother and himself. He knew he would surely leave this child in Vietnam when he went home, and that troubled him deeply.

He wondered what he should do. Of course he would stay in Vietnam as long as he possibly could and postpone making any hard decisions. Perhaps he would send Lien money for the boy's support, once he finally did leave. But he could never marry Lien. She did not want marriage to an American if it meant she had to leave Vietnam. And Aspby, a professional soldier, had no intention of burdening himself with a motherless child.

"I no come, sleep night here anymore," Aspby announced. Lien nodded. "I come daytime, eat, sleep, give you sausage, eggs." Lien nodded again. "Sausage and eggs"—*xuc-xich* and *hot ga*—had become their private language for sexual intercourse. He switched to Vietnamese. "I go work now. Come back Saturday morning, seven o'clock."

"I understand," she answered in her own language. "Maybe Saturday afternoon we will all go and eat beef seven ways? Would you like to come?"

"All *right*!" Aspby exclaimed. "Beef seven ways" was just that, beef prepared and served seven different ways, and a very popular meal with the Saigonese.

"But I no come Saturday. I go work. Come Monday, twelve o'clock."

Lien nodded. "Good" Vietnamese girls never went into public with Americans except under very special circumstances, as when the American was their legitimate husband or a friend of the family and the entire family was present. But Lien did not consider herself a "good" girl, and neither she nor Aspby cared what anybody thought about them. So they frequently dined out, studiously ignoring the snide remarks directed at them.

Gently, Aspby kissed his son and left through the trapdoor that led, via a steep set of wooden steps, to the back door of the modest two-story building in which Lien's apartment was located. He stepped into a narrow alley and walked the short distance to Le Van Duyet Street, where he stood on the curb, waiting for a cab.

Aspby took a pack of Pall Malls out of a pocket, flicked his Zippo, and lit one. He had had the lighter ten years. When he had cleaned his room out at the Metropole he had searched high and low for his lighter, determined not to leave without it. Once, in 1962, he had been caught in a police raid on a whorehouse. He had made a spectacular escape through an open window, clutching his clothes in one hand and his Zippo in the other. His glasses he had left behind, but they could be replaced. The lighter could not; it contained too many memories, and it was part of him.

Eventually a cab pulled up and Aspby got in.

The Tenderest Service

JACK KELLEY DID HIS MILITARY DUTY WELL BECAUSE he liked it. As the number-two NCO at the Free World Military Assistance Office—Jim Aspby was number one because he had made his grade several months before Jack—Jack was responsible for handling classified papers, keeping the general correspondence flowing smoothly, and maintaining the archive that was used by his officers to keep track of what they and their predecessors had been doing to assist the various Free World Forces contingents in Vietnam.

Both Jack and Aspby had been assigned to the liaison office as the luck of the draw. At first Jack had been leery of the job. He knew Aspby slightly and considered him too straight for comfort. But after a few weeks he was pleasantly surprised to discover that he and Jim Aspby complemented each other perfectly. Aspby kept the big problems off Jack's back by running interference with the senior officers, while Jack kept the papers moving and fixed little problems for the office. Jack was a master at scrounging and getting things fixed ahead of schedule, and these official activities never interfered with his own private business

Jack liked every aspect of his job. He was thorough and meticulous in his work and kept his records neat and up-to-date. He knew where to find every piece of paper in his safes, but he had set up his filing system strictly according to regulation, so anyone could use it if they had to. He was open and straightforward in everything he did—except when cutting a deal for profit, and then he could be very devious.

Other people, American and Vietnamese, worked for Aspby and Jack, but their activities were strictly subordinate to the two noncoms, who knew better than anyone how to do every job in the office. This worked out well for the junior enlisted men, who could always count on plenty of time off because the two sergeants could run everything by themselves when they had to.

Although neither NCO had any formal education beyond high school—now more than fifteen years behind them—both were exceptionally well read, for soldiers. As single, long-service enlisted men, they had had plenty of time to read, and they enjoyed it. Like Chaucer's Oxford student—and they had both read *The Canterbury Tales*—each kept a score of books to read at his bedside before bed at night. Aspby even carried a book with him wherever he went. The capacious pockets of the jungle uniform trousers proved very convenient for this purpose.

The liaison office proved especially conducive to reading because it was through Jack that the Allied contingents received their share of free paperback books purchased through a U.S. military recreation fund. The two read everything: novels, historical works, romances, science fiction and fantasy, westerns, and mysteries. Whatever was inside a box of purloined books was gone through cover to cover. They often discussed what they had read and, in their own way, became rather astute literary critics. Over the years, this general reading had given them a fairly broad education, and reading so much good writing had made them capable writers—to the extent anyone had to be in the army. They could spell correctly, knew how to construct a grammatically correct and complete sentence, and could string these sentences together into coherent paragraphs. For military writing, that is all one needed to know.

It was Jack's fluent command of English that caused General Ton to come up with a novel idea: Jack would listen to the general read English aloud and would correct his pronunciation. Lieutenant General Tran Ngoc Ton was the Vietnamese army's chief representative to the Allied headquarters contingents. He was an energetic, capable man with not enough to do, so he enjoyed his whims. The request for Jack's services was duly made, and Jack's colonel enthusiastically endorsed the idea. So every Wednesday afternoon Jack would report to General Ton's office and listen to him read slowly from back issues of American magazines.

This particular afternoon the general was reading from *Time* magazine, the "Essay," in fact, which this week was something about men's hairstyles, "Longer Hair Is Not Necessarily Hippie."

"... might all conform to the book of Levi-ty—Levit-eye—" The general faltered and glanced up at Jack for help.

"That's Leviticus, sir, Lee-vit-i-kus, a book of the Bible."

"I have heard of it before," said the general. "There are many books in your Bible, aren't there?"

"Yessir. Let's see—Genesis, Exodus, Leviticus . . . yes, it's the third book of the Old Testament. The first five books were supposed to have been written by Moses, and in Leviticus, he gives the ritual law to the Jews. The law was administered by the men of the tribe of Levi, so that's why the book's called Leviticus."

"How interesting, Kelley! I did not know you were a scholar of the Bible."

Jack cleared his throat nervously. "Well, I'm not,

really. It's that when I was a kid I was forced to sit through a lot of Sunday-school lessons."

"What kind of school is that?"

"Well, in most Christian Protestant churches, General, the little children don't go to regular church services on Sunday, but they go to Sunday school, where they're taught all about Bible stories."

General Ton nodded. "It says here that in Lee-vit-i-kus, 'Ye shall not round the corners of your heads, neither shalt thou mar the corners of thy beard.'"

"Yessir. That's Leviticus nineteen, twenty-seven," Jack answered from memory. General Ton looked at him wonderingly. Red-faced, Jack explained how the books of the Bible were organized into chapters and verses. He did not explain that as a ten-year-old he had won a prize for memorizing more of the Bible than any other child in his Sunday-school class. He did not understand many of those passages at the time and still did not, but now, almost twenty-five years later, he could still quote them by rote.

"How curious," General Ton said, and then laughed. "You know, Kelley, this quotation reads just like an army regulation."

The general read on. "'Flowing locks were once a symbol of vee-rill—veer—'"

"That's vi-ril-atee, it means 'manliness.' It comes from the Latin, *vir*, a man."

General Ton nodded and continued, "'As the story of Sampson bears witness.' There is a footnote here. 'It is sometimes forgotten that after Dee-lil-ah's—'"

"That's pronounced Dee-lie-lah, sir."

General Ton set the magazine down and leaned back in his chair. "Now, tell me please, the story of this Sampson and Dee-lie-lah, Kelley."

"It's another story from the Old Testament, sir, from the book of Judges, chapter sixteen, as I recall." Jack told the story with verve. It was one of his favorite biblical tales. He admired the way the Old Testament Jews always got back at their enemies. Jack transmitted his enthusiasm to the general, who was excited himself yet also a little bit alarmed by the explicit violence, cruelty, and vengeance of the story, not to mention Jack's evident relish of the terrible details.

When Jack had finished, General Ton sat rigidly behind his desk. "Kelley, this story, do many Americans know it well as you do?"

"Oh, yessir, we all know it. It's part of our culture, our folklore, regardless what our religious background is."

"Thank you, Kelley, but I think that will be all for today," the general said in an even voice, but inside he was tremendously excited. He was certain that the story of Sampson and Delilah was extremely significant and prophetic. It had come to him as Jack spoke, and the general saw the implications clearly: No matter what happened to them, the Americans would always expect their hair to grow back, their strength to return. They were an optimistic people. If the Communist darkness spread here and finally won, perhaps he would go to America. After all, it was the Americans who were keeping freedom alive in the world. So if he had to leave this dear land— A tear came to his eye, and he quickly looked away so Jack would not see.

After Jack had departed, the general took out his copy of *Kim Van Kieu* and began to read.

Sawdust and Bitter Melons

"**T**HESE AMERICANS, BROTHER TANG," GENERAL Ton said, "are a brilliant and energetic people with souls like us, but their army has none; it is a vast machine that blunders along ponderously, but if it is permitted to work long enough, it will destroy the Communists sooner or later."

"Ah, brother Ton"—Colonel Tang sighed through a cloud of cigarette smoke—"will it last that long?" Colonel Tang, a short, round, jovial man, was General Ton's principal aide. They had been friends many years, so they addressed themselves in Vietnamese as *anh*, "brother." They were sitting in General Ton's villa, enjoying a drink after a long day.

"No," the general replied with a sigh. Colonel Tang nodded. "That means," the general continued, leaning forward over the ornate lacquerware coffee table that separated them, "that we must see to the preservation of our families."

47

"We've already seen to that, but what about *us*?"

"The Communists couldn't kill me at Dien Bien Phu" —the general shrugged—"and they won't get me now." But Colonel Tang knew the general had been very fortunate to escape the doomed garrison at Dien Bien Phu. He had been one of the last of the wounded evacuated from the besieged French bastion, otherwise he would surely have perished there.

"We will see the end coming, and after all is said, I don't think even the Americans would abandon us," the colonel said.

"Not on purpose. But I've studied American history. Those people have very short memories. Don't count on them for anything."

Colonel Tang mashed out his cigarette and lighted another immediately.

The general leaned back and studied his glass. "The American army's officer corps is one of the worst in the whole world," he said.

"They don't think very highly of us, either," Colonel Tang remarked dryly.

"No. They think we don't know how to fight, don't *want* to fight. But these American officers, I've known many of them over the years, and they're little machines, tiny robots. They make all the proper noises about the 'ethos' of the officer corps, but at heart they're businessmen. 'Racks for coats and sacks for rice.'" The old expression described those who put their mundane affairs before moral and ethical considerations. "Not one of them, not one in a hundred, has the courage to stand up by himself and endorse an unpopular opinion or disagree with a superior. The best articles in their professional journals are written by junior officers. But once their careers are secure, they stop thinking *for* themselves except when they're thinking *of* themselves."

Colonel Tang was silent for a moment. "Well, they are good at what they do. I think they're one of the best-trained armies in the world. I've been through some of their schools. And during the last big war, they took on the Axis powers and won."

"Yes. I shouldn't be so harsh on them. But you see, they only have one speed and that is fast forward, unlike the Communists, who adapt their strategy to the circumstances. In our country the Americans are fighting a superb World War Two combat. Right now Ho Chi Minh is making the mistake of trying to match them, and he will never win that way. But if he can hold out long enough, the Americans will lose heart."

"I see it coming already, with these peace demonstrations in the United States."

"Precisely! The American war protesters are better allies for Hanoi than either the Russians or the Chinese. They gnaw at the vitals of America while Hanoi's military allies only chip away at her armor. It is all so terribly sad. Have you studied much American history?"

"Yes, in an effort to understand them. Americans are an easy people to admire, from the distance of their history."

General Ton nodded. "Yes. Lincoln, I admire Abraham Lincoln more than any other man in history, theirs or ours. He was great because he did not disjoin his vast power from his remorse at having to use it."

"Washington was another," Colonel Tang offered. "He could have had great power, but he gave it up for principle."

General Ton got up and took the colonel's glass to the bar, where he refilled it from a bottle of Johnny Walker Red Label Scotch. "You know, the Americans I really like are these sergeants," the general said as he handed the colonel his drink.

"Aspby? Kelley?"

"Yes. But any sergeant. Most of them, anyway. The American NCO has something his officers don't. First, the ones I've seen don't seem to worry like their officers do about promotions, schooling, assignments. I think the Americans call that sort of thing 'ticket punching.' And when a sergeant tells you something, generally you can be sure it's the truth."

"And I've noticed another thing," Colonel Tang said. "When an American NCO talks to you, you can tell if he likes you or not. But with his officers, they're all smiles and careful, precise English, but when you're out of sight, they laugh at you."

"How well I know," the general replied dryly.

"What about Aspby? I already know what you think of Kelley."

General Ton laughed. "Kelley! He loves life! I respect that in any man. But Aspby is a bit more complicated. He is a very guilty man. He has had at least one child by a Vietnamese woman, did you know that?"

"Yes. The woman is 'a rose picked off the wall,' am I right, General?" Colonel Tang laughed.

"Well, let us call her a woman of 'easy virtue' instead of a prostitute."

"Aspby has been in our country for a long time. Most Americans who stay here pick up a permanent woman. Personally, I am in favor of that. At least it gives them some feeling for us, if not some understanding of our culture."

"Well, my guess, brother Tang, is that he doesn't feel very comfortable, being a father. He can take the woman or leave her, but I think he's worried about leaving Vietnam without the child."

"You know, strange that you should mention it, but several times Aspby has made as if he wanted to talk to me about something serious, and then he's stopped himself and brought up something routine. I thought he might have some personal problem to discuss, but I could not figure out why an American sergeant would come to a Vietnamese officer with a personal problem. Now maybe I see."

"He has a personal Vietnamese problem." The general chuckled. "Next time he wants to talk, encourage him. Tell him what he should do."

"And what *should* he do?"

"How do *I* know?" General Ton laughed. "That's why I have an officer like you on my staff!"

Colonel Tang drove himself through the quiet and darkened streets. It was after the curfew hour, but he had a special pass that allowed him through checkpoints and roving police patrols. The pass was a necessary accouterment to being an aide to General Ton, because frequently the general entertained diplomats and other important people who liked to party into the night. When Colonel Tang was not kept up late by the general and his friends, he used the pass for his own purposes.

Like many Vietnamese who could afford it, Colonel Nguyen Van Tang lived several lives. In the daytime he was an efficient and accomplished staff officer, juggling myriad details and requirements and putting out the numerous small fires that plague every organization. Two or three nights a week he was a playboy, wining and dining and spending in the best restaurants and cabarets in Saigon, places so exclusive and exotic, some of them, that even old hands in Vietnam like Jim Aspby never knew of their existence.

Thinking of Aspby, Colonel Tang shook his head. He was a good man, but so naive, just like so many professional military men. Aspby knew so very little of the world. He had wisdom when it came to dealing with men like himself, but he knew almost nothing about the rest of humanity.

Colonel Tang's own focus in life was his family, his dowdy little wife and their seven children. He told his wife virtually nothing about his affairs; he never took her out to dine, never introduced her to his foreign friends. She kept his home and their children, and both he and she knew that Colonel Tang would always return to them, no matter where he wandered.

Born in 1925 in Thu Dau Mot City, the capital of Binh Duong Province a few miles west of Saigon, Colonel Tang would be forty-two years old in December, as the Westerners counted birthdays. His family owned land, lots of it throughout South Vietnam, and they had supported the French during their suzerainty. When the French left in 1955 and South Vietnam became independent under President Ngo Dinh Diem, the Nguyens supported him until the military coup of 1963. Since then, they had supported whichever faction happened to be in power—Nguyen Van Thieu since September of that year.

The new president was no relative of Tang's family. Nguyen is a common surname in Vietnam. Actually, few Americans realized that Vietnamese names are written directory style, with the surname first. While everyone called him President Thieu, which was acceptable in Vietnam, that was really like calling President Johnson "President Lyndon" in the United States. Thieu was actually surnamed Nguyen. So widespread was this ignorance of something so basic to Vietnamese culture that some Americans deeply involved in Vietnamese politics and military affairs even listed their Vietnamese friends' names backward in the indexes to their published memoirs.

Colonel Tang was apolitical. As close as he came to holding an opinion at all was his virulent anticommunism. He liked Americans more than other foreigners, but, in the aggregate, not much more. Indeed, he was an expert in American history and culture. A graduate of several officer schools in the United States, including the prestigious Command and General Staff College, he admired and liked individual Americans very much, but he saw America's presence in Vietnam as a mere eddy in the long river of the country's history. He was convinced that America would not stay long in Vietnam, and he had no doubt about what would happen when the Americans left.

So he had been assiduously engineering a way out, an assignment to the military attaché's office at the South Vietnamese embassy in Paris. Why Paris? It was more cosmopolitan than anywhere else. Tang liked French culture, understood the French, and besides, with a large expatriate Vietnamese community, his family would fit in there more quickly than in most other places. Finally, he had large amounts of money in French banks.

He glanced at his watch. It was past eleven, but still early enough to visit a cigar smoker. He turned left on Tran Quoc Toan Boulevard and then right on Duong So Twenty-one, where he pulled into a driveway and got out of his car. He pressed the bell at an iron gate set into a high masonry wall and identified himself to a watchman inside. The gate rolled ponderously open, and he was permitted to drive through.

"Cigar smoking" was a Vietnamese euphemism for one of the specialties of this exclusive establishment. Americans called it by a variety of crude names, one of them being "blow job." But here women practiced fellatio as an art with numerous exotic embellishments, making the act far more exciting than an ordinary "around the world." The denouement of this drama came when the hostess pulled from her customer's fundament at the moment of orgasm a beaded chain that had been carefully inserted during the distraction of the exquisite preliminaries. The sensation, it is said by connoisseurs, is heavenly.

Another specialty of the place, which Tang had tried only once, consisted of a woman and a complicated arrangement of ropes and pulleys attached to a wicker basket with a slot in the bottom. The woman positioned herself over this aperture and the man slid underneath, inserting himself into the girl. She performed the act by hoisting herself up and down using the ropes and pulleys.

On the one occasion Tang had used this system, the thing had collapsed, possibly from overuse and too infrequent safety inspections, injuring him painfully but, fortunately, not permanently. The worst thing about the disastrous event was that the girl had found it amusing, until she realized how grievously and embarrassingly the colonel had been injured. Always a good sport, Tang afterward permitted himself a laugh.

He had not bothered to explain the bruises to his wife, and she wisely had not asked.

The family was all asleep when the colonel finally arrived home.

Cosmopolites without a Plea

"I KNOW SOMEDAY YOU HURT ME, JACK," ANA CHIN said. She and Jack Kelley sat in a booth in a corner near the entrance to Sonya's. Sonya's was at the end of a short cul-de-sac, just off Dong Khanh Boulevard. The sound of the heavy traffic outside was muted by the whir of the air conditioning and the voices of the other patrons.

"I'd never hurt you, baby!" Jack protested.

"I mean, you hurt me here." Ana touched her well-manicured fingers to her left breast. Jack shrugged. He couldn't fight her low-key hysterics.

"Eat your soup, Ana, you'll like it," Jack advised. Ana sniffled and looked away quickly, daubing a tear that clung to her left eyelash. Jack glanced around furtively, to see if anyone had noticed.

"Sweetheart, stop crying, will ya? You keep that shit up and somebody's gonna think I'm a real bastard, you understand?"

"Jack, I tell you true. You leave me, I die! Oh, I—I

don't know *what* I do, you leave me, Jack!" Ana put her hand on Jack's forearm and squeezed his arm again. Jack winced. She had strong hands for such a small woman. Ana looked him full in the face, her eyes wide and brimming.

Jack Kelley was not a man of refinement, but he liked Sonya's because it was a place where discriminating men went for good food, drink, and the companionship of women who could converse on a level above the ordinary Saigon bargirl's prosaic, "Hey, GI, you buy one dwink? You no buy, you numbah fuckin' ten cheap Charlie cocksucker!"

The clientele at Sonya's consisted of American and Australian officers and noncoms. For a modest corkage fee, and with the understanding that mixers would be bought from the house, steady patrons were allowed to keep their own whiskey behind the bar. The bottles were *never* tampered with and were *always* on hand when called for.

Of five steady hostesses employed at Sonya's, Ana Chin was the most popular, though not because she was more beautiful than the other girls or because she dressed better than they. She was a desirable woman because she had the ineffable something called "class," and among Sonya's patrons, that was much in demand. Men bought her drinks and considered themselves honored if she joined them for dinner, just so they could savor her presence for a time. Some pursued her lustfully and lavishly, imagining that she was as accomplished in the arts of love as she was in the social graces. Yet none of the coterie who hung out at Sonya's could boast of having done any more than talk to the delightful Ana Chin. She had had her lovers, but they had all been men *she* had picked for her *own* reasons. She simply was not the kind of woman who could be had for blandishments. But when she fell, she fell hard, and she fell for Jack Kelley.

Jack was not a lady killer, no Don Juan trying to work out his sexual inferiorities by amassing a roster of conquests. He was however, cavalier in affairs of the heart.

Ana loved him, but he had other women on the hook. At first she had been no more than an unexpectedly gratifying experience; he respected her physical beauty and the way she could use her body, but love was not a word in Jack's lexicon. Not that he was an ungrateful lover. He never had sex with any woman for whom he didn't feel some regard, even affection. When a woman gave to him he gave back to her, if only for the moment, and sometimes, after he'd departed from a woman's arms, even long afterward, Jack found himself still thinking about her, and he'd smile. When people who didn't know him saw this bemused look on his face, they assumed he was a relaxed and happy man without a care in the world.

But one man who did know him once said, "You're tryin' to find yer momma, Jack. That's why you chase skirts all the time, you're tryin' to crawl back into the cunt you came from. That'll get you into a lot of trouble, boy! You'd better go easy on the chicks, give 'em up, turn to drink or gambling or something. It's safer."

"What! Give up women? Are you crazy? I couldn't live without pussy! Why, I need cunts the way other guys need meat and potatoes, whiskey, beer, the fucking air itself!"

"Yeah?" Jack's friend answered. "Well, someday one of 'em's gonna put it to *you*, and that'll be all she wrote. How many different girls you got on the string right now? Six? Christ, Jack, how can you handle it? Do you promise 'em marriage, eternal love? What happens when one of 'em believes your line of bullshit?"

"Well, what if I do?" Jack responded defensively. "I love 'em all, and if I was true to only one of 'em, the others'd think it unfair as hell. What does a cunt know about arithmetic, anyway? I have something they want, and I believe in sharing."

The other man snorted. "I don't know when I've seen a heart as big as yours, Jack."

Yet the more Jack got to know the Chinese girl Ana, the more she grew on him. He found her exquisite to look at, and she was an artful and resourceful lover. But ever since Ana had fallen in love with him, it had become a trial for Jack to go into Sonya's while she was there. She clung to him and cried on his shoulder in front of other people, and that embarrassed him painfully. There were proprieties to be observed in Saigon's barlife, and when Ana's façade crumbled, that unnerved Jack. He had a full bottle of Johnny Walker behind the bar, and when that was gone, he promised himself he would quit Sonya's and never return. It would be hard. He really liked the place, and he had done a lot of successful business there, but it would be far better for both of them that way—no ugly parting scene, no public display of emotions. And Jack had observed before that the Saigon barmaid's heart mended quickly.

The first time Kelley had gone to Sonya's, Jim Aspby had taken him there. They had been playing cribbage in the office one afternoon when the subject of a place to go that evening came up.

"Thirty-one for two." Aspby played an ace and pegged two points. "Let's go out like decent people tonight, Jack, and have a good feed."

"Fucking seven for a go." Jack played his last card and pegged one point. "I'd rather get laid, James," he replied.

"Fifteen two, fifteen four, and double run for dozen," Aspby counted, and pegged his points in the rapid, fluid manner of an experienced cribbage player. "Gotta have some fuel in the belly before you exercise that old whang, Jack," he pointed out reasonably. It was painfully obvious to Jack that Aspby was pleased with himself for holding such a good hand. Jack shook his head in disgust. He took in Aspby's lightning count with one swift glance: two aces, a deuce, a trey, and a ten spot on the cut made a dozen points.

"I got a fuckin' pair of ladies for two." Jack threw two queens, a seven, and a four onto the table and pegged his two points. "But in the cribbage I got"—he scooped up his cribbage eagerly—"nine-fuckin'-teen! You lousy, lucky shit!" Jack threw the cards on the table, a king, jack, nine, three; he'd thrown the nine and the three in there himself, and now he wished he'd thrown the queens instead. Aspby laughed as he shuffled the cards for a new hand.

"C'mon, Jack, let's hit Sonya's tonight. You'll like it. No bitches hustlin' Saigon tea, good food, and you drink free, outta my private bottle. Also you can meet the finest hostess in all of Saigon, the redoubtable Ana Chin."

"Will she let me eat her pussy?" Jack sneered as he scraped up the cards. Aspby was thirty points ahead of him in the game. Jack wanted to play, not chatter about Aspby's favorite hangout.

"Mmmm. Mebbe, Jack, mebbe. But Ana's a hard cunt to crack, old buddy."

Jack glanced at his hand: the jack of hearts, three fives, a six, and a seven. He swallowed hard, threw the six and the seven into Aspby's cribbage, and cut the deck. Aspby turned over the five of hearts.

Jack cleared his throat. "Well, mebbe we could peek in at Sonya's tonight, Jimbo." He swallowed again. The five of hearts had given him a hand of twenty-nine points, a perfect cribbage hand.

Aspby said something else about Ana Chin, but Jack did not catch it.

"Brother James"—Jack grinned wolfishly at Aspby— "I will go with you tonight, and yer beautiful Chinese girl'd better not turn out to be another of yer fucking nineteen hands."

Nineteen is an impossible hand in the cribbage count, cribbage players' jargon for zero or a hand with no points in it at all. Jack won the game that afternoon, and eventually he won Ana Chin, also.

But their first meeting was not auspicious. Ana had been whirling about the crowded restaurant, stopping at tables, taking a drink here, a bite to eat there, waving to acquaintances at other tables. Aspby introduced Jack to her as she swept by their table. She smiled and offered her hand to him. He was surprised at the strength in that hand. Then she was off to another part of the room.

"That girl's got a pistol shooter's grip," Jack said admiringly as Ann swirled away.

"A good looker, too, huh?" Aspby seemed just a bit too eager to have an opinion, and Jack wondered if he'd had the woman in bed and wanted to brag about it to someone. "I've never screwed her, Jack, but by God I've tried! She's inviolate, I'm sure of it. Frankly," he added with genuine sadness in his voice, "I think she's already got a steady."

"Well, she is a good-looking woman. You're right about that." And she was, he thought. She dressed sharp, and she carried herself well. And then Jack promptly forgot about her.

He forgot about her, that is, until the following Saturday, when he went back to Sonya's by himself. He did not go back specifically to see Ana. He returned because he liked the place, and had decided to start doing business there. But he also hoped that Ana might be there.

And she was. And it was early in the afternoon. And there were no other customers in the place.

Mrs. Chen, the owner's wife, was sitting placidly behind the cash register, totaling the receipts from the night before. Mrs. Chen was fiftyish and tending slightly toward plumpness. She had very bright and intelligent eyes.

Jack sat at the bar and surveyed the place in the mirror. Ana and two other hostesses were amusing themselves with conversation at the opposite end of the bar. One was very tall and buxom and wore the Chinese *cheong-sam*, with a slit up the skirt that revealed some rather handsome thighs. The other was a slightly built woman with finely chiseled facial features who wore a Vietnamese *ao dai*. Ana was wearing a Western-style skirt and blouse.

A bartender quietly polished glasses.

"May I leave a bottle behind the bar, ma'am?" Jack asked Mrs. Chen.

"Yes, sir." She smiled. "Weren't you in here, several nights ago, with Mr. Aspby?"

Jack was astonished that the woman remembered him at all. He handed her a paper bag containing a fifth of Johnny Walker Red Label. "Would you please write your name on this slip of paper?" she asked, and handed Jack a pen. He scrawled his name. Mrs. Chen added some Chinese ideograms, put a rubber band around the bottle, and placed it behind the bar with several dozen others, all nicely labeled with their owners' names.

"Oh, excuse me, Mr. Kelley, would you like a drink?" Mrs. Chen asked.

"Yes, ma'am. Make it a double and ask the girls down there what they would like to have."

Mrs. Chen summoned the bartender and issued him rapid instructions in Chinese. Expertly he mixed Jack a double Scotch and soda. When he served the women they acknowledged Jack's generosity with thanks. Jack smiled, genuinely pleased with himself. He couldn't help noticing Ana's beautiful legs.

"You speak English very well," he said, turning back to Mrs. Chen.

"I should"—she laughed—"we lived a dozen years in Seattle."

"Seattle, Washington, U.S.A.?"

"Yes. We got out of China in forty-eight, and relatives sponsored us to go to the States. We worked in my brother-in-law's restaurant there."

Jack nodded appreciatively. "Are you U.S. citizens, you and your husband?"

"No, we carry Republic of China passports, but our son is an American citizen. He grew up in Seattle." She shrugged her shoulders. "He's a spec five at the Third Field Hospital, at Tan Son Nhut."

"He's in the *army*?" This conversation was becoming more extraordinary every moment.

"I'll introduce you some night, when he's here," Mrs. Chen volunteered.

Jack finished his drink and ordered another, a single this time.

"Thank you for the drink," Ana Chin said, taking the stool beside Jack's.

"You're welcome, Ana." Jack smiled. "Have another one?"

Ana nodded and ordered another orange drink from the bartender. "You come here before, I think, with Mr. Asspee?" she inquired. Again Jack was surprised and very pleased that someone remembered him after such a brief meeting.

"Yes. Jim and I work in the same office together. He brought me here to meet you, as a matter of fact."

It was Ana's turn to smile. Her teeth were perfectly even and very white. She fingered the single strand of pearls around her neck while she regarded Jack frankly. He in turn stared at her hand, with its clean, well-manicured nails.

"These not real," she said with a shrug, thinking he was looking at her necklace.

"Well, ah—"

"You been here long time?" she asked, meaning Vietnam.

Ana's skirt had pulled up about two inches above her knees, revealing very nice thighs. Her skin was white, almost ivory.

"Well, I—I've been here about eighteen months this time, Ana."

Ana crossed her legs. She rested one foot on a rung of Jack's stool. They were now sitting very close to one another. Jack inched himself just a little closer before he even realized he had done it. It just seemed natural that he *should* be closer to this woman.

Ana placed a hand on Jack's forearm. "You very nice to buy us a drink. I know first time I meet you, you nice man. What your name?"

"Jack. You call me Jack, Ana." Her hand was cool and soft on his arm. He remembered how strongly it had gripped his that night of their first meeting. An iron hand in a velvet glove, he thought.

"You must come more often, Jack." Ana smiled.

"You betcha," Jack replied, and gently touched the rim of his glass to Ana's.

In the following weeks Jack established himself at Sonya's. He began doing business there. Gradually he and Ana formed a warm friendship and began spending more and more time sitting together at the bar or in one of the booths. She never asked Jack for a drink or money, and she never mentioned the subject of sex. But when they were sitting together at the bar or one of the tables, she permitted him to place his hand on her thigh and caress her legs. Indeed, often his hands wandered too far above her knees to be entirely casual visitors.

Their kisses were chaste and exchanged only at meeting and parting, but Jack knew it was only a matter of time.

It was Jack's sense of humor that first endeared them to each other. One day she told him she had been shopping for a new pair of shoes, but the ones she wanted were just too expensive. Jack thought Ana had good taste in shoes. She always wore Western-style high heels, which gave an accentuation of her calves that he thought very sexy. Besides, she wore them naturally, like an American woman. Jack had noticed that when most Vietnamese women wore Western-style high heels, they looked awkward.

"Well, Ana, why don't you go to the market, buy one shoe for half the price of a pair and pick up the other one later, when you have the money."

"Oh, Jack, you crazy! Nobody buy only *one* shoe!" They laughed immoderately over the joke, and Jack knew in the instant of Ana's gay laughter, the way she looked at him, that there was much more between them than a simple-minded little jest. In spite of himself his pulse raced, and he knew he wanted very badly to bury himself in this delightful woman. Their hands touched, and Jack thought he could feel a new warmth there now.

"Jack, Jack," Ana asked hesitantly, "maybe Sunday afternoon, you come see me?" Ana blushed. The last words were uttered in such a small voice Jack could barely hear her. "We have lunch, my place, okay? I fix a good lunch for you." Ana laughed a little too loudly.

Jack remained outwardly clam. "Why, sure, Ana, what time?"

Suddenly he felt very sorry for Ana Chin and ashamed of himself. Here was this beautiful and intelligent woman begging him to come to her apartment for an afternoon. For some reason, she had decided to give him the invitation a hundred other men had sought after vainly, would have paid large sums for. Jack knew from previous experience that once he'd had Ana he'd cool toward her quickly enough. How long would their relationship last? he wondered. And then what would Ana do? How many other fickle boyfriends would she pick up? Eventually, her beauty and charms wasted, she'd find herself a worn-out businesswoman, sitting behind the bar in some dingy dump, keeping the receipts and trading jokes with men years younger than she.

But Jack's reverie lasted only a few moments, and then his thoughts leaped ahead to the weekend.

Mrs. Chen smiled from her place behind the bar.

Jack fidgeted all week.

He'd noticed that the more he went to Sonya's and the more friendly he'd become with Ana, the less he'd seen of Jim Aspby there.

"What's the matter, Jim? You getting to dislike Sonya's or something?" he asked one afternoon. They were sitting in the vault, where Jack had his office. Jack's job was to keep track of a large number of rather sensitive documents maintained by their office.

Aspby shrugged. "Oh, I dunno, Jack. Seems like I got other things to do after duty, you know?" Jack pulled a loose-leaf binder from a shelf and began checking a register of incoming documents against a stack of papers from the safe.

"Well, I sorta miss you down there, ole buddy."

"Yeah. Jack, this document seems to be missing Annex A."

Jack leaned over and looked at the thick sheaf of paper secured with a wire staple. "It's unclassified"—he pointed to the table of contents—"and I let Major Sims in the Korean Plans Office keep it over there."

"Ummm, better just make a note of that."

"Why the fuck worry about it? Jim, what's wrong with you? You're as nervous as a whore in church, for Christ's sake."

"Um, well—"

"Come off it, brother James, you're fuckin' jealous, ain'tcha?"

"Well, Jack, I wouldn't put it that way. It's just—"

"You really like Ana, don't you? You were tryin' to get into her pants, and then I came along and screwed it all up for you."

Aspby's face reddened. He cleared his throat, leaned back in his chair, and looked steadily at Jack. "Jack, we've known each other a while, now, haven't we?"

Jack nodded. "So what?"

"Well, we get along pretty good, don't we?"

Jack shrugged his shoulders again.

"Well, Jack, you make me nervous is all. I know how you handle your women. Yeah, I really like Ana, and from what I see, she more than likes you. I know you're gonna hurt her, Jack, and that makes me sad. I don't go into Sonya's anymore because I don't want to see you two together is all."

"Well, when I'm finished with her, she'll be there for you, ole buddy," Jack said quietly.

"Goddammit, Kelley, that's not what I mean!" Aspby shouted, and slammed the register closed with a bang.

"Calm down, Jim, calm down," Jack soothed. "This is life, Jimbo, and I, just like you, have to play things as they lay. Ana is a very special woman, and I'm gonna see where this goes with us. But don't go gettin' all moral and high on me, buddy, 'cause that knife cuts both ways, you know."

Aspby's face flushed. He knew Jack was referring to Lien and the child he'd had by the Vietnamese girl. Often he'd asked himself what she would do when eventually he left Vietnam for good, and the fate of the child bothered him more than he liked to admit even to himself.

"Yeah, Jack"—Aspby grinned sheepishly—"I guess I was out of line there. Let's forget I said that." He took a breath. "You gonna let me whip yer ass at cribbage today, Jack-o?" He tried to make his voice sound hearty.

Jack glanced at his watch. "Hey, gettin' on toward time to make a run out to MACV." Once a day Jack acted as a courier between their office and the sprawling Military Assistance Command headquarters at Tan Son Nhut Airbase. He stood and lifted a .45 automatic out of a weapons rack along one side of the wall. The rack contained several M-16 rifles, carbines, and .45-caliber pistols. Bins held ammunition clips, and thousands of loose rounds were stored in boxes under the rack. Jack selected a .45, checked the action, and scooped up two full clips. He began strapping on a shoulder holster.

"Why don't you use one of your own weapons, Jack? Your three fifty-seven is more reliable than any of those old beat-up forty-fives there." Aspby nodded toward the rack full of weapons.

"Nah. When I do Uncle Sam's work, I use Uncle Sam's hardware. How's that Browning auto I got for you comin' along?"

Jack had sold Aspby a Browning 9-mm automatic pistol at a very reasonable price, and Aspby carried it with him whenever he was on duty. "Great little weapon. Hope I never have to use it."

The subject of Ana Chin did not come up again. But the rest of that week she was all Jack Kelley could think about.

After enjoying an early supper at Sonya's that Tuesday, Jack decided to have Phu, his Vietnamese driver from the Free World Military Assistance Office, drive him uptown to a quiet bar he knew off Nguyen Hue

Boulevard for a few drinks. Phu rarely spoke, but he was dependable and could negotiate the traffic in Saigon like no one else Jack had ever seen.

"Hey, Jackie boy! Give a GI a lift?" a familiar voice rumbled behind him as Jack climbed into his jeep. Jack cringed. The voice belonged to Warrant Officer Harry Scheldt. Goddamn the luck! Jack thought.

"Hey, Harry! Sure," Jack replied, feigning pleasure. "Where ya goin'?"

"Where am I goin'? Where am I goin'? Jackie boy, it's *Tuesday*, and on *Tuesdays*, ole Harry shoots craps up at the Plaza!"

Jack tilted the seat forward, and Harry clambered into the back, wheezing and breathing heavily as he shifted his bulk around to get comfortable. The reek of whiskey was strong on his breath.

The crap games at the Plaza Bachelor Enlisted Quarters on Tran Hung Dao Boulevard were an institution. Thousands of dollars passed hands up there every Tuesday night, and it was rumored that Harry, when he was hot, won hugely; it was also rumored that somehow he cheated.

"That Chink broad of yours, Jack, what's her name?"

Jack stiffened. He did not like the way Harry referred to Ana.

"Ana, Harry," he replied reluctantly.

"Yeah, Ana." Harry rolled the girl's name deliciously into two syllables. "Does she give you a decent blow job?" Harry laughed immediately. "Just kiddin' ole buddy, just kiddin'!" He clapped Jack on the shoulder with a massive, hamlike palm.

Jack did not mind giving rides to common soldiers. In fact, he made it his policy to give a lift to any lower-ranking enlisted man who looked lost in the big city, especially if he was wearing a combat unit patch on his shoulder. On the other hand, he never offered rides to fellow Saigon commandos, but he could not get rid of Harry, and besides, the Plaza was on the way.

Harry was also an old Saigon hand. Jack had known

him slightly back in 1962. Harry had been a staff sergeant then. Subsequently, he had applied for and gotten a warrant officer grade. Jack considered warrant officers failed NCOs who did not have what it takes to get a real commission.

Warrant officers were a breed apart in the army. They had all the privileges of officers, but they never commanded; they were specialists in technical fields. Jack considered that the better sort flew helicopters, but the farts were ordnance, communications, and administrative specialists, mere craftsmen, not soldiers. And the worst of the lot, the most useless in Jack's opinion, were the administrative warrants. To Jack, all warrant officers were shirking responsibility. They couldn't work with troops like NCOs, and they couldn't lead men like officers were supposed to do, so they became technicians and got fat and disrespectful.

Now Harry shuffled papers somewhere within General Westmoreland's headquarters. Somehow he never seemed to have any work to do because he could be seen gallivanting all over Saigon during duty hours. If that was not sufficient reason to despise him, he was ugly, fat, and cruel. He had the cunning and the morals of a jackal, and that made him dangerous as well. But Harry had made a fortune in the Vietnam drug market, and Jack, because he wanted some of that money, tolerated, even cultivated, Harry's acquaintance. More and more, however, he was coming to wonder if the effort was worth the loss of self-respect it cost him to be civil to such a creature.

"How's things been goin', ole buddy?" Harry asked.

"Still workin' for pennies, Harry," Jack answered, hoping Harry would catch the hint. As usual, he did not, or if he had, he was careful not to let on.

Fireworks were going off everywhere. As they paused at a traffic light, a large firecracker exploded nearby, and Harry started violently. "Goddamn fuckin' idiots! I hope the little shits blow *all* their fingers off! I'd like to see 'em all with their little peckers cut off."

Jack sighed. In a little while it would be Tet, the lunar new year, a very special holiday for the Vietnamese, something like Christmas, Thanksgiving, and New Year all combined. It was a time for visiting relatives, giving gifts, and starting all over again. For the last several years, because of the war, the South Vietnamese government had not permitted the use of fireworks in observance of Tet, and military personnel had to accept restricted furlough privileges.

But this year, the Year of the Monkey, would be different. A truce with the Communists was to go into effect soon, and everyone believed this one would endure through the holidays. So South Vietnamese soldiers were being given permission to return to their homes to observe the new year, and everyone was shooting off fireworks throughout the cities. It was almost as if the war had come at last to Saigon, and Jack thought that if the Communists were to break the truce and attack, most people would ignore the gunshots until it was too late, under the impression they were only firecrackers going off.

"Smell that disgusting shit?" Harry asked, gesturing vaguely at some market stalls along the sidewalk. Jack smelled nothing out of the ordinary, but he knew that his nose had become accustomed to the city's smells and that those odors offended some Americans to an extreme.

Jack was well aware of the sanitary problems rampant in a city the size of Saigon in the midst of a war, under the oppressive pall of dust and hydrocarbons mixed with the reek of garbage, but he was also aware of other odors, exotic and wonderful: noodle soup simmering over charcoal fires in little street-corner stalls; the haunting fragrances of hidden flower gardens wafting over high walls into narrow, sun-baked streets; the smell of paving stones drying in the sun after a shower; and a galaxy of other, delicate, ineluctable aromas that were basic ingredients of the city's ambience.

Now they were passing a theater marquee. Loudspeakers dinned the screeching and wailing music of *cai luong*, the popular Vietnamese opera.

"Goddamn people don't speak no human language I ever heard," Harry muttered sourly. Jack thought *cai luong* silly and noisy, as inane as any American popular music, but he respected the traditional Vietnamese folk music, which he thought was beautiful, and he never tired of hearing the Vietnamese language spoken. "Lazy fucks," Harry said of no one in particular, but meaning the whole Vietnamese people. Jack looked at Phu for a reaction, but the driver's face remained impassive. It was clear to Jack that when they worked for themselves, the Vietnamese were among the most industrious people on the face of the earth. The constant flow of traffic and other activity in Saigon's streets proved that and was the main source of excitement in, and set the tempo for, Jack's own life.

"Well, it's not like in the old days, huh, Harry?" Jack remarked, trying to lighten the conversation.

"Yeah. In the 'old days' there wasn't so much American money in the black market," Harry snorted.

"Well, Harry, that money's there for anybody who wants it," Jack hinted. Harry did not reply. Jack sighed. If the Saigonese were corrupt, well, so was he. The Vietnamese only wanted what he and Harry already had, and there was plenty of that to go around.

"Hey, Jack," Harry said suddenly, "I know a guy, wants to buy a couple of thirty-eights. Can do?"

"Sure, old buddy," Jack replied with false enthusiasm. "Have him give me a call in the morning." Chicken feed, Jack thought. But he would have to follow through now. That's the story of my life, he told himself. He was just too talented at putting people with things for sale or trade in touch with others who wanted to buy or barter. It had started years ago, when he discovered he was adept at scrounging. He thought about the quartermaster operation at Ft. Sherman. That had been fun but not very profitable. I'm just too kind-hearted to make money off decent people, Jack thought.

He took out his handkerchief and mopped the sweat from his brow. It came away stained black. The dust from Saigon's pulverized streets, mixed with the exhaust fumes from thousands of vehicles, clung to his skin in a fine coat of grime. Sure as hell isn't like the old days, Jack told himself ruefully. Those days had been back in '62 and '63, before the city had swelled with refugees and Americans, before the stately tamarind trees had been cut down to widen the boulevards. Jack believed as a matter of faith that those days would come again, just as soon as the war was over and all the Americans, save a small garrison of which he planned to be a member, had gone home at last and the country would be at peace again. Eagerly Jack awaited the renaissance.

"Seven come eleven, baby needs a new pair of shoes!" Harry chortled as Phu pulled to the curb in front of the Plaza. Jack stepped to the pavement and tilted his seat forward so Harry could get out.

A block behind them, unnoticed by either man, a black Chevrolet sedan with civilian license plates pulled to the curb. The driver was a grim-faced, heavyset man in ill-fitting civilian clothing, another American. He had followed them from Cholon. He was watching them now closely.

Immediately they were surrounded by half a dozen of the ubiquitous street urchins that infested the neighborhoods frequented by Americans. Grimy, homeless waifs, they made a precarious living begging and stealing from American servicemen. Jack felt sorry for the children, but at the same time they embarrassed him, too. They were a constant reminder that there was something wrong in Vietnam, that the wrongness had to do with the war, and Jack would not even be there had it not been for the war. That made him feel responsible for the children.

"Hey, you GI! You gimme one hunnert pee, okay? You gimme Salem, okay?" the small boys shrieked, crowding as close to the two Americans as they could get. Jack's hand automatically went to protect his wallet, just in time to frustrate some tiny fingers plucking at his right rear pocket.

"*Di-di*, you little shits!" Harry bellowed, shoving his way through the children.

"Hey, fuck you, GI!" one of the boys shouted. Harry's face reddened, and he swung an open-handed blow at the child, who, laughing, dodged it nimbly. Frustrated, Harry kicked at the boy closest to him. The child howled in pain as the blow connected with his shin. "Fuck your sister!" the boy screamed at the big American. Harry lunged for him, but he hopped away, shouting curses fluently at the warrant officer.

"Hey, hey." One of the boys pulled on Jack's arm. "You wanna fuck my sister? *Beaucoup* pretty babysan. Five hunnert pee, okay?"

"How old your sister?" Jack asked, feigning interest.

"Young, young! Fipteen, fipteen! She babysan! Okay, you? We go now."

"She got the clap or the siff?" Jack asked.

"No! No! She clean girl!" the boy shouted back.

Jack produced a one-hundred-piaster note, worth less than a dollar, and handed it to the boy. "Go home, little brother," he told him in Vietnamese. The child took the bill and ran down the street. The others flocked around Jack, and he gave the oldest one, who could not have been over twelve, a fistful of crumpled small-denomination notes. "Share this with your brothers," he admonished the boy in Vietnamese, "and leave us alone." The boys scampered off obediently.

Harry shook his head. "Jackie my boy, you have been over here far too long," he wheezed. "When you goin' home, huh?"

"I am home, Harry. I am home," Jack muttered.

As Phu pulled away from the curb, the big man in the black sedan remained where he was, watching Harry Scheldt. He knew Jack well, but he knew Harry better, and it was Harry he was after.

* * *

It was raining Sunday when Phu picked Jack up. Jack loved Saigon in the rain. Rain relaxed him and made him feel easy. He loved the sound of it falling in the trees and the swishing sound car tires made as they plowed through the wet streets. The monsoon in Saigon never got as bad as it did in other parts of the country but was more like the extended summer storms he knew back home.

Ana's apartment was in a big building along the left-hand side of Nguyen Lam Street, a block before it ran into Tran Quoc Toan Street and not far from the Phu Tho Racetrack. It was a busy little street. Jack had Phu drop him off a block away.

Nguyen Lam Street was narrow and crowded with foot traffic. Every bit of space along the curb was filled with vendors' stalls and eager shoppers. As Phu pulled away from the curb, Jack was forced to seek shelter from the rain under the awning of a shop selling dried fish and squid. An ancient, emaciated Chinese man sat behind bales and stacks of dried sea creatures, smoking a ragged, hand-rolled cigarette. His smile revealed several gold teeth. He gestured with a bony forefinger at his own close-shaven scalp

"We must share the same barber," Jack said dryly, and smiled back. The man laughed and nodded vigorously, as if he understood and shared the joke. The bartenders at Sonya's had been patiently schooling Jack in the Cantonese dialect over the last weeks, and he decided to try his Chinese on the old man. "*Tsing-Tsang, nay ho ma,*" he said, hoping it really meant something like "Good day, old gentleman." He did not trust his tutors not to foist off an obscenity on him disguised as a scrap of polite Chinese. To be sure, he followed the Chinese with "Hello, Grandfather. How are you?" in Vietnamese.

The old man's smile broadened, and he bobbed his head several times. Impulsively, Jack dug out a half empty package of Pall Malls and shook out several cigarettes, which he offered to the old man. The man's ancient eyes widened in surprise and gratitude, and bowing his head again, he held out a palm. The fingers of the hand were stained with tobacco, the nails dirty and broken and the flesh of the palm covered with calluses representing years of hard work. By contrast, Jack's own hand looked like an overgrown baby's.

"T'ank you ver' much," the old man said. He pronounced the unfamiliar words carefully and distinctly. The smile had left his face, and he regarded Jack openly, speculatively. His eyes were deep set, very bright and intelligent. Jack marveled at the transformation and wondered if the old man were calculating how much money he could skin this big, dumb American for.

On subsequent visits, Jack always stopped to pay his respects to the old fishmonger, even buying some dried squid from him, which, to Ana's vast amusement, he dutifully ate for snacks.

Giving the old man a casual salute, Jack stepped back into the street and resumed threading his way down to Ana's apartment building. Its corridors were as busy as the street outside. Children rampaged up and down the narrow, high-ceilinged hallways; old women, burdened under loads of wet laundry or packages of foodstuffs for the noontime meal, hobbled up and down the narrow stairway. Because most families in Vietnam lacked means of refrigeration, they had to shop for food nearly every day.

Jack climbed laboriously through this vast crowd of very young and very old people to the third floor, where Ana's apartment was located. The corridor leading to her room was dimly lit and cool. Radios blared, children screamed, and the odors of kerosene and charcoal cooking fires, the precursors of the lunch hour, enriched the still air.

Jack paused before Ana's door. He felt very conspicuous standing there, and he was well aware of the many pairs of coal-black little eyes fixed upon him. He had the uncomfortable feeling that whatever happened behind that door at lunchtime would be the major topic of conversation among every family in the building by suppertime. A woman emerged from an apartment just down the hall and, looking at Jack over her shoulder, shooed several children inside. The door slammed with a bang.

Hitching his pistol belt firmly about his waist, Jack knocked.

Ana opened at once. "I think maybe you not come," she whispered, opening the door just enough to let him in. Jack stepped through quickly. The first thing he noticed was the light, a subdued, mellow yellow, filtering through curtains Ana had fixed over the room's only window. The window was open, permitting a slight breeze to ruffle the curtains. Muted street noises came from below.

The second thing Jack noticed—and the sensation that stayed with him ever after—was the aroma. The dominant fragrance was of bath powder, a lilac-scented bouquet fresh and inviting that reminded him of warm and leisurely baths, the physical lassitude of long hot soaks combined with the excitement of vigorous towelings. Under this were other delightful scents: the sweet incense of joss sticks smoldering before a tiny Buddhist shrine atop a dresser; perfumes and aromatic toilet waters; the crisp, clean smell of fresh linen. Ana took his hand and led him to a comfortable rattan armchair by the window. To Jack, the short walk across the tiny room seemed like wading through a warm embrace. He took off his pistol belt and placed it on the floor, under the chair, where he also stowed his fatigue cap.

"Would you like a beer?"

He nodded, and Ana opened the door of a small Japanese refrigerator, the gift of a former boyfriend, he realized, and took out a cold bottle of "33." The beer was expertly poured into a tall glass so there was less than an inch of head to top it off.

Ana was wearing slippers, white silk pantaloons, and a white cotton jacket with a high collar and full-length loose sleeves. A rose embroidered in red over the heart added a splash of color. Her shoulder-length, raven-black hair was kept neatly in place by a red ribbon.

"I cooking for you now, Jack. You stay here, maybe ten minutes, I come back." Ana picked up a metal tray holding several covered dishes and, balancing it carefully, eased open the door. She turned and smiled coquettishly at Jack as she went out, softly hooking the door with a foot and closing it expertly behind her.

Jack sighed and scratched his crotch absendmindedly.

The room was larger than he first took it to be, about twelve by fourteen. Along the wall to his right was Ana's bed, covered by a tightly drawn sheet. The billowing mosquito netting had been drawn back, and it swayed languorously in air currents kept constantly in motion by an old ceiling fan that swish-swished comfortingly overhead. The opposite side of the room was taken up by a dresser with huge mirror and a stand-up wardrobe, which Jack assumed contained Ana's clothing. The tile floor was partially covered by a rattan carpet decorated in floral designs. The rattan table in front of Jack was covered with a thin piece of glass and flanked by two other comfortable armchairs, also made with rattan.

The shelf beneath the table held several cheap magazines, on the covers of which handsome Oriental men and women embraced or advertised such products as toothpaste and cosmetics. Idly, he flipped through one. It was all in Chinese and, judging from the photographs, consisted mostly of articles and stories about movie stars. In a little box containing editorial information was an English inscription: "Printed in the Republic of China."

The meal Ana prepared for Jack was indifferent, and soon afterward he had trouble remembering what he had eaten. There was a piece of tough, overcooked meat that was supposed to pass for steak, a fresh salad of green and red vegetables. Jack had been hoping for fried rice and noodle soup. Ana did not eat herself but attempted to keep a desultory conversation going as Jack plowed dutifully through the food, muttering insincere compliments about Ana's cooking.

Both knew the meal was only a ritual, an obligatory prefatory rite to what Jack had really come for.

After eating, Jack quietly sipped the remainder of his beer.

"You have girlfriend?" Ana asked, feigning indifference to the answer.

"No," Jack answered honestly.

"Maybe you would like . . . ?"

"Life is lonely sometimes, Ana."

"I had boyfriend once, his name Frank. He go back home maybe one year ago. He say he come back for me." Ana sighed. "Do you think he will?"

"No, Ana, I don't think he will."

Ana nodded. "He was nice to me, Jack," she said wistfully.

Jack grinned. "How could anyone not be nice to you?" Ana looked small and helpless sitting there, so plainly asking him to be her man, to keep her, to pay the rent, buy her things, even love her if he could, but that would not be an essential part of whatever bargain they struck that afternoon. Ana wanted Jack to try her goods, and if he liked them, maybe he would come back to stay.

Suddenly Jack was reminded of the birdhouses he had made when he was a boy. He would painstakingly fix them in trees in the backyard and then watch breathlessly to see if the birds would be attracted to them. None ever was, and now Jack remembered his poignant disappointment. Later his father had given him an air rifle, and he'd used it to kill the spiteful, ungrateful little creatures. It was not an act he liked to be reminded of.

"Maybe you like lie down, Jack? Rest for a while?"

It was the invitation Jack had been waiting for. He admired Ana for the way she made the move, a perfectly natural and friendly gesture, much more graceful than simply flinging off one's clothes and fucking.

His back to Ana, Jack undressed, folding his uniform meticulously and depositing his things on the floor near the foot of the bed. He stripped down to his shorts and sat on the edge of the mattress.

Ana stood presenting her now naked body before him. Half-aroused since he had come into the room, the sight, the smells, the whole atmosphere completed the process. With some difficulty he managed to slip off his shorts. He was surprised and gratified by the pleasant ache throbbing between his thighs.

Ana Chin was everything Jack Kelley had imagined she would be. Her body was like sculptured ivory, all the right curves in just the right places. Her nipples presented themselves like hard ripe little rosebuds, begging caresses. Her vulva was covered with a luxuriant growth of fine black hair, something Jack had seldom seen on any Oriental woman and something that excited him enormously.

Ana's thighs, sliding along Jack's, bumped his engorged organ and made it smack with a hollow *thwap* against his belly. Ana laughed, and they fell back onto the bed. She sucked his nipples gently and squeezed him tenderly with one hand. He rolled on top of her and pressed himself fiercely against her.

Then he forgot everything—the time, the place, the circumstance; he forgot everything except the beautiful woman who now lay beneath him, responding to his every kiss and caress. She rolled her head slowly back and forth, moaning and gasping softly. Jack lost himself in gentle, tender foreplay as Ana opened her wonderful body to him like a delicate, scented sandalwood box crammed with amazing treasures, each one of which Jack withdrew, examined, savored as if the richest, ripest pomegranate ever extolled by a prophet—and they were. They were sweet and delicious, and the sweetest and most delicious of all was that wonderful, magical, enchanted forest where he drank her ambrosia as Ana ran her hands wildly over his close-cropped head, calling his name aloud, giving no thought to the neighbors, the war, or the world. They were lost beyond recovery in the sheer ecstasy of themselves.

And at last, instinctively picking just the right moment, Jack intersected the arcing parabolas of their ecstasies and engrossed himself in Ana Chin and wrote his passion for her in long, racking spasms that forced the air from his lungs. His perspiration mixed with hers in sinuous, delightful rivulets that dampened the sheets beneath them, and something fabulous passed between them, embracing them and enfolding them in its sensuous fabric and changing them both a little, irrevocably and forever.

At nine P.M. Jack stumbled down the darkened stairwell to the street and hailed a pedicab to take him home. He half drowsed on the long ride through the dark wet streets, even at that hour, still crowded with the hustle and bustle of one of the busiest, most exotic, and most dangerous capitals of the world. Jack Kelley, man of the world, soldier of fortune who never changed allegiance, a veteran of two wars, a successful wooer of women from Stuttgart to Seoul, had never encountered a woman like Ana Chin. He had lost forever part of his vital essence in that little room on Nguyen Lam Street, and yet what he had lost had, at the same time, been replaced by something Ana had given him, freely and joyously, without any strings attached.

Jack Kelley knew then that he was destined to see a lot more of Ana Chin, and that it would be a long time before he ever thought about another woman again. He stretched luxuriously, causing the pedicab driver to smile wryly. But it wouldn't be *that* long, he promised himself.

This Foreshadowed Food

"THE LENGTH OF A MAN'S PENIS IS DIRECTLY PRO-portional to the length of his nose," Mrs. Ba informed her luncheon guests. The old woman chuckled as her chopsticks plied the rice bowl and scooped up globs that she stuffed eagerly into her mouth. She did not chew betel nut, as did many Vietnamese women her age, so her teeth were pearly white, not stained black.

Lien laughed, thinking how true the old woman's formula was. Aspby's nose was *this* long, and his penis was *that* long! Yes, Mrs. Ba was right.

"John's penis is not very long, but it's thick," Thu volunteered. Thu was Lien's friend and neighbor.

"Just like this piece of *thiet heo*?" Mrs. Ba teased, fishing a succulent chunk of pork out of the meat dish. It was long and quivered suspended between the old woman's chopsticks, dripping droplets of juice back into the bowl. Mrs. Ba dipped the pork into the *mam thom* and popped it into her mouth. The sharp, fishy-smelling shrimp sauce added flavor to the boiled pork.

"Is John's prick hot, too?" Lien joked. Thu's face reddened. Mrs. Ba laughed around her mouthful of pork and rice. "Thu, sometimes you are so naive," Lien laughed, shaking her head.

"Well, Thu, you've told us everything else, so come —how big are John's balls?" Mrs. Ba asked. Thu, who was at that moment sampling the *canh chua*, a soup made from pork bones and tomatoes, coughed violently as some went down her windpipe, but even as she did so, she held out her arms, hands up, as if hefting two huge melons. Mrs. Ba shrieked in laughter and even the normally restrained Lien had to cover her mouth with one hand.

Thu drank some water, to calm her coughing fit.

Lien helped herself to a liberal portion of *com*, steaming hot rice that was white as driven snow, and Mrs. Ba belched loudly as she attacked two plates of fruit, one heaped with *duu hau*, the other *xoai*. The watermelon and mangos were delicious, sweet and rich and cool, a perfect dessert for the meal they had just consumed.

The luncheon was not a special event. Mrs. Ba dined frequently with Lien and Thu, as they rented rooms in her house from her. In fact, the three did other business together as well—mostly selling black market items, including currency and goods from the American post exchange system.

"Well, the upshot of all this penis talk is that *we* are the ones who have to pay for sampling them, no matter how big they are," Lien said. Mrs. Ba nodded sagely. Both the younger women had had babies by Americans. The men would leave someday without either children or the children's mothers. The mothers knew it. Mrs. Ba had seen it before, first with the French, then the Japanese, and then the French again, after the end of World War II. Since 1961, it had been the Americans. All soldiers were the same to her, regardless of their nationality: oversexed and enormously hungry.

Lien and Thu were ruined women. No decent Vietnamese family would allow a son to marry women who had had children by a foreigner.

"Where are you going for Tet?" Mrs. Ba asked no one in particular.

"To Can Tho, to visit my mother," Thu answered.

"I'm taking Tan and going back to Nha Trang, to see father," Lien replied. Tan was the son Aspby had given her.

"Do you think Tan is old enough for such a long trip?" Mrs. Ba asked.

Lien shrugged and drank some water. "Why not? He's fifteen months now. That's old enough to travel."

"How long does that trip take?" Thu wanted to know.

"We'll leave around five A.M. and if all goes well, we'll get into Nha Trang before dark; maybe twelve to thirteen hours."

"Buy your tickets before you leave," Mrs. Ba advised, "to reserve yourself a seat."

Lien shrugged. "I always buy the tickets at the station. Besides, the driver is a friend of mine, so no problem."

"How much does it cost?" Thu asked.

"Five thousand dong," Lien said. "My Jim has given me the money. That's twenty-five dollars. Not very much to an American."

"It may be dangerous," Thu warned.

"This year we will have a truce with the Viet Cong. It should be safe."

"Whoever told you *that*?" Mrs. Ba asked, more sharply than she intended. The younger women looked in surprise at her. "You can never trust the Communists," she admonished. "I know them. I remember when they took over in the north, back in '54. It was bad for everyone who had supported the French but worst for the women who had taken Frenchmen for lovers." This statement struck fear into the other two, and Mrs. Ba saw in their eyes all too clearly the question they were afraid to ask. Mrs. Ba relented. "If the Americans leave Vietnam," she assured them, "we shall survive. I survived, back in '54," she went on firmly. "It wasn't easy, but I came south, and I brought some gold with me. Haven't I been successful since then?"

"Yes, but if the Communists take over here . . . ?" Thu ventured timorously to give voice to the unthinkable.

"Then we will go elsewhere, child! To America, or to France, perhaps. I have a good friend with French citizenship and connections in Paris. And I have money. Well, girls, let's stop all this depressing talk. It is almost Tet and we should start the new year off properly. We want nineteen-sixty-eight to be the best year of our lives." Lien and Thu nodded their agreement.

"But remember this," Mrs. Ba said, "If anything does happen—politically, that is—I will take care of you and your children if your men do not. I have no living relatives and you are my 'substitute' family. You know that. And I haven't survived in this country for fifty years without learning quite a few tricks. Trust me. There is no man alive who can get the better of this old woman."

Lien nodded. She could trust Mrs. Ba. They had known each other a long time and the old woman neither threatened nor promised lightly. She was a good friend and an implacable enemy. Lien knew that a Chinese businessman had cheated Mrs. Ba in a big transaction many years before. Mrs. Ba's revenge had been to hire some thugs to kidnap the hapless merchant. She had personally supervised the hacking off of his testicles.

After the meal the three women retired to their respective chambers for a siesta. Lien lay under her cooling fan, waiting for sleep to come. The housegirl had taken Tan to the market with her while she did the shopping, so the apartment was quiet.

Lien thought about the trip to Nha Trang. It would be long and the bus would be crowded. At least she would not have to travel alone. Her good friend, Miss Thuyet, would be coming along all the way. She considered buying the tickets in advance, as Mrs. Ba had advised, but decided she would buy them at the station as planned.

Lien was not looking forward to this trip and wished

she could stay in Saigon to spend the holidays with Aspby. But when he was gone, as surely he would be someday, her family would still be there.

Thinking about Aspby reminded her of one of his most annoying idiosyncracies. In her imagination she could see him, lying in bed hour after hour, absorbed in a paperback book. When he was reading Aspby was oblivious to everything else. Sometimes Lien fostered a real jealousy toward his books. When he is into them, she thought, he is not into me. She chuckled, pleased with the pun.

Her eyelids grew heavy. Maybe taking a book along to read on the trip to Nha Trang would make the time pass more quickly, she thought. She sighed. Sometimes she wished she knew how to read.

Subterranean Freight

"AWRIGHT, GENTLEMEN," ASPBY ANNOUNCED, "MY game is jacks or better, all the way. That is, if you don't open on jacks first time, it's queens next, then kings, and finally aces 'n' back to jacks. The ante goes up, too, dollar on jacks, two bucks on queens, three kings, four aces. Got it? Okay, here they come."

It was early yet, not quite eight P.M., and Aspby had been in the game since around seven. It was a floating poker game, and it went on every night of the year at the John Houston. Gambling and drinking were the two great pastimes of the American army in Vietnam.

"I see there's a big peace rally at Berkeley again," one man commented.

"Aw, what's new, Al? Buncha college kids, professors, perfessional peace activists, who gives a shit?"

"That's right, man. Long as we're winnin' this war, who cares what the peaceniks does?"

"Hanoi loves it," said the fourth man in the game,

"they think it means we don't have the guts to stick this war out."

"Cards coming, fellas," Aspby announced. Quickly, deftly, he dealt each man a small pile of five cards each. The room grew silent as each scrutinized his hand.

"Who dealt this shit?" one asked.

"I don't have a hand, I've got a foot," someone else groaned.

"You're a worthless dealer," commented another.

"I've got five of a kind, all different," one said, chuckling.

"Openers, gentlemen?" Aspby inquired politely.

"I open fer a buck," announced the man to Aspby's immediate left. He tossed a crumpled bill into the ante. So, at least a pair of jacks, Aspby thought. Each of the other men, despite their complaining about the quality of the cards he had dealt to them, raised the opener, so that when it came Aspby's turn to bet, he owed the pot four dollars.

"It's on you, Jim, four bucks, unless you fold or raise," the man to Aspby's right reminded him.

"I know, I know, I'm just tryin' to figure you guys out is all." He studied his cards. He had a pair of kings.

"I think they should ban all antiwar demonstrations back home," the first man said. "It's bad for morale 'n' gives aid and comfort to the enemy."

"If we did that shit, how'd we be any different from the Communists?" another wanted to know.

"Sure, but you can't fight a war and debate it at the same time," countered the first.

"This is not a declared war, buddy," a third chimed in. "Maybe it should be, but LBJ thinks he can fight it and win without a declaration of war from Congress."

"He couldn't get one, pardner," said the fourth player. "No matter what, the American people don't see North Vietnam as any real threat to us, and let's face it, it ain't."

"I'm in," Aspby announced, and counted out four

bills, which he threw into the pot. "Cards to the gamblers."

The man to his left took two. Something with a kicker? Aspby wondered. Three of a kind, maybe.

"I'll play these," the second man announced smugly. Is he bluffing? Aspby wondered. No, he couldn't be. At the very least he had two pair and was trying to conceal his hand by standing pat. But more likely he really had a straight or a flush.

The third man took three cards, an honest player, Aspby told himself, and the fourth man took only one. Maybe two pair there, an open-ended straight or four cards to a flush. Players one and two were the ones to worry about.

Aspby dealt himself three cards to his pair of kings. They all waited for the opener to bet.

"I'll tell you guys how to win this war," the opener announced. "You take all the Vietnamese you know are with us, see, 'n' you evacuate 'em to boats in the South China Sea. Then you take atom bombs and obliterate everything left behind." He paused dramatically. "And then you sink the ships!" He laughed.

"Grab 'em by the balls 'n' their 'hearts and minds' are sure to follow," said another, also laughing.

"We oughta send some divisions into Cambodia and Laos and tear up the Ho Chi Minh Trail," said one.

"I say pound the piss out of North Vietnam," the fourth man chimed in. "We ought to go after everything that moves up there."

"And no truces!" shouted the first player. "We hit Hanoi with everything we got, show 'em we mean business and got the muscle, *then* and only then we talk 'truce,' and the terms will be withdrawal of North Vietnamese troops from South Vietnam."

Throughout this exchange, Aspby had not looked at his cards. He shuffled them together patiently, waiting for the opener to bet. Grimly, he bet a dollar and was raised by the other three men in their turn. These guys mean business, Aspby told himself. He picked up his small stack of cards. The one on the bottom was the king of spades. Three kings! That was encouraging but probably not worth calling on. Slowly, very slowly, he squeezed the next card out from behind the king. Two of spades. The third and fourth cards were the two kings he had been dealt. He hesitated to look at the fifth card.

"C'mon, for chrissakes, shit or get off the pot!" the opener demanded.

"I think our first mistake in this war was we didn't jump in with both feet in sixty-five," said the third player. "Instead, we dribbled in here, a few men at a time, so all the Commies gotta do is match us move for move. We telegraph our punches."

"Well," the second player said, "we're afraid China'll come in with a milliion men on the side of the North Vietnamese, like they did for the Koreans in 1950. Believe me, buddy, I was on the Yalu that winter, and I'll never forget it."

"I was in Korea, too, in fifty-two and fifty-three, and believe *me*, those Korean winters were a bitch," announced the first player. "But at least here it's *warm*. Big fuckin' difference, lemme tell ya."

"Well, let me tell you all somethin', and that is, China'll never come in this time," the fourth man said. "They won't come in because they really don't love the Vietnamese, nor do the Vietnamese like them so much, and they know we won't drive north of the seventeenth parallel and try for their borders like we did in Korea. If MacArthur had stopped at the thirty-eighth parallel, after Inchŏn, the Chinese never would've come in."

"Yes," said the opener, "and if old Harry Truman had had the balls, he'd have let Mac wax them when they did, hit their bases in China, and blast their field armies with nukes. We're doing the same shit in this war now, givin' the Commies all the sanctuary they need to build up their forces."

Aspby squeezed the fifth card out from behind the deuce. It was the king of hearts. *Four kings!*

"Yeah," another man commented, "we never seem

to learn, do we? Remember in Korea, the Eighth Air Force'd bomb them during the daytime, and at night they'd send out a bunch of coolies to rebuild the roads, clear the passes, construct fords across the rivers where we knocked out the bridges, and before morning their men and supplies would be rollin' to the front again. Same goddamn thing is happening now."

"Ahem," Aspby cleared his throat. "I call and raise you all back a dollar."

"Not me, by Christ!" the first man said disgustedly. "I've got trips—aces—and I'm folding 'em, you bastards." He showed his three aces and tossed his cards into the center of the table. The second man called without comment, but the third raised Aspby back while the fourth player called that raise and looked expectantly to Aspby for the next move.

Aspby raised back. An excited chorus of curses and exclamations escaped the remaining players, but they all called Aspby's raise. He savored the moment. Dollar bills and change lay heaped in the center of the table. Only a straight flush could beat him because he knew three of the four aces in the deck had already been played. And he knew there was no straight flush in this game because if there were, the man who had it would have continued raising until doomsday.

"I got four gentlemen," Aspby announced, laying his cards on the table. The second player whistled and showed a ten-high club flush. "Got it on the deal," he said.

"Who'd ever have thought it?" the third man wondered aloud. "My poor sainted momma—may she rest in pieces—told me there would be days like this one." Slowly, sadly, he flipped four threes and the case ace onto the table.

"To hold *four of a kind* and get beat!" exclaimed the fourth man. "It makes me feel better." He showed three queens and a pair of eights. "Caught the third queen on the draw," he remarked to no one in particular.

Aspby scraped in the money, singing, "Bringing in the

sheaves, bringing in the sheaves, We will come rejoicing, bringing in the sheaves!" Then he said, "And I will tell you what, my friends, we will win this war. I know it in my bones. We hold all the fucking cards! We're waxing 'em everywhere, and we're gonna win. And now that I am ahead, I am going to Wiseman's for a spot of supper. Any of you fools wanna chow down, the tab's on me."

Aspby was having a vivid dream. He was standing in a long line of naked people. They were inside what seemed to be a vast factory of some kind. At the head of the line was a loading dock with a short flight of metal steps leading to a small door. From somewhere outside the building came a menacing roar, as if a titanic wind or tidal wave were rushing relentlessly down on them. He *had* to get through that doorway and to the safety beyond! But the line was moving too slowly, and none of the others seemed particularly concerned about the danger.

He awoke with a start. His first thought, the dream images still fresh in his mind, was, Well, I wonder what Grandma would've made of *that* one? Then he realized something in the room was dreadfully wrong, though it took him a moment to realize what it was. He was covered from head to foot in grease! It was ridiculous, but there it was nevertheless, he could feel it in his hair and on his arms and everywhere, and it had even stuck his sheets together.

Quickly he reviewed the events of the night before. After the card game he had gone over to Wiseman's, a cheap GI dive opposite the Lucky BOQ on Ngo Quyen Street, where he'd eaten a big bowl of their delicious Chinese noodle soup and had had five or six Scotch and sodas. He clearly remembered hailing a cab later and riding back up Tran Hung Dao to the John Houston. He had considered stopping by to see Jack Kelley at the WhiteStone, just down the street from Wiseman's, but he remembered disregarding that plan in favor of getting to bed, so he couldn't have been drunk; he hadn't fallen down somewhere in an alcoholic blackout and rolled in a pool of grease or oil.

He raised a hand before his eyes. Yes, there it was, grease or oil, caked all over his fingers and on his wrist and arm. He brought the arm closer and smelled it.

It was dried excrement. The truth dawned upon him. He'd had a bowel movement while sleeping, and he'd been lying in the stuff for hours. Now he could feel it around his buttocks and between his legs. He hoped it was the big bowl of soup and all the Scotch, and not his dysentery returning.

He got out of his bed, stripped the sheets, and bundled them into the shower. He washed himself off thoroughly and was rinsing the sheets out when suddenly the lights went off. He stood there in total darkness, cursing quietly. Power outages were common in wartime Saigon, but the cursing made him feel better.

He remembered a piece of candle in the shaving cabinet. He fumbled matches from his bedside stand and, lighting one, found the candle among the razor blades and cans of shaving cream. It was a pitiful little thing, about the size of a birthday candle, but it gave off enough light so that he could finish rinsing the sheets. His maid would wash them for him in the morning, but he could not tolerate giving them to her all covered with excrement.

"What a way to fight a war," he muttered as he hung the sheets in the shower to dry. He turned his mattress over and spent the rest of the night under a light blanket. His new roommate never said a word, and by the time Aspby got back from work the next afternoon, he was gone.

The next morning, haggard from lack of sleep and still embarrassed by what had happened, Aspby stood disconsolately on the corner waiting for Jack to pick him up. Fifteen minutes beyond the usual time, he realized Jack was not coming. With a mounting sense of frustration, he hailed a motorized cyclo. Cyclos came in two types: three-wheeled pedicabs and three-wheeled motorized versions; in both, the passenger sat in front of the driver and, in case of accident, was the first to fly. Aspby could tell the good cyclos from the bad ones because the good cyclos had firm, reasonably clean cushions to sit on.

"Take me to Tran Quoc Toan Boulevard," he said as he got in.

The driver turned left on Petrus Ky Avenue, beside what used to be the old U.S. Military Assistance Group compound. Aspby had worked there in 1962, and he could never pass the spot without memories flooding back upon him. Today it was headquarters for the Republic of Korea forces. Frankly, the place never looked better. The ROKs had patched up the walls and put on a new coat of whitewash.

The driver slowed before the Vinh Vien Street intersection. Aspby was horrified to see looming ahead of them a gigantic mound of garbage. Apparently it had been accumulating by the roadside for days, and now it filled the roadway with a vile, viscous mush of pulverized rotting vegetable matter that had the consistency of mud.

Just before the monstrosity, a taxicab sat, its engine idling. Apparently the driver couldn't make up his mind whether to plow through or to back up and find a way around the garbage. The cyclo pulled up behind the cab, and that made up the driver's mind for him. He rammed the gears into first and plowed through, mushy garbage splashing away from his wheels like water from a ship's prow. His passenger, an elderly Vietnamese woman, screamed in protest, but finally the cab burst through into the clear on the other side.

Seeing that it could be done, the cyclo driver began revving his engine. Aspby turned to remonstrate with the man, but he only grinned wildly. Then they hurtled forward at top speed.

"Jesus Christ, *no!*" Aspby screamed, forgetting momentarily the Vietnamese for "stop," but before he could jump free, the cyclo slammed into the garbage with a solid impact. Aspby pulled his legs up and cowered as far back in the seat as he could. Two mountains of variegated, reeking filth loomed over his head on either side of the narrow, undulating pool of slime covering the roadway. The cyclo's engine picked that precise moment, when they were smack in the middle of the mess, to die.

Aspby let out an involuntary half scream half shout, and behind him the cyclo driver muttered as he tried frantically to kick life back into the engine. The stench was nauseating, overpowering, and cloying. Everywhere around him were old fruit peels, chicken bones, indescribable mounds of maggoty substances writhing within inches of his nose.

To get out now, they would have to *walk* through the stuff. "You dumb bastard!" Aspby shouted at the cyclo driver. "You goddamned motherfucking bastard!" Aspby gagged on the stench, and a rising wave of nausea cut off his curses abruptly.

Suddenly, the cyclo engine started. Carefully, the driver revved it a few times and then shifted into gear, and they spurted forward. An instant later they broke free of the garbage.

Aspby collapsed back into his seat, his uniform soaking with perspiration. He still wanted to throw up, but soon the fresh air blowing into his face restored him and he was himself again.

He had known about the garbage piles for some time now. They were just another sign that the city's administration was breaking down under pressure of the increasing tempo of the war and the thousands of refugees who were every day crowding into Saigon.

Something had gone out of the life of this city, to be replaced by—what? An intricate balance had been upset, and the fact that his once beautiful garden of Saigon was turning into a reeking garbage dump was an ill wind indeed. Jim Aspby knew something terrible was coming, and it frightened him.

Half a Bag of Poems

GENERAL TON SIGHED DEEPLY AND REVERENTLY closed the covers of the little book. He had had it so long it was part of him now. His father had given it to him on his fifteenth birthday. He could not imagine life without it.

The general closed his eyes and leaned his head back. He stayed like this for many minutes. Then he opened the book and read: "By lamplight turn these scented leaves and read a tale of love recorded in old books." He rolled the delicious words through his mind, savoring the purity and elegance of the beautiful language.

As often as he read Nguyen Du's classic *Tale of Kieu*, he never tired of its beauty, truly the highest flowering of Vietnamese literature. And yet what a mystery how the old scholar-poet and sometime diplomat at the court of Emperor Gia Long had managed to take such a really pedestrian story, borrowed from a second-class Chinese potboiler, actually, and turn it into an epic of such magnificence. In every line the mundane and trivial became magic prisms through which the poet revealed universal truths about men and women searching for the perfect in a cruel and imperfect world.

General Ton had spent a good deal of his life contemplating the nature of heroism and genius, and he had come to the conclusion that they were the same. Both the hero and the intellectual genius did things few other humans could, the one acts of bravery, the other acts of creation; both were positive forces in the world, given freely for the benefit of humanity at large. When men and women managed to surpass themselves in that way, they assumed the dimensions of gods.

General Ton believed that when ordinary people contemplated the deeds of such persons, it was possible for them to be uplifted by vicariously sharing the hero-genius's achievements.

General Ton urged his American friends to read *Kieu*. "This poem will help you to understand us," he told them. "In *Kieu* you will find our emotions and character laid bare, and you will begin to understand our concept of personal morality and public obligation." Sadly, they never took his advice. Instead, they smiled politely and never brought the subject up again. He knew they scoffed at him instead, barely forgiving his love of the poem as an eccentricity.

Years before, when he had had a field command, his American adviser had injudiciously remarked within the hearing of a staff officer who understood English, "How the hell can these people win a war when one of their best officers goes around mooning over some doggerel about a goddamned prostitute?" General Ton did not know what hurt him more, a trusted and valued friend referring to the Vietnamese as "these people" or to the *Tale of Kieu* as "doggerel."

Americans, he had concluded, were men of action living in a world where emotion and personal morality, because they could not be quantified—incarcerated in regulations, encased in legislation—were meaningless. These people, so admirable in so many ways, were prisoners of a vocabulary that included "logistics," "maneuver elements," and "ammunition supply rates," at one end of the spectrum, and "sucking" and "fucking" at the other.

He knew there were probably plenty of Americans who could appreciate Nguyen Du's image of the scholar, Kim, alone in his "icy-metal cold" book-lined study, unable to drive Kieu from his haunted mind. Ton shivered inwardly as he recited the lines by heart: "He drained the cup of gloom: it filled anew— / One day without her seemed three autumns long." Unfortunately, the Americans who could appreciate such delicious metaphors knew nothing about ammunition supply rates, and in the present circumstances, his beloved country needed logisticians, not poets.

He thought of the conversation with Colonel Tang on the subject. How inextricably the fate of the fictional Kieu was bound with the fate of the real Vietnamese. Could the poet have been speaking directly to the present-day Vietnamese when he had Kieu say to her mother, Dame Vuong, "Your daughter's doomed to live / On foreign land and sleep in alien soil." No wonder the mother "let out a shriek / That would pierce heaven, crying for redress."

General Ton sighed. Life must go on. "Sergeant Long?" he called. An elderly, bespectacled master sergeant appeared silently in the doorway.

"Have Colonel Tang come in here, will you?"

Colonel Tang was a comfort in these times of sadness. The general knew all his friends' faults, too. Good friends always know each other's weaknesses.

"Are the preparations for the barbecue about finished?" he asked as Tang entered the office.

"Yes, elder brother," the colonel replied. In public, Colonel Tang always referred to his general in the most respectful terms. But he gestured casually with one of the cigarettes he always kept burning. The staff had a private joke that he had somehow invented a method for keeping a cigarette burning even while he slept—and could smoke it, too.

"Good, good. How's the guest list coming along?"

"Excellent, sir. Everyone who received an invitation has responded, most of them affirmatively."

General Ton nodded in satisfaction. "Who's *not* coming?" Colonel Tang recited a short list of names, mostly high-ranking Vietnamese government and military officials.

"Very good! I did not want those people anyway."

"We must observe the proprieties." Colonel Tang smiled.

The general nodded. "On your way out, tell Long to have Corporal Ong bring me my beer now, will you?" Once a day, just before lunch, General Ton permitted himself the luxury of one cold bottle of beer. "Ah, I'd almost forgotten," he added. "Will you be seeing Sergeant Kelley today?"

"I am sure that I will. You will see him tomorrow for sure, when he comes in to listen to your reading."

"Is Wednesday upon us so soon? Well, speak to him privately for me, brother Tang, will you? I hear he's been gambling with my enlisted men again, and losing. I know he can afford to lose, but I don't want them taking advantage of Kelley's naiveté, either."

Colonel Tang had known about these games for some time. After duty, Jack had been known to hunker down among the enlisted men of General Ton's staff and drink beer and play cards with them. They played a version of poker in which each player tried to make the three best hands out of thirteen cards, a maddening game that depended more on strategy and psychology than knowledge of the odds to win. The hands were arranged in descending order of importance, and the two highest in any hand won. Jack could never resist putting a full house on top rather than breaking it up to strengthen the remaining hands, especially the last one, which had only three cards to it.

"Excuse me, sir, but I think Kelley loses because he's

a poor card player. I would hardly describe him as 'naive.'"

"Well, I'll tell you something else about Kelley. Of all the Americans I have ever met, I think he is one of the few who could, if he ever would, read *Kieu* and really appreciate it."

Colonel Tang's mouth dropped open. *"Kelley?"* he almost shouted. "Is elder brother having one of his little jokes at my expense?"

"No, no, no! I tell you, he has the instinct, the heart —yes, the heart to grasp *Kieu*. Its literary metaphor, no; he's not a schooled man. But the soul of the poem? Yes, our Kelley is capable of appreciating that."

Colonel Tang fumbled unsuccessfully for the right words.

"Anh ba," General Ton admonished with a forefinger, addressing Colonel Tang as his "younger brother" half in jest, "trust my judgment in this. *Kieu* and long experience have taught me how to evaluate human character."

Colonel Tang conceded with a slight nod of his head.

"Well, brother Tang, this has been an exceptional day for you, has it not?"

"Sir?" Colonel Tang thought he had not heard the general correctly.

"Today. An exceptional day for you, eh?" The faintest hint of a smile played around the edges of the general's lips.

"I do not understand—"

"You have been wrong *twice* in one day, my friend! And for you that is a most exceptional event, eh?" The general laughed with good-natured brightness.

Colonel Tang's face reddened slightly, and to cover the embarrassment of allowing himself to be caught in another of the general's little jokes, he pretended nonchalance by flicking cigarette ashes onto the floor.

Of All the Martial Blest

For Oates, RETURNING TO VIETNAM AS THE EIGHTeenth Division's sergeant major was a special honor. It was his third war with that division. He had been following the Eighteenth's progress since 1966, when it had first deployed to Vietnam. The Second Battalion of the Thirteenth Infantry Regiment was now part of the division's Third Brigade, which he knew well. He had been with it at Normandy. And he would be with it now, operating near the provincial capital of Suc Lo, just a few miles east of the Cambodian border.

Halfway between Suc Lo and Bu Lon, the division base camp, is the hamlet of Ga Chet, base camp for the First Brigade. With the First Brigade is the Thirtieth Infantry. Oates had been a rifle company first sergeant with the First of the Thirtieth in Korea in 1951, and he had been one of the last Americans to evacuate Seoul in the face of the advancing Chinese Communist army. The Eighteenth Division was full of bittersweet memories for Oates. It was where his regiments lived.

As for his battalion, its battle honors included a U.S. Presidential Unit Citation. The "PUC," as it is often called, is the highest decoration for valor any army unit can receive. To earn it, a unit must have displayed in combat a degree of heroism equivalent to that required for an individual soldier to win the Distinguished Service Cross—the second-highest award for individual heroism. The battalion's campaign credits read like an honor roll of American military history: Manassas, Antietam, Chancellorsville, Gettysburg; against the Modoc and Bannock in the Indian wars; Santiago, Cuba, in the Spanish-American War; the Aisne-Marne, Meuse-Argonne, and Château-Thierry in World War I; Normandy, northern France, the Rhineland, Ardennes-Alsace, and central Europe in World War II.

And since March 1966, Vietnam.

The Eighteenth U.S. Infantry Division was an awesome fighting machine. Its three infantry brigades consisted of twelve battalions supported by two armored battalions, six artillery battalions, an aviation battalion, various reconnaissance units (armored, long-range patrol, and ranger), and eight support battalions, including medical, supply and transport, engineer, signal, maintenance, administration, and military police companies. Beefed up for Vietnam service, the division numbered more than 22,000 men.

The typical infantry battalion in the Eighteenth Division consisted of four rifle companies (designated A through D), a headquarters and headquarters company, and a combat support company (Company E), in all more than 900 men. Each rifle company had an authorized strength of 6 officers and 158 enlisted men armed with a variety of weapons: six 7.62-mm machine guns; twenty-four 40-mm grenade launchers; nine .45-caliber pistols; 149 M-16 rifles; three 81-mm mortars; and three 90-mm recoilless rifles. The ninety-six man support company provided additional firepower in the form of four 4.2-inch mortars and twelve portable flamethrowers as well as the rifles and sidearms the men themselves carried.

This potential devastation, supplied at the expense of the American taxpayer, was supplemented by any weapons and equipment the individual infantryman could capture, trade, beg, borrow, or steal during his endless peregrinations. Thus the men slogging through the jungles in search of an elusive enemy carried with them an assortment of rifles, shotguns, pistols, and revolvers manufactured in the United States, Communist China, the Soviet Union, and various European countries.

The division's area of operations extended west from Saigon to the Cambodian border, principally within that part of South Vietnam known as the III Corps area to the Americans and South Vietnamese, Military Region IV to the Communists. The land there is generally flat and dry and consists of jungle, paddy, and extensive rubber plantations. It is bisected by the Saigon River flowing west to east from Cambodia into the South China Sea and in 1967 straddled in the Eighteenth's TAOR, tactical area of operations, by the First Brigade at Ga Chet and the division headquarters farther downstream at Bu Lon; one of the division's missions was river security, and for this task it had developed a sophisticated set of riverine assault tactics that proved extremely effective against enemy forces using the riverway.

The division sat astride one of the Communists' main infiltration routes from Cambodia into the national capital region, and aside from riverine operations to secure the Saigon waterway, the men of the Eighteenth engaged in constant patrols, reconnaissances, search missions (called "search and destroy"), and large spoiling operations in coordination with other U.S. and South Vietnamese forces.

Opposed to the U.S. Eighteenth Infantry Division was the Viet Cong Ninth Division, consisting of the 271st, 272nd, 273rd Viet Cong Main Force regiments and the 101st North Vietnamese Regiment, perhaps six to eight thousand men. In addition to these forces, the enemy also had the Military Region IV headquarters and its First and Seventh battalions under the 165th VC Regiment as well as the Phu Loi Local Force Battalion and numerous local force companies to call out to battle. These soldiers were well armed, led, and organized; though they always fought well, the Viet Cong Ninth Division was no match for the U.S. Eighteenth.

The problem was to pin it down long enough so that the Americans could bring their superior firepower and numbers to bear. The enemy commanders were masters at avoiding such confrontations, at massing their men where the Americans were weakest and striking when conditions were to their advantage, then withdrawing before the Americans could redress the odds in their favor.

In nearly two years of fighting throughout the area, the Americans had hurt the Ninth Division badly, killing more than 3,000 of the enemy at a cost of 653 of their own.

In his first six months as the division's sergeant major, Oates had made his presence felt. As he told his noncommissioned officers, "I've been shot at and hit and shit at and hit, but that's my job, and it's yours as well. I don't want to hear of any noncom in a line company leading his men from the rear, and I don't want to see any NCO anywhere else in this division sitting on his rear." Oates always paused here for effect. "And that includes the NCOs in the division and brigade headquarters, too, by God! *Especially* them!"

Oates himself set the example by spending most of his own time visiting the troops. He especially enjoyed dropping in unannounced on remote outposts. He'd usually get there by hitching a ride on a resupply helicopter flight near the end of the day and would then spend the night with the men in their forward positions. "My clerk runs my office," he told his NCOs, "and don't bother to call there for me 'cause I ain't there most of the time. You got anything to tell me, hold it. I'll be by to see ya soon enough, 'n' then you can tell me in person."

Oates affected the dress of the combat infantryman.

He never put starch in his jungle fatigues but just had them washed when they needed it and wore them rumpled and faded. Starched uniforms were the symbol of the rear and anathema among the division's fighting men. Neither did Oates wear underclothes, which in the jungle only rotted and chafed anyway. But he could not reconcile himself to going without socks. The infantrymen had good reason not to wear socks on their feet, which were wet most of the time, but Oates, who could dry them out when he wanted, kept his socks a small secret vanity.

In six months, Oates had been wounded twice, but not very seriously either time. Once his helicopter had been hit by machine-gun fire while approaching a "hot" landing zone (a helicopter landing zone under enemy fire was called "hot"), and the second time he'd been spending the night at a base near the Cambodian border when he had stopped a small fragment from an incoming mortar round.

The men of the Eighteenth Division loved Sergeant Major Oates because he came out where they lived and fought and shared their food and their hardships, but most of all because he understood them. And Oates understood them because in nearly twenty-five years in the army, he had never forgotten his own origins. He had never forgotten what it is like to be the lowest man on the military totem pole, despite the fact that as sergeant major he had the respect of generals and colonels throughout the army and in the Eighteenth Division, everyone, from General Foster right down the chain of command.

Sergeant Major Billy George Oates possessed that rare ability, found only in the smallest handful of enlisted leaders of an army, really a sixth sense, that enabled him to size up a man almost by looking at him. After a few words with a private soldier, Oates could tell if he'd been paid on time, had family problems, was getting along with his squad and platoon leaders, or gave a hang one way or another about the army. Oates could go into any rifle company in the division and, after an hour of talking with its men, tell the company commander who his problem children were and which of them he could rely on as his best enlisted soldiers. He was a constant source of amazement to the officers and a pure inspiration to the enlisted men.

Just pursuing what he considered the course of his normal duties had made Oates a legend in the division, but what happened at Fire Support Base Charlie immortalized him.

"Jonesy, I'm goin' up to Charlie," Oates told his clerk at six-thirty one morning as he grabbed his hat and headed for the door of the wood-frame hut that was his office. Specialist Fourth Class Clarence Jones looked at his sergeant major quizzically. The day had hardly started yet.

"You been up there twice this week already, Top," Jones said.

"Yeah, well, this'll make the third time, then. I wanna take up these compassionate reassignment papers on that kid, PFC Cleveland, with the Seventh Arty. And also"—Oates winked conspiratorially at his clerk—"I got a 'presento' for Sergeant Major Pat Ryan of the Fourth Battalion." Oates nodded toward the small handbag he was carrying. It contained the reassignment orders for the PFC and a fifth of Jack Daniels Black Label bourbon for Sergeant Major Ryan. Oates anticipated helping Ryan drink it. Today was his forty-sixth birthday. They had served together before; their wives were friends, their children had gone to school together.

"When'll you be back?"

"When I get back," Oates answered nonchalantly. He jammed his boonie hat over his head at a jaunty angle, gave Jones a mock salute, and stomped to the door.

Fire Support Base Charlie had been carved out of a hillside in the thick forest halfway between Ga Chet and Suc Lo, near the abandoned hamlet of Suoi Ba, to provide artillery support for operations west from there to Cambodia.

First C Company of the Fourth Battalion, Tenth Infantry, hacked its way into the site. After securing a perimeter, they created a landing zone by blasting enough trees to open a hole in the triple-canopy jungle. Helicopters inserted a team with a bulldozer from the Sixty-fourth Engineer Battalion, and they cleared the hillside in two days. The artillery guns were airlifted in, slung beneath Chinook helicopters.

In the ensuing weeks, the base fired thousands of rounds of explosives into the enemy and along his infiltration routes through the area. Six 105-mm howitzers could hit targets in any direction up to six miles away, while heavier 155s could reach positions up to eight miles distant, and because FSB Charlie's fire plans were interlocked with those at Suc Lo and Ga Chet, no Eighteenth Division unit operating westward of Bu Lon was without artillery support.

And the Communists did not like it. So in June 1967, the commander of the Viet Cong Ninth Division decided to do something about FSB Charlie. His staff planned and calculated carefully and rehearsed endlessly for an attack and with infinite caution made their dispositions. By August they were ready.

The flight to FSB Charlie took only fifteen minutes. It seemed the helicopter had only just gotten clear of Bu Lon and achieved its cruising altitude, and then it was descending for its approach to the base. There had been some light rain earlier in the morning, but the sun was out now and the air was fresh and cool up here at a thousand feet. Oates was the only passenger. The door-gunner crouched behind his M-60 machine gun, enjoying the ride. The passenger compartment was littered with crates and boxes and bags of material and supplies and personal items for men at the base. He noticed a gray canvas mail sack with a tag on it for a SP5 Carson Timberlake, B/3/16 Arty and wondered if it was a whole sack of mail for just that one man.

From the air, FSB Charlie was a horrid gash in the surrounding green dotted with square and circular formations that looked like the excavated ruins of some ancient civilization. Up close, they resolved into neatly constructed fighting bunkers, command posts, fire direction centers, and, dominating everything, the gun emplacements themselves.

The base was roughly oblong, measuring about 250 meters in length and less than 100 meters in width; the outer perimeter was about 600 meters in circumference. It ran roughly north to south with the 155s at the northern end and the 105s at the southern sector. The chopper landing pad was at the northern end of the perimeter.

Each gun position was really a small fort with parapets and trenches. They could be defended individually if the perimeter were breached in an attack. The positions each held a heavily sandbagged ammunition bunker, a fighting bunker for protection, and a personnel bunker where the artillerymen lived. The infantry had constructed a series of bunkers protecting the perimeter of the base. Claymore antipersonnel mines, trip flares, and rolls of concertina wire placed well outside the defended perimeter gave added protection against infiltrators, and even farther out were listening posts manned at night. But in the months since Charlie had been dug out of the hillside, it had never been mortared, and the frequent patrols conducted throughout the area had not turned up even a shred of enemy activity.

Oates was aware of all this, but still he felt nervous visiting Charlie. It was just too quiet. In his guts he knew the enemy would hit there someday—they were only waiting for the right time.

Considerable care had been taken in constructing the infantry battalion command post bunker. Access was provided by two short flights of stairs that twisted at a right angle so that in the event the base were overrun, grenades or explosive charges could not be hurled directly inside. The engineers had gouged the bunker out of the hillside and constructed the entranceway stairs. The command post itself was a good five feet below the surface of the earth and proofed against a direct hit by anything the VC could fire at it.

As Oates descended the stairs he was met by a rush of fetid, moist air. "We couldn't live down here in the daytime without ventilation," Ryan told him, "so we got this messhall fan from somebody in Saigon. A guy named Kelley. Said he knew ya."

"Well, I'll be go to hell! Yeah, ole Jack Kelley. He'll give you Irishmen a bad reputation."

The working space inside the bunker was quite large, although crowded with men and equipment. Radio operators and clerks wearing only shorts sat with sweat streaming off them at their consoles and desks. "Hard to work with paper down here in the daytime 'cause your sweat sticks you to everything," Ryan commented.

About half the space underground had been converted into a makeshift briefing room with folding chairs and a raised platform with a blackboard and maps of the area. Naked light bulbs strung from cables crisscrossing the room provided light. Oates had been inside once before, and he was familiar with the way it was arranged. The bunker's electrical power was provided by a gasoline generator dug in some distance from the command post; the electrical cables were buried in the ground. The generator failed quite often, so Coleman lanterns hung everywhere, ready for use.

The radios could be powered by batteries, but their operation and maintenance were the responsibility of radiomen from the division's 118th Signal Battalion. In the event that either the battalion commander needed to communicate during a power outage or enemy fire destroyed the bunker's radio antenna system (erected away from the bunker itself so as not to draw fire), several PRC-25 portable radios had been stacked on shelves. The PRC-25, or "prick twenty-five," as it was called, was the standard infantry two-way radio.

The battalion commander and Sergeant Major Ryan lived in the command post bunker, which was manned around the clock. The battalion's personnel (S-1) and intelligence (S-2) officers shared a small room off to one side where they worked; the operations officer (S-3) had a somewhat larger space.

"It gets almost livable in here, once the sun goes down," Ryan said over his shoulder as he led Oates to his living space.

"How's morale, Pat?" Oates asked as he unfastened his pistol belt and hung it from a post in the corner.

"Couldn't be better. It's been good duty up here, Goats. Too good, if you know what I mean." Oates nodded and sat beside Ryan on the shelf carved out of the earth that was his bunk.

"Mind if I stay over tonight, Pat? I'll take the first chopper out in the morning."

Ryan nodded. "Sure, glad to have ya. But it's gonna be mighty boring around here." Ryan hesitated. "Billy, I got this feeling," he said.

"Like what?" Oates was too good a soldier to pooh-pooh another's premonitions.

Ryan shrugged. "Like I dunno. Nervous, I guess."

"Any grunt who's been in the war zone more 'n' two months with no action is bound to get nervous. You think Charlie's planning something?"

"Yeah. Our intelligence types and your boys up at division are worried, *not* 'cause they're on to anything, but because they *ain't*. The Ninth Division's been too fuckin' quiet recently."

"Sergeant Major Oates!" a voice called. Oates and Ryan stood up politely for Lieutenant Colonel James P. Dickerson, the battalion commander. Dickerson was a lean, muscular black man who had been commissioned from West Point when black faces were rare there.

The colonel spent very little of his time in the CP, although his nickname, "Dugout Dick," a malapropism if ever there was one, had stuck simply because he *did* risk his life with his men. Soldiers are perverse in nicknaming their leaders, and the men in Dickerson's battalion favored it as a kind of in-joke: only *they* knew it was not descriptive of the man. As one young sergeant put it when Oates asked him about the nickname, "Well, what the fuck? We don't want the folks back home to know how much we really love our old nigger colonel."

"Good to see you again, Colonel." Oates shook hands.

"Sergeant Major Ryan takin' care of you, Top?"

"As always, Colonel. Rally 'round here after chow tonight, sir. I got a little something special for you 'n' brother Ryan here."

"You got it, Top." Dickerson laughed. "I sure as hell ain't goin' very far." He swept his arm in a circle, indicating the narrow confinement of FSB Charlie. "Right now, though, I'm goin' over to Alpha Company's positions. Care to come along?"

"I'll join you later, sir. I should visit the cannon cockers for a while first, drop off some personnel papers."

"Good enough. See ya later." Dickerson gave the thumbs-up signal and threaded his way outside.

In the early afternoon Private First Class Clarence Cleveland of the Seventh Artillery, a huge smile on his face, boarded a helicopter for Bu Lon and the United States. More than a thousand men of the Viet Cong 271st and 272nd regiments rested quietly under the thick forests surrounding FSB Charlie, secure in hidden bunkers and tunnels so cleverly concealed nobody suspected they were there, and listened to the chopper receding noisily toward the southeast.

In midafternoon the 272nd Regiment, in coordination with the 101st NVA Regiment, made a feint toward elements of the First Brigade patrolling north and east of Ga Chet, too far for the guns of FSB Charlie to support them. A fierce firefight erupted, and General Foster, back at Bu Lon, ordered additional elements of the First Brigade, supported by a battalion of the Second Brigade, to block the enemy escape routes. The battle raged inconclusively until after dark. The radios at FSB Charlie chattered all afternoon as the battle progressed. Toward dark someone at division headquarters remembered that a whole battalion of infantry was sitting at FSB Charlie, so one company was quickly airlifted into an overnight blocking position along a likely withdrawal route in the direction of the Cambodian border where they sat with other units and did nothing all night long.

It was the break the enemy had been waiting for.

Just after dark the VC 273rd Main Force Regiment, the reserve for the attack, crept into the vicinity of Suoi Ba hamlet and took up its positions. The 273rd mustered 1,421 men, and with its arrival, the enemy now had more than a three-to-one numerical superiority over the Americans on the nearby hillside.

Colonel Dickerson called for a briefing of his remaining commanders and platoon leaders just after dark. "Otherwise, with all those people in here, we'd suffocate," he joked. Meanwhile, the messhall fan whirred away, keeping the temperature down in the low nineties.

The briefing was to explain what was going on elsewhere in the TAOR, how the battle raging there might affect them at FSB Charlie, and also to reassign perimeter defense responsibilities now that they were one company shy. "We were in fat city before, with a whole battalion to defend this place," Ryan said just before the briefing started. Oates nodded. They were still in good shape. After talking to the men all day long, he had concluded they were vigorous and alert, more than a match for anything the VC could throw against them.

An hour after the meeting Dickerson, Ryan, and Oates inspected the perimeter defenses. They did not get back to the command post until nearly ten P.M.

"Long fuckin' day," Dickerson said with a sigh as he took a folding chair beside Ryan's bunk. The colonel himself slept on a folding cot placed behind some ponchos hung from telephone wire strung between two wooden supports that held up the roof.

Oates fetched his handbag from a makeshift bunk he had set up next to Ryan's niche—an air mattress and a poncho liner someone had loaned him—and fished out the bottle of Jack Daniels. "Happy Birthday, Patrick, and many happy returns," he said, pouring a dollop of the whiskey into a canteen cup and passing it to Ryan.

"Colonel?" Oates offered another cup to Dickerson.

"Gimme a little water to cut it," the colonel said. Ryan poured water from a canteen. "No ice?" Dickerson joked. "Happy Birthday, Sergeant Major." He raised his cup. They drank.

"Arrgh, damn good stuff!" Dickerson shuddered. "How the hell old are you, Top?"

"Too old, sir," Ryan quipped. "Nah, I'm forty-six today. I was twenty-one when they bombed Pearl Harbor, 'n' I'd already been in the army a year at the time."

They talked for nearly an hour. Colonel Dickerson sipped slowly from his cup, nursing the whiskey along; Oates and Ryan both had two more shots during the conversation. They talked about places they had been and people they'd known over the years. They speculated about where they would go when they left Vietnam.

"This is it for me," Ryan announced. "Three wars 'n' yer out in this man's army."

"Well"—Dickerson sighed at last, rising—"it's time to go out and tour the battle front. I have miles to go before I sleep and promises to keep, saith the poet. Comin' along, Pat?" He clapped a hand gently on his sergeant major's shoulder.

"Can I resist the call of duty?" Ryan laughed and stood.

"Bedtime for me," Oates said.

Ryan and Dickerson walked out of the bunker.

Oates stretched out on his cot, settling his body comfortably onto the air mattress. It squeaked and sighed as he shifted his weight around on it. He sighed. It had been a long day.

A tremendous explosion rang through the CP like a thunderclap, sending a rush of wind down the stairway, lifting loose pieces of paper into the swirling air. The light bulbs swayed drunkenly and flickered.

"Jesus Christ, that was close!" someone yelled. Men jumped up from where they had been sleeping or reading paperbacks and groped for weapons. Radios made reports and desperate calls for reinforcements from the perimeter. "There's ten thousand motherfuckers out there!" one infantryman screamed, and then his radio went silent.

"Where's the colonel?" asked a bleary-eyed captain. Oates recognized him as the battalion operations officer. He'd been snoozing behind the blackboard on the briefing platform. From outside, the men in the bunker could hear the thudding of impacting mortar rounds.

"He and Ryan went outside to inspect— Oh, Jesus—"

The lights winked out, plunging the CP into complete darkness. After a few seconds of cursing confusion, someone got a Coleman going. Oates could smell gasoline burning and guessed an incoming mortar round had found the generator.

"Someone loan me a weapon?" he asked. Nobody answered, so he grabbed the first one he saw. He snatched several clips from someone's field desk and ran toward the door.

"The colonel and Ryan went out just before the first round went off," he told the operations officer. "I'm gonna check 'em out." But the operations officer was already at a radio, calling for air support and yelling questions and orders to the perimeter defenders.

Oates slammed a clip into his M-16, chambered a round, and flicked the safety to "off," then cautiously ascended the stairs. The mortar round had exploded just outside the bunker, doing very little damage to its structure. A number of sandbags were ripped open, and that was all he could see at first in the wavering light of flares drifting above the base.

Two bodies were sprawled in front of the entrance. A thick cloud of smoke from the burning generator drifted over and he coughed. He knelt beside one of the men. It was Ryan. Oates could tell the man was still alive by the throbbing of an artery in his neck but couldn't tell how badly he'd been hurt. Before Oates could check on Colonel Dickerson, he happened to glance to the north. What he saw horrified him. Swarms of enemy infantry were pouring out from between the bunkers and were headed straight in his direction. He remembered that a 105-mm gun stood somewhere a few yards to the south of the CP bunker. He ran that way and jumped over a sandbagged parapet.

Four men were laboring to manhandle their gun to fire at the enemy on the northern side of the base. Oates slung his rifle and stepped between two of the men heaving on one of the gun's trails. "Beehive on the north perimeter!" he shouted.

"Fuckin' A!" a heavyset black soldier screamed at him.

The beehive artillery round, known as the XM546 antipersonnel projectile, is filled with over eight thousand fléchettes, or small metal darts. The rounds had been employed before in Vietnam to stop ground attacks like this one, and in constructing FSB Charlie, the infantry bunkers had deliberately been built up from the rear to protect the men inside if the guns ever had to fire at targets within the perimeter.

Oates threw himself against the parapet and began shooting methodically at the enemy closest to him. They were very close. He thought he hit some, but there were so many and they were moving so erratically he could not be sure. Several other rifles popped as artillerymen piled out of their bunker and joined the sergeant major.

"Die, you bastards!" the black gunner shouted, and fired his gun. There was a great crackling and whining noise as the fléchettes cleared the ground before the muzzle. It seemed that momentarily the noise of battle ceased and was replaced by an awesome moaning sob as dozens of the enemy were cut to pieces by the terrible ammunition.

"Gimme another!" the black gunner screamed even before the casing of the first round was free of the breech. He loaded and fired again. The gunners around him whooped and screamed, and the black soldier slapped Oates on the back. "Did you see them mutha-fucks! We wiped 'em *out*!"

A parachute flare drifted slowly overhead. "Hey!" the black man exclaimed, "You Sergeant Major Billy Goats Oates, ain't ya? Pleased to meetcha. I'm Staff Sergeant Sylvester C. Robinson, gun chief here." They shook hands solemnly under the flare light as the fighting raged all around and the fate of FSB Charlie hung precariously in the balance. Other guns belched elsewhere, sending fléchettes crackling and screaming into the men of the Viet Cong Ninth Division; other men emptied their weapons and fought hand to hand for their lives, but here, at this lone gun, the battle was won.

"Man," Robinson exclaimed to his men, "we kin tell our kids we fought with Billy Goats Oates tonight!"

"Man," Oates said, "I can tell *my* kids you saved my sweet ass tonight."

The fighting did not die down until dawn. What the new day revealed was that FSB Charlie had been re-duced to a shambles. During the night more than six hundred mortar rounds had been fired into the perimeter, all of them extremely accurate. But hundreds of enemy dead littered the ground.

Jet fighters and helicopter gunships had been over-head almost from the beginning of the fight, and now the forest around FSB Charlie smoldered and reeked of na-palm and high explosives. All morning long unarmed hel-icopters called "slicks" brought in supplies and ferried out the dead Americans and the wounded of both sides. Fifty Americans had died in the attack, and over one hundred had been wounded. But four hundred and thirty-six dead enemy soldiers had been counted on the battlefield along with six wounded. Nobody ever knew how many had been carried off, but later intelligence re-ports indicated that several hundred litter cases had been transported across the border into Cambodia.

The 271st VC Regiment, the spearhead of the attack, had been knocked out of the war for months to come. After its bloody repulse, the enemy commander had ordered a withdrawal to the northeast, and during the retreat his command had been further punished by the U.S. Air Force.

Dickerson and Ryan were among the first wounded taken out. Oates saw them loaded on a helicopter. Both had been unconscious, but a field medic told him they had a fighting chance.

Much later the division would be awarded a battle streamer embroidered "Suoi Ba," in honor of the defense of Fire Support Base Charlie, and Dickerson and Ryan would be there to see it presented.

Oates sat for a while on a sandbag pile outside the main CP bunker, working on the bottle of Jack Daniels. Ryan would not be drinking it, so he figured he might as well take a few pulls. Men wandered dreamily over the smoking landscape, some collecting weapons, others hauling bodies around. Some repaired damaged bunkers, and still others sprawled wherever they could, in the sleep of total exhaustion.

Soon photographers and generals began arriving, first the Army Signal Corps cameramen and then, after it was determined the base was safe, civilian newsmen. Oates recognized General Westmoreland himself, accompanied by General Foster, but he made no move to approach them. Though he knew Westy personally—and admired him—this morning he wanted nothing to do with generals.

Later, at the helipad, when space became available on an outgoing chopper, Oates climbed aboard. Then the legend that always surrounded Billy George Oates was embellished with another detail: Oates sitting dazed in the chopper, an open bottle of whiskey dangling from one hand.

Oates's last impression of Fire Support Base Charlie was a small American flag fluttering from a radio antenna where some signalman had put it during the night. It snapped bravely in the breeze. Seeing it made Oates feel good. He took a long pull from his bottle.

Cellars of the Soul

Harry Scheldt was as happy as a fly in a privy. He had wangled the next two days off, and he intended to take as much of that time as he needed to swing one of the biggest deals of his career: penetration of the HJO— Herman Johnson Organization.

The HJO had been in existence for about ten years. It had been organized and was led by a coterie of black drug dealers and distributors and operated in every part of the world where significant numbers of U.S. service-men were stationed. The HJO had cornered a large slice of the drug market in Southeast Asia, with connections in P'yongyang–Seoul, Peking–Hong Kong–Taipei, and especially Saigon–Pnompenh–Vientiane–Bangkok. The organization was also active in Europe and the Middle East.

The HJO did business with anyone who paid. Some of its best patrons were high-ranking South Vietnamese government officials, a situation that ensured virtual im-munity of operation in that country; the U.S. government could only target its military associates, over whom it had direct authority.

Harry's mob connections in the States had commissioned him to tap into the HJO, and to that end, for some weeks past, he had been assiduously cultivating the HJO's Saigon representative, an elusive black man known to Harry only as "the Hawk." Harry caught a cab on Hung Vuong Boulevard, just where it crossed Su Van Hanh Street, half a block from the Seven Seas Bachelor Officers Quarters, where he lived. "Khanh Hoi," he wheezed as he climbed into the backseat. The driver nodded and proceeded toward the Saigon docks. Harry did not bother to cover his trail, and when he turned half around in the seat to peer out the back window, he wasn't surprised at the unmarked black sedan following several car lengths behind. Harry turned forward and smiled. "Dumb fuckin' cop," he snorted contemptuously.

It was a long ride to the docks.

The driver crossed into the Saigon harbor over the Ben Nghe Bridge and drove along Trinh Minh The Street, keeping the Saigon River on his left. At Nguyen Thanh Hien Street, Harry directed him to turn right and, soon after that, left onto Ton That Thuyet Street. The Kinh Te Canal was on their left now, and they were moving away from the harbor. They were on the south side of an island formed by the Saigon River to the northeast, the Ben Nghe Canal to the northwest, and the Kinh Te. The island was a warren of warehouses and shanties, and somewhere in there was the Saigon bastion of the Herman Johnson Organization.

The Hawk had told Harry to get out at a certain spot along Ton That Thuyet, a beer stall along the curb, under a huge dentifrice advertisement. Harry was instructed to wait there for an escort. He paid the cabbie and waddled into the stall, which was really no more than an awning stretched over the curb. Harry eased himself onto a rickety wooden stool and ordered a beer, wiping the perspiration from his forehead.

"Fuckin' niggers sure live in a rough part of town," he muttered. He wiped the mouth of the beer bottle with one hand and drank greedily. He finished the beer in two enormous swallows and ordered another. He paid the ancient woman who ran the place with a two-hundred-piaster note, nonchalantly waving away the change.

Harry belched loudly, drank his beer, and looked down the street for the black sedan. Yep, there he was, a block away, pulled to the side of the road. Harry shook his head. He could barely make out the figure sitting behind the wheel, but Harry did not need to see the man to know who he was. He imagined the heavyset, grim-faced figure, sitting there in his car, cursing probably, pounding the wheel with his fist out of frustration. All the cop could do now was watch; this was as far as he could go without a battalion of military police because he was in Herman Johnson territory and wouldn't last five minutes off the main street. Dumb cop or no, Harry knew his tail was not stupid enough to follow him farther.

Harry raised his beer bottle, waved at the sedan, and drank.

It was getting dark. Harry looked around for anyone who might be his escort. There was no one. "I got time," Harry told the old woman sitting behind the arrangement of empty packing crates that served as a counter. She smiled and nodded as if she understood English.

An hour passed. Harry worked on his sixth bottle of beer, fuming inwardly. He knew the Hawk was only playing it cool, but making him wait so long was more than just irritating. It was insulting.

"Hey, man, you Harry?"

Scheldt started and looked up to see a slightly built, light-skinned black man standing just beyond the edge of the awning. His hair looked red in the dim light, and his face was freckled. He stepped into the light, and Harry noticed that his face was flushed and his pupils contracted almost to pinpoints.

"You take me to the Hawk?" Harry asked.

"Yeaaah, man. Follow me."

Harry lumbered to his feet and followed. He trotted a short distance down the street toward where the sedan was parked and then turned right, up a side street. Before turning the corner himself, Harry waved at the tail again. "Happy dreams, asshole!" he shouted.

His guide crossed the street and followed it north for about a hundred yards. Then he disappeared up a narrow alley between two warehouses, and, huffing and wheezing, Harry followed.

"Hey!" Harry gasped. "Slow down, will ya?" The guide turned and waited impatiently for Harry to catch up. He shifted his feet constantly, and his head swayed back and forth as if he were listening to a persistent tune inside his head. All the while he grinned and chuckled. When Harry was up with him he resumed the pace, Harry struggling after, face streaming perspiration.

The passageway they were negotiating was narrow and very dark. Water splashed under their feet, and high damp walls towered over them on both sides. They passed innumerable doorways, all tightly closed. The very faint light of a half-moon filtered down from the night sky. Harry tired of trying to mark the twistings and turnings and finally admitted to himself that he was hopelessly lost. Afterward he concentrated on keeping the bobbing white shirt of his guide constantly in sight.

At last they arrived at a large building with several vehicles parked in front of it. Harry was as relieved to see the vehicles as any explorer lost in the jungle who stumbles across welcome signs of civilization.

They climbed a short flight of concrete steps to a platform that ran the length of the building. At the opposite end the guide stopped by a metal door and whispered something to someone at a peephole. The door swung open and admitted them into the dim recesses of a vast warehouse. Harry caught a fleeting glimpse of open space piled with crates and boxes, and then he was whisked down a dimly lit corridor. The man who had let them in, Harry noted, had been heavily armed.

Harry's guide stopped at a door and knocked. A huge black man opened it and stared at Harry with bloodshot eyes. "You Harry Scheldt?" he rumbled. Harry nodded. "Okay, Skeeter," the big man said to the guide, "you off duty for tonight." He handed him a small plastic bag. Skeeter snatched it gratefully and scuttled off down the corridor. Harry suddenly realized the man was a junkie.

The big man held the door for Harry, then stepped into the large office behind him, slammed the door shut, twisted Harry's arm painfully behind his back, and slammed him hard against the wall. Harry was big and enormously strong himself, but the man who had him now seemed made of solid rock and tempered steel.

"What the—" Harry protested, and grunted with pain.

"Easy, skinny," the man rumbled. Expertly he frisked Harry. "We can't take no chances wif anybody. Mebbe you got a gun, a wire, who knows?"

"Goddammit! I'm a legitimate businessman!" Harry shouted to the wall. "Tell 'im, Hawk! Call 'im off, will ya?"

"He clean," the guard announced, and let Harry go.

"Hello, Harry," said the Hawk. Harry spun around, massaging his arm, a curse starting to roll off his tongue. What he saw turned the expletive into a soft bubble of air more like a sigh than a curse.

The man standing before Harry looked like a black version of Mr. Clean.

"I am the Hawk, Mr. Scheldt. Forgive our stringent security precautions, but these are dangerous times. Won't you come into my private office?" He ushered Harry inside. "Melvin"—the Hawk turned to the guard —"send in the rest of the staff, please."

Harry had never met the Hawk in person. His previous contact had all been on the telephone.

The Hawk's office was magnificent—and air-conditioned. He offered Harry a seat in a plush leather chair and took one himself, behind his enormous teakwood desk.

"Before the staff arrives, let me explain something, Mr. Scheldt.

"Because we are all ex-military people, we have, uh, a 'very special' relationship with America's servicemen abroad. We're very jealous of that relationship, consider it our prerogative, and desire to keep it to ourselves. But we're also desirous of expanding our distributorship, and that is why we agreed to permit you to come here tonight.

"You realize, of course, that I myself am only the head of the Saigon office, and I cannot make any deals."

"Neither can I," Harry replied.

The Hawk smiled coldly. "But we can feel each other out tonight, make some preliminary negotiations, have a pleasurable intercourse, if you will, and report back to our superiors. We can relay terms and conditions, and in time, perhaps, strike up a bargain that will be mutually acceptable and quite profitable to all concerned."

Three men entered the office, two blacks and an Oriental. The Hawk introduced them as Leonard, his chief of staff; Elbert, his operations officer; and Mr. Nguyen, his "liaison officer." The handshaking was perfunctory. None of them smiled, and all looked very hard at Harry. But Harry had expected that.

A slack-faced white American with long greasy hair then entered with a tray of mixers. He opened a rich mahogany bar in one corner and asked the men for orders. After mixing and serving the drinks, he departed at a nod from the Hawk.

"We support quite a colony of American deserters here in Saigon," the Hawk said. "Most of them have habits and Vietnamese women. For our help in maintaining both, they perform certain valuable services for us, sometimes as couriers, sometimes as messengers. Occasionally the most trustworthy of them handle certain, uh, more violent details on our behalf." The Hawk paused long enough to light a cigar. "It's a 'symbiotic relationship,' you might say," he continued, shaking out the match. "That young man who was just in here is a former soldier in the Hundred and First Airborne Division who one day had enough of the war. He's been with us how long now?"

"Six months," Elbert answered. "We operate like a military organization, Mr. Scheldt," he continued. "We expect the mos' high degree o' loyalty and personal dis-e-pline from our people, and if we do not receive that, we kills 'em. Zero defects permitted, as we say in the army these days." Elbert's laugh was very nasty.

"Perhaps we have all had too much of this war," Mr. Nguyen offered.

"Precisely who are you 'liaison' to, Mr. Nguyen?" Harry asked, sipping a large Jack Daniels and Coke.

Mr. Nguyen stared coldly back without answering. Harry grinned. It's bad enough, he told himself, I have to deal with niggers, but then they have to slip this fucking slope in on me. Harry saluted Mr. Nguyen with his glass, still grinning.

"To business, gentlemen," the Hawk said briskly. The others shifted their weight in the chairs and cleared their throats.

"Precisely what is your line?" Mr. Nguyen asked, not yet willing to give up the showdown.

Harry's smile broadened. "I'm a middleman, Mr. Nguyen."

"Are you not also an officer in the U.S. Army?" Mr. Nguyen smiled back.

"For the present, Mr. Nguyen." Harry grinned.

"Very nice cover." Now Mr. Nguyen positively beamed.

"Almost as good as being somebody's 'liaison officer,' wouldn't you agree, Mr. Nguyen?" Harry shot back.

The sparring match was over. Mr. Nguyen saluted Harry with his glass.

"We respect what your organization has done," Harry said. "We are interested in what we can do for each other, and there just might be the possibility of a very profitable business arrangement between your people and mine, providing we can come to terms."

The talk went on for another hour. Three more times the long-haired deserter was summoned back to mix drinks for them.

"How you gonna smuggle so much shit as we can provide back into the world widout losin' mos' of it?" Leonard asked at last. It was the question to which they were all hungry to know the answer.

Harry smiled archly and wagged a forefinger at the man. "That's *my* baby, but I'm workin' on it, I'm really workin' on it." Harry chortled like a schoolboy with a nasty secret.

"I have very good vibes about all of this," the Hawk announced at last. "Harry, suppose we call it a night. We will each of us make his separate representations to our superiors and arrange another meeting soon, to iron out the final details. Yes, yes, my man"—the Hawk rubbed his hands together—"my vibes are definitely positive tonight." The others agreed with their leader. The atmosphere was now relaxed and casual, and there were plenty of smiles and handshaking all around. Harry felt very good, too, and very proud of himself.

"I would like to ask one favor," Harry said. The Hawk looked at him questioningly; the others stared suspiciously. "There's a certain army cop, a Warrant Officer Prudhomme to be exact, who has been bugging me no end. He followed me partway here tonight." The others snorted derisively at the suggestion any cop could be so stupid. Harry's expression turned apologetic.

"You gotta understand, gentlemen, as an active army officer, I am vulnerable. You have protection, I don't. If I get busted, our deal goes down the tubes, for the foreseeable future, anyway."

"We know that fuckin' dude," Leonard interjected. "He got a blood for his partner."

"Yes," the Hawk added affably enough, "we know Mr. Prudhomme, a dedicated professional, but largely ineffective. We're working on, ah, neutralizing him. Not because we're afraid of him, you understand," he added quickly, "but we were anticipating your concern." The Hawk smiled.

"Kill him," Harry said in a flat voice.

"Ah, Mr. Scheldt." The Hawk held up a hand. "I said we were working on the problem. We will do what has to be done, I can assure you."

"And now, Harry," the Hawk whispered, "I have prepared a treat for you, to kind of seal the preliminary agreement we have managed to reach tonight. It is just a tidbit, but something I know you will enjoy."

"Sure, Hawk, what've you got in mind?" Harry was immediately suspicious again. Nobody ever gave him something for nothing.

The Hawk's smile revealed two large rows of perfectly white teeth. "My dear Harry, please come right this way."

The room was large. It had been fitted with a makeshift stage at one end. Several overstuffed chairs sat about the interior within a few feet of the stage. Harry was shown to one in the front. The Hawk seated himself directly behind Harry. Then, except for one bright spotlight that bathed the stage, the other lights were turned off, leaving Harry Scheldt in profound darkness.

Center stage was occupied by a low, narrow table about four feet long. For some reason this table excited Harry, and his insides rumbled in anticipation.

A black man and two white men, escorting a petite Vietnamese girl between them, stepped into the light from the left. The men wore tights and nothing else. Their genitals bulged prominently behind the fabric. The girl was naked. The men held her firmly and propelled her toward the table, to which they lashed her facedown with telephone wire. Harry's pulse quickened.

The two whites, judging from their loose expressions and the puncture marks on their arms, were obviously a pair of the Hawk's addicts, but the black man's expression was alive and interested as he supervised tying the young woman down. He snapped his fingers, and a much older woman stepped onto the stage from the right. She was Oriental, of indeterminate age, her hair lank and unkempt; her large breasts drooped ponderously, and when she smiled at the audience, which she could not see, large black gaps showed in her mouth where teeth had once been.

In one hand she carried a large artificial penis attached to a belt. Grinning lewdly, she fastened the contrivance about her hips. The grotesque instrument bobbed obscenely before her as she positioned herself behind the girl on the table. While the two white men held the girl down, the woman situated the device with one hand and, with the black man pushing her from behind, began to insert it into her victim.

At the girl's first scream of terror and agony, Harry had an erection. He sat transfixed, his heart pounding and his trousers swelling painfully. The girl's piercing screams filled the room, reverberating from the walls and ceiling and engulfing Harry in pure ecstasy. The old bawd, experiencing her own peculiar orgasm, thrust and pushed wildly, shouting incomprehensible encouragements to the squirming woman beneath her. She reached the height of her own frenzy as her victim's strength waned and diminished to groaning sobs, and then, spent, she collapsed upon the young woman's back. Both lay in a kind of embrace for several long moments, one gasping in pain and terror, too exhausted to protest or resist anymore, the other softly kissing her victim's sweat-bathed neck, their perspiration mingling in greasy rivulets that spattered and stained the table beneath them.

Without further ceremony, the black man stepped in front of the girl, looped a length of wire about her neck and slowly strangled the life out of her.

Harry groaned and gripped the arms of his chair; his head lolled to one side as his body suddenly went rigid and a dark stain spread down the inside of one thigh. His sweat-soaked shirt clung damply and obscenely to the back of his chair. The men on the stage untied the dead girl's corpse and bundled it off the stage. One of the white assistants, Harry noted dimly, was the same long-haired deserter who had served them drinks earlier.

"Did you like it, Harry?" the Hawk whispered from behind. Harry groaned. "We conduct this little theater on occasion, for special friends. You are now a special friend. If you want, you will be invited to another performance sometime soon."

"Y-yes!" Harry gasped.

The Hawk smiled in the darkness and placed a hand on Harry's damp shoulder. "Mr. Nguyen gets the young ladies for us from the villages down in the Delta," he explained in a soft, relaxing voice. "We will dispose of her in the Saigon River, where the currents are swift and deep, and if she should ever come to the surface, who will know? Who will care? There is a war on, you know." The Hawk laughed, and his laughter stirred a response deep in Harry Scheldt's innards.

The Hawk's big hand caressed Harry's neck gently. He let the hand linger there for several moments. The stage light had been dimmed. The other guests had departed, one part of Harry's mind told him. He did not care. He had room only for thoughts of the Hawk sitting there so close to him in the dark. He smiled deep inside himself. From the first time he had heard the Hawk's deep voice over the telephone, he had liked the man, felt strangely drawn to him and eager to meet him in the flesh. The Hawk had power, and Harry loved power as much as he loved money. He was now in the Hawk's power, and he knew he was not the first to succumb to it. But he was not angry, he was not afraid.

"Harry," the Hawk whispered, "Harry, my man, are you ready?"

"Yes!" Harry exulted. His breath came deep and fast, and the swelling was back in his trousers again. "I am ready!" He sighed.

The Hawk stood up.

* * *

The young man was trembling and sweating. He blinked his eyes painfully at the bright light. A wave of nausea hit him, but he managed to suppress it. He squinted and shaded his eyes with one hand. Where the fuck is Tom? he wondered. He trembled again and groaned softly.

This trip to the outside world had required all of the self-control the young man had managed to retain through the weeks of horror. If this meeting had not been prearranged, he never would have had the endurance to make it. Special Agent Frank Fitzgerald, U.S. Army CID, had become a heroin addict, and he knew if he did not get out now, this very afternoon, he never would.

Frank had been under deep cover for the past ten months. He had volunteered for the assignment, fully aware of the terrible danger it entailed. That he had been able to get this far without being discovered was a testament to his courage and dedication.

The army had given him a complete new identity, returned him to the States, sent him back through basic training and advanced infantry training, and then reassigned him to the 101st Airborne division in Vietnam as a rifleman. He had served two months in a line company, been wounded twice, and decorated with a Bronze Star for valor. None of this had been part of the plan, but, as planned, he had "deserted" and made his way to Saigon.

And then the phony needle tracks with which he had come to Saigon had turned into real ones. He had been good at faking it at first, puncturing himself with sterile needles, pretending euphoria, imitating withdrawal symptoms, but the Hawk had been watching him closely. Frank sensed he suspected something, and he knew that the Hawk did not need anything more than suspicion to cut his throat.

Frank was young, healthy, and in good physical condition. He was sure that if he could only maintain his cover a little while longer he would get the evidence the army needed to close down the Saigon branch of the HJO and do the organization irreparable damage elsewhere as well. He had sacrificed too much to get into the HJO to blow it by getting himself killed.

Frank Fitzgerald, of his own free will and because he had a job to do, started shooting heroin. He had been confident he could control his dosage and get out before he developed physical dependence on the drug. He had been wrong.

A black sedan pulled to the curb and Frank got in. He leaned back in the seat and uttered a long, groaning sigh. The stocky, florid-faced man driving looked at him questioningly.

"Frank, you look awful," he said, glancing at him suspiciously out of the corner of his eye as he skillfully guided the car through the hectic traffic. "What's wrong?"

"I'm through. I'm not going back in there." Suddenly Frank doubled over with pain. "Oh, Jesus!" he gasped. He was sweating profusely and trembling violently. "Pull over! I gotta puke!"

The driver pulled quickly to the curb. Frank pushed his door open and retched into the gutter. Finished, he lay back exhausted on the seat. The big man reached over quickly and wrenched back the sweat-stained sleeve of his shirt. Frank's arm looked as if it had been used as a punching bag.

"Oh, no, Frank! You didn't!" the big man groaned. He rested his hand on the steering wheel.

"Tom, I had to," Frank gasped. "I'm sorry. I held out as long as I could, but that Hawk, man, he got me on the stuff! That motherfucker is the devil himself! Lookit me, man, I'm a fuckin' junkie!" Frank held out his pitifully bruised arm and began to sob. The big man sat quietly, staring out the windshield. After a while Frank began to babble, "I *got* to have the shit now, Tom, I got to you got to get me *out* o-u-fucking-t of there, man, *out* oh Jesus fucking Christ Tom I got to have it or I'll die." He began screaming incoherently and pounding his fists into the dashboard.

Vietnamese passersby gawked curiously at the two Americans.

"Wh—what's that *smell*?" the big man asked. When he recognized the odor he stared horrified at Frank, who began nodding his head violently and laughing hysterically.

"I shit my pants, Tom, I shit my fuckin' pants I can't help it the horse does that to you oh God Tom I gotta have a fix for the love of Mary Joseph and Jesus help me or I'll die!"

"You won't die, Frank," Tom said, and started the engine. The smell was so bad the only way he could get rid of it was by getting the air circulating through the open windows.

Frank gradually became more coherent. "Last night, Scheldt was there. I heard most of what they said." Frank told him all he could remember. Tom listened attentively.

"But Scheldt didn't say how he was gonna get the stuff back into the States?"

Frank shook his head. "No. He didn't say last night, but if only I coulda stuck it out, I'da found out. But Tom, that ain't the worst of it." He told him about the girl. "And I had to *help* with it, Tom. I knew what I was doing was evil, but I couldn't help myself. I need the shit so bad I'd have let 'em do it to my own sister, my mother, for a fix. The only reason I been able to hold out since last night's 'cause I knew you'd get me into detox."

"You just hold on a little while longer, buddy, 'cause we're on our way to the medics most skosh."

A gaggle of young schoolgirls trotted by, swinging their leather briefcases crammed with books, laughing and talking gaily among themselves without a care in the world. Their little wooden shoes made a clack-clacking on the pavement, and their long black hair, secured by silver clips at the level of their shoulders, bobbed in time to the swinging of their heads. The sight of the children steadied the big man. They were a bright spot of sanity in a very crazy, very nasty world.

Tom Prudhomme and his partner, Bill Washington, sat on either side of Frank's bed. A doctor had given him something to ease his withdrawal symptoms, and he was relaxed and fairly alert.

"Frank, my man, you are one brave motherfucker." Washington smiled. He placed a big black hand on Frank's shoulder and squeezed.

"Aw, man, I blew the whole thing," Frank said weakly, but he smiled his thanks back at Washington.

"You're gonna be okay," Tom reassured him. "Detox won't be any fun, but you'll be back on your feet before you know it, back on the job as good as ever."

"Next time, Chief, why don't you get someone else to go under?" Frank whispered, and grinned. Tom and Bill both laughed. "They say I'm goin' to Japan in the morning, fellas."

"Yeah, you lucky bastard," Prudhomme agreed.

"I guess it's good-bye, then, huh?"

"Naw, only *auf Wiedersehen*, as we used to say in ol' Deutschland: not good-bye, just 'until we meet again,'" Washington said.

"And we are goin' to see your ass again, Frank, bet on it," Tom said.

"You are one brave man, ol' buddy. I'd be proud to serve with you again," Washington whispered.

Outside it was still light. Prudhomme was physically exhausted and in bad need of a cold beer.

"Bill, what say we stop in at the China Doll and grab us a couple of beers?" he suggested to Washington.

"Okay by me, Chief."

They walked down Tran Hung Dao Boulevard and waited for the light to change in front of the Saigon Motors Hotel, opposite the International BEQ.

"The old Saigon Motors"—Washington laughed, nodding his head toward the building behind them—"that's where I first fell in love in old Saigon, back in 1962."

"Jesus, Bill, were you here then? That makes you kinda an old hand in these parts."

"Sure do," Washington agreed. "Heh, heh, that girl's name was Snow, and for years I used to tell the brothers how one mornin' in Saigon I woke up six inches in Snow." Washington laughed. "Man, she give me a dose of the clap one time, thought I'd *never* get rid of it."

"Bill, if I was tellin' the story, I'd say I woke up in *nine* inches of Snow."

Washington laughed again and slapped Prudhomme on the back. The light changed, and they started across the street.

"Bill, what kind of a fuckin' world do we live in, anyway?" They threaded their way through a crowd of Vietnamese, Prudhomme talking over his shoulder to Washington, loping to keep up with him. "I mean, young men are dying out there in the paddies while scum like Scheldt pull their shit and get away with it."

Several off-duty military policemen lounging outside the International called out to them by name and exchanged greetings as they passed.

"Oh, it's not such a bad world, Tom. We see scum all the time, so we think the world is all scum, right? But every time I look at pictures of my wife and daughters" —he slapped his wallet—"I know it's a *good* world, at least in one small corner it is." Washington felt uneasy. He did not like the way Prudhomme was taking all of this, the way he was talking about it. There was something, an undercurrent, maybe, that disturbed him. Well, he told himself, everybody gets the nerves sometimes, even a rock like Tom Prudhomme.

"You know what really burns me up, though?" Prudhomme went on. "People only remember the shit. I went ashore at Iwon, on the east coast of North Korea, with the Seventh Division in November 1950. I was with the Seventeenth Infantry, and we made it as far north as Hyesanjin, almost to the Yalu, and then the Chinks came in and knocked us right out of the war. We made it back to Hungnam, forty-some days later, fighting all the fuckin' way. It was so cold, Bill! I thought I never would be warm again. I got out on the USNS *Heinselman*, December eighteenth, 1950. The point is, people don't even remember Korea anymore, Bill, but they'll remember this fuckin' place forever!" Prudhomme waved his arm at the street scene all around them.

"Yeah," Washington said, sighing dramatically, "people sure do have short memories."

Later, when he was alone, Prudhomme cleaned his revolver very carefully. First he inspected it for rust. In the tropics weapons rusted quickly and had to be cleaned often. Too much oil makes them rust more quickly, so when he was finished at last, he coated the weapon very lightly with oil, reloaded it, and put it back into its holster.

He sat on the edge of his bed and hefted the gun. One shot, and he could rid the world of Mr. Harry Scheldt; two, and he could do for the Hawk, too, whose real name was Martin Robinson.

Naw, forget it, he warned himself. But the daydream forced itself back into his mind. He could not use his own gun. For that gun he would need a clean weapon. He saw himself in his imagination, loitering on a street corner somewhere, Harry and the Hawk pulling up beside him, the gun coming out, pointing it into their surprised faces, pulling the trigger, the bullets striking them. He shook his head. Never happen. But if I needed a clean weapon, I know someone who can get me one that could never be traced, he thought.

Mocking the Midnight Bell

THE HIEN DOI WAS A REMARKABLE PLACE.

It was situated just off Nguyen Hue Boulevard, along Huynh Thuc Khang Street. Asphy had discovered it quite by chance one day and stopped in, attracted by the glass-and-ironwork façade and the bright and airy interior.

Aspby and his old friend Gregory Pappas were sitting in the Hien Doi, waiting to be joined for lunch by a reporter named Sheridan from a Charleston newspaper. "About as appropriate as Grant from Richmond," Pappas quipped.

Unlike most long-service noncommissioned officers, Pappas had a college education, obtained on the GI Bill after the Korean War. He spoke French well, and the army had sent him to language school for a year to learn Vietnamese. He boasted that he was the only left-handed Greek master sergeant in the United States Army.

Pappas had one of those shadowy intelligence jobs, which required him to work primarily with Viet Cong

defectors, taking them on propaganda operations into remote villages and recruiting others for the Kit Carson
Scout Program. The scouts he placed with various U.S.
infantry units, where they had proven remarkably useful
on combat patrols. "Set a Commie to catch a Commie, I
always say," Pappas remarked.

"Well, where the hell is he?" Aspby demanded, looking at his watch.

"He'll be along any minute now."

"Can he find his way here? I don't think a cherry boy
newspaper fart knows his way around Saigon well
enough to find this place."

"I'm having one of the boys from the center drive him
over. Relax. If you want to feel nervous, think about all
this glass around us." Most places in Vietnam that catered to Americans did not have glass in their windows
to guard against fragmentation in the event of a terrorist
bombing.

"Relax yourself, Greg. Americans almost never come
here, and I'm sure the proprietor pays his taxes to the
VC regularly." Most Americans in Vietnam believed Viet
Cong terrorists avoided bars and restaurants that made
contributions to their cause, and indeed, some of the
more conspicuous watering spots in Saigon, prime targets, had never been bombed.

"Okay, Jim, it's all set up for tomorrow. We meet at
the center at oh six hundred."

"Right. I've got the rest of today off. I'll hop a cab
early tomorrow and meet at your place."

"Fuck that. I can put you up in my room tonight, 'n'
we can leave together in the morning."

"Fine." A short, bespectacled man with wavy black
hair entered the restaurant.

"That's him!" Greg said, and stood up. "Charlie, over
here!"

Aspby laughed. They were the only customers in the
place.

Sheridan had a good smile and a firm handshake,

which impressed Aspby. Introductions were made and beer was ordered.

"What do you fellas recommend I eat?" Sheridan asked. There was a note of deference in his voice that pleased Aspby. He had never before been this close to a reporter, and he wondered what impression he was making on the man.

"Well, what's the mood back home?" Pappas asked after the plates had been cleared and cigarettes lit.

"Pull out," Sheridan answered. He had eaten with gusto, as if full meals were not a feature of his daily life as a journalist touring Vietnam for his paper.

"Pull out? Who's for pulling out?" Pappas asked, and he and Aspby exchanged glances.

"Everyone," Sheridan replied. "Congressmen, government officials. Vietnam is a quagmire. We've gotten in too far, and the politicians especially want to wash their hands of the whole affair. Remember, I was based in Washington before my paper sent me over here, and I can tell you that's what the people back there want."

"But we're winning!" Aspby protested.

Sheridan shrugged. "Sorry to tell you this, fellas, but they don't think so back home. Tell me this, you're both professional noncoms. What would you do if the U.S. pulled out of this war tomorrow? Would you do like the French in Algeria? You know, pull a coup?"

Aspby's mouth fell open. Sheridan's question was the most preposterous he had ever heard and betokened the reporter's profound ignorance of the American military man.

"We are bound by our oath of enlistment to defend the Constitution," Pappas said softly. "The American army's NCO corps, just like its officer corps, is totally apolitical. A *coup*?" Pappas laughed. The thought was ridiculous.

"I don't mean to strain your credulity, but you asked my opinion and I gave it," Sheridan said defensively.

"Charlie," Pappas said gently, "you've got a lot to learn about the American soldier. But you wanna find out how the war's goin'? My Vietnamese and I are going on a propaganda operation tomorrow. You're invited."

"Now you're talkin'!" Sheridan exclaimed. "When and where?"

"At the center, make it oh six-thirty, give me time to get 'em cranked up."

"All right!" Sheridan smiled and drank some beer. "Adventure!"

"It'll be pretty secure, I'm afraid. The One Hundred Ninety-ninth Light Infantry is going to provide security; we'll be in their area of responsibility. The Vietnamese will be in charge. Major Luang will go along."

"Major Luang is in charge and he's going along, but you set it all up, right?" Sheridan grinned.

"Yeah. I'm his adviser, after all."

"Greg, I hear you're really a colonel and you're working for the CIA. Is that true?"

"Now where the hell did you pick that information up?" Pappas asked, and winked at Aspby. That rumor had been circulating among the Vietnamese for a long time.

"At the center this morning."

Pappas nodded. "Charlie, I'm impressed. You know how to dig shit out, don't you? But actually I'm just a lowly master sergeant. I was assigned to the center for two reasons: I speak Vietnamese, and I was available."

"Okay," Sheridan said as if he were closing the cover on a mental notebook. "Mind if I bring a photographer tomorrow?"

After dinner they went to Pappas's room. He'd arranged for an extra cot for Aspby to use until morning. They were feeling mellow from a big supper and several very good drinks.

"Greg, you went to language school, right?" Aspby asked.

"Yeah. So what?"

"Well, did you ever hear of a book called *The Tale of Kieu* or something like that in Vietnamese?"

"Sure. But it's not a book, like a novel or something; it's an epic poem. It's egregiously boring stuff. Why?"

"Because General Ton is always harping on it. He told my colonel he should read it, and the old man asked me what it was all about, as if I'm some expert on Vietnamese culture."

"You should be, as long as you've been here."

Aspby snorted. "I only know how to get along with these people, I don't really understand anything about them. But what's this *Kieu* all about?"

Pappas shrugged. "*The Tale of Kieu* is to the Viets what Shakespeare is to us. It's a story about a decent young girl who is forced to sell herself into concubinage in order to save her father from an unscrupulous mandarin. It's full of sobbing men and tough broads. We had to read some parts of it in language school at Monterey, but I didn't find it to my taste."

"So what's so hot about the book—I mean poem?"

"I suspect the Vietnamese love it because they see it as a metaphor for Vietnam. Kieu in the poem *is* Vietnam, sold, enslaved, raped. This poor country has a history of getting its little ass kicked. But the story ends happily—sort of—with Kieu reunited with her true lover and her family. The story's strong on family and interpersonal relationships, very Confucian. And the language of the poem, to the Vietnamese, anyway, is surpassingly beautiful. Every Vietnamese who makes it as far as high school reads the thing until it comes out his ears."

"Sobbing men and tough broads," Aspby mused. "What a combination."

"Yeah. In this country the men sob a lot and write poetry while the women run things."

"C'mon, not quite that fucking bad!"

"Well, okay, but when a country's one great literary

hero is a fucking woman, what does that tell you about its men, huh?"

"Goddamn you, Gregory!" Aspby shouted into Pappas's ear. "I went to all the trouble to get permission to go on this fucking operation, and it'll have to be canceled because you're too fucking drunk to make it!" Pappas began to slump forward in his seat, but Aspby grabbed him and held him upright as the jeep rolled through Saigon's early-morning streets toward the center.

"Garangimis," Pappas muttered.

Aspby was not quite sure himself when he had finally gone to sleep, but it had not been long enough ago; he was still half-drunk, although moving around and shoving Pappas into his gear and pouring him into the jeep had revived him somewhat.

The gate guard waved them through when he recognized Pappas. Aspby helped his friend out and, by holding him up, managed to stagger halfway across the parking lot before Pappas stopped. To the great amusement of the watching Vietnamese, Pappas vomited copiously.

Major Luang came running down the steps of the headquarters building.

"What is wrong with Gregory?" he asked, genuine concern in his voice.

"Uh, he's just had a bit too much to drink, Major. Can you help me get him upstairs and out of sight?"

"Coffee! Coffee!" Greg mumbled.

"We will have to cancel the operation," Major Luang said in exasperation.

"I can still go," Pappas protested. "I need coffee."

"Okay, Major, let's get him inside and force some coffee down him, but you're right. We'll never be able to get him sober by oh seven hundred. And goddamn, the press will be here by then! We'll have to hide Greg somewhere and tell Sheridan he's got the shits or something. Jesus, what a farce!"

Major Luang and Aspby stumbled up the steps and into the headquarters building. An orderly produced a cup of black liquid at Major Luang's command, and it was thrust under Pappas's nose.

"Mmmm, nhaa, that's better," he slurred.

Aspby sat at the table opposite Pappas. "What a night, eh, Jim? More coffee, please!" Pappas gulped down the second cup and held it out for a refill. "I never missed a day's work in my life because of booze, and today's no exception," he said. By the fourth cup he was beginning to look human again. Aspby marveled at the transformation.

"Awright," Pappas bellowed suddenly, "let's get this fucking show on the road!"

"My, you are a ball of fire this morning." Sheridan grinned from the doorway.

"Ah, Mr. Sheridan"—Major Luang shook the correspondent's hand warmly—"we were just having coffee. Won't you join us?"

"Jim, Greg." Sheridan nodded at the two sergeants as he took a place at the table.

"We'll be ready to go in a few minutes," Pappas rumbled, and slurped some more coffee. "I ain't worth a shit in the morning without my cupa coffee," he added, a huge, stupid grin on his face.

"I apologize, gents, but my photographer couldn't make it," Sheridan said as he sipped his coffee. He made a terrible face and then whispered in Pappas's ear, "Confidentially, Greg, this is the worst coffee I've ever had in my life!"

"Don't be a goddamned fool, Charlie," Pappas roared. "It's ambrosia! It's ambrosia!"

The Fourth Battalion, Twelfth Infantry's base camp was the worst shantytown Aspby had ever seen, but the infantrymen did not seem to mind it much. "We move around a lot," one informed them as the armored personnel carrier, commonly called an APC or a "track," roared into the center of the camp.

They dismounted and walked in a group across an open space to the battalion tactical operations center. On the way Aspby peeked into some of the bunkers. Except for the elaborate stereo systems and tape decks the soldiers had installed, their living quarters looked straight out of World War I.

Inside the TOC maps were spread on tables. While Pappas and Major Luang discussed their requirements with the battalion operations officer, Aspby stood at the back of the crowd, feeling out of place. Sheridan busied himself taking down the names of several clerks who sat typing up journals or working at map overlays. These were real soldiers here, Aspby realized, not support types. At the same time, he realized that the troops in the rifle companies thought battalion headquarters was a rear-echelon hideout for military incompetents.

"Okay," the operations officer said, "we've arranged to give you a squad from Delta Company, Lieutenant Pebbles's platoon. You shouldn't need any more than that because Ap Ba's pretty quiet just now, wouldn't you agree, Frank?" The S-3 deferred to an elderly-looking captain, who was the battalion intelligence officer. The S-2 chewed his pipe calmly and nodded his agreement.

"Bob here is going to accompany you." The S-3 nodded toward the psychological operations man, a tall, bespectacled captain.

"Yep," said the psy-ops man, "and we're takin' a couple of Doc Ramsey's medics."

"Major Luang, Sergeant Pappas, good luck out there," the S-3 said, folding up his maps. "You shouldn't have any trouble, but if by chance you do, you can get us on the horn and we'll be there most skosh."

"This'll be a good one, Jim." Pappas slapped Aspby on the back once they were outside.

"Greg, how the fuck did you do it? A while ago you were dead from alcohol poisoning, and now you're a dynamo."

Pappas winked and increased his stride to catch up with Major Luang. Everyone, including the infantry squad, the psy-ops officer, and the two medical personnel, climbed aboard the personnel carrier. The medics would pick up their own jeep and equipment back at the Binh Chanh turnoff, where they had transferred to the track.

They reached the village of Ap Ba around noon. Their convoy looked impressive rolling into the place with its three jeeps and armored personnel carrier, possibly the largest motorized force the villagers had seen since the French occupied the country. Aspby had spent the trip from the battalion base camp riding along on the APC while Pappas and the officers rode in one of the Vietnamese jeeps.

Pappas, Aspby suddenly realized, was the brains behind this whole operation. Aspby was surprised to note a twinge of professional jealousy on that account. Pappas had the same MOS—military occupational specialty—as Aspby, an "administrative supervisor"—a glorified clerk —but somehow he had gotten himself assigned to the center, and he had changed. He was not just a high-ranking clerk anymore, but a man who could get others to do things for him. Major Luang was in titular charge only. Aspby recalled how the major had wanted to cancel the operation because he had thought Pappas was too sick to go.

The infantrymen, with some of Major Luang's men, spread out to secure the village perimeter while the American and Vietnamese medical personnel set up their equipment in the center of the village. Major Luang produced a portable loudspeaker and began calling the people together. "Attention! Attention!" he shouted. "Bring us your sick and injured. We have American and Vietnamese doctors here. Come forward! There is no obligation for this service. We are your government, and we are here to help you."

"One of the biggest lies in any language," Aspby whispered into Pappas's ear, " 'I'm from the government, and I'm here to help you.' "

Pappas laughed. "We probably won't get anything out

of these people today," he explained. "Nobody would ever dare to come up and blab in front of all these witnesses anyway, because if there are any VC in this crowd, and you can bet your sweet ass there are, the informant would be dead by morning."

"But the village looks so friendly," Aspby protested, looking around at the crowds of laughing children and smiling old people.

"It is now, but when the sun goes down, who knows? And it is officially in a pacified area, so we know a lot of the villagers are friendly toward us. But whose side are you going to support when someone shoves an AK-forty-seven into your gut, no matter where your true loyalties lie? We hope that if we treat these folks decently now, maybe someday one of them will give us a piece of information on VC or NVA troop movements that might save American lives."

And the people did come forward that day, in large numbers. Aspby wandered among their humble houses. The village had a population of more than two hundred souls, he estimated. It was located at the end of a dirt road two kilometers from the larger hamlet of Ben Luc, itself only a thousand meters from Highway 4. Rice fields spread around three sides of the village; the western edge of Ap Ba was bordered by a vast field of elephant grass. The air was fresh and clean, and the place reminded Aspby very much of the villages he had seen back in 1962 with the old MAAG, north of Saigon.

Children crowded around him, their tiny, dirty fingers beseeching gifts. "Mr. American! Mr. American!" they shouted. "Give us candy? Give us Salem, okay?" Aspby was sorry he had not foreseen this and brought something with him. In the old days, when they had moved through villages up near the Cambodian border, if the children were friendly, the village was friendly.

Aspby walked back to the carrier, where the driver sat, his legs dangling over the side, an open can of C-rations in his hand.

"Can you spare some chow?"

"Sure, Sarge," the driver replied. "Case o' Cs inside the track, climb in and get some." Aspby rummaged around in a carton and fished out a few bars of chocolate and some tiny boxes of chewing gum, which he shoved into a pocket. Selecting a can of tuna and noodles for himself, he joined the driver.

"How long ya been in-country?" he asked the driver, a private first class. The man's thick, hairy forearms had been burned a deep mahogany by the tropical sun, and his short blond hair was bleached almost white, indicating quite a long time in-country.

"Ten months, Sarge," he answered. "You?"

"Uh, three years in May, this time."

"Jesus Christ, long time!" The driver looked at Aspby curiously. "Seen much action?"

"Naw, not even when I was out in the field, back in sixty-two and sixty-three. Didn't see any in Korea, either, except when the city of Pusan burned down once."

"Two wars and you ain't seen any action?" the driver marveled.

"I don't need to get shot at to know I don't want to be." Aspby chuckled.

The driver laughed. "You ain't dumb."

"How about yerself? You seen much action in the past ten months?"

The driver shrugged. "Some. Had a track blown out from under me once by a command detonated mine, got a couple o' Hearts. We see a lot of real small stuff in the Hundred Ninety-ninth, nothin' like I hear some of the guys catch up north. We see a lotta ambushes and sometimes a little heavy shit on search 'n' destroy ops. But me, I'm gettin' outta here in two months, standin' up and with all my parts intact."

Aspby laughed and spooned some tuna and noodles into his mouth. "Well, there's a cease-fire comin' up at Tet. That'll give you guys a breather. Been on R and R yet?"

"Yeah," the driver answered enthusiastically. "I went to Bangkok—that's 'bang cock,' and mother, did they!

Boy, can them Thai girls fuck! These gook broads are like fuckin' a sweaty pillow, you ever notice?"

"Yeah. But Thais are gooks, too, ain't they?" Aspby's eyes crinkled about the edges in merriment.

"Oh, hell no, Sarge!" the driver answered seriously. "The Thais are real people. These Vietnamese are gooks." The man pronounced Vietnamese "Viennese." He noticed Aspby's 9mm auto revolver. "Heeey! You got a piece and a half there, Sarge! Kin I touch?"

"Sure." Aspby drew his hand gun and handed it to the man, barrel pointing straight up.

"Beautiful!" the man exclaimed. "A real hogleg." He ejected the clip and worked the slide a few times. "Light as a feather," Aspby said. "Hardly know I'm carryin' it most of the time."

The PFC nodded and handed the piece back to Aspby. "Where'd you get it?" he asked.

"From a friend."

"Kin you get me one, Sarge?"

"Well, maybe. Yeah. But why? You're leaving in two months."

"Yeah, well, you see, I kinda extended my tour and I forgot to mention it. I get thirty days free leave home 'n' then transfer outta combat duty when I come back. I saved enough money to buy a new car since I been here, and another six months will gimme a nice nest egg."

"Okay. You see that big master sergeant over there, the guy I came out here with?" Aspby pointed to Pappas, who, with Major Luang's help, was talking earnestly to an old man.

"You mean the guy with two left feet?" the PFC asked. Aspby laughed loudly. Greg's feet were rather large. He was an awkward man who shambled, and quite often his feet did not both go in the same direction at the same time, especially when he had been drinking.

"Right. He'll tell you how to get in touch with me, and I'll put you in touch with the guy who got this piece for me. He charged me a hundred and fifty bucks for it. Hey, what's your name, anyway?"

"Roger Farnsworth."

"Well, PFC Farnsworth, I'm SFC Jim Aspby, pleased to meetcha." They shook hands. "Where you from?"

"Williamsport, PA."

"I've been through there. Nice place."

"Nicer than this shithole." Farnsworth gestured toward the nearby rice fields. "Well," he corrected himself, "maybe some of it's real pretty country."

Sheridan climbed up on the track. "Hey, Jim, I'm the one's supposed to be doin' the interviewing."

"Roger Farnsworth, meet Charlie Sheridan, the real enemy," Aspby said.

"Typical lifer attitude," Sheridan replied, nodding his head toward Aspby. Farnsworth laughed.

A large number of village children had gathered about the track, and they squatted silently in the shadow of the behemoth, staring up at the Americans. Aspby threw a handful of candy bars and gum onto the ground. The children screamed and shouted and scrambled for the sweets.

"That's rather patronizing, don't you think?" Sheridan asked.

Before Aspby could reply, Pappas climbed up beside them and spoke.

"Do you remember the story Boswell tells about being out with Dr. Johnson in the streets of London? Johnson would give all his spare change to the poor, and Bozzy asked him why he did it. 'They'll only spend it on gin,' Boswell complained. Johnson replied, 'Pray, why deny them the only bit of pleasure in their lives?'

"No, Charlie, it's not patronizing at all. Whaddya think we should give these kids? Journalism lessons?"

Sheridan shook his head. "Gregory, they threw away the mold when they made you," he said.

"We go now! We go now!" Major Luang shouted. The security men returned to the convoy from their positions. With a quick good-bye to Farnsworth, Aspby jumped to the ground and found himself a seat in one of the jeeps. He was joined by Pappas, Major Luang, and the psychological operations officer. As they rolled back down the road toward Ben Luc, the villagers of Ap Ba waved and shouted, "Good-bye!" and, "Thenk you!" in English.

"We'll stop at Ben Luc for a while," Pappas told Aspby. "We want to talk to the village chief there. He's been very cooperative with us in the past, and the medics can do a little civic action among the people."

"It's been a good morning," the captain remarked. "Those people were genuinely grateful for the help we gave them today. We gave out quite a lot of stuff back there."

"Did anyone come forward with any intel?" Aspby asked.

The captain grinned and handed Aspby a slip of paper. There were some words in Vietnamese scrawled on it. "What's this?" he asked.

"It is telling us who the main VC contact is in the village," Major Luang replied.

Aspby stared at the slip of paper and handed it back to the captain. "What are you goin' to do about him?" he asked.

"She," Pappas corrected. "She'll be taken care of."

Nobody mentioned the incident again.

They parked in the center of Ben Luc. The hamlet had a proper marketplace installed under a huge corrugated tin roof. Because it was siesta time, few of the stalls were open, but Aspby's eye caught one where beer was sold.

The village chief came out to greet the visitors, and while the others followed him to his home for tea, Aspby sidled inconspicuously over to the beer vendor.

"How much for a Beer LaRue?" he asked in Vietnamese.

"One hundred dong," the vendor replied with a take-it-or-leave-it shrug of his shoulders. It was robbery, but Aspby would have paid twice as much for a cold bottle. He found a wooden bench and sat down. The beer tasted absolutely wonderful. He drank nearly half the big bottle without stopping for a breath of air.

Out in the square the sun blazed down furiously, but under the roof it was cool and there was a breeze. Aspby looked down the main road. Off to one side, half in a ditch, an armored personnel carrier rusted, the victim of an ambush. He had noticed it there when they came through earlier in the day. Beyond the track two infantrymen crouched in the shade of a palm tree. The others were nowhere in sight. Aspby finished his beer and walked up the road toward the blasted track.

The track had belonged to an Arvin unit, and it had been taken out by an armor-piercing round of some kind. The projectile had punched right through the side armor, and all around were pockmarks gouged in the metal by the shaped charge when it detonated. Aspby wondered what had happened to the crew and passengers. The ramp was down in the rear, but he could see nothing inside. He tried to imagine what had happened here. Had the men all died, and if so, had it been quick? Were some wounded? Did any survive? He marveled at the courage of the enemy, to fire a rocket at such a monster. If the VC gunner had missed, it would have been all over for him!

"Thanatopsis, Sergeant Aspby?" Sheridan asked quietly. Aspby jumped.

"Thana-what?"

"Thanatopis. Contemplation of death. You know, like the graveyard scene in *Hamlet*, regarding Yorick's skull —'Alas, poor Yorick, I knew him,' or something like that. I wonder what happened here."

"Hmm. Looks like some of our Allies got wasted."

"Well, I don't like to think about it too long. *We* aren't safe home yet, are we? I'm going to talk to those two GIs up there. Would you come along with me?"

They walked up the dusty road.

"Hot," Aspby muttered.

"Sure is. That Pappas of yours, he's quite a fellow, isn't he?"

"And your next question, Charlie, is, 'What is a man like him doing in the army?'"

"Or you, for that matter."

"I'm in the army because I like it, and I'm in Vietnam 'cause I love this fucking place. Seriously, I love it here. This is *my* war. It's been part of me since March 1962, more than five years now. Lookit me. I'm no hero. I'm a glorified clerk's what I am, Mr. Sheridan. But I'm *proud* of what I am. I'm proud to be allowed to wear my country's uniform; I'm proud the army lets me serve here in Vietnam; I'm proud of what the United States is tryin' to do here, and so long's I can contribute somethin' to what we're doing, this is where I want to be."

"You and Pappas—"

"And I'll tell you something else," Aspby rushed on, "the army's got something nobody else's got, unless it's the marines and maybe a few swabbies and a few flyboys, 'n' that's real heroes, guys who got the papers to prove it. In the army I rub shoulders with real heroes. I work with them, and I got their respect. My boss is an air force light colonel. He got the Distinguished Service Cross in World War Two. He respects me for what I do, and I respect him for what he's accomplished, not just 'cause he's a colonel an' I'm a sergeant. And you know what? I *like* to do things for the guy, even though he's an asshole at least twice every week. Sometimes oftener. And that kid I was talkin' to, up on the track? He's only a PFC, but he's got two Purple Hearts, ten months in-country, and he just *extended*. He's a hero in my book, and I like talking to guys like that. I figure if I stick around in the army long enough, some of these guys' courage and dignity and honor might just rub off on me and make me a better man than I would be otherwise."

Sheridan took a deep breath and let it out. "You and Pappas, you're two of the most unusual people I've ever met. Do you think someday we could sit down over a beer and do an in-depth interview for my paper?"

Aspby was flattered. "Sure. You name the place and the time."

The two infantrymen were still crouched in the shade beside the road. One, cradling an M-60 in his arms, looked out over the paddy while the other gazed off into the brush beside the road. "Man, I love dingin' gooks with muh pig," Aspby heard the machine gunner remark to his partner. They looked up quickly as Sheridan and Aspby approached.

"Where you boys from?" Sheridan asked heartily. Then he asked them a string of casual questions, which were answered laconically.

"Think we'll win this war?" the reporter asked suddenly, watching the two closely for their reaction.

"Who gives a shit?" the machine gunner snorted. "I go home in two months. Ain't that right, Clyde?" he asked his partner. The other man laughed.

After a few more questions Sheridan said he wanted to return to the village.

"Rather uncommunicative pair," he remarked dryly as they trudged back down the road.

"They're good kids. Probably didn't want to say anything in front of a lifer like me."

"You call yourself a 'lifer,' Jim. That's an interesting word. What does it mean to you, as a professional soldier?"

"Means I'm in the army until it ain't fun no more."

"Fun? Do you call this fun? Do you really mean to imply that an intelligent man like yourself likes boring, nasty work at the world's worst pay?"

Aspby shrugged. "When I don't like it anymore, I'm gone."

"It doesn't bother you that most Americans would rather not be in your shoes?"

"No. In fact, I get my jollies thinking I'm keepin' some poor dumb son of a bitch alive back home, takin' his place over here. You know the three things a professional soldier doesn't need? He doesn't need a wife, a car, or civilian clothes."

"Jim, back home they're calling people like you baby-killers."

"Well, fuck them. Look." Aspby took off his cap. "Notice the way I cut my hair?" He ran his hand over his short hair. There was less than an inch on the top of his head, and the sides above the ears were virtually shaved bald. "We call this a 'whitewall' haircut, Mr. Sheridan. Can you see why?"

Aspby put his cap back on. They were walking past the ruined personnel carrier now. Sheridan trudged along quietly, waiting for Aspby to continue.

"Short hair's practical. No fuss, no bother. I comb it with a washcloth in the mornings and go to work. In the tropics, short hair's comfortable, except when you get too much sun, like today." He rubbed the back of his neck tenderly. "But this haircut is also a symbol, Mr. Sheridan."

"Of what?"

"Well, it means you reject civilian life. You reject the nine-to-five mentality. You don't worry anymore about a paycheck, your family, your status, your car, your home, any of that mundane civilian shit. When you make up your mind to be a professional soldier and you get shaved like this, you withdraw from the world, so to speak."

"Like a priest or a monk?"

"Well, I don't know if I want to carry it *that* far. No, that's not what I mean. Well, maybe a little."

"Your hair makes this statement wherever you go, then?"

"Yeah. Or worse." Aspby laughed. "People think you're a fuckin' gyrene."

Sheridan shook his head. "I've talked to other NCOs, Jim, but those guys, unlike you and Pappas, could only speak in monosyllabic grunts."

"Sure. Who wants to say anything serious in front of a liberal, elitist media representative, Charlie? If you don't fuck up what they say, you're sure to shit on it."

Sheridan laughed. "Do all the pros think like that?" They were back in the village square now.

"Probably. Most of 'em won't talk much about how they feel, not to an outsider, anyway. It's too personal. Besides, flag waving, talking too much about patriotism and all that, anyone who does is considered either crazy or phony."

"Ever read *From Here to Eternity*?"

"I read it. You're thinkin' of that first sergeant, what was his name? Burt Lancaster played him in the movie. Well, that was the army before World War Two. Jones did have some regular service, but the people he described were ones he'd met in the army of the thirties. I didn't find the NCOs in Jones's book typical of the ones I've known. Ever read a book by William Goldman, *Soldier in the Rain*?"

"No." Sheridan jotted down the author's name and the book.

"They made a movie out of that one, too, starred Jackie Gleason and Steve McQueen. Read it. Master Sergeant Maxwell Slaughter's the kind of NCO I'm talkin' about." Aspby noticed for the first time that Sheridan's nose had turned a flaming red since morning. "Hey, Charlie, looks like you got a bit too much sun yourself."

"Mount up! Mount up!" Pappas shouted. Engines began to rev and roar, and the security teams came trotting back into the village.

"Guess it's time to go now, Jim. I'm serious about that beer and talk."

"Sure. See you back in Saigon." They shook hands. Aspby never saw Charlie Sheridan after that.

Pappas and Aspby were having a Sunday brunch at the Hien Doi. Large golden mounds of scrambled eggs flecked with ham heaped their plates; a pile of toasted French bread sat in a basket to one side of the table; cold "33" beer rounded out the meal.

"I was really impressed with how you handled the Ap

Ba operation, Greg," Aspby said around a mouthful of ham and eggs.

"I'm glad to hear that, Jim, because I wasn't too sure how well I'd handled it." Pappas stuffed a large chunk of French bread into his mouth before taking a long pull at his beer.

"You were magnificent, vintage Pappas, Gregory."

"Ah, that's really good to know, Jim, 'cause that morning I was still so drunk from the night before I can't remember a fuckin' thing that happened that day."

The breakfast dishes had long since been cleared from the table. Pappas and Aspby were drinking their way to Monday morning. They had finished seven beers apiece, and it was still a long while to noon. Pappas fumbled a disheveled Camel from its crushed pack. After lighting it, he blew a cloud of smoke across the table into Aspby's face.

"Greg, for a guy who's got a college degree, you are a fuckin' slob."

"Jim, for a guy who doesn't have a college education, you are too smart to be wasting your time as an NCO in this fuckin' army."

"Yeah, same-same you, ole buddy. But seriously, what is a guy like you doing in the army?"

Pappas drank some beer. "It sure isn't for the money." He laughed.

"Fact is, Greg, I'm makin' a base pay of about a thousand dollars a month. Then you gotta consider hostile fire pay, rations, overseas pay, no income taxes because I'm in a war zone, and free mailing privileges. And you're doin' a little better 'cause you're a master sergeant. But that's not bad. When I first came in the army, anybody making a thousand bucks a month was doing pretty good on the outside."

"How much are you worth dead, Jim?"

"Ten thousand smackers," Aspby replied immediately, and drank some more beer.

"And when you rotate back to the States you lose all

those nice perks, so your take-home pay goes down to way under a thousand a month."

"I ain't never goin' home. I love it here."

"Me too. But that's not the point. War is what a soldier does, but when he's not fighting one he spends his time training for war. And they can't pay me enough to put up with the garrison routine back at Bragg or Dix; maybe SHAPE headquarters in Paris or army attaché duty in Copenhagen, but fat chance I'll ever get to any of those places. No, our next duty after Vietnam's gonna be some place like Baumholder or Grafenwöhr in Germany or Ft. Leonard Wood or some such place back in the States, where you eat chickenshit for breakfast, lunch, and supper until it comes out of your ears."

"So why are we in the army then?"

Pappas finished his bottle of beer. "When I was a kid, my dad used to take us to visit a friend of his, an ex-sailor in the German merchant marine. This guy lived in a cottage on the lake near where we lived. One day, when he and Dad were well into a case of beer, the old Kraut said he'd got out of the merchant marine 'cause an old salt had warned him that if he didn't, the sea would get into his blood, and he'd wind up spending the rest of his life on ships. I guess the army's just got into my blood, that's all."

Aspby nodded. Then an idea struck him. "Say, when we get tired of this place, let's go back to my quarters, and we'll work on a fifth of Jack Daniels I've got stashed there."

"My dear friend"—Pappas saluted Aspby with his glass—"your words are drops of music as pour liquor in the soul."

"Hey, very nice! 'Drops of music as pour liquor in the soul.' Is that original?"

"Naw. Something I remember from *Kim Van Kieu*."

"I thought you said you didn't like *Kieu*."

"Was I drunk or sober when I told you that?"

"Sober, for sure."

"Then I lied. *Kieu* is world-class poetry, old buddy.

Shame is, we in the West don't know it. Problem is, you either gotta get a very good translation or learn to read Vietnamese exceptionally well."

Aspby was suddenly struck by another thought. "Hey, can you recommend a good translation for me? Maybe if I read it, I can impress General Ton."

They were sitting in Aspby's room, drinking bourbon out of dirty plastic cups.

"Did I ever tell you about Master Sergeant Charles C. Williams?" Pappas asked. His face bore the heavy, serious expression of a man well into his cups.

"Yeah, at least fifty times."

"Well, you're gonna hear it now for the fifty-first time. It was August 1950 and we was in some hills just behind the Naktong River and t' whole fuckin' North Korean Army was pushin' us t' hell—"

"Goddamnit, Gregory! We're in Viet-fucking-Nam, not Korea! You wanna tell a war story, tell one about Viet-motherfucking-Nam!" Aspby shouted.

"—right fuckin' outta Korea," Pappas continued. "I was with Foxtrot Company, Seventh Infantry. We was part of the Second Division, remember th' ol' Second Division, Jim? I was eighteen years old 'n' I thought I'd live forever." Pappas laughed sarcasticaly. "I found out real quick in Korea just how fragile human life really is. Well, an officer from battalion grabbed a bunch of us—sixty or seventy of us—'n' tol' us to dig in on this hill about six hundred yards east of the river."

Pappas got unsteadily to his feet and poured himself a large dollop of whiskey. Swaying gently, he stood between the beds and went on with his story. Aspby lay back and went to sleep. Pappas rambled on, shouting and whispering to the air, oblivious of time or circumstance. He was back in Korea again, a frightened young infantryman. He waved his arms wildly and bourbon sloshed onto Aspby's face.

"I was with the group that got cut off and ol' Williams was the rankin' man with us by then. He took charge.

Boy, he was everywhere, a one-man army! Even after he got shot and paralyzed from the waist down, he lay in his hole and shouted orders and encouragement to the rest of us; even gave up his water and rations so others could keep up their strength for fighting.

"Man, the fucking gooks came at us, again and again! We shot 'em down like dogs! They got into our perimeter a few times and we fought 'em hand to hand!" Pappas punctuated his words by jabbing his fist violently in the air.

"That night we decided to make a break for it. There was only about twenty of us left then and we were almost outta ammo. We wanted to carry Williams down with us, but you know what? He fucking refused! Refused," his voice quavered. Pappas fell silent, his mouth hanging open slackly as he stared transfixed at the baseboard. He stood like that for a long time. "He said he'd be too much of a burden," Pappas continued in a whisper, "and make it easier for the gooks to spot us if we carried 'im down. He was right, but nobody wanted to leave 'im up there for the gooks to get him. The fucking gooks! We found a lot of our guys later who'd been tortured by the miserable little motherfuckers! You know what they did? They burned their fucking family jewels off with gasoline! Do you think any of us wanted to leave ole Williams up there to face that?"

Pappas nodded his head sowly and mumbled to himself. Then he continued speaking aloud: "Ol' Williams says, 'Never mind 'bout me, boys,' he says, 'just load m' carbine, stick the muzzle under m' chin 'n' leave me here. I know what to do when the gooks come for me.' So that's what we—"

Aspby rolled over and groaned in his sleep.

"I said," Pappas shouted, "I said, 'I wonder what ol' Williams thought about, layin' up there, waitin' for the gooks to come for him?'"

Pappas stared intently into his whiskey glass for a time. Whatever he saw in there seemed to sober him up momentarily. "You asked me earlier today why I stayed in the Army, remember? Well, once you see courage and sacrifice like Charles Williams's, you're never the same again. I realize now that on that hill above the Naktong River in that summer of 1950, I was in the presence of God. Williams's act transcended human courage, Jim. Transcended it! I was touched by God that day. It was a terrible kind of glory, Jim. Whoever said God was gentle 'n' nice? Bullshit! God scares the shit out of you! But," his voice lowered to a confidential whisper, "it was glorious, Jim and I loved it. I loved it. I mean"—his voice broke—"not even Christ, who is God, died better 'n' ol' Williams that day. I mean, you only see that kind of shit"—Pappas was having trouble getting his breath— "you only see that kind of thing in the military, Jim. Only in the military. That's why I'm still in. I'm lookin' for God."

Pappas collapsed to the floor with a tremendous crash, knocking over the whiskey bottle, which shattered into a thousand fragments. Pappas lay there oblivious to the broken glass and spilled whiskey all around him.

Aspby rolled over again and mumbled, "Fuck 'em all but six."

Pappas began to snore loudly.

Just Man Raging

"CHIEF, THE COLONEL WANTS TO SEE YA," THE MP operations sergeant said as he stuck his head inside Mr. Prudhomme's office. "And he wants you to bring the Scheldt and Herman Johnson files with you."

Prudhomme shrugged and took the two thick files out of the cabinet where he kept his open cases. He was not scheduled to brief the provost marshal on the cases, but the old man was the type who asked for impromptu updates when he thought to, which was often on important cases like these two.

"C'mon in, Tom." Colonel Langhorne motioned for Prudhomme to take a seat beside his desk. The warrant officer sat down, holding the two case files loosely in his lap.

"Those the files I asked you to bring, Tom?" Langhorne nodded at the cases.

"Yessir."

"May I have them?" The colonel put them in the middle of his desk but did not open them. "How's Frank Fitzgerald?"

Prudhomme shrugged. He'd briefed the colonel on Frank's condition only yesterday morning. "He's in Japan now, sir. He'll be okay. We shouldn't expect to see him back here, though."

"What went wrong, Tom?"

Prudhomme thought for a moment. The air conditioner in the window hummed. Outside the sun beat down and it was hot and dusty, but in here it was cool and quiet. "I dunno," he answered shortly. "I guess Frank felt he was being watched too closely to fake it, so he took some smack to make it look real. I suppose he figured a few doses wouldn't hurt 'im. I guess he thought he'd be comin' out soon enough anyway. I guess, I guess, I guess," he said bitterly. "I guess I guessed wrong."

"Don't blame yourself, Tom." Colonel Langhorne leaned back in his chair. "The decision to put Frank in there was made a long time ago by someone else. I wouldn't have gone along with it, but I wasn't in charge here then, and you only did what you had to do. So did Frank, God bless him." The colonel shook his head sadly. "How many times did you see Frank while he was in there?"

Despite Colonel Langhorne's soothing words, Prudhomme saw this line of questioning as criticism of the way he had handled the case. "Maybe once a week, Colonel. Well, I *talked* to him that often, at least, but it wasn't easy for him to get out of that fortress they've got down there in the docks area. I think I'd actually seen him only once in the month before he came out the other day. Otherwise I'd have noticed the symptoms and made him come out sooner."

"Okay." Colonel Langhorne leafed through the Herman Johnson file idly.

"Colonel, they murdered a young girl in there, the night before Frank came out. He saw the whole thing. They murdered her for Harry Scheldt's pleasure."

The Colonel looked up sharply. "Yeah, and our only witness is in the drug farm back in Japan, Tom. Now how the hell do we build a case in that situation? Take this back with you." He handed back the HJO file. "This one"—he tapped the Scheldt file with a forefinger—"is closed as of right now."

Prudhomme caught his breath sharply. *"Closed? Wh—"*

"Closed, goddammit!"

"But sir! I don't understand! We have enough in there to put Harry Scheldt in Leavenworth for the rest of his life! How come 'closed'?"

"Tom, don't make this any harder on me than it already is. I've been ordered to close this case, and as of right now, it is no longer an open file. You are off it. We're all off it. Don't fuck with Harry Scheldt anymore."

Prudhomme stared at the provost for a long moment. "On whose authority is my case being closed, Colonel?"

"On a hell of a lot higher authority than I have, Tom. Don't ask me any more questions. Harry Scheldt's got friends in high places, and they'll shit all over us if we don't lighten up on him. We're soldiers. We follow orders. I'm following mine, and you will follow yours: the Harry Scheldt case is officially closed, and you will have no further contact with him from this point on. Understand?"

Tom Prudhomme sighed. "Yes, sir, I understand. No further contact with that murdering bastard traitor Harry Scheldt, may God damn his soul to hell."

"That's more like it, Tom. Sarge!" the colonel called out, and the operations sergeant stepped into his office. "Take this file and close it, please. Forward the final report of investigation to Scheldt's commanding officer with the standard remark, 'Case closed due to lack of evidence,' and I'll sign it." The sergeant nodded, took the file, and left the room.

Colonel Langhorne sighed. "Tom, I'd like nothing more than to go into that nest over there with the whole battalion and clean those fucking sewer rats out, every last one of 'em. And I'd string Harry Scheldt up by his balls, if I could."

"But you can't."

"No, I can't. But the U.S. government and several others are after the Herman Johnson Organization, and they'll get 'em, sooner or later. The work you and Fitzgerald have done will help."

"Yeah, Colonel, and meantime Scheldt gets away."

"For the moment, Tom, only for the moment. Lookee here." Colonel Langhorne held up a brown manila envelope. "My orders were to close the file, Tom, so I closed it. You saw me close it just now, right? But nobody told me I couldn't make a copy of the fucking thing and send it to a friend of mine back in Washington. This friend"—the colonel grinned—"works for somebody who ain't no friend of people like Scheldt, and Harry's friends won't do him no good with these boys."

Prudhomme smiled for the first time. "Colonel, you're a sly old rascal, aren't you?"

"Yes, I am."

"When did you make the copy?"

"Early this morning. I may be just a colonel and I may only be the provost marshal for this command, but I'm real good at running a copy machine all by myself. But you still aren't happy about this, are you, Tom?"

"No, sir. I want Scheldt for myself. Think I should go see the chaplain with my problem, Colonel?" In the army, when a man is told to go see the chaplain about a problem, he is being told, "Tough shit," and Prudhomme knew the colonel would understand his remark in that light.

"Aw, Tom, don't pull that shit on me," Colonel Langhorne groaned with a sincerely pained expression on his face. "No more Harry Scheldt, Mr. Prudhomme, that's all."

"Fat chance, Colonel." Prudhomme grinned.

After a moment, Langhorne grinned back. He had known Prudhomme for many years, and he respected him profoundly. "Tom," he said carefully, "I guess what you mean by that is if you're a cop and you see a crime being committed, well, you're bound to act. But be very careful, Tom, *very*."

Long after dark that night, Prudhomme, in his black sedan, tailed Harry Scheldt to Sonya's, then pulled his car over to the curb a block away and waited. Sooner or later, he would see a crime being committed, and, in the colonel's words, he would be bound to act.

"Hiya, Ana banana, why'n'tcha siddown w'me?" Harry Scheldt's enormous catcher's mitt of a hand fastened onto Ana's arm as she passed by the booth where he was sitting.

Ana had seen Harry often at Sonya's, but he had never before spoken to her—or to any of the women in the place, for that matter. Nonetheless, she had always feared the ugly American warrant officer and shied away from him whenever he was in the place.

"Sorry, no can do now." She tried to smile and pull her arm out of Harry's hand. He tightened his grip ever so slightly, but it increased the pressure on Ana's arm so much she winced with the pain.

"C'mon, coitus blossom, siddown wid old Harry for a while, huh?" Harry tugged at her arm and drew her inexorably into the booth.

"No!" Ana protested, her voice louder than she had intended. Several heads turned in her direction. Mrs. Chen paused at her accounts and looked up with a worried expression on her face; two Australian warrant officers dining quietly at a nearby table glanced toward the booth and pushed their chairs slightly away from the table. They were big, sunburned men, and they looked hard at Harry lolling in his booth. Harry grinned wolfishly back at them.

"Jack come soon. I must go now," Ana protested desperately. Harry snorted and tightened his grip. Ana gasped with pain and stumbled into the booth.

"What the hell is going on here?" Jack demanded. It

was as if he had appeared from nowhere, almost at Ana's bidding. His face was flushed, and he held himself as if he were a mastiff straining at a leash. Ana's eyes desperately implored him to do something to help her. "Let her go, Harry!" Jack demanded.

Harry's face registered surprise. This preemptory, demanding Jack Kelley was not the same fawning man he had come to know. "Fuck off, Jack," Harry wheezed nonchalantly. "I ain't got no time for peanut vendors like you." He drew Ana to his side and leered up at Jack, daring him to do something.

Like a man who has been holding a bad dinner inside him too long, all Jack's loathing for Harry Scheldt came rushing out.

"You fat fucking pig!" he screamed, and threw himself at Harry. He kneeled on the tabletop, scattering the glasses and condiment bottles onto the floor, and rained blows into Harry's face. Harry was so astonished, he let go of Ana, who shot into the aisle and began screaming for the patrons to come to Jack's aid. She was well aware that Harry outweighed her man by more than a hundred pounds.

Harry recovered from his surprise and, ignoring Jack's blows, grabbed him by the waist and slowly lifted him into the air. Jack continued to swing, but now his fists hit only the thick muscle and fat padding of Harry's arms and shoulders. Slowly, slowly, Harry lifted Jack above his head and tossed him like a sack of potatoes onto the nearest table, where the two Australians happened to be eating. They jumped to their feet, cursing as the table toppled over and spilled Jack and their half-consumed dinner to the floor.

Jack lay there stunned, his uniform festooned with food scraps. Slowly, he picked himself up. The two Aussies offered their help, but Jack waved them away and got to his feet by himself. Harry Scheldt, elephantine and menacing, loomed in the wrecked booth only a few feet away; Ana stood to one side, screaming in English and Chinese. She scooped up a teapot from a nearby table and bounced it solidly off Harry's head, but Harry hardly noticed.

Jack glared at Harry. To the other customers, Harry Scheldt had never looked more dangerous. He was a leviathan with the strength of several men. Noodles from a bowl of Chinese soup clung to Jack's head and shoulders, giving him the appearance of a body just washed up from the ocean; one particularly long and juicy strand hung from an ear, swaying and jiggling as if it had a life of its own.

Harry Scheldt began to laugh.

Jack unbuckled his pistol belt and swung at Harry with all his remaining strength. The butt of Jack's revolver caught Harry with a sickening *thwunnnk* on the right temple. Harry's eyes went wild and then rolled back into his head, and he collapsed with a crash into the booth. Ana screamed victoriously, but as Jack stumbled forward, the other patrons decided at last to intervene. The Aussies disarmed Jack and restrained him while others rushed to Harry's aid.

"Kelley, you ain't long for this world!" Harry shouted as several men helped him to his feet. Tenderly he massaged the swelling on the side of his head and glared at Jack. There was such hate and malevolence in his expression that Jack began to feel unnaturally frightened. For an instant Jack thought he saw something behind Harry's eyes that seemed profoundly, almost supernaturally, evil, and then it was gone and it was just nasty old Harry again, raging and cursing.

"You—you and that cunt of yours, I'll get both of you for this, I swear it!" Harry wheeled on Ana. "*You*, I'll fix yer little ass, bitch! Yeah, your little *ass*!" Harry wheezed. Spittle flew from his purple lips, and Ana stepped back quickly. Breathing more heavily from emotion than exertion, Harry shook off the men around him. "I'm leavin', I'm leavin'," he rumbled, rearranging his clothes. Someone passed him a damp cloth to apply to the bump on his head, but he threw it contemptuously to the floor.

The crowd parted to let Harry out. He lumbered menacingly toward the door, and the crowd warily gave him all the room he needed. No one mentioned the possibility of damages. At the door Harry turned and pointed a rigid forefinger at Jack. "Asshole! You're gonna regret what you did!" And then he swirled out into the humid night air.

The activity among the diners, which had been frozen since the fight began, resumed once again. Waiters and cooks rushed to restore the upset and damaged furniture and to clean up the food spilled on the floor. Ana and several of the other girls offered Jack handkerchieves and damp face towels to clean himself up, and the Australians, who knew Jack well, pounded him on his back and pumped his hand, shouting, "Bloody good fight, old cobber! You give the bloody bastard what for, mate! You're a dinkum gent, Jack, here's to you an' Ana!"

Meanwhile, Harry Scheldt stumbled down the street to the Lucky Bachelor Officers Quarters, where he made a telephone call.

Ana stood on Dong Khanh Boulevard, anxiously searching the late-night traffic for a taxi or a pedicab. She had desperately wanted Jack to take her home in his jeep, but Jack, elated and enormously proud of his fight with Harry, had gotten himself drunk with the Australians, and they had had to escort him back to his quarters. That had been over an hour ago, and during that time Ana had sat disconsolate at the bar, fretting and worrying. She knew Harry Scheldt had meant what he said.

"I will have Mr. Chen take you home tonight, Ana," Mrs. Chen offered.

"Oh, no, that will not be necessary," Ana protested politely. "I am not afraid at all. That man is just like a toy balloon, full of hot air and noise. I am perfectly safe, Mrs. Chen." But Mrs. Chen knew better. She tried unsuccessfully to convince Ana to let her have her husband take her home, but Ana refused adamantly. Mrs. Chen sighed and gave up at last, reflecting that her Ana had the pride and stubbornness of a man.

Now Ana began to regret she had not taken Mrs. Chen's offer. When the other girls had climbed gaily into taxis and pedicabs, they had begged Ana to come with them, but Ana, under the influence of some perverse imp, had refused. She stamped her foot impatiently. Where were all the taxis when you needed them? She looked up and down the street, a desperate, sinking feeling in the pit of her stomach. She had the uncanny feeling she was playing a part and not in control of anything that would happen tonight.

Suddenly a black Citröen sedan separated itself from the traffic and pulled to the curb. Things happened so fast Ana had no time to react.

Harry Scheldt, agile and quick despite his bulk, leaped out of the backseat and pinioned Ana's arms tightly to her sides. "Ever been on the stage, ya little bitch?" he whispered. "Well, you're gonna put on a private command performance fer old Harry in a little while, and all the screaming in the world won't help you once it starts. And oh, yes, little bitch, you *will* scream." Harry chuckled in anticipation at the thought of a naked Ana tied to a tabletop. The big, beautiful black Hawk had promised Harry he could administer the coup de grâce himself, and Harry intended to perform it with as much imagination as his lust and ingenuity could muster.

Ana did not understand much of what it was Harry had been whispering, but she knew by instinct that if he got her inside the sedan, it would be like entering the portals of hell itself. There was nothing she could do! Harry held her so tightly she could hardly breathe; she kicked her legs weakly as he lifted her off the sidewalk and propelled her headfirst toward the gaping door. She tried to scream, but no sound would come. Ana stared in wild terror at the darkness inside the back of the car; she imagined she saw it *move* to make room for her in there. Harry cursed foully as Ana's bladder involuntarily emptied its contents down the front of his trousers, and he pushed her viciously backward. Ana's head bumped the roof of the car, and Harry stepped back a pace. As he did, he felt something cold and round pressing into the back of his head.

"How're you doin', Harry?" a voice whispered into his ear. There was the sharp click-cluk of a revolver hammer being levered back, and Harry Scheldt froze. "Let 'er go, you fat fucking pig, or I'll blow your head off right here." Instantly Harry released his grip on Ana, and as soon as her feet touched the pavement, she darted under his arm and flung herself across the sidewalk and up against the nearest wall, as far away from Harry Scheldt as she could get.

"Now tell your chauffeur there to beat it, Harry," Prudhomme growled.

"Take off! Take off!" Harry rasped, and slammed the door. The driver sped away into the traffic and left them standing on the corner. Prudhomme stepped back quickly, his weapon poised, waiting for Harry to turn and face him.

"Prudhomme, your ass is grass for this," Harry hissed.

"Why, Harry? 'Cause I called you a fat fucking pig? Everyone knows you are one."

Harry studied Prudhomme, judging the distance between them, but he decided not to take the chance. "That's the second time tonight someone's called me that," he muttered.

"Oh? *Fifty* times in one night wouldn't be enough, Harry."

"You're real smart, aren't you, Prudhomme?"

"Naw, Harry, just a dumb fucking cop. But I'm in charge right now, so beat it before I kill you."

"You won't always be in charge, Prudhomme," Harry warned as he began backing carefully down the street. Then he turned and lumbered away. At the end of the block he hailed a taxi and, as he got in, whirled and threw the finger at Prudhomme.

Prudhomme laughed, eased the hammer forward, and

stuck the revolver back into the holster under his shirt. Then he walked over to Ana.

"You're Jack Kelley's girl, aren't you?"

Ana nodded mutely. Despite the fact that her hair was disheveled and her face streaked with tears, Prudhomme noticed how beautiful she looked in the pale lamplight. He felt an impulse to hold her tight and kiss her wet cheeks. Instead he marveled at how lucky Jack Kelly was to have such a woman.

"Well, where is Kelley?"

"He have big fight with fat man. He get drunk and go home."

Prudhomme shook his head. Jack had the guts to take on a murderer like Harry Scheldt, but not the sense to realize how much danger he and his woman were now in. Still, Prudhomme was deeply pleased because long ago his sixth sense for judging character had told him that when the chips were down, Jack Kelley would do the right thing. Instinct is very important in police work.

"Do you and Jack live together now?"

"Yes. No. Jack, he come see me, but we not living togedder. Someday soon, Jack take me wid him and we leave Vietnam," she said proudly, defiantly.

"Yeah? Well, right now we got a problem, and that is how to keep you safe from Harry Scheldt."

"I have gun!" Ana announced.

"What! With you now?"

"No, at home. Jack, he give it to me."

"Well, ain't that just like Jack Kelley? But can you really shoot a gun? Have you ever shot one before?"

"No, but Jack, he tell me how, and that fat fucking pig, he come to my place, I kill him eight times," Ana raged.

Astonished, Prudhomme looked at Ana for several seconds and then burst into genuine laughter. Soon Ana began laughing, too, and they stood on the sidewalk, holding onto each other and laughing.

"Okay, honey," Prudhomme managed to gasp at last, wiping tears from his eyes, "we're gonna go and find your man, sober his ass up, and then I'm gonna drive you both over to your place."

They walked hand in hand down the street, and suddenly Prudhomme shouted, "'I kill him eight times,'" and they began laughing again.

The MP on duty outside the White knew Prudhomme by sight and assumed he was working on a case.

"Good evenin', Chief"—he saluted Prudhomme—"what's up?"

"Can I leave this girl in the lobby for a while? I gotta talk to someone in here, and I don't want to leave her alone in the street, you get me?"

The MP waved them imperiously into the lobby, giving Ana an appreciative once-over as she walked by. Prudhomme found Ana a chair in the lobby and then got Jack's room number from the night clerk on duty there.

"You wait here, Ana. Don't move. I'm gonna get Jack, and then I'll take you home."

Jack's room was on the top floor. The elevator, like all the elevators in the buildings the army leased in Saigon, wasn't working. He climbed the five flights of stairs. The corridor leading to Jack's room was very dark. From behind him, on the other end of the building, he could hear a card game in progress. The voices of the men playing were muffled, but Prudhomme knew they were playing cards by the steady plink-plink of the plastic poker chips they were using.

Halfway down the hall he almost stumbled over a man sleeping on the floor, a master sergeant, too drunk to get his door open and sleeping it off in the corridor. Prudhomme shook his head. These enlisted people, he thought wryly, are almost as bad as the officers.

Prudhomme did not bother to knock on Jack's door, which was unlocked, anyway. When he flicked the lights on, he found it empty.

"What the—" he said aloud. This was an unexpected complication. But Jack had to be somewhere in the building because there was his jacket and pistol belt, tossed carelessly on the bed. The card game!

Prudhomme trudged back down the hall. The drunk had rolled over in the meantime and was sleeping with his nose pressed into the baseboard.

There were six men in the game. They were playing seven-card stud, and judging from all the chips in front of him, Jack was winning at the moment. Too bad, Prudhomme thought.

"Remember me?" The warrant officer loomed over the players, and the room fell silent. Jack, still half-drunk, looked up in surprise, and then a grin spread over his face. "Purdome? Pudman? From Fort Sherman! Sure, I remember ya, Chief! How're ya doin'? Siddown. Someone'll be droppin' out soon enough."

Prudhomme shook his head. "Can I talk to you a minute? Outside?"

Jack glanced uncertainly at the other players. "Sure."

"Aw, fer chrissakes, Jack, at least bet your hand before you go!" someone protested.

Jack looked quickly at his cards and then threw a five-dollar bill into the ante. "Take it or leave it, boys!"

"Let's walk down to the end, there, where it's more private," Prudhomme told Jack once they were outside. "Now I don't have much time to explain all this to you, Jack, but I'm workin' on a hot case. It involves Harry Scheldt, and now you and Ana are involved because of that fracas you had with Harry back at Sonya's earlier tonight. Both you and Ana, but especially Ana, are on Harry's shit list, and you don't have any idea how nasty Harry Scheldt or his friends can be."

"Ana? Man, I don't—"

Prudhomme grabbed Jack by his undershirt and slammed him hard against the wall. "Not one fucking word! Now listen to me." He told Jack all about the incident between Ana and Harry Scheldt. "It's a good thing for you that I was on Scheldt's tail. Jack, you're a first-class asshole, did you know that? Not a bad guy, a decent guy, really, but nevertheless, you're a fucking idiot.

You're still drunk, aren't you?" Prudhomme could smell
stale whiskey on Jack's breath. He sighed. "Okay. Can
you still handle yourself?"

"You told me not to say anything."

"Goddammit, Jack—" Prudhomme raised his fist
threateningly.

"I can handle myself, I can! Don't get upset!" Prudhomme let him go.

"I got Ana downstairs right now. You go collect your
things, 'cause you're gonna stay with her tonight, okay?
I'll drive you over there."

"I'll drive myself, if you don't mind."

"Okay. I'll follow you and make sure you get there in
one piece."

"You're very serious about this, aren't you?"

"This is more serious than I hope you ever have to
find out, Jack," Prudhomme said in a low voice. For the
first time since the one-sided conversation had started,
Jack felt fear.

"Chief, thanks. I'm not so good at apologizing, but I
owe you one."

"You don't owe me anything, Kelley. I know a lot
more about you than you realize. Now let's get going."

"Hey, I just remembered! I had three aces goin' in! I
gotta finish that hand."

Prudhomme laughed. "Cards, whiskey, and women.
Jack, you're headed for perdition."

By the time they were ready to go, the drunk was
standing up, relieving himself against the door to his
room. "Jesus," Jack muttered in disgust as they walked
past him, "that's not even his room."

No Balm in Gilead

WHEN PRUDHOMME TELEPHONED JACK IN HIS OFFICE the next day and asked him to "drop by" for a while, Jack agreed at once, although it meant he had to cancel an important meeting with one of his clients. Beside his desk, wrapped in a neat, stubby package, was a Thompson submachine gun he was yearning to sell to a client from Pleiku.

The previous night, Ana had told him in graphic detail what had happened in the street outside Sonya's, and Jack realized how much he owed Prudhomme. The deal with the Thompson could wait. Jack grabbed his hat and left the compound as soon as he hung up the telephone.

Prudhomme's office was too small for him and the black CID agent sitting at the other desk. There was barely enough room for the two of them, a couple of chairs, and two filing cabinets. The black man stared at Jack intensely from the moment he walked into the tiny office. This made Jack nervous. He was sure Prudhomme wasn't going to charge him with anything, but he had reason to fear too much scrutiny by anyone else. In the time since he had arrived in Vietnam, Jack Kelley had broken just about all the rules there were.

"Kelley, I know you from somewhere," said the black man, glowering at him.

"Uh, Bill, could you leave us alone for five minutes?" Prudhomme asked.

Bill nodded, gathered up some folders he had been working on, and stepped to the door. "I'll remember," he warned Jack as he went out.

Prudhomme settled back in his chair. "You know Bill Washington?" he asked, nodding toward the black man's desk.

"Hell, no! Never laid eyes on him before just now."

"Just checking. I thought you might have run afoul of the law somewhere before." Prudhomme grinned. "'Course, I ran a check on you a long time ago, Jack. You're a lucky shit. Your record's clean as a whistle. Not even a traffic citation."

Jack shrugged. "I just never did anything really big, is all. Besides that, Chief, I have never, ever fucked anybody!"

"I know that, Jack. Just keep it that way."

"Hey, Chief, I love you like my brother, but is this why you called me down here?"

"Last night you said you owed me one. Well, I need your help, Jack."

"You got it."

"Get me a gun. I want a three fifty-seven magnum, if you can swing it, a thirty-eight special will do if you can't. Make it a four-inch barrel, in good shape. I'll be in the bar at the Plaza next Thursday at nineteen hundred. Bring it to me there. Put it in something inconspicuous, like a paper bag. Don't ask any questions, and never say anything to anybody about this. Here's a hundred bucks, your going price, I believe?"

Jack stuffed the money into his pocket.

The door opened and Washington stepped back in. "Hey, Kelley, I remember you now! You were at Ferris

Barracks, at Erlangen, Germany, back in fifty-six or fifty-seven, wasn't you. I *knew* I remembered you! I never forget a face, even if you white folks do all look alike. Boss"—he turned to Prudhomme—"this is the guy who gave Tom Riley the one and only put-down ever! You shoulda seen it! I laughed so hard I thought I'd split a gut!"

"So you're the one who named old Riley 'Super Senior Sarge,' huh? By the way, Jack, meet Spec. Seven Bill Washington, my partner part of the time and stick-buddy all the time."

"You were at Erlangen in those days?" Jack asked Washington as they shook hands vigorously.

"Yep. Ninth CID. I was in the audience that morning, suffering through TI and E like everybody else, until you livened things up for us!"

"And how do you know Riley?" Jack asked Prudhomme.

"We just know 'im," Prudhomme answered cryptically. Jack, astonished, wondered what kind of trouble old Riley had gotten himself into with the CID, but he knew better than to ask.

"Jack, you sure pick big guys when you decide to tangle with someone, don't you?" Prudhomme asked. "You're a hard man to figure out." He shook his head. "Now hit the streets. And Jack?" Jack paused, looking back at Prudhomme. "Jack, take good care of Ana. You're a lucky man to have a girl like her." Prudhomme winked and made a small pistol out of his forefinger and thumb.

"Chief, *you're* a difficult man to figure out, did you know that?" Jack said as he stepped through the door.

Washington waited all day for Prudhomme to tell him what was up, but when the old warrant officer kept his silence, Washington began to speculate. He knew how Prudhomme had saved Ana from Harry, and he knew there was some kind of special relationship between his partner and Jack Kelley now. But what had Prudhomme said to Jack that was so secret he had been asked to leave the room? And what could they have transacted in such a short time? The only thing Jack could do for a man like Prudhomme, if they were transacting business, was to get him a gun. Now why would a CID agent go to Jack Kelley for a gun? There could be only one reason. Prudhomme wanted a gun that couldn't be traced.

Bill Washington was worried. First, he knew how frustrated Prudhomme was about the entire HJO investigation, particularly Scheldt's involvement. Second, he knew how hard Prudhomme had taken Fitzgerald's addiction and the loss of the information he had been feeding them on the HJO; Prudhomme blamed himself personally for the whole debacle. And third, Colonel Langhorne's summary closing of the whole case had really hit Prudhomme hard.

Now Prudhomme calls in Jack Kelley, arms merchant. They talk for about two minutes, and Jack leaves. Washington had caught the gesture Prudhomme had made with his hand, making it into a pistol, and Jack's parting words, "You're a difficult man to figure out," seemed loaded with innuendo.

By degrees, a very nasty thought was creeping into Specialist Seventh Class Bill Washington's mind. He would have to keep a close eye on his partner from now on. If Tom Prudhomme were going around the bend, he, Bill Washington, would just have to be there in time to pull him back.

That night Prudhomme stayed late. He sat at his desk, cleaning his revolver. Why did he hate Harry Scheldt so much? he asked himself. It wasn't Harry, after all, who was the kingpin in the HJO investigation, it was the Hawk. The Hawk is the one I should hate, but I don't, he thought. He wondered why he had never become so involved in a case like this before, and the worst part of it was, he had hated Harry long before he knew for sure what a bucket of slime the man really was.

This hatred, it was just—he couldn't put his finger on

it. There was something about the man that instantly
kindled dislike in Tom Prudhomme, and the longer he
had worked on the case, the more he had come to hate
the man. That Harry Scheldt was also a warrant officer
and a professional soldier had something to do with it.
Harry had betrayed the army and his comrades. But that
was only part of it.

I am not in control of myself when I think like this, he
told himself. Hatred was warping his judgment, and if he
could not control it, it would ruin him. He knew that,
and still he seethed. He rammed the bore brush hard
down the barrel until it slammed into the fire wall behind
the cylinder. Then he yanked it out, and a thin spray of
oil discharged into the hot, still air. It smelled good,
clean.

He needed the gun from Kelley, he thought. Then he
yelled to himself, "Dammit, call it off!"

Prudhomme rested his head wearily in his hands. He
had a terrible feeling he was no longer in charge, that
events were propelling him forward into an unknown future. He was being driven. The worst of it was, there
was no one he could talk to. He dare not tell Washington, because Bill, if he couldn't talk him out of it, would
tell Colonel Langhorne, and that would be the end of his
days as a CID agent.

Pastor Bennett would know how to deal with this
conflict, but the Lutheran minister was twelve thousand
miles away. Tom Prudhomme had never felt so alone, cut
off from both counsel and confidence. He wanted to
weep.

And the worst part of it was, prayer had not helped.
Always before, prayer had proved effective against de-
spair. But this time temptation was proving just too
great. He had called upon the Lord for help, and there
had been no answer. He felt rejected, like poor old Saul.
If I carry this through, then I will be rejected by the
Lord, just like King Saul when he disobeyed the prophet
Samuel, he warned himself.

Prudhomme closed his eyes and prayed silently.

Nothing. Zilch. Blank wall. He opened his eyes. It was just no good.

Goddammit, he thought, stop feeling so sorry for yourself! I have to work this out on my own! Stop crying like a kid and act like a man. If God won't tell me what to do, then He must mean I have to find the way by myself.

He sighed and picked up the revolver from the newspaper where it lay on his desk. Dirty cleaning patches lay spread about, and splotches of bore cleaner and oil dotted the latest edition of the *Stars & Stripes* Far East edition. He carefully wiped the excess oil from the weapon, then stuffed the newspaper and the dirty patches into the wastepaper basket.

Handling the weapon, cleaning it, had made him feel a little better. But he had made his decision. It was foolish, maybe dangerous, but he had to give his faith one last try.

"Chaplain, I believe I have seen the devil."

Chaplain (Major) Cleaneth Williams shifted his weight uncomfortably and regarded the man on the other side of his desk. He was stocky, florid, in his forties, and dressed in casual civilian clothes suitable for the tropics. It was hot in the small office, despite the asthmatic wheezing of the air-conditioning unit in the window just behind the chaplain's desk. Chaplain Williams had been in Vietnam nine months. For the past two he had been a staff chaplain in Saigon, and he had had a head cold all that time because every day he was exposed to the air-conditioner, which blew a constant stream of damp air onto the back of his neck.

"I apologize for the arrangement of this office," Williams said, gesturing helplessly, "but the only way the furniture can fit in here is if my desk goes in front of the air conditioner. That way only I get the benefit of the thing, and my visitors all hate me for it." He smiled wanly and blew his nose into a Kleenex.

"I don't mean that I saw the devil in a red suit with

hooves and horns, Chaplain," his visitor went on. "No. He's a man, a very unusual man, but if he ain't the devil walking like a man, well, then my ass—uh, excuse me, Chaplain—is a Chinese typewriter."

Chaplain Williams shrugged off the slip. "Even in my line of business I don't hear much talk about the devil these days, Mr.—Jones did you say your name was?" His visitor nodded. "Pray continue," the chaplain said, and smiled.

"I'm serious," said the stocky man, his face reddening.

"So am I. But you know, if I got up this Sunday and delivered a sermon that even *hinted* that evil is really a force external to man's psyche, much less personified in the form of the traditional Satan, the command chaplain'd probably have me under medical care before Monday morning."

"I understand." Mr. Jones nodded. "Let me rephrase my statement. I've been in the army for eighteen years, and I worked on a big-city police force as a detective before I was drafted in 1950. I've seen it all, every nasty thing one person can do to another. But here, in Vietnam, for the first time, I've encountered a man so evil that I've become personally involved in the case. Before, the evil that other men did sort of washed off my back. I got some of them; others got away."

"Uh, you are some kind of law-enforcement officer, Mr. Jones?"

"Some kind."

"And now? This time? With this man?" Williams asked.

Mr. Jones shook his head. "This guy'll get away. He's *protected*," Jones added bitterly.

"'Protected'? How do you mean?"

"It's not important, Chaplain." Jones rubbed his arms and shifted his weight in his chair. "What's important is that I know what this man is, and I know he deserves justice. But there's no way I can do anything about him, legally."

"So why come to me, Mr. Jones? Take the matter up with the proper authorities."

Jones took a deep breath. "Because I have this urge to kill him, Chaplain."

Williams grunted. After a moment he spun his chair around and fiddled with the air-conditioning vent, turning it away from himself. He turned back toward his visitor and leaned his arms on his desk, where the perspiration left damp stains on his blotter. Now the chaplain understood his visitor's need for anonymity. The temperature in the small office seemed suddenly to have gone up several degrees.

"Do you think you can kill Satan, Mr. Jones?"

"No, Chaplain, but I sure can kill the guy who works for him."

"Mr. Jones—may I call you Tom?"

"Sure, please do."

"Tom, you cannot destroy evil."

"Probably you can't, Chaplain," Jones said bluntly.

"So why do you think *I* can help you?" Chaplain Williams held his hands up in bewilderment.

"I came to see you because I want to know *why*."

"Why what, Tom?"

"Why God lets guys like—I can't mention his name. I want to know why God permits evil."

"I don't know," the chaplain answered.

"You're a hell of a lot of comfort, Chaplain."

"Well, there's more to it than just that—"

"Chaplain"—Jones's voice rose—"I've lived all my life with human tragedy, none of it accidental, and I've seen the human shit that infests our so-called society, and it all comes to a head in this guy. And you know what I've learned in all my years dealing with human scum? The wicked get rich and fat and live long lives, and good men die young! Now Chaplain, I would like you to explain to me how in *hell* a good and loving and all-powerful God, the way you sky pilots are always telling us he is, can permit that kind of thing in the world he created?"

The air conditioner wheezed behind the chaplain's back, and Jones stared at him, expecting some answer.

"Tom, you see victims and a man who you say is the perpetrator of horrible crimes. You see the broken bodies and ruined lives that society casts up out of a sea of troubles. And I see broken spirits." Williams paused. "People come to me with dashed hopes and ruined lives, looking for reassurance and explanation, just like you. I help some; others I can't."

Williams reached for another Kleenex and blew his nose forcefully into it. Jones waited patiently for him to continue.

"So you want to know why evil."

"Why?" Jones echoed.

"Well, first off, Tom, don't blame God. You can't expect to get good things from Him and not get bad things, too. After all, He's in charge, and yes, He permits evil. But remember, men are always too ready to interpret God's providence in their own terms, to explain what things are consistent with His character and what are not, and they argue with opposing consciences by appealing to God's so-called authority, which is really their own."

"Okay, Chaplain, I understand all that. And excuse me for getting upset a minute ago. But you see, I'm agitated like never before because of what this man represents and what he's doing to *us*. He's into drugs in a big way; murder, too—murder so disgusting, Chaplain, I can't describe it to you!" Jones hesitated before going on. He expelled a breath and gestured helplessly with one hand. "He—he buys drugs from Communist agents —he knows who they are, and he buys from them, arranges deals with them—to sell death back home in the States and to GIs over here, men who are out there fighting the war! And the money the Commies make goes to buy stuff to kill our men. And *he* is making money hand over fist! Do you see?"

"I see, and I believe you are right to resist this man's evil. We all must hate it as you do yourself. But Tom, if

you take the law into your own hands, then it is *you* who
will have succumbed to evil. We may inveigh against
God for permitting men like this What's-his-name to in-
fect society, but only God can quell the rebellious forces
of evil in the cosmos. We humans can only try to transcend it. We cannot stand up to it toe to toe and slug it
out and expect to win."

Jones made an impatient gesture. "But how can I
'transcend' it?" His spirits were sinking fast. This chaplain was not at all like Pastor Bennett. He did not have
the spirit. His faith came from the mind, not the heart.
There was no consolation in this man, no comfort. God's
presence was not in this room.

Chaplain Williams sighed. "I'm full of confusion, too,
Tom. Yeah, I'm the 'sky pilot,' I'm supposed to have an
'in' with God. But like you, I look for good and see only
evil, and when I pray for the light, there comes all too
often only darkness. I *know* God speaks to me from the
Scriptures, but I don't always *hear* Him. I'm afraid my
answer will not be very comforting, Tom."

"Let me have it anyway, Chaplain."

"You transcend evil by never speaking wickedness or
uttering deceit, keeping your integrity and holding fast to
righteousness. You don't strive against God, and you
don't expect Him to give you any account of His matters. God's ways are inexplicable, and what you and I
define as 'good' and 'evil' has some other meaning for
Him."

"'Righteousness'? I don't even know what that is!
Chaplain, I just refuse to believe in a god that obscure.
I'm sorry, I can't accept that."

"Well, do you believe in General Westmoreland?
When's the last time he deigned to explain anything to
you personally? Yet you accept his authority and you
follow his orders. Why, then, is it so hard to imagine a
God as inscrutable as General Westmoreland?"

"But Chaplain, Westy's a *man*, like you and me! He's
not God!"

"But Tom, so is What's-his-name a man, whom you hate so much."

"Well, I believe in God, Chaplain, I really do. But this God you describe to me, I just can't accept the unquestioning obedience to something I don't understand."

"Excuse me, Tom, I was being a bit sophistical with you. Sure, I see what you're saying. I couldn't accept the idea, either, first time I heard it. I was just a PFC then, during World War Two, and I was an infantryman at the time. You know, war brings ordinary folks close to suffering, and that makes 'em ask the kinds of questions you're asking. Satan's always been going to and fro at will, but in wartime we get to see him close up, and that shakes all our comfortable ideas about man and God in the universe all to pieces. You know this man you hate is only one piece of crud to be washed up in this war."

Jones's face took on a pained expression. "What does any of this have to do with the war? You're beginning to sound like one of those woolly-headed liberals back home, telling people they ought to give up and let the Commies run all over Southeast Asia."

"No," Williams said firmly, and slapped his desk. Jones started. "Those are the moral relativists, the people who are trivializing evil. It's preposterous and frightening that today, when evil is about to overcome us completely, we hear less and less about it from the pulpit."

Williams blew his nose into another Kleenex.

"You see, like you, Tom, I believe in the devil," Williams continued. "If you ever quote me on that, I'll deny I said it." He smiled. "Oh, I don't believe in Satan as a person who manifests himself to human beings, but I believe in an intelligent and purposeful force in the world that is inimical to mankind, and that's the devil. I don't believe the devil limits God's power in the universe, either. God permits him to function, and the purpose of that is to test us, maybe, for reasons beyond our understanding.

"What's-his-name is evil, as is this war—all wars—

and What's-his-name is God's way of testing you, Tom, just like this war tests us all. Whether you clap him into jail, whether you kill him, whether or not we win this war or lose it is not what really matters. What matters, Tom, is if we're faced with evil, do we give in or do we transcend it. Why evil? Maybe there is evil in order to lead us to good."

"Chaplain, I—I just—" Jones gestured helplessly. "Look: How do we deal with a horror like the Nazi death camps, then? How do you 'transcend' an evil that terrible, huh, Chaplain? I mean, it was armed men who destroyed Hitler, it was force that overcame his evil. How do you tell a victim in a concentration camp to escape from his fate by 'transcending' it? Is it possible to 'transcend' guards and barbed wire and run like hell?"

"Tom, you ever know any death camp survivors? I've met a few. They are humble, gentle people, not towering terrors of revenge and hatred. Isn't that odd? Me, if I'd been in one of those camps, I'd want to kill every German in the world. I know I am too weak to go through something like that and not hate because of it."

Jones threw a questioning look at the chaplain.

"The survivors *did* transcend Hitler's evil, don't you see? They transcended first by simply surviving and second by not becoming like their persecutors. They were Jews, these folks, but still the most perfect Christians I've ever met.

"Are you completely sure this anger of yours is righteous after all? Might it not really be impelling you to do wrong? Tom, do not become like this man, What's-his-name."

Williams took the last Kleenex and blew his nose again. He rattled the empty tissue box sadly and threw it into his wastepaper basket.

Jones shook his head slowly. "I just can't believe it, Chaplain."

"I warned you my answer wouldn't make you feel much better. You know, the prophet Jeremiah asked, 'Is there no balm in Gilead; is there no physician there?

Why then is not the health of the daughter of my people recovered?' Well, Tom, there is no balm in Gilead, not for us.

"Don't kill this man, Mr. Jones. Do your duty, but do not take the law into your own hands. Be careful that in this sea of human misery called life you don't drown the eternal of your own soul."

Jones sighed. "Thanks for yer time, Chaplain. One last question?"

"Sure, Tom."

"How can you live with such a bleak philosophy?"

"Bleak?" Williams laughed. "Not bleak, Tom. It's frightening and bewildering, yes. But it's also glorious, Tom, utterly glorious, and I am secure in that because there is hope. I know that my Redeemer liveth, and that He shall stand at the latter day upon the earth."

"What is all that supposed to mean, Chaplain?"

Chaplain Williams snuffled. "That's faith, Tom, that's faith."

"There ain't a rebel in all o' North Carolina if I cain't drink this here bottle o' whiskey!" the drunk shouted defiantly to the entire room, throwing back the contents of a full shot glass.

"Who's your friend?" Jack asked as he took the stool next to Prudhomme.

"Some asshole. He says he's gonna drink that whole bottle of bourbon by himself. He's had eight straight shots since I've been here. You bring the piece?"

Jack handed the paper sack to Prudhomme. "Just what the doctor ordered."

Prudhomme opened the sack and inspected the contents briefly. "Thanks, Jack. Now forget all about this."

The drunk fell to the floor with a tremendous crash.

"Well, see you in church," Jack said, getting up and stepping gingerly around the unconscious figure on the floor.

"S'long, Jack," Prudhomme muttered.

Jack stared down at the drunk and then up at the bottle of whiskey he had been drinking. More than half of it was gone. "Hey," he called to the bartender, who was calmly polishing glasses, "you better call an ambulance for this guy here."

"No sweat," the bartender replied, "him do dat every night."

Of Paul and Silas

THE STREET DOOR OPENED AND GAYLORD STROLLED in. He went straight to the bar, his green beret cocked jauntily over his forehead. He looked neither to the left nor to the right as he weaved his way between the closely packed tables. At the bar, he ordered his customary Chivas on the rocks and, when he was served, sipped it reflectively, surveying the other customers in the huge mirror behind the bar. He was one of Jack's best customers in the small arms trade.

"Excuse me," Jack said to Ana, grateful for the opportunity Gaylord's arrival had given him, "I've got to talk to Gaylord for a minute."

"You *always* talking him!" Ana pouted.

"Baby, it's only business; I'll be back in a while."

"Always 'business, business,' Jack!"

"I gotta make hay while the sun shines," he said, and realizing Ana wouldn't understand the colloquialism, explained, "I gotta make money, Ana."

"'Make haiti while the sun shines'?" Ana repeated.

"'Hay,' Ana, 'hay.' You know, money. We say 'make hay' for 'make money.' 'While the sun shines' means 'opportunity,' so it all means 'make money when you can.' Get it?"

"'Make hay while the sun shines.' Oh, good, Jack, you teach me nice new English phrase! You go see Gaylord now, Jack. I wait for you."

Jack hesitated before getting up. How little it takes to please this girl, he thought. Whatever am I going to do about her? When she was cloyingly possessive, as she had just been, Jack almost hated her, but at other times, like just now with the little English lesson, she was the most precious thing in his life. He realized suddenly that either he would have to abandon Ana Chin or take her home with him. There was no other way to settle their relationship. Impulsively, Jack almost blurted out, Get your passport and buy a plane ticket, we're skipping to Taiwan! But he held back. There was business afoot.

"How's it going?" he asked, sliding onto a stool beside Gaylord. Gaylord did not answer. "You buyin' anything these days?" Jack inquired casually.

"I need three three point fives with ammo," Gaylord said after a moment, speaking to Jack's reflection in the mirror.

"I got three, with twenty rounds each," Jack answered quickly.

"How much?" Gaylord spoke in a low, almost inaudible, conspiratorial tone of voice. He watched Jack closely in the mirror.

"Fair market value, maybe even a little less," Jack said, trying to sound offhand.

"Balls!"

"Take it or leave it, buddy. You won't get a better deal unless you go out 'n' steal 'em." Jack almost added "yourself," but he caught the slip in time.

"They're *already* stolen, Kelley."

"They're *captured* weapons, my friend," Jack countered. "The Viet Cong took 'em from the South Vietnamese, and we took 'em back. Well, I don't ask questions. They're for sale, and that's good enough for me."

Jack knew little about Gaylord except that he was somehow associated with the U.S. Army Special Forces in Vietnam. He wore the subdued metal rank insignia of a specialist seventh class—the same pay grade as Jack —and packed a Browning 9-mm automatic in a shoulder holster under his left armpit. He had met Gaylord through a mutual acquaintance some months before, and they had done business several times since. Gaylord paid cash on delivery, and Jack's instinct told him he could trust the special forces man.

For his own reasons Gaylord wanted three 3.5-inch rocket launchers with ammunition. He wanted them very quickly and very badly, and he did not want them from official sources. Jack suspected that he got the money for such purchases from some contingency fund. Everybody knew that the sneaky Petes were deeply involved with the Central Intelligence Agency in Vietnam and, like the agency, had money to buy certain kinds of untraceable weapons on the black market. Jack did not care what they would be used for.

"You can pick 'em up day after tomorrow," Jack said.

"Okay. We go in my jeep. I check 'em out thoroughly before I pay. What time do I pick you up?"

"Nineteen hundred. I'll wait for you on the corner of Dong Khanh and Ngo Quyen. Bring money. That'll give us plenty of time to do our business, especially since they've lifted curfew for Tet this year."

"Okay, comrade army sergeant." Gaylord finished his drink and stood up.

"I'll go see my main man in a little while and make the arrangement." Gaylord nodded and walked out. During the entire exchange he had not once looked directly at Jack.

Out on Dong Khanh, Jack looked up and down the street for his Vietnamese driver, Phu.

"Howdy, Kelley, you keepin' out of trouble?" a voice asked. Jack whirled and saw it was Dan Vinson, a mili-

tary policeman he knew slightly. Vinson and his partner
were conducting a foot patrol of the GI dives in the
neighborhood. Vinson was a big, well-muscled man who
at first glance could easily be mistaken for a brainless
cop. But Jack knew Vinson better than that. The man
had a quick wit and a degree of intelligence, and because
of that, Jack was sure Vinson always knew more than he
ever let on. That made him a threat, but still, Jack liked
the MP. He kept his mouth shut for one thing, and for
another Jack's instinct told him Vinson was the kind of
man you could trust in a pinch.

"Me? Keepin' out of trouble? That's not my style,
Dan," Jack joked.

Vinson nodded and permitted himself a wry smile.
"Well, Jack, you keep yer ass down 'n' yer powder dry,
hear?" Vinson touched his right hand to his helmet liner
and resumed walking down the street in the direction of
the Capitol BEQ.

Jack spotted Phu then, parked half a block up the
boulevard. Phu was supposed to be a general-purpose
driver, assigned each trip by a common motor pool dis-
patcher, but Jack had "appropriated" him as a sort of
personal chauffeur. This was strictly unauthorized, but
Jack knew how to get around the rules.

Jack wondered for whom Phu was really working. He
was too intelligent, too observant, and he understood
English too well to be just another ordinary motor pool
flunky. Jack suspected he was a planted intelligence
agent, despite the fact that he'd actively finagled to get
Phu's service himself. Anyway, Jack hoped Phu was an
intelligence operative and not a police undercover man.
The intel boys were okay, in Jack's book, because they
minded their own business. Meanwhile, he didn't mind
their keeping an eye on his activities.

"Phu-oi!" Jack shouted. Phu started his jeep and
pulled it up in front of where Jack stood. "Pham Ngu
Lao, and *di-di mau*!" Jack shouted as he climbed in. He
added the injunction to make haste out of habit. Most
Americans had the impression the Vietnamese were an

indolent, backward people, despite the everyday evidence to the contrary. Jack had fallen into the mind-set in spite of the fact that he knew better.

Jack did not know the address on Pham Ngu Lao Street to which he was going, but he did not need to know it. He only needed to know the general location.

Jack indicated the spot where he wanted Phu to let him off. "Phu, wait here. Thirty minutes—*ba muoi phut*—I come back. Okay?" Phu nodded. Jack could never resist using the few words of Vietnamese he knew. He could not speak the language very fluently, but he had a vocabulary and his pronunciation was good, although he knew only the southern dialect.

Phu watched Jack walk down the street and disappear into the mouth of an alley beside the Mondial Hotel. He sighed and glanced at his watch (a Seiko self-winding model with calendar and luminous dial). Jack had given him the watch as a present, and he was very proud of it. He lit a Camel (Jack also kept him well supplied with American cigarettes) and then took out a small notebook from a rear pocket.

In his notebook Phu recorded the time, date, and place. He knew where Jack was going—had been there himself—and the name of the man he would see there. The alley led into a torturous maze of closely packed slum dwellings that covered the entire two-block area between Pham Ngu Lao, Bui Vien, and Tran Hung Dao.

When he was finished with his notes, Phu removed his trip ticket from the glove compartment, thought for a moment, then entered a fictitious destination—the 218th Medical Dispensary on Tran Hung Dao. The mileage would be about right. This was a bothersome game, falsifying trip tickets, but necessary. Many Vietnamese employed by the Americans as drivers obtained use of their vehicles for unauthorized purposes and cheated on overtime by falsifying trip tickets regularly and forging authorized signatures. Phu felt sorry for them. He had to do it to keep up appearances, but the regular drivers did it for a living. Well, soon he would be assigned to other work, something to do with destroying the Communists, whom he hated passionately, and not spying on the stupid Americans, whom he, like most Vietnamese, tolerated as a necessary but disturbing factor in his life.

Jack treated him well, Phu reflected. No matter what he might think about Americans as people, they were generous; stupid, but generous. Phu often wondered how such a race could ever have gained so much power in the world. The Communists Phu could understand. They were ruthless murderers who craved power and dominance. But the Americans made a big show about not wanting anything for themselves out of this war, and Phu half believed they really didn't. So why were they investing so many lives and such large sums of money in his poor little country? It was a mystery to him.

Phu inhaled deeply on his Camel. Ah, he reflected, the Americans make good cigarettes! And, he reminded himself, although the watch he wore on his wrist was made in Japan, he would not even have the instrument except for the American presence in Vietnam. The Americans are better people than the French, Phu thought, thinking back to his boyhood.

How well Phu remembered the indignities his people had suffered under French colonial rule. The funny thing about the French was that they were quite civilized and decent except when they owned you. Now his father had worked for the French, really *worked* for them, endured their curses and supercilious treatment for coolie's wages. But Phu, in the time he had "worked" for Jack, had come to think of the American as *his* creature.

Phu chuckled to himself. Despite everything, he liked this dumb American and would miss him when he was gone.

Jack returned in thirty-two minutes. The American sergeant was very punctual, as Phu had noted several times. Jack seemed well satisfied as he climbed into the jeep. He smiled broadly at Phu. "Bach Dang Quay," he announced. Phu nodded and started the engine. "I'm gonna have a little chow at the My Canh," he added, patting Phu on the shoulder. The My Canh was a floating restaurant on the Saigon River, moored along the quay between the Majestic Hotel and the Club Nautique, although it was moved frequently.

Jack was understandably happy. He had just arranged for the purchase of the rocket launchers for Gaylord, and his profit margin on the deal would work out to be considerably higher than he had originally estimated.

Phu followed Pham Ngu Lao Street to where it joined Tran Hung Dao—by the railroad station, which was a local joke; trains had not used the station in years because the Communists were constantly cutting the tracks. He turned right, down Ham Nghi Street to the waterfront. As they were turning left onto the quay, Jack noted with alarm that the area around the restaurant was blocked off by police and soldiers. Red lights flashed on emergency vehicles, and a crowd stood about gawking. A Vietnamese military policeman was diverting traffic away from the scene, and he indicated that Phu should bear to the left, up Nguyen Hue Boulevard and out of the area.

A flatbed truck, moving fast, emerged suddenly from among the official vehicles—jeeps, ambulances, police cars—clustered about the My Canh. Two white-uniformed Vietnamese national policemen perched on the running boards, piping shrilly on their whistles and gesturing furiously for the traffic to make way. Jack was horrified to see a number of bodies covered with blood-stained white sheets on the bed of the truck. The corpses bounced and jiggled obscenely to the movement of the vehicle.

The truck slowed to a stop within inches of where Jack sat. His eyes were drawn to a lifeless hand protruding from under one of the sheets. He guessed from the well-manicured fingernails that it belonged to the corpse of a young woman. Circles of lighter-colored flesh on three of the lifeless fingers revealed where rings had evidently been roughly pulled off. A premonitory sense of death tingled up Jack's backbone, and the hair on the back of his neck rose. Before he could see any more, the truck driver shifted gears and sped off up Nguyen Hue Boulevard.

"Goddamn! They hit the My Canh again?" Jack asked. Phu grunted affirmatively. As they drove up Nguyen Hue, Jack glanced over his shoulder at the front of the My Canh. The façade looked as if it had been riddled with shotgun pellets fired from close range, the characteristic effect of a Claymore-type antipersonnel mine. Jack settled back into his seat, and his left hand automatically went to the butt of the .357 holstered by his side. For a few moments both men were silent as Phu skillfully maneuvered the jeep in and out of the early evening traffic.

"Where to now?" Phu asked in the unaccented English he claimed to have learned in public school. Jack did not reply at once. He took off his cap and ran his fingers through his closely cropped hair. "Goddamn, the VC really know how to fuck up a guy's evening," he said.

Jack had Phu drop him at Wiseman's. His room, in the White Bachelor Enlisted Quarters, was only down the street and within easy "staggering" distance—that was how he planned to go home, staggering drunk.

The bombing of the My Canh had upset him. The thought that had he finished his business with the arms merchant only a few minutes sooner one of those bodies might have been his own also contributed to depression. He could not rid his mind of the horrible, fascinating memory of that dead woman's hand, sticking out from under the sheet. He found himself wondering what she had looked like in life—what she looked like *now*—how big her breasts were, what her legs looked like, whether she was a good lay. It was as if he had gone into a beautiful garden and found there, coiled under the most fragrant flowers, a deadly serpent waiting to strike.

The heat and light and noise in Wiseman's were a comfort. Jack ordered one Scotch and soda, and then he had two more in quick succession. At Wiseman's one could order real whiskey from the bar. In most GI joints one drank only beer because the bar whiskey was always watered, but not at Wiseman's. The bar was a curiosity. It was owned by a Chinese who had picked a Jewish-sounding name, and sometimes you could have your fortune read there by a South Korean army officer speaking to the mamasan in fluent Vietnamese while she translated what he said into very good English. The Korean had predicted that before he was forty, Jack Kelley would experience "a great sickness."

The alcohol made Jack feel much better.

It was after dark when Gaylord picked Jack up. Gaylord's jeep was battered and dirty. Jack settled himself gingerly into the greasy, canvas-covered, springless passenger's seat.

"Which way?" Gaylord asked. Jack told him to drive along Ngo Quyen Street to Hong Bang Boulevard, and he would direct him from there. Gaylord backed recklessly into the flow of the early-evening traffic, without bothering to look behind or to the left. Obviously, Gaylord had been driving in Vietnam quite a while, because he did it just like a Vietnamese, with one foot alternating between the brake, gas, clutch pedals, and his right hand working the gearshift. The jeep engine coughed and sputtered. "Gotta get this thing a tune-up someday," Gaylord muttered.

"I know a guy'll do it for you real cheap," Jack offered automatically. Gaylord gave him a dirty sidelong glance.

"Nervous?" Gaylord chided, observing how tightly Jack gripped the crash bar.

"Nah. I just want both arms relatively undamaged when we get to the meeting place. Easier to count the money that way." Jack grinned wolfishly at Gaylord, but Gaylord drove steadily onward, poker-faced.

They crossed Tran Quoc Toan Boulevard to the east of the Phu Tho Racetrack and drove into the Phu Tho

Hoa area. The traffic began to thin after that. Before long, Jack had Gaylord turn onto a heavily rutted, pot-holed dirt road that bordered an immense open field. It was very quiet and dark along the road. Gaylord switched to his high beams.

"Do you really know where we are?" Gaylord asked.

"Sure. I've been here plenty of times."

"This is fuckin' VC territory, Kelley."

"No sweat whatsoever. You've been in lots tougher spots than this before, haven't you?"

Gaylord did not answer. Jack found himself amused by Gaylord's apparent nervousness.

"There's a dead-end turnoff just ahead. They'll be waiting for us at the end of it."

Gaylord pulled to the side of the road, parked, and shut off the engine and lights.

"Hey! We're still a hundred yards from the turnoff!" Jack protested.

"Yeah, but we park here and walk the rest of the way in. I don't want anybody to know too far in advance that we're comin'."

"What're you sweating, anyway? This is just routine business! You can trust these guys. I've dealt with them plenty of times before."

"You have, but *I* haven't. Besides, I don't much care for the territory they chose to deal in. They coulda un-loaded their shit in some alley back in town. We're half-way to Cambodia, for chrissakes."

Jack sighed and climbed out of the jeep. He began picking his way carefully along the road and stopped at the turnoff to wait for Gaylord, who had been deliber-ately hanging back.

"You go in first," Gaylord whispered as he came alongside Jack.

"What for?" Jack asked in his normal tone of voice.

"You just go in first," Gaylord hissed. "I'll be some ways behind you." Jack decided not to protest, but Gay-lord's crazy insistence on acting as if this piece of utterly routine business were actually an operation in enemy territory had begun to irritate him.

There were a few houses standing along both sides of the dead end, but all of them were dark. Jack paused for a moment. There was no sound at all on the humid night air. He fought down a sudden feeling of the creeps and walked a few paces farther down the roadway. Ahead he could just make out the shape of a vehicle—a Land Rover, he knew from previous trips—sitting squarely in the middle of the road. "S-ss tt! Thien?" he whispered. There was no reply. Jack whispered Thien's name again. This time somebody dismounted quietly from the Rover.

"Kelley?" The speaker's voice did not sound like that of the arms merchant, Thien.

"Yeah. Is that you?"

"Yes."

"Well, let's have a light, Thien-oi! My friend's . . ."

The darkness exploded in a brilliant flash. A white flame lashed out from the Land Rover. It was accompanied by a thunderous crash that seemed to detonate precisely in Jack's left ear. He was so startled that he did not realize he had been shot at or that he had fallen down until he felt his buttocks squishing in the mud. Two more cannonlike blasts lashed and roared at him, but the shooter's aim was off slightly, and the slugs plowed into the mud a little to Jack's left. Still, they were close enough so that he imagined he had actually felt them ripping through the air past his left ear; he clawed frantically at his holstered revolver.

Three more shots erupted, and then Jack had his gun out. But before he could return fire, several shots cracked from behind him. Whoever had been shooting at Jack screamed shrilly. Immediately, someone else, using the Rover's hood as a firing rest, returned Gaylord's shots. His first rounds were aimed at the muzzle flashes of Gaylord's automatic, but Gaylord had rolled away from his firing position as soon as he had squeezed off his shots.

This new shooter, who was using an M-2 automatic

carbine, apparently thought his fire-selector switch was
on semiautomatic. But the carbine was set on full automatic and got away from him, and the rest of the burst
sprayed harmlessly up into the air. The muzzle flashes
from his weapon gave Gaylord a good target, and he put
three quick rounds into the man. The carbine clattered
across the Rover's hood and splashed into the mud.

The silence was deafening. "Shag ass!" Gaylord
shouted from the roadside. Still clutching his unfired
.357, Jack jumped to his feet and pounded down the
center of the road, unmindful of the ruts, potholes, and
muddy puddles. There was no movement from the
Rover.

Gaylord was already seated in his jeep with the motor
running when Jack ran up, grabbed the windshield
frame, and swung himself into the passenger's seat in
one fluid motion—the most athletic thing he had done
since his teens. Gaylord jammed the gears into reverse,
backed up, slammed into first, and hurtled the jeep back
toward the main road. Jack was unaware of his head
striking the canvas top as the jeep lurched and bounced
violently along, while Gaylord raced through the gears
and the engine made roaring, grinding noises.

Behind them lights began to flick on in the houses.
Dogs barked, children cried, and men shouted. But before anyone back there could have seen them, Gaylord
had reached the main road. He made the right onto the
hardtop on two wheels, and then they were breezing
their way back to Saigon.

Jack tried to light a cigarette, but his hands shook so
badly he spilled half the pack to the floor before he could
extract and fumble one into his fingers. It required a
conscious effort of will to control his shaking long
enough to flip open his Zippo and get a flame.

"Nervous? First time you been shot at?" Gaylord
asked.

"Y-yeah," Jack stammered. He sucked smoke into his
lungs.

"You get used to it," Gaylord said matter-of-factly.

They were both silent for a few moments. Jack seemed to be floating along, suspended somewhere between sheer terror and wild exhilaration.

"Funny thing, now that it's all o-ov-ov—" Jack shook his head and began again, "Now that it's all over; but I've been down there before, about this same time of night, and the other times, there was always plenty of people around, you know? Lights on all over the place, and kids playing in the road and all that. Funny I didn't notice the big difference this time, huh?" Jack's voice quavered as he spoke.

"Yeah." The tone in Gaylord's voice was heavy with sarcasm. "If you'd said something before, you might've saved us a lot of trouble. You might've saved yourself *that*." He indicated bloodstains down the left side of Jack's face. Jack rubbed his cheek on that side, and his mud-stained fingers came away smeared with blood. For the first time he was conscious of a throbbing in his left earlobe. Gingerly, he reached up and was horrified to find that he did not have a left earlobe anymore.

"Jesus Christ! I thought the crusty stuff on my neck was mud!" Jack's voice was tinged with awe. Gaylord laughed. "Maybe you can get yourself a Purple Heart for it. 'Course, you can't tell anyone how you *really* got clipped, but knowing you, Kelley, you'll come up with a likely story."

"What I don't understand is why Thien'd want to double-cross us on this deal. Hell, there wasn't enough money involved to make it worth killing for." Jack stopped short. His own words brought him to the fact that Gaylord had probably just killed two men and definitely saved his own life.

"Uh, by the way, that was pretty quick work on your part, back there. Thanks." Jack stared ahead, and Gaylord did not bother to acknowledge the thanks. They drove in silence for a few moments. As Gaylord stopped on the edge of Hong Bang Boulevard, waiting for an opening in the traffic, he said, "That was no double-cross, Kelley."

"How do you know that?"

"You said it yourself. There's no cash in zapping either of us, 'specially not *me*. Whoever those guys back there were, they didn't even know I was around. That's why you 'n' me're still breathing and they're not. I hope. But they opened fire soon's they knew it was you. Naw, Kelley, those two were waiting to get you, and my bet is they weren't trying to ice you for cash."

"Why'd—"

"You tell me! You know what kinda shit you're into better 'n' *I* do!" Gaylord fixed Jack with an accusing look. "Well, okay, hotshot, where do you want off? Your quarters?"

"Yeah." A terrible sinking feeling in his guts told Jack that Gaylord was right. But who wanted him dead? And more important, why?

Gaylord pulled the jeep to the curb about half a block beyond the entrance to Jack's quarters. Jack got out on wooden legs and was on the sidewalk before he realized that Gaylord was saying something to him.

"I said, 'Forget about them three point fives,' okay? They're just too expensive at your prices, know what I mean?"

"Uh, yeah. Oh, and thanks, Gaylord, thanks a lot, okay?"

"Don't fuckin' mention it," Gaylord sneered.

Jack was not even aware when Gaylord drove off. He was so ill he wanted to vomit and almost did, right there, in the street, but he was able to hold it until he got to his room.

"How the hell'd you get this?" the army doctor asked.

Jack shrugged. He could pretend nonchalance. He had had all night to invent a story and regain some of his composure.

"I was drinkin' in a Vietnamese bar last night. Some rangers got into a fight, 'n' one of 'em pulled a forty-five, shot the place up. Guess a bullet clipped me. I wasn't aware I'd been cut so bad at first, I was so busy shagging my ass outta there."

The doctor glanced up at him sharply. "You shoulda come in right away, Sarge."

"Well, sir, the whole thing happened so fast, and I was lit up enough so's not to notice how badly I'd been cut until I woke up this morning."

The doctor grunted. Such things were common enough. "Well, nice clean wound, anyway. We'll clean 'er up a little, put in a stitch or two, and you should be okay—Maybe a little lopsided for a while. Bitch of a place to apply a dressing, though. Hurt much?"

"Yessir. A little."

"Umm. I'll give you some antibiotics, and you come back in a week so I can check the stitches and see how well you're healing up. If the thing swells up on you and begins to hurt, come right back in. We can't allow it to get infected." He continued to examine the wound. "Too bad you got this in a barroom brawl, Sarge."

Jack caught a cab to work, as Phu had not reported in that morning. This was distressing for two reasons. First, it meant Jack would have to find his own way to work, but worse, it pointed the finger at Phu as the one who had set him up. At first Jack had thought the ambush had been Harry Scheldt's doing. Now he was convinced it had been Phu, and that he had been a plant all along. For the first time in years, Jack did not enjoy the ride through the Saigon traffic.

"What the fuck happened to you?" Aspby shouted when Jack at last walked into the office. Jack beat a hasty retreat into the vault. Aspby followed him.

"Jack, you look awful. What happened?" Aspby said with genuine concern.

Jack mumbled the same phony story he had given the doctor. It was such a transparent lie that Jack couldn't imagine anybody believing it, but Aspby did.

"Jesus, Jack, you oughta stay outta those Vietnamese

places. Do you feel well enough to work the rest of the day?"

"Oh, hell, yes, Jim! I'm okay." Jack feigned heartiness. But he really did feel terrible, not so much from the throbbing in his ear or the ignominious memory of the ambush that had caused it, but from the undeniable fact that someone wanted him dead. He was afraid and disoriented. It was as if he had just pulled back the covers on his bed, anticipating a good snooze, and found a rattlesnake coiled there ready to strike.

During the next few days, Aspby became increasingly alarmed at the change that was coming over his friend.

"I know goddamned well that chunk out of your ear is not what's bothering you, Jack," he finally said one afternoon.

"Nothing's bothering me, Jim," Jack replied defensively.

Aspby just stared at his friend.

"Well, shit," Jack said after a moment, and then told him the real story.

"Oh, Jesus, Jesus," Aspby whispered after Jack had finished. "No wonder you look like a hunted animal! 'N' you don't have any idea who tried to ice you?"

"Shit, who knows?" Jack answered wearily. "Like Gaylord said, I'm into so much shit it's hard to tell. But I never crossed anyone I know of, and I never hurt anyone, either. At first I was sure it was Scheldt, Jim, 'cause I know he's got it in for me, but when Phu didn't show up for work the next day, I figured it must have been him or whoever he's working for."

"I think it's politics," Aspby said suddenly.

"Huh?"

"Well, I suspect we're all being watched by somebody some of the time. You're always goin' out to General Ton's villa, 'n' you deal with all sorts of shady Vietnamese and Chinese types. I bet you got picked up on somebody's surveillance operation, and they figured you for a big fish."

"Aw, Jim, I don't know. I'm just a small-potatoes guy!"

"Whoever wants you dead doesn't seem to think so," Aspby said pointedly. "No, I tell you, Jack, I think you got on the Vietnamese CIA's list 'cause you're a confidant of General Ton. Hell, it's an open secret they put him down here because nobody trusts him not to try to pull a coup if he ever gets a troop command again." Aspby nodded. "I'll bet that's it. They probably figure you're U.S. CIA yourself, working with the general to cook up a coup."

"Then suppose you tell me what I can do, huh?" Jack replied. "I can't just live out the rest of my tour creeping between the White and this place. And I can't go in and ask the army to curtail my overseas tour, either. Christ, wouldn't that look hilarious on a personnel action: 'Request curtailment of EM's current overseas tour because his criminal activities have made him some nasty enemies who are trying to kill him.' Now wouldn't the boys at Department of the Army get a kick out of somethin' like that?" Jack laughed nastily.

"Okay, okay, calm down. First thing you do is you take a long leave. How much time you got on the books, Jack?"

Jack shrugged. "Sixty days, maybe more."

"Good. Put in for a thirty-day leave and go back to the States. Relax. Visit the Pentagon and politic for a curtailment. You don't have to give 'em a reason. Hell, you've been here for *years*, Jack, you don't owe anybody anything."

Jack was still unsure. "What do I do if I gotta come back and finish out the six months remaining on my tour?"

"Jack, in thirty days this'll all blow over— Hold it! I just got an idea. You go ahead, type up your leave request, and I'll get the colonel to sign it. Then you hand-carry it out to MACV headquarters. You stick close to the flagpole until you take off, see, and meantime, I'll pull some strings out at MACV myself, so if you can't get Department of Army to pull you out of here, we'll transfer you to another part of the country for the rest of your tour."

"Oh, yeah, like where? The fucking Big Red One? I'll take my chances in Saigon, not out in the boonies with the grunts! Did anybody ever tell you there's a real war going on out there? At least here there's only a few guys tryin' to get me. Out there I'd have all of Ho Chi Minh's finest tryin' to wax my ass."

"C'mon, Jack," Aspby pleaded, "I'll get you a billet up at Nha Trang, with Second Field Forces, or even out at U.S. Army headquarters. Long Binh ain't that far up the road, but it's as secure as Fort Knox. It's a bit dusty and nasty"—he shrugged—"but what the hell?"

"Oh, thanks," Jack replied sarcastically, "you're sure one hell of a fine buddy!" Immediately he regretted having said that. "No, sorry, Jim, I didn't mean that. You are a good friend. I'm finally beginnin' to breathe again, for the first time in days. Thanks, buddy." They shook hands.

But there was something else on Jack's mind. "Jim . . ." he began, then hesitated, unsure of how to say what was on his mind. "Jim, what am I gonna do about Ana?" he blurted out. "I can't leave her here like this. What if Scheldt makes another grab for her?"

Aspby grinned. "Why not take her with you?"

"Up country, you mean?"

Aspby nodded. "Sure, easy."

"And if I don't come back from leave?"

Aspby shrugged. "Would you take her back to the States, Jack?"

"You mean *marry* her?" Jack asked, incredulous. "Jim, I'm in the fuckin' *army*. The army's all I ever knew. A soldier don't need a *wife*! What the hell's got into you?"

"Don't worry, then. If you leave her behind, I'll take care of her."

"I *bet* you will!" Jack said angrily.

"No, asshole, I don't mean *that*! I'll work somethin'

out to protect her. Maybe Colonel Tang can make an arrangement. We'll get her out to Taiwan, if we have to. Meanwhile, we can put a watch on her, have someone escort her around, until the heat dies down. Your buddy at CID, Purdome—is that his name?—maybe he'll help. The MPs are good at doin' little favors for someone they like. I'll talk to Colonel Tang. Don't worry about it anymore."

Jack's request for leave was approved immediately. He would fly on a military contract flight departing Bien Hoa Airbase, twenty miles northeast of Saigon, on Thursday, February 1, 1968, only a few days away. He relaxed then. He knew he was going to make it. The Vietnamese CIA could not touch him in the States.

Jack drove himself around Saigon now. Each night he parked his jeep close to his quarters, and in the mornings he checked it thoroughly for boobytraps. It was a harrowing experience because each time he was certain he would find a bomb attached somewhere.

Jack arranged to take off the thirtieth of January. Preparing for his departure consisted of packing one very small bag and drinking a lot of whiskey.

He was still worried about Ana, but he had faith in Aspby's word. Maybe, he began to think, things would turn out right after all.

The Future Never Spoke

Gᴇɴᴇʀᴀʟ Tᴏɴ's ʙᴀʀʙᴇᴄᴜᴇ ᴡᴀs ᴀ ɢʀᴇᴀᴛ sᴜᴄᴄᴇss. They always were. The general hosted at least two each year, and all his friends attended. This one was no exception.

Jack drove his jeep into the parking lot in front of the general's villa, found a vacant spot between a Mercedes-Benz with diplomatic license plates and a Land Rover belonging to the Australian Army Forces. Jack decided not to go in right away. He lit a cigarette and sat in his jeep, contemplating the other vehicles in the lot. Most of them were chauffeur driven, and the Vietnamese drivers had all gathered down at one end of the lot to smoke and gossip.

There was money here tonight and power, plenty of it, Jack reflected. His battered old U.S. Armed Forces jeep was a sorry sight next to the gleaming sedans parked in the general's parking lot. A sudden burst of laughter from the general's courtyard attracted his attention. The laughter was male, raucous, certain, powerful, like the cars around him.

Now suppose somebody saw *me* coming in here to-night, Jack mused. What would he think about a lowly American army sergeant mixing with all those powerful people in there? Would he believe Jack Kelley was in-vited as a friend of General Ton, a friendship due to the general's whims? Or would he think that Jack himself was . . . well, something more than just a lowly American army sergeant?

Maybe Aspby was right after all. Maybe somebody had Jack Kelley figured as some sort of undercover agent.

Jack took a final drag on his cigarette and tossed the still glowing butt onto the parking stand, where it disin-tegrated in a spectacular shower of orange sparks, dis-mounted from his jeep, and walked purposefully into the courtyard.

A goat was roasting slowly on a spit over a charcoal fire in one corner of the courtyard; about twenty-five guests were present. They represented quite a mixed bag, and several nodded casually to Jack as he walked by. Near the fishpond, in the center of the courtyard, several Americans in fatigue uniforms were talking. One, Jack recognized as a popular broadcast specialist from the Armed Forces Radio and Television Service. General Ton had seen him doing the evening news, decided there was something he liked about the man, and invited him and his friends to the barbecue.

"Kelley!" a huge voice bellowed, and Jack winced. It was Colonel Burns, the deputy chief of the Free World Military Assistance Organization, and he was already several drinks ahead of everyone else. "C'mon over here, Sarge," Burns demanded. He introduced Jack to a group of officers standing in a small circle around him as "The finest scrounger in the United States Army." They shook hands. Jack stood there awkwardly, wanting very much to put his hands in his pockets. He did not know how to socialize with officers.

"So you're the famous, or should I say 'infamous' Sergeant Kelley?" one of them asked. The speaker was a tall, spare army lieutenant colonel wearing immaculately pressed and starched jungle fatigues; his boots glistened with polish.

Jack bridled instantly at the colonel's words. "Good folks think I'm famous, Colonel; bad ones think I'm infamous."

"Lieutenant Colonel John Rakes," Colonel Burns introduced him.

"Colonel will do." He nodded at Jack.

"Not yet, John, not yet." Burns winked at Jack. Rakes smirked.

"Well, I see you're an AG officer, Colonel," Jack remarked, gesturing with his glass at Rakes's insignia of branch, the shield of the army adjutant general's corps.

"Yes," Rakes said uncomfortably. "I was infantry, but I changed branches," he added, and then promptly regretted it.

"Twinkle, twinkle, little shield, keep me off the battlefield," said one of the other officers, laughing. Rakes's face reddened.

"Staff work's pretty important," Jack said. "You gotta have somebody run things when all the men are off at the war."

The other officers laughed, but Rakes, at whom it was aimed, was not amused by the remark.

"I understand you're rather, *adept* at getting things for people," Rakes said pointedly.

"I steal from the officers and give to the enlisted men, if that's what you mean, sir."

"That's *not* what I meant, Sergeant," Rakes responded sharply. Then he smiled to cover his anger. "Do you also fix up little boys with little girls?"

"What else is there, John?" Burns shouted gleefully. He was enjoying the scene enormously. Jack was great entertainment at parties because you never knew what he would say next.

"No, Colonel," Jack said over the laughter. "I fix up men with men. Are you interested?"—wrong thing to say, but Jack said it anyway.

"What!" Rakes shouted.

"Kelley!" General Ton exclaimed, walking up before Rakes could say anything more. The officers stiffened at the general's approach and stepped aside deferentially to permit the crisp little man to join them. Immediately the atmosphere changed as the officers became attentive and respectful.

The general was wearing slacks and a garish Filipino sport shirt; his jet-black hair, always carefully groomed, looked as if it had been sculpted to fit the contour of his head.

"Well, gentlemen, is all to your taste this evening?" the general asked. There was a chorus of enthusiastic assent. "Just wait until the lamb is ready! You will enjoy it enormously, I assure you. It is being prepared according to an Algerian recipe I learned when I was a student in France years ago."

"How long were you in France, General?" asked Colonel Rakes in fluent French.

"Oh, I do not speak French anymore, Colonel, on principle," General Ton answered. "Not since 1955, the year they gave us over to the Communists."

"Excuse me, General," Rakes apologized.

"Never mind, never mind, Colonel! I think it is an excellent thing that an officer know one or two languages besides his own. My not speaking French is, how do you say, an 'idiosyncracy'? Purely personal and most inconvenient at times." General Ton laughed merrily. "You know, if I were to stop speaking the language of those who have betrayed us over the years, I would be speaking *no* language by now—especially not my own."

The Americans laughed politely, but they were embarrassed by General Ton's remark. How had America ever betrayed Vietnam? they wondered.

"Now, gentlemen"—the general clapped his hands together brusquely—"I would like to borrow Sergeant Kelley for a moment. Would you . . . ?" He extended a hand toward the house, and Jack walked on ahead of him. They disappeared through the front door, the general's arm laid familiarly across the sergeant's shoulders.

Rakes stared after them.

"I hope I get that sergeant of yours in my battalion, when I get one," he told Burns. "I'll take the starch out of him," he added darkly.

Burns laughed derisively. "John, *if* the army gives you a battalion and you want to save your career, pick anybody else before Kelley. He knows all the little NCO tricks that can screw up a commander six ways to Sunday. He'll fuck you forever simply by carrying out your orders to the letter, John. Stay away from NCOs like him, and if you can't, cooperate with 'em."

"Honestly, Bobbie," Rakes snorted, "I've never heard such bullshit in my life." He finished his drink and stomped off to get another.

The general's study was quiet and comfortable. He motioned Jack to sit in a rattan chair drawn up to a low lacquerware table. "What are you drinking tonight, Kelley?"

"Scotch and soda, sir."

General Ton mixed Jack's drink. "'Deep and mean are those who hate and smile,'" the general quoted from *Kieu*. He handed Jack his drink.

"What was that, sir?"

"That lieutenant colonel you were talking to when I walked up. Who is he?"

Jack still seethed over the encounter with the supercilious officer. "I don't know, sir. Some friend of Colonel Burns, I suppose."

"He was no friend of yours, Kelley. Stay away from him." The general sat opposite his guest and crossed his legs.

"I intend to, sir."

"Thank you, by the way, for this Scotch." The general raised his glass.

"Oh, it was nothing," Jack protested. Actually, getting the whiskey had been a big problem, but Jack solved it at the cost of a 1.5-kilowatt generator traded to one of his special forces contacts at a remote camp in the Central Highlands.

"Kelley, do you remember Vung Ro Bay?" the general asked. Jack nodded. At Vung Ro Bay, on the South China Sea, a steel-hulled trawler loaded with supplies for the Viet Cong had been captured in February 1965.

"Those weapons, plus thousands of others we've captured from the enemy over the years, are in a warehouse not very far from here," the general said. "We give them away, mostly to foreigners as souvenirs or 'war trophies.' All perfectly legal, you understand. I could get some for you."

Jack thought for a moment. What was the pitch? Whatever it was, Jack trusted General Ton. "Chinese copies of the Tokarev TT thirty-three pistol would be in very great demand, sir. SKS carbines will sell well, also. Automatic weapons I can't use, not in the souvenir market, cause you can't take 'em home. But could you part with any AKs?"

The general shook his head. "No, my friend, only semiautomatics."

"Oh well, just a thought. I *could* use the pistols right away. Say, ten to begin with?"

"You shall have them, with leather holsters and extra ammunition clips. We will discuss the carbines later. If you would join me here for dinner next Wednesday, I will have them ready for you." The general clapped his hands together loudly, indicating the conversation was over.

Jack had no idea why General Ton had brought the subject up. He did not intend to ask, either. The general, for his own reasons, had decided to bestow a little favor on him, and why not? Kelley was a trustworthy friend.

General Ton rose, and then he sat down again abruptly. Jack hesitated, then he also sat down.

"My problem, Kelley," the general began, "is that in Vietnam, the most highly politicized country in Asia, I am a man with no politics. I am a soldier, that is all. But nobody believes that, and so I am not trusted. I should be commanding an army corps, not buried in this meaningless 'liaison' assignment. I am an exile in my own land," he added dryly.

Jack did not comment.

"Politics is a very unstable profession, especially in Vietnam," General Ton continued. "I don't play, but I can be played with, if you understand." Jack understood. "So I take certain precautions. Of my five sons, one is always abroad, in case anything happens at home. I keep accounts in foreign banks. So"—he shrugged—"I do what I can for my friends, and I bear my personal burden as manfully as I am able." He paused. "Let us go outside now and eat and drink and enjoy what life we have left to us."

Back outside, the party was in full swing. In one corner, Aspirant Truong was doing his impression of an elephant, to the vast amusement of a small group of Thai and Filipino guests. Jack walked up to the group and placed his hand on the shoulder of Master Sergeant Quinto, the finance sergeant on the Filipino headquarters staff.

"How goes it, José?"

"Ah, Jim! Good, good! And you?"

"Okay. José, what can I do for ten cases of San Miguel? I have this friend—"

"Done!" Quinto said with a short nod. "A couple of my boys, they could use some pistols?"

"Good. Let's talk about it tomorrow, okay? Meanwhile"—he nudged a Thai sergeant by the name of Fuangchoelai—"be careful of this fellow here, José. He's a dangerous man."

* * *

Colonel Tang paused to chat with this group, waved or spoke casually to someone he knew in another, but he was in fact, more preoccupied with Jack Kelley's problem than with his guests. The simple fact is, he thought, Kelley is Kelley and General Ton is General Ton; no mystery, no danger to anyone except perhaps themselves. He had told his superiors that a thousand times, it seemed, but they had their own preconceived notions and apparently refused to believe him. They took his periodic reports and divined meanings from them that were never intended.

It was disgraceful, the way Colonel Tang's controllers, anonymous men in the South Vietnamese Central Intelligence Organization, took the evaluations of a mere field agent like that bogus driver of Kelley's over his own more reasoned and accurate appraisals, the colonel thought.

That damned Phu had them believing Kelley was some sort of undercover agent sent to work with General Ton, draw him into some conspiracy to overthrow Thieu and his government. Such idiocy! the colonel raged.

The CIO was fully aware of General Ton's capriciousness in selecting his associates, but at bottom they simply refused to believe that any lieutenant general in any army, even their own, would ever stoop so low as to pick a mere sergeant for a friend. Therefore, in their weak and twisted minds, Jack Kelley was a dangerous plant.

And now they had gone and tried to assassinate Kelley! Such stupidity was incomprehensible, and to make the whole thing even worse, Kelley had been ready for them, and now two of their best agents had been killed and there was nothing they could do about it without giving the whole thing away. Colonel Tang was delighted that Kelley had escaped. Perhaps, he told himself, he should warn Kelley? No, that would be foolish, and besides, the sergeant could take care of himself; he had demonstrated that very well the other night.

It was General Ton he was worried about. The time had nearly come when he might have to warn the general. Perhaps not, though. The general knew he was being spied on, might even suspect it was him. He was a wily old rascal. He claimed not to play politics, and he did not, but Tang knew his general as a very shrewd politician and a superb strategist. If he suspected his chief executive officer was a CIO plant on his staff, he was showing good sense by not letting on and keeping him around. If you know who the conduit is, you can always feed him what you want others to know. Without realizing it, Colonel Tang smiled.

Just then a voice interrupted his thoughts.

"May I talk to you privately, Colonel?" It was Jim Aspby.

"Certainly, my son," Colonel Tang answered, falling into their father-son routine.

"I have this personal problem," Aspby began, and told him about Lien and his son.

"Marry the girl," Colonel Tang advised.

"I'm afraid that is not possible, sir. She—we are not—I mean, neither of us want marriage."

"That certainly complicates things, James. I assume this liaison of yours was just casual at first, an 'arrangement' that became complicated when she got pregnant?"

"Yes, exactly."

"Women get pregnant out of wedlock all the time, James," Colonel Tang said. He had dropped the father-son banter as soon as he realized how serious the conversation would be. "Why should you worry? It is the nature of a man to sow wild seeds and forget about them."

"Well, I can't do that, Colonel, I just can't. Yes, I thought I would at first, but that was before he was born. And now, well . . . well, dammit, he's my tiny drop of blood, and I just can't run off and leave him."

"Hmm. I am very pleased you have the confidence in my judgment to seek advice from me on this problem, Jim. But this is neither the time nor the place to discuss such things. Let me think it over and we'll talk more next week, at lunch. Agreed?" Colonel Tang patted Aspby affectionately on the arm and excused himself.

The waitresses were laughing hysterically by the time they were through with the main course.

"What the hell's wrong with them?" Aspby asked, mentally surveying everything he had done since they sat down, to see if he had committed some gross social blunder. No, his fly was not open; he was an expert at using chopsticks; Colonel Tang had ordered the meal in Vietnamese, so he knew they had not mispronounced some key word and ordered something impossible and disgusting.

Colonel Tang lit a cigarette. "They are laughing because you ordered the soup as the *first* course. We always eat it last. And not many Americans ever come in here, so you're a bit of a curiosity."

"That's *all*? My God, I thought they were laughing at the size of my nose or something!"

"No. In fact, they think you are quite handsome. And that brings us to what we were discussing the other night. Shall I go on?"

"Please do."

Colonel Tang drew on his cigarette and drank some tea. "I notice that you Americans love the sun. You're always trying to get a tan, to make your skin darker. Why is that?"

"I guess we think it makes us look healthy, young, athletic. I don't know. I don't like too much sun myself."

"We Vietnamese are just the opposite, James. We turn very dark in the sun and those of us who can, avoid being out in it too much because in our country a light skin is a highly prized attribute of beauty. The rich can afford to stay indoors while the poor labor in the sun and their skins turn dark. A white skin is also a sign of social status among us."

"My son's skin will be light. Are you saying this is to his advantage?"

"No. We Vietnamese are a very narrow-minded people when it comes to other races. We consider ourselves superior to all others. Among us, mixing blood is tabu. A Eurasian child in Vietnamese society is an outcast, looked down on, denied his birthright. If your son grows up Vietnamese, he will never achieve legitimate success in our country, even though he may be able to live well, in spite of the enormous prejudice we have against his kind."

Aspby looked down at his beer and made no comment.

"It is not easy, this decision you must make," Colonel Tang said softly. "But I am telling you the truth. Don't forget, though, that we love children in this country. For the near future, your son will be well taken care of, spoiled, actually, because everyone will dote on him. His mother and whatever family she may have will always love him and lavish affection upon him. But he will not go very far, and he will begin to experience the bitterness of his mixed racial ancestry as he grows into manhood."

"So what do you suggest I do?"

"James, if you love this child, and I think you really, truly do, take him back with you. If you must marry this woman to do it, I will help you in every way I am able, and that will be considerable; so will General Ton. He has many powerful friends who can help expedite your cause through our government bureaucracy."

"But what if Miss Lien—excuse me, I never told you her name, I guess." Colonel Tang smiled; he had known the woman's identity for months. "But what if Miss Lien absolutely refuses to go, to marry?"

"She will not refuse. If she does at first, leave the rest to me."

A huge weight seemed suddenly gone from Jim Aspby's soul, and his spirit soared with joy and hope. "I—I guess I didn't realize how much this has been bothering me, Colonel Tang," he said. "Yes, by God, I will! Thank you, Colonel Tang! Thank you very much!"

They shook hands, Aspby enthusiastically pumping

the colonel's arm until it hurt, but the American's happiness was so genuine Tang could not resist sharing its certain warmth. Aspby was so American, Colonel Tang reflected, so preoccupied with morality and wanting so much to do what was "right," so confident that there *was* a right way, and that once found, it could be pursued. How easily life's bewilderments and complications melted away for these people! They believed something, and magically it was true. All is well with the world!

Fiddlers' Green

"**S**IR, I'M GONNA HOP A FLIGHT TO SAIGON FOR A couple of days," Oates told General Foster. "See if I can get some assignments for some of our boys who'll be going home soon. I think I can get General Westmoreland's sergeant major to make a call back to Department of the Army, grease the skids a bit for these guys."

General Foster nodded and sipped at his Scotch. "Put in a good word for me while you're down there." He laughed. "Jesus, Goats, take a week! You deserve some time off. How long've we been here now? Eight months. And I bet you haven't even thought about your R and R yet, have you? You're overdue. You could have Mary meet you in Honolulu."

Every soldier in Vietnam was authorized one rest and recuperation, R&R, trip, not chargeable as military leave, during his year there. Most single soldiers took theirs in places like Hong Kong, Sydney, Bangkok, Penang, Kuala Lumpur. But a favorite with married men was to have their wives meet them in Honolulu.

Oates shook his head. "Naw. Not for me. I can sweat it out for one year, sir. I'll relax a bit in old Saigon. That's about as far away from here as I want to get, until time to go home, that is."

"So you're goin' to Fiddlers' Green on me, huh?"

"'Scuse me, sir?"

"Fiddler's Green, Top, as in the old Sixth Cavalry song:

Halfway down the trail to hell, in a shady meadow
    green,
—Are the souls of all dead troopers camped near a
    good old-time canteen,
And this eternal resting place is known as Fiddlers'
    Green.

Sure you don't remember that, Goats?"

"Well, only because you've been singing it for nearly forty years, General." Oates laughed.

General Foster noticed that Oates's drink was nearly empty. "Make yourself another, Sergeant Major."

"How 'bout a bourbon instead? You know, sir, Scotch is an officer's drink, and I feel peculiar having one." He mixed himself a Jim Beam and water at the tiny wet bar. They were sitting in the living room of General Foster's trailer. It was nearly midnight. They had these private sessions, the old general and his trusted sergeant major, quite regularly, to exchange views and information about the people and the activities in the division.

Oates was frank in his evaluations, and the general appreciated that. It gave him a chance to find out what was really going on among the enlisted men in the division.

"I heard a good one today, sir."

"Oh? Let's have it." General Foster's sense of humor was earthy and lively. The dirty joke was a specialty of his.

"Young lieutenant, just married, receives his orders for the 'Nam. He's heard about all the temptations over here, so he promises himself he'll be a good boy during his year. First three months're okay, but the second three are pretty bad. Still, he takes a lot of cold showers and gets through it somehow. Masturbates a lot. Finally comes time for his R and R, and he arranges for his wife to meet him in Hawaii. He can barely hold it back, on the plane, anticipating getting her into bed. He's almost in a frenzy when the plane lands at Honolulu, can hardly walk off the damned thing. There she is, waiting for him. He grabs her, pushes her into the rental car, and whisks her off to the nearest motel, where they strip unceremoniously and fall into the bed."

The general listened carefully, head cocked, a tiny smile on his lips.

"Now this young stud's been nearly nine months without any pussy, so no sooner does he get it in, and he pops his nuts, and she says"—Oates screwed up his eyes and imitated the falsetto patois of a Saigon bargirl—"'Choi-oi, honey, you fini too quick!'"

General Foster roared his laughter. "Oh, Jesus, Billy, that was *bad!*"

"So now you see why I don't want to go on R and R." Oates chuckled.

The general laughed some more. He sipped his drink and then said, "Top, you ever think about committing adultery?" Oates was the one person General Foster trusted enough to ask such a question. Oates realized the general was implying that a problem had come up and he wanted his advice.

"No, and I'll tell you why. My marriage oath is a bond of faith, sir, and I take it as seriously as I do my oath as a soldier to defend the Constitution. If I can't be true in my personal relationships, how the hell can I be true in my military ones? Once you start cheating or lying, where does it stop? Some can do it, and it doesn't seem to bother 'em, and you know a few like that are in this division right now; we've known 'em in other places, too. Maybe they can get away with it for a long time, but if a man keeps cheating, sooner or later it catches up with him."

"Goats, let's put this into a hypothetical situation. Suppose an officer, a personal friend, gets carried away? What do you do? Ruin his career over an indiscretion?"

Oates guessed instantly whom the general was talking about. "Talk to 'im first, General, warn him. But if he continues, can him. It's like an officer or a noncom getting drunk in front of his troops. It may happen once, but never let it happen twice, or everyone'll lose respect for him. A leader, especially one who's married, doesn't have to prove his manhood or that he's one of the boys by screwing every doughnut dolly or every village washerwoman around the camp."

General Foster's eyebrows shot up at the mention of "doughnut dolly," because the officer in question was having a torrid and indiscreet affair with one of the attractive young Red Cross volunteers working at the Bu Lon field office.

"You know him, don't you?"

"Yessir. And if you and I know, then every GI in this whole division knows about the colonel's indiscretions. It's the talk of our small town. Send him back to the States, but go easy on the girl. He's a handsome devil, and she's only twenty-one and fresh out of college. I say God bless her for coming over here in the first place. If only she'd been getting it on with some private in a line company instead of a goddamned staff officer in base camp, she'd deserve a medal."

General Foster laughed. "Well, thanks for playing devil's advocate for me." Oates knew the general had decided to send the philandering colonel home. Now he frowned at his drink, and Oates realized there was something else bothering him.

"You know, the intelligence boys are a bit antsy. There seems to be a lot of enemy activity up in the northern provinces."

"You think the bastards'll break the truce?" Oates asked.

The general shook his head. "No, but be ready for some big action after Tet. I think they're goin' to use the holidays to get into position for an all-out push sometime later, probably in February. Oh, there'll be 'incidents,' as there always are, shots exchanged here and there, maybe even some small attacks, but I think the big event will come later."

"You can handle things without me, then?" Oates smiled.

"You taught me real good"—the general laughed—"now get your tail out of here for a few days, Sergeant Major, and leave the war in this sector to me and my troops."

The next morning Oates placed a call to the MACV sergeant major on the direct line in the general's trailer.

"Frank, you old bastard, how the hell are you?" Oates shouted when the sergeant major came on the line. The two were not friends, but they had a grudging respect for each other.

"Who is this?" the MACV sergeant major asked, not recognizing the voice and highly annoyed. Oates smiled. He'd gotten the old fart pissed off at the start. That was good. The initiative was with him.

"Billy Goats, Frank. How're ya?"

"Goats! I shoulda known! I'm great, hope you got the drizzling shits."

"Nope. I'm coming down to see ya tomorrow, Frank."

"Oh, fuck me! To what do I owe this honor?"

"I want to ask for some favors for some men of mine, maybe a voice back at DA, to get 'em assignments, the usual tricks."

"Okay, Goats. What time will I see you, providing I can't invent some excuse not to be here when you come in?"

"I'm catching a chopper out of here at oh seven thirty-five, ETA Tan Son Nhut oh eight hundred. How do I get from the pad to your office?"

"Take a fucking taxi, like everybody else. No, I'll

have my jeep pick you up there. I presume you'll be coming in at the Hundred Twenty-fifth Aviation's pad?"

"Roger-doger, old codger. See you then."

"Not if I can pay the VC enough to shoot your ass down on the way in." The line went dead.

Oates chuckled and flashed the division switchboard. "This is the sergeant major," he told the operator. "Get me Tiger switch in Saigon, please." He waited, listening to the clicks and whistles and groans as the division switchboard operator tried to put his call through. A terrible roaring noise came through the receiver that caused Oates to wince.

"Sorry, Top," the operator said, "but I'll try to put your call through again. I'll call you back when I make the connection."

"Fine. I'm on the general's line." Oates hung up disgustedly. How could the United States, which had sent men around the moon and put an army in Vietnam, not be able to install a simple telephone system that worked? The telephone rang sharply, and Oates picked it up at once.

"Go ahead, Top, Tiger on the line."

"Tiger operator, sir," a sweet Vietnamese voice announced. Oates could just barely hear her, although she was less than forty miles away.

"Give me two thirty-five, Tiger," he shouted. The line clicked several times, and Oates could hear it buzzing on the other end. An American-sounding voice answered at last, but the connection was so bad he couldn't understand what it was saying.

"Is Sergeant Aspby there?" Oates screamed. The answering voice said something in reply as Oates strained to hear, but there was no further response.

"This is Lion, sir. Are you working?" announced an intermediate switchboard operator.

"Working, working, Lion! Don't cut me off!" Oates screamed. Too late. The line was dead. Oates sighed and looked at his watch. He had the entire morning at his disposal.

"Shall I try again?" the division switchboard asked. Oates knew the young man. He was assigned to the division's signal battalion, and he'd just come back to Vietnam from a month's emergency leave in the States. His father had died. "Yes, Sergeant Baxter, give it another try. I'll stand by here."

When Aspby at long last came on the line, his voice sounded far, far away, and apparently he could barely hear Oates.

"I gotta talk quick, Jim, 'cause they'll cut me off surer 'n hell," Oates hollered. "I'm comin' down tomorrow. Can you put me up for a few days?"

"Sure, Top, at the John Houston. One of the guys I know there is on R and R this week. When you comin' in?"

Oates thought he understood the question, but he couldn't be sure. This was like communicating with the spirit world, he told himself. "After lunch sometime—"

"Tiger. Are you working, sir?"

"Working, working! Tiger, you cut me off, I'll bite your tits off!" Oates shouted, but the line had already gone dead on him.

Despite the fact that it was Saturday morning when Oates arrived at the sprawling MACV headquarters complex near Tan Son Nhut Airport, the place was in full operation. General Westmoreland's policy was that so long as there was a war going on, his headquarters staff would work a minimum of twelve hours a day, seven days a week. Many of his people routinely put in eighteen-hour days, and everyone who worked in the headquarters consoled himself that long hours were better than getting shot at.

Oates finished his business with the MACV sergeant major quickly. Frank regularly made calls to the assignment managers back in the Pentagon, and he had a list of names Oates had given him. "What now, Goats?" he asked.

"Well, frankly, Frank"—the MACV sergeant major winced at that—"I'd like to see a little of Saigon, renew my acquaintance from the old days."

"Good. I'll put a jeep and driver at your disposal for as long as you're here. Where you staying?"

"At the John Houston, in Cholon."

Frank frowned. "That's for nobodies. I can get you a room at BEQ number three, with the other top graders."

"Naw, Frank, I don't want to spend my time with a bunch of fat-assed rear-echelon lifers. I'll stay with the troops, thanks just the same."

The room Aspby had arranged was nice, although Oates felt uncomfortable using another man's bed. He dropped his bags there and spent the rest of that day hitting the bars around town. He was surprised at how many Americans there were in those places, and the sun was still shining. That night he and Aspby drank with the Australians and other foreign NCOs in the Free World Military Assistance Compound on Tran Quoc Toan Boulevard, next door to the Buddhist Institute. On Monday the twenty-ninth, Oates rested. That night he and Aspby got roaring drunk in Aspby's own room at the John Houston.

On Tuesday the thirtieth, Oates slept late, intending to catch a flight back to the division in the late afternoon. Around ten A.M. the Vietnamese desk clerk knocked on Oates's door, announcing a telephone call for him in the lobby.

"Frank here, Goats," the MACV sergeant major announced. "The shit's hit the fan, old soldier." Frank's voice exuded enthusiasm.

"Whaddya mean?"

"The Tet cease-fire's been canceled, and all U.S. units are on full alert. All hell's broken loose up in the I Corps, and we may even catch some of it down here," he chortled. "Shit, last time I had as much fun as this we were evacuating Seoul as the Chinese Reds were comin' down on us!"

"Christ. I'd better haul ass back up to the division ASAP."

"Not a chance today, Goats. Everything that'll fly is either up in the air or committed. Better just stay where you are until I can get you a flight back up to Bu Lon. Uh, by the way, sorry about this, old pal, but you better send my jeep back out here, pronto."

"Roger. You let me know when I can get outta here, okay, Frank?"

"Sure, Goats. Gotta go now."

Oates hung up. He'd never felt more frustrated in his life. A big—really big—fight was brewing, and here he was, stuck in Saigon.

Oates spent the rest of the day drinking beer and playing tonk with some black noncoms in the roof garden. Although he was curious, he did not inquire why these men were off duty in the middle of a workday. He recognized one of them from a time years before, when they had served together in the Third Infantry Division, in Germany. This was Oates's introduction to the group, and after the obligatory round of reminiscences, which overcame the barriers of race and rank, the sergeant major was allowed to play. By the time the game was over, he was on a first-name basis with all of them. As he walked back down to the lobby, to try calling Frank for the latest news, he reflected that this bonhomie was probably due in large part to the fact that he had lost twenty-five dollars in the game.

He could not get through to MACV, and on the second try he gave up for good. He knew Frank had his hands full just now and did not need a stranded field rat bugging him. Until the MACV sergeant major called him back, Oates was prepared to cool his heels.

Before going to bed for the night, he cleaned his .45 automatic. As a precaution, he jacked a round into the chamber, put the weapon on safe, and laid it on the nightstand beside his bed.

At shortly past midnight, January thirty-first 1968, history took one of its irreversible twists, and the United States began spiraling down into the dark at the end of the tunnel in Vietnam. The great Tet offensive had begun.

Making Haiti

T HE DRESSING ON HIS LEFT EAR WAS REPLACED NOW by a small bandage. Jack was getting ready to leave Vietnam.

On Wednesday he visited the Chase Manhattan military banking facility at the Cholon Post Exchange Compound. As always, there were long lines at the bank, but they moved quickly. Jack got into the one that appeared shortest. The man just in front of him was carrying an M-60 machine gun slung over one shoulder; the other men were also heavily armed. Jack's .357 hung heavy on his left side. The only restriction on carrying firearms into the bank was to clear them and put them on safety before entering. Nobody had ever tried robbing the place.

Jack withdrew $2,500 in military scrip. He did not bother to convert any of it into Vietnamese piasters. Two thousand he planned to leave with Ana, in case he didn't come back; the rest would pay his traveling expenses. Ana, he knew, could convert the military payment certificates into whatever currency she wanted, at a much higher rate on the black market than any bank would give her.

He had always been very careful to keep only as much money in his account as he could reasonably explain. Still, over the months, his account had swelled to a respectable balance. The proceeds from his illegal transactions he deposited in a bank back in the U.S., in an account under his brother's name. The last time he had checked, there was over forty thousand dollars in that account. He used various methods to transfer this money home, but the most reliable was to fold a few greenbacks into a personal letter and send them through the mail. Jack always required payment in greenbacks from his bigger clients because the money was easier to dispose of that way. He converted his Vietnamese currency into U.S. dollars through black market contacts.

Back in his room, hidden in a suitcase, Jack had over five thousand dollars in green, which he planned to take with him on the flight home.

He left the PX compound through the Hung Vuong Boulevard gate. He turned right, walked through the Nguyen Tri Phuong intersection to where his jeep was parked. Dozens of vehicles were drawn up along the block, mostly military jeeps and trucks. Swarms of street urchins begged money and candy from the soldiers or offered their services as watchdogs over the vehicles while the men were shopping in the PX.

Jack had promised a boy a hundred piasters if he would watch his jeep for him. The child and several of his companions were sitting in the vehicle when Jack walked up.

"Hey, you, GI! Where you going now?" his watchdog asked as Jack unfastened the padlocked chain he kept about the steering wheel to deter thieves.

"Cholon, kid. Clear your friends outta here now. G'wan, scat! scat!"

"Hey, mister, you take us wid you? You go Nguyen Hoan Street? We go Chinese movie, lotsa fighting!"

"I can't take you kids to the fucking movies!" Jack protested, laughing.

"No, no, *we* go movie, *you* go home. You give ride, you give ride, okay?"

Jack regarded the boy with amazement. The suggestion was so novel it intrigued him. The situation reminded him poignantly of his own childhood, when, if you were under twelve, you could get into the best movie in town for only a quarter. He had always felt sorry for these children, most of whom were orphans, but now he felt a certain understanding and kinship with them.

"Good heavens! The children are going to the movies, no?" he said in Vietnamese. The boys shrieked delightedly and piled back into the jeep.

"Okay, kid," Jack shouted to the watchdog, who appeared to be in charge of the others, "you tell me where to drop you boys off, okay?" He guided his jeep into the traffic and drove off in the direction of Nguyen Hoan Street, trying to remember if he'd ever seen a movie theater there.

He did not notice a nondescript Vietnamese army jeep pulling out of the parked vehicles at the end of the block to follow him. Inside were two soldiers dressed in fatigues. Neither of them wore any insignia of rank. If Jack could have seen them he might have been impressed by the hardness in their faces. They pulled alongside him at a stoplight. Jack, chatting and laughing with the children, never saw them.

"Not now, not with all those children," the driver hissed at his passenger, who was holding a fully cocked .45-caliber pistol between his legs.

"Damn these Americans," the gunman muttered, frustrated; he had other things he would rather be doing than tracking this one all over Saigon.

"Patience, patience," cautioned the driver. "Sooner or later he will expose himself."

The light changed and Jack, to the vast amusement of his tiny passengers, peeled rubber as he darted through the intersection.

"He drives like a madman!" the gunman complained.

"These Americans, they all think they're Grand Prix champions." The driver chuckled. "We shall continue to follow him, and we will get him when he is on foot."

The gunman put his weapon on safe and slipped it back into its holster. "I am hungry, Dat," he informed the driver. "The sooner we get rid of this man, the sooner we can eat. If he is going home now and he stays there any time at all, I will eat some *pho*." His stomach rumbled at the thought of the delicate rice-noodle soup, laced with thin slices of beef, flavored with onion and pepper and a dash of *nuoc mam* sauce.

By noon Jack had finished his packing and wandered into the lobby.

"Some shit's goin' on up in the northern provinces," the sergeant who managed the White BEQ announced importantly as Jack stepped into his office. He threw himself insouciantly into an easy chair opposite the manager's desk and picked up one of the girlie magazines the sergeant kept beside the chair in an old cardboard box.

"Looks like they canceled Tet up in I Corps," said the manager. "Somethin' big goin' on up there, Jack."

"Yeah. I leave tomorrow mornin', Frank. After that they can shove this whole fucking place."

"*You*? Jack Kelley, the Saigon kid, rotating stateside? I can't believe it!"

"Not rotating, Frank, just a month's leave. But I'm goin' t' work on scaring me up a nice assignment elsewhere, maybe Seventh Army or somewhere else in Germany. Maybe Panama, on second thought, Frank. Yeah, Panama. I like the tropics and dark-skinned women."

"But Jack, whaddya know about this business up north? Seriously."

"Frank, seriously: somethin's *always* goin' on up north; the marines're constantly catching hell across the DMZ up there. So what?"

"Nothin', I guess. I just feel antsy."

"You mean you don't have enough work to do around here, Frank."

"No, what I mean is, I'm nervous. Do you think there's anythin' to be worried about, Jack? Seriously, now."

"Frank, seriously: no. I leave outta Bien Hoa tomorrow at thirteen hundred. I gotta be at the Koeppler Compound at oh eight hundred to check out. What am I gonna do the rest of today, huh?"

"Get drunk?" Frank suggested.

"Goddammit, I'm goin' to walk over to Sonya's! Wanna come along?"

"No thanks, Jack, I've got the duty right here. Bit early to be going anywhere, huh?"

Jack looked at his watch. It was then a little past one. He still had half a bottle of Scotch behind the bar. He would finish that and, when she came to work, give Ana the money. He would tell her it was "insurance" money. He would not tell her he was going to try to get himself reassigned, once back in the States. He would deal with the emotions of that eventuality when and if it came to pass.

It was just past three in the afternoon when Jack finally walked into Sonya's. The lunch hour crowd was gone, and there was not another customer in the place. None of the girls were there yet.

Mrs. Chen smiled from behind the bar. "You are early today, Jack," she commented.

"I'm going back to the States tomorrow, Mrs. Chen—just for leave—so I took today off. When will Ana be in?"

Mrs. Chen shrugged. She had been watching the romance between them closely.

Jack finished his drink and ordered another. "Can you put a record on for me, Mrs. Chen?"

Obligingly, Mrs. Chen put on "Lara's Theme" from the soundtrack of the motion picture *Dr. Zhivago*. Jack liked it; so did Ana. They often requested the record when they were there together and business was slow. The music made emotions surge through Jack Kelley's mind. He *had* to get out of Saigon, there was no question about it, but what would happen to Ana? His attachment to her had grown strong.

"Another Scotch, Mrs. Chen. Make it a double, will you?"

"I hear there will be trouble with the Communists this Tet," Mrs. Chen said, leaning across the bar. "There has been nothing official on the radio yet, but people are saying there is a surprise offensive going on up in the Da Nang area. Is that true, Jack?"

"We'll handle 'em, Mrs. Chen." Why did people think he knew anything about it?

"It is possible none of the girls will come today, Jack. Tomorrow is Chinese New Year, too, and besides, people are nervous. It's everywhere, this nervousness. Can't you feel it?"

"Naw; I'm not so hot at feelings."

Mrs. Chen regarded him silently for a moment. She would never forget how he had flown into Harry Scheldt's face to protect Ana. "I think you are," she replied firmly.

"Not me. How about a drink?" She accepted a tiny glass of crème de menthe. They toasted and drank.

"How is it with you and Ana, Jack?"

"Great, Mrs. Chen, just fine. You know, if she's not here by, oh, five, guess I'll go out to her place. I have an early plane to catch tomorrow."

"Ana is a very good girl, Jack. You won't find many like her. She comes of good family. They lost everything in forty-eight, when we had to flee China. They came here. You know the old joke about the contest, where first prize is one week in Philadelphia and second prize is two weeks in Philadelphia? Well, coming here for any Chinese is like two weeks in Philadelphia."

Jack chuckled. "You Chinese don't consider yourselves citizens of this country, do you?"

"We are citizens, many of us, since President Diem declared us so a few years ago. But you are right, every Chinese heart is really back in China, even if they've never seen it or, like Ana, were too young when they left to remember it very well. Ana has a Taiwanese passport, did you know that?" Jack shrugged. "You and her should have taken a vacation in Taipei. That would have been very nice for both of you."

Jack ordered another double.

"You are coming back here, aren't you, Jack?"

"Yeah! Sure. What's wrong, Mrs. Chen? Are you matchmaking or something here?"

Mrs. Chen smiled. "Yes, I am. You and Ana were made for each other. I see these girls of mine tossed aside so regularly by their American lovers. I think sometimes I am responsible and maybe we shouldn't have them in here at all. It's so sad."

"Hey! I told you, I'm comin' back! This is just home leave for me. I haven't been back to the States in three years. I got family, too, you know."

"Of course, Jack. Just don't hurt her, please. She really loves you. I've seen her other boyfriends, and she never reacted to any of them like she has to you."

The record ended. Some other customers crowded noisily up to the bar. Jack knew two of them. He was grateful for the interruption and joined them in several drinks.

"Man," exclaimed one of them after a while, "did you notice there's hardly any traffic in the streets this afternoon? I've never seen old Saigon so quiet."

"Well, tomorrow's Tet, asshole! The slopes're all home gettin' ready for the New Year," the other explained.

"No traffic in the streets?" Jack marveled. He had not noticed on the way over, but now that it had been mentioned, the traffic had been rather light. If anything, it should have been heavier than usual. This was his fourth Tet in Vietnam, and always before, even when the government had refused to lift the curfew, the marketplaces and streets had been thronged. "Hey, either of you heard anything about the VC breaking the truce up in the I Corps?" he asked suddenly.

"No. Whaddya you know about it?"

"Nothing, really, just rumors."

"You can never trust those Commies."

"I'll drink to that," Jack said, laughing, and toasted the others.

Soon the other two excused themselves. After they left, Jack judiciously moved to the opposite end of the bar so he wouldn't have to listen to any more of Mrs. Chen's talk about Ana. But he couldn't get Ana off his mind.

A month with her in Taiwan? What a possibility! Why didn't I think of that before? he asked himself. The more he thought about it, the more he realized that he really did not want to return to the States after all. If he were to be transferred out of Saigon when the leave was over, he could take Ana with him there.

No, he told himself, his orders had been cut, and he was scheduled to fly out tomorrow. He was primed to go; it was too late to change anything. Of course, he *could* change his plans, if he really *wanted* to. It would take a day or two, but tomorrow he could go out to headquarters and have them issue new orders, authorizing him leave in the Republic of China.

He had more than seven thousand dollars within his immediate reach. What a time he and Ana could have with all that money. People he knew who had been on Taiwan said it was a wonderful place.

How long would it take her to get ready? he wondered. Mrs. Chen had said she had a Taiwanese passport. Did that mean she was a citizen of the Republic of China? If so, she could leave tomorrow or on the first flight out of Tan Son Nhut. Maybe setting the trip up would take a few days more. So what? It had now been a week since the ambush, and nothing had happened. Maybe the heat was off. Anyway, who said the Vietnamese CIA was after him? Maybe the two who had ambushed him were nothing more than insignificant hoods trying to make themselves some quick money. If so, he was in the clear, thanks to Gaylord's shooting.

Jack was feeling very good. His powers of reasoning had never seemed better. Every detail around him was sharp and clear; even his sense of touch seemed enormously improved. He stroked the butt of the revolver at his side, and it felt good, alive, like a pet.

The next time Jack noticed, it was six o'clock and the place was crowded. But none of the girls had come to work.

"All U.S. troop units have been put on full alert!" someone shouted over the hubbub. The announcement was greeted with laughter, and men crowded to the bar and ordered more drinks. So the Tet truce really has been broken, Jack mused. So what? Tomorrow he was on his way to the States. Or Taiwan. Decisions, decisions, he reflected.

At nine he made a boozy farewell to Mrs. Chen and very carefully threaded his way through the tables to the door.

Once outside, the night air enfolded him like a wet blanket. He staggered and then carefully regained his balance. He looked to the end of the alley. Nothing was moving along Dong Khanh Boulevard. He congratulated himself on being able to see that far after all the whiskey he had drunk. With growing assurance, he walked the short distance to his jeep. He didn't bother to inspect it but climbed in, unlocked the chain, and threw it into the backseat, where it slammed to the floor with a great crash that echoed eerily in the quiet street. Jack looked around. Still nothing stirred. He shrugged and started the engine.

Once under way a sense of euphoria came over him. The breeze felt so good he was moved to sing an old song as he motored happily down the thoroughfare:

"Oh, my lover he was a logger, no man like him
    lives today:
 If you'd pour whiskey on it, he'd eat a bale of
hay."

A block behind followed the Vietnamese jeep.

"He's going to his girlfriend's," the gunman remarked.

"How do you know?"

"I know these Americans. Besides, where else could he be going at this hour?"

"Then we will have to kill them both," the driver said. The gunman checked his .45.

Master Sergeant Long was really a clerk, so he felt very awkward with a .45 slung around his waist, but General Ton had ordered him to check the area outside his villa. He knew how to load and prepare the automatic pistol for firing, but he had never actually shot such a weapon before. In the years he had been with General Ton, he had had no reason to carry a firearm, and he preferred it that way.

It was very quiet, too quiet. A moment before, he thought he had heard a shout from the nearest villa, about seventy-five yards from the general's. It belonged to a high-ranking government official. Long stood in the parking lot and listened. It was very dark out there. Something was wrong, the elderly sergeant could sense it. There had been these rumors all day long. . . .

Long shook his head. No use thinking about such things now, he would only frighten himself.

The lights along the walls around the general's home were bright enough close up, but they did not penetrate very far into the shadows. Long drew his pistol, jacked a round into the chamber, and set the safety. He knew he should complete the circuit of the walls, but he decided not to go any farther; the thought of walking around the other side of the property, where the grass was high, did not appeal to him at all just now.

He was stepping into the courtyard when an arm grabbed him around the head from behind and pulled his neck back cruelly, exposing his throat to the knife swiftly drawn across it. The pain was not as great as the surprise, Long noted as he crumpled to the ground. If this is death, he thought, it's not quite so bad. People were jumping over him, and someone reached down, grabbed him roughly, and dragged him out of the way. Very dimly and very far away, he could see the light shining in the general's study window. In his outstretched fingers he still firmly clutched the fully cocked and loaded pistol. Gradually the light went out.

General Ton was mixing himself a drink when the first Communist soldier burst into his study. Several others crowded in after and fanned out around the room, quickly encircling him with the muzzles of their automatic rifles. The general's hand froze in midair, tiny silver tongs suspending a single ice cube over his empty glass. He let the tongs fall, and the ice cube tinkled merrily in the bottom of the glass. He lowered the hand.

"Up! Up!" shouted a soldier, gesturing with the barrel of his rifle. The general raised his hands to the level of his shoulders.

Then came the report of a single pistol shot from somewhere in the house. It was followed immediately by a burst of automatic weapons fire. General Ton took an involuntary step forward.

"Back! Back!" the soldier ordered. Reluctantly, General Ton moved backward. His wife screamed his name, and he stepped forward again but stopped short before the gun barrels.

An officer entered the room. He ordered two of his men to tie the general's hands behind his back. Roughly, they forced his arms behind him and tied his hands tightly with a strip of telephone wire. General Ton winced as the wire cut painfully into his wrists. Blood trickled down his fingers and dripped onto the floor.

"I am Captain Sa of the Party Committee of the Two Hundred Forty-first Main Force Battalion, People's Liberation Army," the officer announced. "This is now a liberated area, and in a few moments a people's court will convene to try you, General Tran Ngoc Ton, for your crimes against the Vietnamese people."

"The trouble with you Marxists," General Ton said

calmly, "is that you are all insects. You have no souls. You fill the ears of the real Vietnamese people with lies and false hope. You and the Americans deserve each other, and you should be out swapping your sawdust for their bitter melons. But at least people can live on what the Americans sell them; nobody can swallow your stuff and live on it." Captain Sa instantly recognized the allusion to a Vietnamese folktale about two swindlers, one selling sawdust as rice bran, the other bitter melons as cucumbers. They met one day and duped each other.

"Take him away!" Sa commanded.

"Wait!" General Ton protested. "There was some shooting a few moments ago. Who—?"

"One of your servants was foolish enough to resist us. He was killed. Now take him into the courtyard."

The guards shoved General Ton roughly from the room and, once in the hallway outside, kicked and pummeled him to his knees. A rifle butt slammed into his head, and he collapsed onto his side. Two soldiers grabbed his legs, flipped him onto his stomach, and dragged him semi-conscious through the front door of his house and down a short flight of steps into the courtyard. His face thudded on the steps as his body bounced over them. A soldier kicked him onto his back while another threw water from the fishpond into his face to revive him.

General Ton felt himself yanked to his feet. He stood dazed, held erect by two Communist soldiers. His once gay Filipino shirt was stained with blood, dirt, and water, and blood welled from the side of his head; his lips were swelling and bloody from where his face had been dragged down the stairs. The officer ordered more water sloshed into his face.

The courtyard was jammed. To one side were his wife and children. His wife was kneeling, pleading for her family. Six of the general's personal staff, all enlisted men, had been herded into another group. They showed signs of rough treatment. Two were missing, the general noted through the fog that seemed to be engulfing him.

A hatful of water splashed into his face, and this had the salubrious effect of reviving him. He realized with perfect clarity what was going to happen to him, and with a desperate, sinking feeling, he also realized there was absolutely nothing he could do about it. He recalled a line from *Kieu* that perfectly described his predicament: "The ant's inside the cup—where can it crawl?" General Ton was now the ant. "I will die bravely," he muttered through his bruised lips, but no one was listening.

The political officer ordered his men to form the prisoners in a semicircle about the general and himself. Ton's head was clear now. He counted twelve enemy soldiers in the courtyard. Now, in the last minutes of his life, small details became very important. He observed the equipment the Communists were wearing and the condition of their uniforms; he noticed the reflection of the light from the windows of his home on the water in the pond; he gazed longingly at the gate to the parking lot, about thirty feet away. It stood wide open. To one side lay a dark shape.

General Ton's guards forced him to his knees. A soldier unsheathed a large machete. Planting both legs firmly, he took a position to the general's right; the political officer stood to his left, back to the gate. So I am to be beheaded, General Ton thought. Good! Disembowelment would have been hard to take. It was important to him that if he die now, he die with dignity. He glanced up at his executioner. The man's face was utterly impassive. "Do it quickly," Ton whispered to him, but the man showed no reaction.

"You will not die just yet," Captain Sa informed him. "First we must have a reading of the charges against you." Sa produced a typed sheet of paper and began to read. The charges started with the general's "betrayal" of the people in 1948, when he was sent to France to train at a military school for Indo-Chinese officers. The event had been planned far in advance, and the Communists had done their homework well. Captain Sa droned on, obviously enjoying the theater of the moment, impressed with himself and reveling in his own sense of power.

"Get it over with, you long-winded fool," Ton muttered.

"Silence!" Sa ordered. He glared down at his prisoner for a moment before continuing. How *young* he is, General Ton thought.

"You were a child when I was fighting with the French at Dien Bien Phu," General Ton said in a nearly normal voice. "You may kill me now, but you and all your men will die, also, and soon."

An exasperated Sa nodded to one of the men holding the general, and he drove his rifle butt into Ton's kidneys. His wife screamed, and the general coughed and retched in agony, tears of pain streaming down his cheeks. Calmly, Sa read on. It was a long list, but far too short for the general.

"For these crimes you are now sentenced to death!" Sa announced at last. "These people"—he gestured to the general's family and staff cowering under the muzzles of his men's guns—"have been called here to witness the execution of justice on a foul traitor." He turned to the man with the machete: "Do your duty, Private Binh."

"Happy New Year, you filthy chamberpot! May you drink Ho Chi Minh's piss for a thousand years!" General Ton shouted. The machete flashed upward.

Somewhere between weaving across Hong Bang Boulevard and pulling onto the sidewalk outside Ana's apartment building, Jack Kelley decided to propose to Ana Chin. He mapped it all out in his head as he drove along. He would give Ana the money as a sort of dowry gift. Then he would return to the States for a week, no more, just long enough for him to see to his financial affairs. They would rendezvous in Taiwan, where he would spend the rest of his leave. He would pull all the strings he could to get himself reassigned to the Military Assistance Advisory Group to the Republic of China, and if that didn't work, eventually he'd bring Ana to the States and they would get married there.

Jack leaped out of his jeep and stomped up the stairs to Ana's floor. While walking down the corridor, the thought occurred to him that she might not be home. No problem! He would wait for her there, right in the hallway, sleep outside her door until she came back. He knocked on her door, quietly at first. There was no answer. He pounded with all his might.

When the door opened at last, Jack was shocked to see Ana's condition. Her eyes were swollen and her hair disarrayed. She stared at Jack, who grinned back idiotically, a wad of bills clutched in one outstretched fist.

"Ana, baby, I'm going back to the States, and do I have news for you!" Jack brushed by the astonished woman and threw the money on the table, where it made a soft thud. Ana caught only the first part of Jack's sentence, and it struck her like a thunderbolt, confirming her worst fears and suspicions.

Jack helped himself to a beer and popped it open. He whirled dramatically, arms outstretched. "Ana, I'm going—"

Jack froze. While his back had been turned Ana had snatched a .32-caliber automatic from her dresser and now stood between him and the open doorway, clutching the gun with both hands. It pointed directly at him, and Ana's arm was rock steady. "Jack, I tell you, someday you hurt me? Now you no hurt me anymore!" Tears streamed down her face. She pulled the trigger.

The gun did not fire. Jack sucked his breath in. The weapon was still on safe. Jack let the bottle fall to the floor. It broke with a crash. Ana stared dumbfounded at the gun. Then she remembered how Jack had taught her to operate it and flicked the safety catch off.

"Ana!" Jack shouted.

The first soldier, his .45 at the ready, stepped through the door. Ana, suddenly aware of his movement behind her, swung around and, before she could stop to think the situation through, shot him between the eyes. The shot split the air with a loud *crack*! and the tiny shell casing tinkled merrily as it spun across the floor. Ana froze, gaping mindlessly at the corpse sprawling at her feet.

The second soldier jumped into the doorway, his pistol leveled at Ana. Jack saw him and reached for his own gun, but before he could yank it free, the soldier's head miraculously exploded in a spray of blood and brains as another gun roared outside in the hallway. The man spun half around and fell through the door onto the body of his dead comrade.

An eternity of ghastly silence passed before the old Chinese fishmonger stepped fastidiously over the two corpses. In one hand he carried an automatic pistol. After checking the corpses to make sure they were dead, he placed it under his shirt.

"I really do not like the Americans at all," he told Ana conversationally in Chinese, "but I like men like these" —he kicked one of the bodies gently—"even less. When I saw them in the street and then realized they were after your man there, I decided to act. It was very foolish of me, I know, to endanger our great offensive—many of my comrades are counting on my being here to guide them through this part of the city—but, your American is a good man, and that makes up for his being an American.

"Now take your boyfriend, get into his jeep, and flee, if you can. Soon many of my comrades will be here, and if they catch you, I will not be able to save you a second time. Besides, I'll do no more favors for my enemies."

The old man bowed formally in Jack's direction, stepped through the door, and closed it quietly.

Jack discovered that his heart was still beating. "What—who?" he gasped.

"That man"—Ana gestured after the old fishmonger with the pistol she was still holding—"said he is a Communist agent. He recognized these two and followed them here. He told me—he said—he could not let them kill you. He said we must leave now, many, many VC coming soon!" Ana began to cry. "I no *want* kill you, Jack, I no *want* kill anybody! But you say you leave me!"

Jack stepped across the room in two long strides and embraced Ana. "No, no, baby," he murmured, "you didn't let me finish! I won't leave you, Ana, not now, not ever. Now c'mon, let's get the *fuck* outta here!"

Jack opened another bottle of beer, which he badly needed, and Ana began to change her clothes.

"Wear something old. We have a lot of traveling to do tonight. Take your passport, all the money you got, and your jewelry. That's it, no more. We gotta travel light."

"But Jack, where we go? I kill policeman! They find me soon!"

"Those guys weren't cops," he snorted. "I don't know what they were, but they weren't cops. I got a friend who'll help us. But c'mon, c'mon! This place is goin' to turn into a war zone."

Jack finished his beer and opened another. Ana changed into a set of black pajamas and then stuffed her money and valuables into a large jute shopping bag. Jack peered cautiously out the window. The street was empty and frighteningly quiet.

"We go now, Jack?"

On the way out Jack scooped up one of the .45s. "Lock the door and throw the key away," he advised Ana. There was nobody in the hallway. Good.

Almost sober now, Jack carefully backed his jeep into the street and rapidly shifted into second gear.

"I'm gonna take you to General Ton's," Jack shouted. "I think he'll help us. If he can't, he'll find someone who will. I'll get you out of this, Ana, I promise."

Behind them a squad of heavily armed Viet Cong sappers was already cautiously trudging down the street under the guide of the old fishmonger. Within hours, the swift Allied reaction to the Tet offensive would pound the entire block into dust, and neither of the two assassins would ever be missed.

Like numerous other government officials, General Ton lived in an exclusive and isolated part of town in the Phu Tho Hoa area, north of the racetrack and near the Chi Hoa Prison. It was accessible from a small road that branched off Nguyen Van Thoai Boulevard. Jack turned onto this road, drove a little way down it, then stopped.

"Why stopping, Jack?"

"I don't know. It's too dark. There's a guardpost just a little ways ahead, but I don't see anyone there." They peered into the dark, but the jeep's headlights revealed no movement about the guardpost. Jack shut the lights off. This is too much like the ambush, he thought.

And then Jack Kelley got mad. He was sick and tired of running. He was finished with people playing around with him.

"You wait here, Ana. I'm goin' to check out the guards. Don't worry, they know who I am." He withdrew his revolver and cocked it. In his left hand he carried the .45.

The barbed-wire gate at the guardpost bunker was standing wide open. Suddenly a burst of automatic weapons fire racketed into the night from somewhere ahead. Jack hesitated to go inside the post. Sweat streamed down his cheeks. He was forcefully reminded of the events leading up to the ambush. Swallowing his fear, he stepped inside the bunker. He stood there quietly, listening to the steady thumping of his own heart. He could see nothing in the dark. He placed the .45 between his feet, shifted the revolver to his left hand, fished out his cigarette lighter, and struck a flame. Two men lay slumped against one wall, their slashed throats gaping obscenely in the flickering light.

Instantly Jack snuffed out the light, snatched up the automatic, and stumbled back outside.

"It's empty," he told Ana back at the jeep. "We can go on from here without any trouble, honey."

"But Jack, I hear big gun shooting!"

"Nothin' to worry about." Jack started the engine and let the jeep slowly roll forward.

Ana placed her hand on Jack's forearm. "Jack, I very scared! You think we die? Many VC come Saigon tonight."

"Yeah, honey, *beaucoup* VC around tonight. Maybe —maybe they kill us, I don't know."

"Jack, I live with you, I die with you, same to me; I *with* you, okay? I love you, Jack, I happy die with you tonight."

Jack looked at the half-moon of Ana's face in the dim light. "I—I love you, too, Ana. I came to your place tonight to ask you to marry me, but you didn't let me finish! We get through this and we'll be together forever, I swear it! Oh, Jesus, honey! I just remembered, I left the money back in your apartment on the table!"

"No, Jack, I have," Ana replied brightly, patting her shopping bag.

Jack laughed, and that eased the tension somewhat.

"Take this." He handed her the .45. "You shoot it the same way you shot the little gun, but this one is bigger and it'll kick hard, so hold tight. If you have to shoot it, just point it at the guy and squeeze the trigger. Okay?"

"I know, Jack," Ana said grimly as she took the heavy automatic in both hands.

The jeep's tires rolled softly over the laterite into General Ton's parking lot. The engine purred quietly in the still night air. Nothing stirred outside the villa's walls, but lights and people were visible in the courtyard.

"What's going on in there?" Jack whispered. Was the general having another of his parties? Over the hum of the engine Jack thought he could hear someone talking. He wondered what he should do.

Master Sergeant Long slowly became aware that he was still alive. He was very weak, though, and his throat burned and throbbed painfully where the knife had been hastily drawn across, but the blade had missed the jugulars.

Long lay still and silent in the grass by the gate. Gradually the dim shapes that clustered and wavered before his eyes became distinct, first those closest to him, then others farther away. General Ton knelt, his arms behind his back. A man stood reading from a paper, and another held a machete. General Ton shouted something, and the machete began to rise.

Long flicked off the safety of his pistol, took a breath, fixed the executioner's head in the V of the sights, and squeezed the trigger. The automatic exploded with a roar and jumped from his hand.

The flash of a pistol made up Jack's mind for him.

"Hold on!" he shouted at Ana, and slamming the gearshift into first, he gunned the jeep straight through the open gate and into the general's courtyard. The vehicle burst into the semicircle like a raging bull. Its bumper caught the political officer squarely in the middle of the back and flipped him neatly right over General Ton's head and into the faces of the two soldiers holding him. Jack slammed on the brakes, and the jeep slowed to a stop in a swirl of dust and gravel, only inches from General Ton's nose.

Ana found herself staring into the eyes of an astonished Viet Cong soldier. She shot him in the mouth. His front teeth disappeared. The bullet gouged its way up into his brain and out the back of his head.

Jack leaped from the jeep and shot the first soldier he saw. The man just stood and stared at him; angrily, Jack shouldered him out of his way and shot two more. The magnum jumped in his hand two more times. Jack was so close to his targets he fired at them on double action. He hit everyone he shot at. It was the first time he had ever fired his weapon.

The courtyard was pandemonium. General Ton's staff and family fell upon their captors with fists, fingernails, and feet. Screams and shots filled the air. Jack threw himself on one man who was firing his AK-47 wildly, knocked him to the ground, and began beating him with the butt of his revolver.

General Ton staggered to his feet and jumped on the political officer's face; he lay on the ground paralyzed from the waist down with a broken back. One of his guards recovered himself and knocked the general down again, giving Ana a clear shot. She leaned around the windshield and shot him squarely in the chest. General Ton's wife raked her fingernails over the face of the other guard while an aide strangled him.

Jack rose unsteadily to his feet and looked at the havoc around him. In one hand he clutched his magnum by the barrel; blood and hair covered the butt. He let it fall to the ground.

General Ton, standing with his hands still tied behind his back, issued orders for his men to collect all abandoned weapons. The general's cook, a corporal named Hoang, had produced a pistol from somewhere and walked about the courtyard, methodically shooting Communist soldiers and screaming, "Danger! There are snakes all over the place!" Someone took the pistol away from him.

The general's wife tried vainly to undo the telephone wire digging into her husband's wrists. Wincing with the pain, he called out to Jack, "Help me, will you?"

The wire was buried deeply into General Ton's wrists and slick with blood. Ana and the general's wife daubed at the blood with handkerchieves so Jack could see to unfasten the wire. The general ignored his pain as he issued orders in rapid fire to secure the perimeter of his villa. All kinds of weapons began appearing: an M-60 machine gun, M-79 grenade launchers, a box of fragmentation hand grenades, rifles, pistols, ammunition.

"I believe in being prepared," he told Jack over his shoulder. "Unfortunately, I should have ordered this done hours ago." Jack managed to undo the last strand of wire, and General Ton sighed his profound thanks. "I have no feeling in my fingers," he remarked as he tried to flex them, "but I believe I will recover. What are hands, compared to the head, eh?" He gestured at the machete that lay on the ground next to the body of his would-be executioner. A tiny hole in the middle of the man's forehead marked where Long's bullet had entered; a large mass of blood and brains clotted the back of his head.

"Kelley, my dear friend, Kelley, did God bring you here tonight? I owe you my honor, my life, and the lives of my men and my family. Such a large debt it is not possible to repay, but I will try."

Jack wiped the blood from his fingers on Ana's handkerchief. "Well, now that you mention it, General, there is one small favor," and he told him all about Ana Chin.

To Fight Aloud

IT WAS TWELVE-THIRTY A.M. ON JANUARY 31, 1968.

At first Sergeant Major Billy George Oates thought it had been the steady swish-swish-swish of the ceiling fan that had awakened him. The mosquito netting around his bed swayed gently in humid night air stirred by the slowly rotating fan. He lay there quietly. The room was nearly dark. Weak light filtered in from lights in the street three floors below.

There was somebody else in the room with him.

Out of the corner of his eye he could see the figure of a man standing just inside the door. Oates could not remember hearing the door open. The figure was dimly silhouetted in the weak light. It carried an AK-47 assault rifle at port arms. Oates recognized it as an AK-47 because of the banana-shaped clip jutting underneath and angling toward the muzzle.

Oates was completely alert now. He forced his mind to block out everything except the enemy standing in the doorway. Because of the way the nightstand was placed in relation to the bed, Oates would have to roll over on his right side to grab the pistol with his left hand. He regretted that he had not put the gun under the pillow. Even then, with death standing only a few feet away, he had to smile at the image of himself sleeping with a loaded automatic stuffed under his pillow.

Then he acted.

He swung his feet to the floor, and carrying the mosquito bar along with him, he lunged before the enemy soldier could swing the barrel of his rifle far enough around to fire directly at his target. The man managed to get off a short burst that smashed harmlessly into the ceiling, but by then Oates was all over him.

Oates knocked the man's legs from under him and threw him to the floor, then pinned him with his knees and sat on his heaving chest. As Oates fastened his big hands around his throat and squeezed, he could not see the soldier's mouth, only hear him gasping for air. He leaned forward, pressing his weight and all the strength of his upper body into the job of killing the man.

The soldier's neck was like rubber in his hands. Oates could feel the frenzied throbbing of the jugulars to either side of his thumbs. Then suddenly the cartilage in the man's throat broke. Blood welled from his nose and throat and spattered over Oates's hands. The dying man gurgled horribly, and his body jerked spasmodically. After a moment, it was over.

Oates was not aware at first that the lights had been turned on and the room was full of Americans in various states of undress. Someone tugged gently at his shoulder. "Hey, man," said a black wearing only underwear and rubber shower sandals, peering awestruck into Oates's face, "that mothafuck' *daid,* man!"

Slowly Oates's surroundings came back into focus. With sweat streaming down his face, he gasped for breath and flexed his arms. There was no feeling in his hands. He noticed, incongruously, a thin veneer of white dust covering everything—plaster gouged from the ceiling when the enemy soldier had fired his rifle. Someone had picked the weapon up from the corner where it had been kicked during the struggle and was hefting it.

"Jesus Christ," someone whispered, "he killed 'im with his *bare hands*!"

Oates tried to get to his feet, and half a dozen arms snaked out of the crowd to help. Someone patted him on the back, and another thrust a freshly opened can of cold beer at him. He drank it gratefully in one long swallow. The men cheered, and Oates was offered a second beer, which he gulped down like the first.

All these details were noted and remembered and became part of the legend that after that night was to spread throughout the army.

Oates looked down at the dead man and saw him for the first time. His eyes had bulged nearly out of their sockets, and his face was discoloring; flecks of blood and mucus stained his upper lip and chin. The man was dressed in black cotton peasant-style pajamas and sandals made from rubber tires. Around his waist was a belt with spare ammunition pouches and potato-masher-type hand grenades. Loaded for bear, Oates thought.

"All these slopes look like kids, don't they?" someone remarked. "Bastard's prob'ly thirty-five 'n' fought more battles than Audie Murphy."

Oates began stripping the dead body of its equipment. "Who's the senior man in this BEQ?" he asked. The dead soldier had been carrying a dozen clips of 7.62-mm ammo for the AK-47. "Who's the senior man here?" Oates asked again.

The men in the room looked at each other and shrugged. Oates stood up and took the AK-47 from the man who had recovered it. He slung the weapon over his shoulder. "How many of you men have weapons?" he asked. At first there was no response, and Oates had to repeat the question twice more before five men hesitantly raised their hands.

Oates searched the faces in the crowd and saw Aspby standing by the door, a big grin on his face. "Jim! C'mere," Oates ordered. Aspby pushed his way through the others. He started to congratulate Oates on his exploit, but the big man silenced him with a wave of his hand. This was no longer the man with whom Aspby had been drinking the night before.

"How many men live in this place?" Oates demanded.

"Christ, Goats, I never counted 'em. Maybe a hundred?"

"Hundred fifty-one swinging Richards. I'm the senior occupant of this building as of right now, and you will take orders from me. Is there a defense plan for this place?"

"Yeah," one of the blacks answered. "It say, 'When the bomb go off, bend way over, grab yo' ankles, 'n' kiss yo' ass good-bye!' " Several men laughed nervously.

"The CQ's got an M-fourteen rifle," someone said.

Oates sighed. "Okay, men, here it is. I'm Bill Oates, sergeant major of the Eighteenth Division. I came into town on business, and Aspby here was good enough to arrange this room for me in your"—here he hesitated slightly—" 'hotel.' So that's who I am and how I got in here. Now I plan to stay alive. How about the rest of you?"

The men stared silently at Oates. Fear appeared on some of the faces as they began to realize the import of a dead enemy soldier lying in the middle of a room in a U.S. Army BEQ facility in the heart of Saigon. That meant something was very seriously wrong.

"This guy meant business," Oates said, kicking the dead man's foot. "Where there's one, there's bound to be more. I think he was part of an assault force, and maybe he got separated from the main body. We'd better be ready to defend this place if his friends come looking for him."

An uneasy ripple seemed to go through the men at Oates's words. "We're going to form our own defense force and be ready to give this guy's buddies a warm welcome if they drop in. I want you men with weapons to go back to your rooms, get dressed, and meet me in the lobby in five minutes. The rest of you go through this building, every room, and wake everybody up and have 'em form in the lobby, right *now*."

Nobody moved.

To Aspby, Oates seemed to have grown larger during the last few moments. Now the sergeant major took a deep breath and his chest expanded, and Aspby had the wild notion that Oates was undergoing some strange metamorphosis right before his eyes.

"Men," Oates said softly, "you may never have been in deeper shit than you are right now. *Get moving*." Oates's words galvanized them, and they jostled with one another getting through the doorway. "Jim, get your own shit together and meet me in the lobby, ASAP. It looks like a long night, and I'll be needing you."

"Jesus, Goats, I knew you had it in you, but . . ." He gestured at the dead soldier on the floor.

"Never mind about that now, James." Oates stepped casually over the body and threw the AK on his bed. Aspby hesitated at the door. He could hear shouting and banging coming from different floors in the building as the occupants were rudely invited to rouse and join the war.

"Goats, we've come a long way since the days playin' cribbage at the Metropole, haven't we?"

"Not even halfway yet, Jim," Oates replied as he put his trousers on.

Only seventy-five men gathered in the lobby, twenty of them armed. Even so, the lobby was crowded. Oates posted two armed men at the door to watch the streets and gathered the rest of them as far back from the street as they could get.

It was one A.M. and deathly still outside. From the roof of the building some men had seen parachute flares drifting just beyond the The Nghe Canal a thousand yards away and large fires burning all around the city. They also reported seeing intermittent flashes at Tan Son Nhut, and from the description, Oates knew they were 122-mm rockets detonating at the airport.

"Somebody said there's a hundred men here, Jim," Oates said. "I only count seventy-five. Are you sure you got them all?"

"Sure. The missing men are either shacked up, working, maybe on leave, R and R, temporary duty somewhere else . . . who the fuck knows?"

Oates nodded. "Okay, you men, shut up!" he shouted. The hubbub gradually died. "Now listen up. The Tet cease-fire is broken, and the enemy's in town. For all we know we're right in the middle of it, or will be soon. I'm taking charge, and you'll all follow my orders."

A long burst of machine-gun fire rattled in the street just outside the doorway, and the crowd burst into pandemonium as men flung themselves behind whatever cover they could find in the lobby.

"At ease!" Oates screamed. "That was an M-sixty, one of ours! Now listen to me, you assholes, and get this into your goddamned fucking heads! We may be cut off in here. If you fuckers want to live through the rest of the night, shut the fuck up, calm down, and do what I tell you!"

The men quieted down. "Sergeant Aspby, here, is my deputy. You guys with guns, follow me up to the roof—not you two at the door there! You stay where you are. Keep a sharp lookout, but don't open fire on *anyone* unless they shoot at us first.

"Jim"—Oates turned to Aspby—"I want you to organize the support we need here. Set up an aid station somewhere protected from small arms and rocket fire. Get the lights out in the hallways and in the rooms. No lights anywhere, except in the aid station and my command post, which will be right here, at the receptionist's desk." Aspby nodded his understanding.

"Nobody's to leave his room unless I say so. The men who don't have weapons or other duties are to stay put and tell 'em not to come out, no matter what. If shooting starts, we don't want to be distracted by assholes running up and down the hallways in the dark.

"Pick some guys, have 'em go through every room

and confiscate all the dried and canned food and drinks. Take inventory of everything in the refrigerators and all the potable drinking water you can find in the building. Oh, if you find any first-aid stuff, grab it. Otherwise, have the medical team tear up bedsheets so we can use 'em for field dressings. If there's a firefight here, there's not a fuck of a lot we can do for serious wounds, but at least we can see nobody dies from bleeding all over the place."

"There's a big first-aid kit right behind the receptionist's desk," Aspby said.

"Good. Secure it. Who's on CQ here tonight?"

Aspby shook his head, and Oates shouted for the charge of quarters. A leathery old man in navy dungarees shuffled forward.

"Are *you* the CQ?" Oates asked.

"I got the watch, Chief," said the little man, thrusting his jaw forward aggressively. His face was a sea of wrinkles, and his voice sounded like a fog-horn.

"Well, who the *fuck* are you?" Oates demanded.

"Bo'sun's Mate Second Class Hargrove. But you kin call me 'Popeye.'"

"Okay, Popeye, you're in the army now."

Popeye snorted.

"That telephone working?" Oates asked him.

"Was earlier tonight, Chief."

"Well, get on the goddamned thing, Bo'sun, and find out what's happening. Try to get MACV. They must have some kind of reaction force available in this command. Anyway, keep the line open, it may be the only link we have to other Americans.

"Jim, get this place organized. You men"—Oates indicated the armed men standing nearby—"you come with me to the roof."

The roof of the John Houston was almost all patio surrounded by a wall about three feet high. The Houston itself was only six stories high, but there were a few other buildings in the vicinity that were taller. The nearest of these was the Hotel Victoria, about two blocks farther up Tran Hung Dao Boulevard, toward the center of Saigon. The night sky all around the city glowed with fires. Some of the parachute flares from The Nghe drifted directly overhead; their canopies were clearly outlined against the night sky. Farther out, beyond the city, tracers spurted back and forth between American aircraft and enemy ground forces. There was a lot of ground fire, Oates saw, and that was very bad. The Communists' tracers were green, the Americans' orange.

The eighteen men who had come up to the roof with Oates milled around, waiting for orders. Between them they had a motley collection of firearms. Oates's AK-47 was the most potent of the armory, followed by the CQ's M-14, an old M-1 Garand, several semiautomatic carbines, and a mixture of .45-caliber pistols and .38 revolvers. One man had a 12-gauge military riot gun loaded with double-aught buckshot. Another had four ancient MK-2 "pineapple" hand grenades, which, he told Oates, he'd gotten from a Vietnamese soldier. Gingerly, Oates took two and placed one in each lower-front pocket of his jungle fatigue jacket.

The Houston, which fronted Tran Hung Dao Boulevard, was bordered on one side by a narrow street that ran in the direction of the The Nghe Canal. The other two sides abutted other buildings, none of them taller than the Houston itself. That was good, because it would give them a clear field of fire if the VC tried to get at them by coming over the rooftops.

Because of the activity in the direction of the canal, Oates positioned the man with the M-1 and several others with carbines behind the wall in that direction. He put six men on the roof, all armed with weapons that had some range. He singled out one, a burly six-footer with a short haircut.

"Who're you?"

"Sergeant James Gibson, USMC."

"What the hell's a marine doing in this place?"

"I'm a classified documents clerk at MACV headquarters, sir," the marine answered.

"Okay," Oates said with a sigh, "you're in charge up here, Gibson. Keep your eye on that side street down there, but don't forget about the rooftops. Don't fire unless you're fired on first, and make sure your shots count. You see anything you can't figure out, have someone come down and get me or Aspby in the lobby. When I get these others posted, I'll have a man with an M-fourteen come up here to give you more firepower."

Oates turned to the rest of his men. "You guys come along with me."

"Hey," called a voice from the stairway, "what the hell's going on here, anyway?"

A tall thin man wearing a cotton bathrobe emerged from the stairwell and walked toward the group. He was wearing rubber shower shoes that slapped incongruously against the tiles. "I'm Master Sergeant Sykes, the senior man in this BEQ, and I want to know what the hell's going on up here." He stopped short and hesitated when he saw that the men were all armed.

"Where've you been, Sergeant? We've been looking all over for you," Oates said.

"I been in my room. Jesus Christ, it's after one A.M.! What the hell's going on here? Who are *you*?"

Oates wondered how this man could possibly have slept through all the commotion or avoided being disturbed by the men he'd sent through the building to rouse everyone. He suspected that the tall sergeant had been hiding in his room.

"We're under attack," Oates told him.

"By who?" the master sergeant asked incredulously.

"By the fucking Girl Scouts of America."

"Bullshit!"

"Sarge, I killed one of 'em in my room, not more than half an hour ago. Where you been?"

"Are you assigned quarters in this facility?" the master sergeant asked, his eyes narrowing suspiciously.

"Sarge, get out of my way," Oates told him.

"What the fuck do you mean, ordering me around?" the sergeant blustered. "Who the fuck are you, and get the fuck offa my roof!" he shouted. He turned to the other men and made shooing motions with his arms. "Go on! Git! Git!"

Oates simply ignored the man. "You other men, come with me. Gibson, remember what I told you." The marine nodded and began placing his men around the rooftop. When Oates made to move toward the stairway, Sykes, emboldened by his own shouting and infuriated that nobody was listening to him, stepped in front of the sergeant major.

"I'm confiscating those weapons," Sykes announced.

"What?" Oates asked.

"Gimme those weapons! C'mon, gimme! MACV regulations specifically forbid the carrying of firearms within the limits of metropolitan Saigon except for those personnel assigned courier or guard duty. I'm not aware of any alert, you guys aren't guards, and I won't have a bunch of armed drunks running around my BEQ. Now gimme those guns or I'll call the MPs." More machine-gun fire echoed from the direction of the canal, but Sykes was oblivious to everything except the tableau on the rooftop.

Oates unslung his AK-47 and slammed the butt into Skyes's solar plexus. The tall sergeant crumpled to the tiles, retching and gasping. Oates gripped him with one hand and lifted him up. "You go back to your room, Sergeant Sykes, and don't bother us anymore," he said softly. Released, Sykes staggered toward the stairs and was never heard from again.

Oates stationed two men with revolvers at either end of the second-floor outside hallway and instructed them to cover the railings and the stairways and to keep their heads down. "Under no circumstances," he warned them, "are you to look over those railings into the street. But if anyone comes over them, don't ask questions. Just kill him."

By the time he returned to the lobby, the lights were out on all the floors and no one was moving in the hallways. A Coleman lantern burning brightly in a little room behind the receptionist's desk was the only light in the whole building. Several armloads of supplies and food lay heaped in one corner, by the stairs—the result of Aspby's inventory.

High up near the lobby ceiling were two small windows that looked out on the side street. There was no glass in them, but they were inset with heavy wire mesh fixed into wooden frames. Oates grabbed two men and told them to rip the mesh out. "We can use those windows to cover the street. They'll make good firing points."

"But we'll have to stand on chairs, to get high enough to see through 'em," one of the men protested.

"Then get chairs," Oates told him.

"But who ever heard of fighting a battle standing on a chair?"

Oates snorted. "Okay. Go get yourself a mop handle, ram it about two feet up your ass, and you can fight the fucking war as a fucking popsicle."

Without a further word, the two set about tearing out the wire mesh.

Oates next checked the men he had left at the front door. They had pulled the steel shutters partway closed and were crouching behind them. One had an M-1 carbine, and the other was carrying a 9-mm Madsen M-46 submachine gun. Oates decided not to ask the man where he'd gotten it.

"You men stay alert out here, and if anything moves, anything at all, you call for me or Aspby. Keep outta sight." He clapped the man with the Madsen on the shoulder and trotted back to the desk, where Aspby and several others were sorting through cans and boxes of food.

"Chief, I got the MACV duty officer on the line," Popeye whispered.

Oates grabbed the telephone. "Sergeant Major Oates here. Who's this?"

"Lieutenant Colonel Grose, MACV duty officer. What's your situation?"

"One enemy KIA, sir. Seventy-five present, twenty armed. No activity yet in this area."

"Good. Top, all hell's broke loose. The VC have busted the Tet truce wide open. I can't tell you much, except they're all over town. We got a report of a ground attack at Tan Son Nhut, some sort of activity around the U.S. embassy, a big firefight out along Plantation Road. I can't help you now, and I think we might just be getting the shit kicked out of us. Try to keep your heads down. I'll try to get help to you when—"

The line went dead. Oates stared at the receiver for a moment. "Help's on the way," he lied to the others. "They know we're here, and they're sending help." He handed the now useless telephone receiver back to Popeye. "Popeye, can you use that M-fourteen you've got there?"

"Does a bear shit in the woods?" Popeye responded. Oates noticed his hairy forearms were covered with enormous tattoos of naked women, sea serpents, and mermaids. "Good. Get up on the roof. There's a marine named Gibson in charge up there. Back him up. And yeah, I think I left the guy with the shotgun up there by mistake. Have him come down here, pronto."

Popeye gathered up his weapon and some spare clips and slipped quietly toward the stairs. Oates realized for the first time that the building had no elevator. That meant someone would have to be found who could run up and down six flights of stairs all night long without collapsing. What he needed was a runner. His eye fell on a young man, well muscled, helping Aspby sort through the supplies.

"Hey, you with the build, come over here," Oates called shortly. "Who are you?"

"Airman Paul Buczkowski, sir. I'm a clerk in the MACV Information Office."

"Okay. You in good enough shape to run up and down these goddammed stairs for me, Paul?"

"Yessir!"

"Good. Keep with me. When I need someone or

something, you carry the word, got it?" Buczkowski nodded. "Jim, how're you doin' over there?"

"Fine," Aspby answered. "We've got enough canned and dried food to feed us for a while. I don't know what's in the refrigerators yet, but probably some meat and fresh vegetables. We've got charcoal braziers, lighter fluid, everything we need for a barbecue."

"How much drinking water?"

"Maybe a hundred gallons in all."

"The tapwater still running?"

"Yeah, sure, but it's not safe to drink, Goats."

"We may need it to put out fires. If the VC do their jobs properly, count on 'em knocking out the utilities anytime soon."

"I found two guys who claim to be medics," Aspby volunteered proudly. "They've set up an aid station of sorts back in the mamasans' laundry room, behind the staircase there."

"Good. Paul, you go back in there and then up the roof. Show yourself to every man on the defense force. Tell 'em who you are and what you'll be doing. Take this with you." Oates unbuckled his .45 and gave it to Paul. "Can you use one of these?" he asked the young airman.

"Sure, I'm quite a good shot with one of these things." Buczkowski flicked off the safety, ejected the clip, and inspected the chamber carefully, catching the round snuggled there in the palm of his hand as he eased back the slide experimentally. Deftly he reinserted the unused round into the clip, slammed the clip home in the butt of the pistol, jacked the round back into the chamber, and put the weapon back on safe. He adjusted the pistol belt a few notches and put it around his waist.

Oates noticed Aspby carrying a handgun in a shoulder holster. "What've you got there, James?"

"Browning nine–millimeter."

"Goddamn, Jim, I'll be damned if I can figure where your commandos get all these peashooters."

"Jack Kelley, mostly. Least, that's where I got mine."

"Jack Kelley! I haven't heard that name in years. What's he doing these days?"

"Well, you know Jack. Wheeling and dealing. But mostly selling illegal firearms to everybody in Saigon. Maybe it's a good thing he got around to me, huh?"

Oates laughed. "Jack fucking Kelley! Well, I wish he was with us tonight, Jim."

"Lotta things I wish we had tonight, Goats. Smoke?" Oates took a cigarette from Aspby, and they both lighted up. "What's the real score, Goats?"

Oates hesitated. "There's some bad shit up."

"What's our chances, Goats?"

"Oh, probably somewhere between shit and syphilis. If we're up against some real VC main force units, they'll be armed to the teeth. That boy I killed up in my room was ready to do some serious fighting. How do you think these guys here would stand up to a whole company of men like that one?"

Aspby swallowed hard but made no reply.

"But MACV knows we're here, and I doubt the VC'll waste any valuable manpower or time on rear-echelon freaks like this."

"Sergeant Major, you'd better come over here," one of the men at the door called softly.

A jeep was coming slowly down Tran Hung Dao from the direction of Cholon. Oates recognized it as a military police jeep, with its windshield folded down and sandbagged. Its lights were off. Two MPs rode in it, one sitting behind an M-60 machine gun. "Jesus, MPs!" one of the men lying next to Oates whispered, relieved. "Let's flag 'em down."

Oates placed a restraining hand on the man's shoulder. "Jim, get me a flashlight." Oates whispered to the men beside him, "It's dark, those MPs are looking for trouble, and you don't want to go running into the street before they know who you are." Aspby produced the flashlight and Oates trained it on the jeep. He flicked it on and off several times. In response, the jeep stopped in the middle of the street, and one of the MPs directed a brilliant floodlight onto the front of the Houston.

"We're Americans," Oates called out. "What's the situation?"

At first there was no reply. The men crouching behind the doors could hear static-laden conversations blaring into the darkened street from the jeep's two-way radio. "Charlie's all over the fuckin' place," one of the MPs shouted back. "Keep buttoned up 'til daylight. We're goin' up to MACV Two Compound, to check out the Koreans." The jeep began moving slowly down the street again.

"Better keep that radio down," Oates warned, but the MPs did not hear him.

"Jesus, I forgot about that!" Aspby exclaimed. "The ROKs're just up the street, in the old MACV Compound! I bet they got *beaucoup* firepower up there! Goats, why don't we just bail out of here and pile into their compound for safety?"

"Just cool it, Jim," Oates answered. The jeep disappeared up the street, hidden by the profile of the building next up from the Houston. Suddenly the flash and bang of a rocket-propelled grenade erupted in the street outside.

"RPG!" Oates shouted. "Jim, come with me! You two, cover us!" Oates darted out the door and ran, half crouching, to the opposite corner. He threw himself flat in a doorway and peered around the edge of the building, up Tran Hung Dao. Aspby threw himself down beside him. The doorway was deep and well protected and offered a good view in three directions.

The jeep lay on its side, surrounded by a pool of burning gasoline. Already the heat was causing the M-60 ammunition to explode. A figure swathed in flame staggered up from behind the jeep, took a few faltering steps down the street, and collapsed inside a widening circle of burning fuel.

"I don't think we're goin' to be doin' much running back and forth between here and the Koreans," Oates said dryly. Aspby's face had gone white and drawn, and he stared, fascinated by the man roasting in the street.

"C'mon, Jim. C'mon! Back to the Houston. We can't do anything here."

"But the MPs—?"

"They're dead. Follow me, and run like hell."

No shots followed them as they dashed back into the hotel building. The other men were standing inside, well back from the street, nervously fingering their weapons.

"You two"—Oates pointed to the man with the carbine and another, the one with the submachine gun—"you get across that street to the doorway we just came from. I want you to lie low in there, check out the street in both directions, and if anybody comes at us from up that side street, give us a nice crossfire."

"How do we let you know if we see anything?" one of the men asked.

"I'll be watching. If you have a message, gimme hand signals, whistle, throw a rock, but no shouting. You keep one eye on this doorway all the time. I'm worried about the VC coming up this side street."

"But who fired the RPG?" the other man wanted to know.

"Don't worry about him. If he'd spotted us, you can bet that round would've landed in here." Oates hoped he sounded confident because he was *very* worried about the enemy soldier who had fired the rocket launcher. Reluctantly, the two men scuttled off across the street to take up positions in the doorway there. Black smoke wafted down the street from the burning jeep, and the smell of roasting human flesh filled the air.

Buczkowski and the shotgunner came up to him. The young airman was shaking with fear; the shotgunner, a much older man, was also visibly shaken and perspiring profusely.

"Gibson says he sees someone comin' up the side street!" Buczkowski whispered.

Aspby's reaction to the news was a powerful urge to throw up. "Let's take a look," Oates said. He went into a crouch and waddled through the doorway. Outside, he stretched himself full length along the pavement and peered over the sandbags. At first he could see nothing. Then dim figures became visible, picking their way slowly along the narrow street, staying very close to the tightly shuttered storefronts along the way. Oates could not tell if they were friendly or enemy.

Oates scuttled backward into the Houston and stood up just inside the doorway so the men across the street could see him. In the dim light he could see them, squatting in their doorway, looking in his direction. He made frantic hand signals toward the approaching figures. They nodded that they understood him.

If it was the enemy, he had them in a three-way cross fire. If he could stop them in the side street, before they had a chance to get into the main boulevard and debouch, he could get enough to make the survivors withdraw. But he had to get them while they were still bottled up and whittle them down very quickly. The idea of just lying low and letting them go by without firing never occurred to him.

"How many of them did you see, Paul?" Oates asked. Buczkowski was crying with fear, and the other men were on the verge of throwing down their weapons and running away.

"Ab—about twenty, I think. I did—didn't ac-actually c-count them."

"You aren't going to let me down now, are you, Paul?" Oates demanded.

"N-no, sir!"

"Fine. Run back to the roof. Tell Gibson to line his men up along the street side but to keep under cover. That's important. Tell him not to open fire 'til I do. Then come back down here. Got that? Repeat it to me." Buczkowski repeated the message, haltingly at first and then more smoothly. "Good, Paul. Take off." Buczkowski covered the first flight of sixteen stairs in three enormous bounds.

Oates's calmness was beginning to have an effect on

the others. "I'll fire first, with my AK. You guys back me up. The guys across the street'll join in. We'll get them in a cross fire and kill pointmen and a few others. That should stop 'em.

"You men at the windows, brace yourselves against the sills as best you can and fire at the targets closest to you."

The Coleman lantern hissed behind the receptionist's desk. "Cut that light off!' someone whispered, and the lobby was plunged into darkness.

The front of the John Houston was barricaded with fifty-five-gallon sand-filled oil drums. A double row of sandbags stacked high on either side of the doorway itself gave additional cover. Oates still was worried about that RPG. If the VC could get only one 40-mm antitank round into the lobby, it would be all over. He had to hope the enemy probe was poorly coordinated. Maybe the troops were lost and just feeling their way around, and the man with the RPG was not part of the column now approaching his position.

Oates wriggled behind one of the drums. The figures were much closer now, only about thirty yards away, coming up both sides of the street. Oates knew them by their weapons. It was the enemy.

"Where the *fuck* are the military police when you need 'em?" he whispered.

Gallanter I Know

"**T**HEY'RE COMING IN! HELP ME!" THE VOICE CRACK-led over the military police radio. The MP sergeant sitting in the jeep parked along a side street just off Tu Do looked at his partner and then checked his watch. It was 0248.

"That was from the embassy, Sarge," his partner observed.

"Yeah. Guess we'd better get on over there and check it out, huh? Damn, I was countin' on this bein' a quiet night."

"Well, not so 'quiet'"—the driver laughed—"with no curfew, this bein' Tet and all, those raunchy GIs raising hell up there." He nodded toward the hotel across the street. It was a well-known institution that catered to Americans, and tonight, in honor of the new year holiday, a noisy party was in progress in the rooftop garden.

The pair had parked opposite the hotel only a few minutes before, and they had been debating the possibility of "checking" the place out. They were more curious than anything else and were suffering from a long tour of duty and a feeling of being left out of the fun everybody else seemed to be having.

"Maybe after we're off duty we can come back down here and have a beer with the boys," the sergeant suggested as his partner started the jeep engine.

They turned left on Tu Do and picked up speed in the direction of the Saigon Cathedral. The driver skirted the northwest side of JFK Square, drove past the Post, Telephone, and Telegraph Building, across Nguyen Hau Street, and onto Dai Lo Thong Nhut or "Unification Boulevard." To his left, south, was the Vietnam Presidental Palace, "Independence Palace."

He turned right and drove across Hai Ba Trung Street, named for the two Trung sisters who died fighting a Chinese invasion army in the year A.D. 43. The American embassy loomed on their left. Straight ahead, north, but not yet visible in the early-morning darkness, were the Saigon zoo and botanical gardens. To the right was a Vietnamese apartment building and a bit farther down Thong Nhut, on the corner of Mac Dinh Chi, the British embassy.

This was the new U.S. embassy, opened in September 1967 at a reported cost of $2.6 million. Construction had started on the new chancery shortly after the old one had been heavily damaged in a terrorist bombing in March 1965, that took twenty-two lives. The new building was a six-story structure fitted with shatter-proof Plexiglas windows to guard against fragmentation in the event of another explosion. Many of the embassy personnel in the old embassy building had been cut by flying glass in the explosion—a car bomb, detonated in the street outside during broad daylight.

A terra-cotta sunscreen covering the front of the chancery was intended to double as a "blast shield" in the event of another attack.

What was loosely called the American Embassy Compound actually consisted of two separate compounds: the main one, with the chancery and its outbuildings, and Norodom Compound, just to the south, which housed the consular buildings. The two areas shared a common wall and were joined by a steel gate, which that night was securely locked. Both compounds were surrounded by an eight-foot-high masonry wall, and the thick metal street gates were bolted and secured by heavy padlocks.

Just to the south of Norodom Compound, and bordering Hai Ba Trung Street, was the French embassy.

The first thing the driver noticed was that there were no Vietnamese policemen on duty at the guard kiosk near the main gate. "Uh-oh, something fishy here," he muttered. A bit farther down the street, near the Mac Dinh Chi side of the embassy compound, what looked like debris littered the sidewalk.

"Stop here," the sergeant ordered as they drew abreast of the main gate. "You're right, this don't look so good," he muttered. For the first time since the plea for help had came in over the radio, both men were beginning to feel nervous. The sergeant got out of the jeep, and he had taken only one step toward the rear of the vehicle when a sniper bullet fired from the apartment building struck him in the back. He spun around, staggered toward the jeep, and collapsed.

"Take cover!" shouted an American voice from somewhere near the Norodom Compound gate. The driver ignored the warning, jumped out of the vehicle, and ran around the front end. His sergeant lay sprawled on the other side of the jeep. He bent over and examined him. His own breath caught sharply when he discovered the sergeant was no longer breathing. I've got to get help, he thought, and reached for the radio microphone inside the jeep. A burst of automatic weapons fire from the apartment building struck him in the back and head. He slumped dead across the passenger seat.

"Sarge! Sarge! Get up, get up!" the charge of quarters shouted in Dan Vinson's ear. Vinson unglued his eyes and looked at his watch. It was shortly past 0300. He felt he had only just drifted off to sleep. "What's up?" he slurred.

"The world's on fire, Sarge, and they need you to piss on the flames," the CQ answered.

"Who do you think I am, Lemuel Gulliver?" he asked sarcastically. Then: "Get the others." Vinson swung his feet to the floor. Staff Sergeant Daniel Vinson, 527th Military Police Company, was the NCO in charge of an eleven-man reaction team billeted at the International BEQ, about a mile and a half up Tran Hung Dao Boulevard from the John Houston.

Vinson slipped quickly into his fatigues, buckled on his .45, snatched his rifle and flak jacket. He hesitated a moment and then stuffed a snub-nosed .38 revolver inside the top of his left boot. The revolver was strictly unauthorized, but it represented a kind of insurance the army couldn't give him. Back down in the lobby, First Lieutenant Frank Radich, the officer in charge of the reaction force, paced impatiently back and forth.

"Dan," he called as Vinson came in, "I've just been talking to the battalion commander. The whole city's going up in smoke. Looks like VC inside the American embassy itself, fer chrissakes."

Vinson whistled softly. "So the Tet 'alert' bullshit was for real after all!"

"Yeah. But as many of these goddammed false alarms we've had so far, I never thought it would come like this. You know, Dan, as of right fucking now we're the *only* U.S. fighting unit inside the whole city of Saigon." The two stared at each other in wide-eyed amazement.

The rest of the men began filtering into the lobby. "Okay, fellas, let's saddle up!" Radich shouted. Outside, they piled into a deuce and a half, the lieutenant up front and Vinson on the tailgate in back. The engine sounded very loud in the quiet night. As they pulled away from the BEQ, Vinson glanced again at his watch. It was now 0317 hours.

The empty streets were menacing. Vinson spent much of his time on Saigon's nighttime streets, and he'd never seen them so quiet before. From different places, but hard to pinpoint, came the sound of gunfire. This is really "it," Vinson thought. He ordered his men to lock and load their weapons.

It took them only a few minutes to drive the mile and a half from the International BEQ to JFK Square. The lieutenant dismounted the men and divided them into two teams. He took one and Vinson the other, and they proceeded cautiously down both sides of Thong Nhut Boulevard. Vinson checked his watch again. It was now 0324. Someone wondered aloud where the Vietnamese police were, and another man laughed derisively.

Vinson knew something was dreadfully wrong as they filed down the wide boulevard. A military police jeep stood unattended right in the middle of the street, opposite the main gate. Judging by the way it was tilted down at the right-front end, Vinson guessed that tire was flat. An excrescence of dark shadow at the right side of the jeep caused a nasty ball of cold fear to form in the pit of his stomach.

"Get down!" Vinson hissed to the three men behind him. They doubled over and scuttled forward. The sergeant's intuition saved their lives, because a burst of automatic weapons fire suddenly lanced over their backs and splatted harmlessly into the middle of the road.

Vinson threw himself into the gutter. Momentarily, the sound of rifle fire was drowned in the clatter of the men hurling themselves behind cover. Vinson knew the fire had come from somewhere on his right, but he hadn't actually seen it himself.

"Dan!" Radich shouted from across the boulevard. "They're over there! Over there!" Vinson turned his head slightly. The lieutenant was gesturing frantically toward a large building set back a little distance from the street. When he looked over in that direction, he could see the winking of automatic rifles. Holy Jesus, he thought, they're shooting at *me*!

"Take your men and get over there!" Radich shouted. Although no one had given any order to do so, several men were busy returning fire with their M-16s, and that had the good effect of abating the enemy shooting momentarily. "Hugh, Pete, give us covering fire," Vinson shouted to two of his men. He pounded the third man on the back, and they both ran down Thong Nhut, keeping close to the cover along the western side of the street. They ran to the right, along a side street that entered the main boulevard opposite the Norodom Compound gate. The shooting from both sides was very intense now, but none of it seemed to be coming their way.

They crouched behind a chest-high masonry wall to catch their breath and figure out what to do next.

"Whaddya see, Jerry?" Vinson panted.

"I think they're shooting from the third or fourth floor, Sarge." There was a burst of shots at that precise moment. "Third floor, Sarge! Third floor for sure!"

Vinson peered nervously over the wall. The building ran roughly north to south, at an acute angle to Thong Nhut. It was six or seven stories high, set back some distance from the main street. Apparently they were approaching it from the rear. Each floor had a balcony open to the outside that ran the whole length of the building. The shooting was coming from the end closest to the U.S. embassy, where the field of fire covering the embassy was least obstructed.

"What's that street that runs parallel to that place?" Vinson asked, nodding his head toward their right.

Jerry hesitated. "Nguyen Du, I think. Yeah, the place fronts on Nguyen Du. I think it's an apartment building."

Vinson nodded. "Friendly fuckin' residents. Okay. We gotta go in fast, from this end. We'll find the stairway and go up single file. Come out into the hallways shooting. Looks to me like only two of 'em. Stay close behind me, buddy."

They scaled the wall, ran behind a small villa and across a lawn to the nearest end of the apartment building. The stairway was open, and Vinson took the steps two at a time, running swiftly and lightly, his heart in his throat. He could hear Jerry's loud breathing close behind. He paused on the third-floor landing. At that moment a long burst from an AK-47, the explosions reverberating painfully inside the narrow stairwell, told him they had the right floor.

Vinson motioned for Jerry to stay close behind him. Up to this point Vinson had not yet fired his weapon. I've got 'em, he exulted silently, stepped onto the balcony, and emptied a full clip on automatic fire into the shadows at the opposite end of the building. He dropped to one knee and, bracing himself against the wall, reloaded, slamming the clip home and jacking a round into the chamber in two swift motions.

Jerry leaned out from behind him and emptied his own weapon. He ducked back behind the wall to reload, and at that moment someone came charging out of the shadows, an AK-47 blazing in his hands. Vinson fired instinctively, almost before he was even aware that the man was coming at him. He did not bother to aim. Great white muzzle flashes split the darkness as both men's weapons roared. Bullets gouged holes everywhere, shattering tile, brick, and wood. Vinson was only vaguely aware of something slicing open the right side of his face; his helmet spun off his head and slammed with a hollow *thunk* to the floor; he could sense more than feel the bullets twitching through his clothing. He was riding a roller coaster high above the earth, thousands of bright flash bulbs and swirling lights exploding before him; he was awash in a roar of sound, flames from a blast furnace licked at his face.

And then it was dark again and unearthly quiet. Vinson sank onto his haunches and let out his breath in a groaning sob. He realized with surprise that he'd been holding it since the instant he'd stepped onto the balcony and opened fire. He leaned against the wall and extended his left leg before him. His holstered .45 pressed painfully into his right thigh.

There was a movement from the man who lay sprawled on the floor a few feet beyond where Vinson slumped. Jerry loosed a burst into him. Vinson could clearly see the bullets striking the man's body. Jerry ejected the clip and fumbled for another. Amazing how quickly these M-16s eat up ammo when you're in a hurry, Vinson thought. Realizing then that he was out of ammunition himself, he bent forward and snatched the .38 out of his boot.

A figure stepped out of the apartment just in front of where Vinson sat. Slowly, it turned and extended an arm accusingly at him. Vinson shot it six times full in the chest. In the muzzle flashes he saw that it was a young woman. Even before her body hit the floor, he knew he'd just shot one of the residents by mistake.

"Holy Jesus, holy Jesus," Jerry whispered. He stepped past Vinson and bent over the girl's body. When he straightened up, he turned and showed Vinson the Soviet Tokarev TT33 pistol she would have emptied into the sergeant's face if he had not shot her first.

"Whew, Sarge, lookit that! You probably saved the both of us! That was some fine, fine shooting."

"Don't thank me, Jerry, thank that asshole Jack Kelley. He sold me the fuckin' thirty-eight for fifty bucks."

A Wave-Tossed Fern

"**Q**UICKLY! QUICKLY! WE'RE LATE AS IT IS," LIEN shouted over her shoulder as she gathered up Tan and her baggage. Miss Thuyet, Lien's friend and traveling companion for the long trip to Nha Trang, scrambled out of the taxi behind her.

"I told you we should have left fifteen minutes earlier!" Thuyet shouted back. Miss Thuyet would have been a beautiful young woman except for the severe scarring of her face, the result of a childhood bout with smallpox. Like Lien, she had come to Saigon from Nha Trang to seek her fortune in the capital city, but unlike her friend, she had not been lucky enough to find an American to support her. So Miss Thuyet pushed drinks at Le Cabanon and took men home with her when they would have her. Lien had advanced her the money for the trip.

The women shuffled down the street toward the bus station, a wide spot along Pham Ngu Lao where it emerges at the Cho Thai Binh, the Saigon Central Market. The sun was not quite up yet, but nevertheless perspiration was already beginning to stain the armpits and backs of the long-sleeve cotton blouses they were wearing. On her right hip Lien carried her fifteen-month-old son, still half-asleep. In her right hand, she half carried, half dragged a suitcase. Over her right shoulder hung a jute shopping bag. Thuyet was encumbered with two suitcases and two huge shopping bags, one stuffed with provisions for the trip.

Both women were dressed like peasants—rubber sandals, loose pantaloons, and loose cotton blouses. The night before, Lien had chuckled aloud that nobody would suspect her of being an American's woman, dressed that way and traveling on the bus, among the hoi polloi.

"But Tan looks like an American child," Miss Thuyet pointed out brightly. Indeed he did, with his white skin and distinctly Occidental nose. But every Vietnamese woman who saw the child adored him, despite the fact that the Vietnamese in general despised Eurasians. Tan had his mother's black eyes, cheekbones, and jawline, but his nose was Aspby's, as were his ears, which stuck out prominently from the sides of his head; he also had his father's fine, silky brown hair.

Lien regarded her sleeping baby and smiled. "I will invent some story, if anyone becomes too nosey. I will claim to be his nursemaid and say that his father was recently transferred by the army to Nha Trang and that I am taking this baby there to join his parents."

"No one will ever believe such a cockamamie story. If the VC stop us, they will kill him."

Lien snorted. Thuyet, who lived a hard life, was sometimes too honest for her own good. "There is a truce for the New Year, did you hear about it?" Lien said, "Besides, I doubt the VC would waste their time on one small child. In any event, I shall put my trust in heaven, the protector of women and children."

More than a dozen buses lined the curb, and the street was awash in a sea of happy faces as people busily crowded aboard while others hawked sundry delicacies for the consumption of the travelers.

"Our bus is Dai Nam number fifty-four," Lien reminded Thuyet for the third time that morning. Number fifty-four was halfway down the line of vehicles, an old Dodge motorbus with a forty-passenger seating capacity. "Thuc-oi! Thuc-oi!" Lien called out to the driver. Mr. Thuc, a thin, brown, wrinkled man in his late thirties, smiled broadly and waved back at Lien.

"Good morning, Miss Lien! Who is your friend?"

"This is Miss Thuyet," Lien introduced her companion. Thuyet smiled up brightly at Mr. Thuc. Miss Thuyet used her perfect white teeth and rich dark hair effectively. Her face was as rough as the surface of the moon, but the rest of her body was celestial in its perfection. Mr. Thuc smiled back. "We'll be having lunch at Vinh Hoa, ladies," he announced. "Would the two of you care to join me then?"

"Yes!" Lien shouted over the heads of the other passengers crowding aboard the bus.

"Good. Pay Mr. Lam there, if you don't already have tickets. He'll have your luggage stowed for you. Hurry up! We'll be leaving in five minutes."

"Here," Lien said to Thuyet," take Tan and get us seats. I'll pay the man and have our bags loaded." Men were frantically securing large baskets of fruit and produce under tarpaulins on the roof of the bus. By nightfall the owners would be selling the fresh fruit and vegetables to the citizens of Nha Trang. Lien paid their fare and saw their luggage placed securely between two large wicker baskets full of fruit.

"Whew!" Lien exclaimed as she slid into the aisle next to Thuyet. "It will be a long trip, but I'm excited, aren't you?" She took her baby back from her friend.

"Oh yes! That Mr. Thuc, Lien, is he married?"

Lien laughed. "I don't know. I think so, but maybe not. He never told me, that I can remember. Why?"

Thuyet shrugged. "Oh, he has to sleep somewhere tonight," she joked.

"Ah, you're shameless!" Lien slapped her playfully on the shoulder. "But you know," she continued in a serious tone of voice, "he is a trustworthy man. We have done some black-marketeering together." Lien nodded. "You will get to know him much better over lunch, and I think you will like him, Thuyet. I think he already likes you." She wrinkled her brow in a mock-serious frown and slapped her friend lightly on the shoulder again.

The first hour of the trip was very pleasant. At the end of Phan Thanh Gian Boulevard they crossed over the Cau Bong Creek and drove north along the four-lane Saigon–Bien Hoa Highway. Traffic was sparse at that hour, and by the time they crossed the Dong Nai River, about twenty kilometers outside Saigon, the sun was well up but not yet high enough to be unpleasantly hot.

On their right passed the sprawling U.S. Army, Vietnam, headquarters complex, the principal army headquarters in Vietnam. Behind the fence that ran along the roadside, vehicles and troops traveled the dusty roads. The complex had been built on the site of an old rubber plantation.

"I remember this place from before the Americans came here in large numbers," a man sitting behind them remarked to his wife.

"It was very beautiful then," she replied. "Young people would come out here and picnic on weekends and holidays. Someone once wrote a song about it." She sang the opening verse of a popular song about a young man taking his sweetheart for a ride along the Saigon—Bien Hoa Highway on his motor scooter.

Lien giggled. The lyrics were very suggestive. In fact, "riding to Bien Hoa" had become a euphemism for sex between unmarried couples.

"But look at it all now." The woman sighed. "Barbed wire, no more trees, terrible red dust everywhere, and *soldiers* all over the place." Few Vietnamese regarded soldiering as a respectable trade. "This place is an ugly scar on the land. The Americans with their army are ruining our country."

"This war is a terrible curse," her husband agreed, "but let us not forget, my dear, that the Americans would never have come here if it weren't for the Communists. If camps like this are what's needed to keep us free from *them*, the price is worth it."

About ten kilometers beyond the Dong Nai Bridge, by the Ninetieth Replacement Battalion, they turned east onto National Highway 1. Now the bus made frequent stops, picking up and discharging passengers. There were no bus stops as an American would think of them; travelers simply hailed the driver and he stopped, if there was room.

To Lien's great satisfaction, Tan was proving a redoubtable traveler. Only once before they reached the town of Xuan Loc, some forty-five kilometers farther on, did his mother have to carry him off the bus to change him. At Xuan Loc they stopped for a ten-minute rest, and the adults relieved themselves.

At the village of Ap Run La, forty kilometers east of Xuan Loc, they stopped again, and people bought refreshments from vendors—soft drinks, sugar-cane stalks, bread, cooked rice. Lien and Thuyet stretched their legs by the roadside.

Off toward the sea, a few kilometers east of the village, Nui Be Mountain jutted half a mile above the plain. The sun was very hot, and as the women looked back along the black-topped highway, the heat shimmered like pools of water on its surface. It was only eight-thirty in the morning.

"Oh, Lien, isn't it beautiful!" Thuyet pointed at Nui Be, a blue-black eminence sprouting above the fields like a scene from an antique Chinese landscape painting. A stiff breeze started up and blew the women's hair away from their shoulders.

"Ahhh, wonderful!" Lien sighed. "This is proving to be such an exciting trip, Thuyet! I'm so glad to have your companionship, dear friend." Lien's heart raced with anticipation at the coming holidays. Her suitcase was crammed with presents for her family. She looked forward to the feasting and visiting to come, but most of all, she thought ahead to being safe once again in her father's home.

They resumed their trip. The breeze coming through the windows gave some relief from the heat and Tan slept comfortably. Soon his mother dozed off beside him, while Miss Thuyet moved to a seat just behind Mr. Thuc, where she made a point of getting to know him better.

About twenty kilometers farther on, where Route 2B branches off from Route 1 toward Ham Tan and the sea, a group of South Vietnamese soldiers from a nearby outpost flagged the bus down.

"Be very careful from here to Phan Thiet," a sergeant warned. A ripple of anxiety passed through the passengers; sleepers awoke and dozers started and everyone leaned forward to hear what was being said.

"What's up?" Mr. Thuc asked.

The soldier was a master sergeant, an older, capable-looking man, and he spoke with authority and confidence. His men were young, boys almost, about a dozen of them, standing around and nervously fingering their weapons.

"The VC have broken the truce," the sergeant announced. "We've lost the radio contact with Ham Tan, where our headquarters is, but there are reports of heavy enemy troop movements between here and Phan Thiet."

"Where's your officer?" Mr. Thuc asked. A few meters off the roadway loomed the outpost, a watchtower surrounded by barbed wire and sandbagged firing points. The yellow and red-striped flag of the Republic of South Vietnam, much the worse from exposure to the sun, rain, and wind, drooped from the tip of the antenna fixed to the roof of the watchtower.

"Our officer?" The sergeant shrugged. "He went off to Ham Tan last night and we haven't seen him since. Who needs him? I can do anything *he* can do, and better. I fought the French," he added proudly, "and since 1960 I've been fighting the Viet Cong. I don't need any boy lieutenant to tell me how to fight."

"But if the VC come here, you don't have any men or weapons," Mr. Thuc said.

"*I'll* know when they come," the sergeant answered with a short nod of his head. "If worse comes to worst, we'll defend ourselves with our feet. These men of mine aren't going to sacrifice themselves for this miserable place. Besides, we have a radio, and before I abandon my post I'll call in air strikes and artillery, providing I can raise anyone on the radio and providing anything can be spared for a place like this."

"Good luck, then, Sergeant," Mr. Thuc said, "and thank you for the warning."

"You are welcome. I don't think the VC will bother you on purpose; they'll be moving too fast to worry much about civilians in their way. What you have to be concerned about is getting caught in the reaction, when our men or the Americans go after them."

As the bus rolled forward, Mr. Thuc's passengers, who had been talking with the soldiers, threw the young men soft drinks, beer, and things to eat from their own supplies for the trip. The two groups shouted words of good luck and encouragement to each other as the bus picked up speed down the highway. A curve in the road cut them off at last.

The flag, drooping from the antenna, was the last sight Mr. Thuc had of the roadside fort. It lingered for a while in his rearview mirror, and then at a turn in the road it, too, vanished, leaving Mr. Thuc with conflicting emotions in his breast. He was a man who cared little for politics and less for politicians. In his view, the government that governed least governed best. He could take care of himself if given half a chance. So even though his government, in its chaos and corruption, governed poorly, it was infinitely preferable to the Communists, who would govern completely and effectively and thereby strangle freedom of initiative.

"I feel so afraid for those men and their sergeant, back there all alone with the enemy nearby," said the husband sitting behind Lien.

"Feel sorry for us, husband. We are traveling *toward* the enemy, not away from him," his wife replied.

Lien was afraid, but her mind was working well. If they were stopped by the Viet Cong, she would obscure her baby's face, and if not, she would attempt to talk her way out of the situation. If the VC had the time and the inclination to interrogate the passengers, they would be looking for soldiers and government officials, not a woman with the child of a foreigner.

The Viet Cong stopped them at the village of Ap Phu Minh, just over the Long Khanh—Binh Tuy provincial border and twenty kilometers beyond the sergeant's forlorn little outpost. A roadblock had been set up just outside the village.

"Everyone remain calm," Mr. Thuc told his passengers.

Tan was sleeping. Gently, Lien drew her straw hat over her baby. Masses of enemy troops scurried across the road. They were marching toward a treeline to the west, behind a Catholic church that loomed massively among the paddy fields. A few kilometers to the east rose Nui Takou Mountain, a breathtaking natural feature soaring two thousand feet above the countryside.

"This is an *army,* not just a band of local guerrillas," the man sitting behind Lien whispered to his wife.

"Where are they going in such a hurry, husband?"

"To attack somewhere, I'm sure. Possibly they'll circle back to the northeast and attack Phan Thiet itself. The Americans have a big airfield there."

"What could have happened? There was supposed to be a truce!" his wife exclaimed.

"Never trust the Communists," her husband whispered.

A small group of soldiers stood by the driver's side of the bus. "We don't have much time," one of them snapped at Mr. Thuc. "Your taxes for traveling through liberated territory will be five thousand dong, payable immediately, in cash."

"You won't take a bank check?" Mr. Thuc inquired.

He knew he shouldn't provoke the man, but he could not resist an opportunity to insert a tiny barb into the inflated officiousness of the little military bureaucrat.

"No jokes!" shouted the Communist soldier. "Five thousand dong. In cash. Now."

"I don't have that much cash," Mr. Thuc protested mildly. Miss Thuyet, sitting just behind Mr. Thuc, was both profoundly frightened and wildly exhilarated. At that moment, she thought Mr. Thuc positively the bravest man who had ever lived, talking back to the Communists like that. But if they find out what *I* do for a living, she thought, it's the end of me for sure. Yet it was evident the Communist soldiers would neither board the bus nor search the luggage because they were in a hurry to get away from the area.

"All right," the tax collector relented. "Pass the hat. Tell your people we want five thousand dong, and the sooner we get it, the sooner you may pass on. Quickly, quickly!"

Miss Thuc offered her straw hat, and it was passed quickly down the aisle. Coins and bills clinked and fluttered like offerings at a church service as each passenger dug for a contribution.

Miss Lien placed a crumpled hundred-piaster note into the hat as it passed her way. She recalled that Aspby had told her that in America, because things were so expensive and people were afraid to carry large sums of cash around with them, they had plastic cards for use instead of real money. She could not remember what Aspby had called these ingenious devices, but she wished now that she had one to donate to the Viet Cong. Let them spend *that*!

The hat was passed to the tax collector, who dumped its contents into a canvas sack without bothering to examine or count it. "You cannot proceed any farther along this road today," he announced.

"Why not?" Mr. Thuc asked, but he already knew why.

"Because we have had to cut it ahead. There may be

much fighting here soon, so my advice to you is take refuge in the church over there. Or perhaps the villagers will permit you city people to squat in their shelters." The tax collector and his men jogged back down the road to the roadblock where another bus was pulling up.

Mr. Thuc turned in his seat. "The road ahead is cut," he informed his passengers. "I recommend we settle ourselves in that church over there until we know what is going on or until we can proceed farther up the road. Do not be alarmed. This has happened to me many times before."

But Mr. Thuc *was* alarmed. It was true that in his years driving a bus he had many times been held up for taxes by the local Viet Cong, but never before had he seen so many of them at one time. Something very big was going on here. The sergeant had been right to warn them not about the Viet Cong, but about the cross fire that might engulf the innocent passengers.

Lien scooped up her baby and got off the bus. She glanced at her watch. It was only nine-thirty in the morning. She looked back up the road. Two more buses were pulling in behind theirs. She became aware of a noise in the air, a steady putt-putt-putt coming from she knew not what source. She ignored the sound and scrambled down into the ditch beside the road. It was not formidable, just a drainage ditch that came about midway to her short thighs, but she was encumbered with her baby in one arm and the shopping bag in the other, and the bottom of the ditch was choked with weeds. Beyond them, a forecourt separated the ditch from the church doors. The people from her bus were clambering across the ditch when a dark shadow drifted overhead.

It was a small airplane with one engine in the front. Lien could see it so clearly! The sun glinted off the windows, and its wings tilted and wobbled in the air currents one hundred feet above them. She wanted to wave at the pilot because she knew he was not with the Viet Cong but chasing them.

The people stood in the ditch, watching the observation plane as it soared above the church. Suddenly there was a bang-swish as the pilot fired a smoke rocket into the treeline just behind the cathedral. Lien started at the noise. There was a babble of commentary from the others. Mr. Thuc glanced at the church, a good one hundred yards beyond the ditch. He alone among them knew what that signal really meant.

"Nobody move! Get down!" he shouted. At first the other passengers hesitated. The church was so close. It beckoned to them; Come in and rest within my sacred walls! it seemed to say to them. The plane banked sharply and flew away toward the sea, leaving them standing in the heat and silence of the early morning. The Viet Cong had all disappeared. The tiny aircraft had flown away as if the pilot had been frightened by something, although no shots had been fired at it. Lien wondered why not. There were hundreds of Viet Cong in the neighborhood, all armed with weapons that could easily have riddled the tiny airplane.

"Down! Down!" Mr. Thuc shouted, and crouched himself in the weeds. The others followed his example. Lien placed Tan between her legs and rested her back against the roadside wall of the ditch. Several seconds passed, and it grew hotter and hotter among the weeds. What was Mr. Thuc afraid of? she wondered, idly fanning herself with her conical straw hat. Tan was awake now, his tiny pudgy little fingers fumbling happily for his mother's nose. She smiled down at her son.

A brilliant spurt of flame appeared in the sky, to the right and just beyond the church. The detonation of a brace of 750-pound bombs in the treeline behind the church racketed the air around the people in the ditch and drowned out the roar of the jet fighter's engines. The concussion of the exploding bombs slammed Lien back against the wall of the culvert. Dirt and small stones trickled down the back of her blouse. She clutched her child tightly and stared up at the belly of the second fighter swooping in over the church steeple. Its napalm canisters exploded two hundred yards beyond her, but she could distinctly hear the roar of the flames, and as the greasy smoke billowed skyward, she imagined she could even feel the heat upon her face.

There were now dozens of people in the ditch. A score or more of them jumped to their feet and rushed toward the shelter of the church. Lien rose to follow them. Mr. Thuc shoved her down hard. "Get back down!" he screamed, running down the line of struggling, milling people, pulling as many as he could back into the safety of the culvert.

The first jet came back firing its 20-mm cannon. The guns howled like the raging of a dragon, and the people now halfway between the church and the drainage ditch appeared to vanish in a mist of pulverized earth. The people remaining behind flung themselves to the ground in real terror. The second jet roared over but directed its cannon into the treeline beyond the church.

The terrible machines made several more passes, but now they worked over the treeline behind the church with methodical fury. Lien peered over the top of the ditch to watch. What she saw littering the foreyard terrified her more than the roaring and crashing of the air attack, which in any event was now directed at the fleeing Viet Cong and not at the civilians around the church.

"How could such a thing be happening?" she asked aloud, but amid the hellish uproar, nobody heard her.

The sobbing, cowering survivors remained in the culvert for an hour after the jets finally roared away toward the north, and that hour was hell. Some frightfully wounded people managed to crawl back among them from the foreyard, and others, too badly hurt to move, shrieked and groaned continuously.

Mr. Thuc was the first among those cowering in the earth to stand and face the horror that lay before them. At that same moment the doors to the church swung open, and the village priest at the head of his parishioners stumbled out into the light. With the help of Mr. Thuc, the priest organized villagers and travelers and did what he could for the wounded. Prayers for the dead, like the bullets that had killed them, fell with equal efficacy upon the believers as well as the non-Christians among them.

"Lien, Lien," Thuyet sobbed, "I'm so relieved you're all right!" They had not seen each other since they got off the bus and into the roadside ditch. Lien set Tan on the nearest pew and embraced her friend warmly. "Ma! Ma!" Tan shrieked in delight, and when the women looked down at him he was gaily passing a clear stream of water straight up into the air. The tension broke, and amid their tears, both women laughed at the sight.

Several entire families died in the courtyard, among them the man and woman who had been sitting behind Lien. She had never seen their faces, but she knew they were most certainly dead because they were the only people missing from Mr. Thuc's bus the next day. By dawn, all the wounded had also died.

At three A.M. the next day, Lien awakened with a compelling need to relieve herself. In the darkness she stumbled outside the church to find a quiet place. It was cool, and the stars were very bright overhead. From far away in the north came the steady thud-thud-thud of artillery firing. The sound comforted her because she realized it was made by either American or South Vietnamese guns. And they were shooting *away* from her and her child.

Finished, she hitched up her drawers and stood. Her eyes had become used to the dark. She was aware of gasping and scuffling nearby, close to the walls of the church. She looked in that direction. There was a moving blotch of darkness near the base of the wall. She stepped a few paces closer and was both surprised and embarrassed to see a woman's bare legs firmly gripping the plunging thighs of a man. The man's trousers were down about his ankles, and his thrusting buttocks seemed to her at one and the same time magnificent and ludicrous.

The man grunted and his body stiffened, and the woman's breath began to come in quick, dry sobs. After a long moment they collapsed into each other and lay still on the ground. Lien turned to go, and the man looked up.

"Sorry," he whispered apologetically.

"Mr. Thuc!" Lien exclaimed, recognizing his voice.

"Lien-oi," Thuyet whispered from beneath Mr. Thuc, "you've caught us at a bad moment."

"I should think it was a very *good* moment." Lien laughed softly.

"Your friend is a very special woman," Mr. Thuc said, quickly pulling up his trousers and zipping his fly shut.

"And Mr. Thuc is a brave man," Thuyet added. He helped her to her feet, and she busied herself straightening her clothing.

"Neither Tan nor I nor Thuyet nor any of the other passengers on your bus would be alive now if it had not been for you, elder brother," Lien said.

"I did what I had to do, little sister. Well, let's get what sleep we can. This will be a very long day." With that, he walked along back into the church.

"I intend to see more of that man," Thuyet muttered as she and Lien found their way through the dark, arm in arm.

They reached the outskirts of Phan Thiet around noontime that day. The road had indeed been cut by the Communists, but the travelers, now swelled to a convoy of five buses and almost two hundred people, dragged trees, bushes, and stones from the surrounding fields and forests, and filled the holes well enough to drive over them when they could not drive around.

Lien knocked on her father's door after dark. That night the old man confided to his daughter that although a foreigner's child, he was well pleased with his new grandson.

Soldier's Prize

PRUDHOMME DECIDED TO MURDER HARRY SCHELDT on Tuesday, January 30, 1968, when Harry would next go to his weekly crap game at the Plaza BEQ on Tran Hung Dao Boulevard. The game was always held in a back room on the first floor of the hotel, at the end of a long, quiet hallway that was convenient to a stairway. Harry went to the games punctually at seven P.M. Prudhomme would wait for him in the stairway and, when he came down the hall, step out and pump six .357-magnum slugs into him. He would wear jungle fatigues, without any rank or patches, and a boonie hat, to obscure his face.

After killing Harry, he would take the stairs to the second floor, walk to the front of the building, then descend to the lobby and depart unnoticed in the confusion. If for some reason Harry missed the game that night, Prudhomme would kill him the following Tuesday.

Prudhomme was confident that if Jack were ever interrogated, he would never admit to selling a gun to him.

By rescuing Ana Chin from Harry Scheldt's clutches, Prudhomme had made Jack Kelley his friend for life. Chaplain Williams might be a different case, he realized, but the chaplain was going home soon, and his mind would certainly be on things other than playing detective. Murders and assassinations were a commonplace event in wartime Saigon, and most went unremarked by the American community in general.

The plan was simple and flexible, and Prudhomme liked it for those reasons. And the best part was that finally he did not really care if he got caught. Although he was not at all anxious to ruin his career and go to jail for murdering Harry Scheldt, that he might did not faze him. It would be worth it to rid the world of Harry Scheldt.

He sat on his bed and loaded the gun with the six 158-grain hollow point shells Jack had given him. He always carried his service revolver with the hammer sitting on an empty chamber so that if he dropped the gun, it couldn't fire by accident. But tonight he wanted all six chambers loaded. He reasoned it might take six rounds to make sure Harry died. He would aim for the head, and when Harry went down he would empty the cylinder into his brain. Prudhomme was a good shot, and he would be firing at such close range he couldn't possibly miss. But the sixth round was insurance.

Prudhomme had gone over the route several times. He estimated the actual shooting might consume seven seconds at most. Harry would never know who shot him.

He put the revolver inside his waistband; carrying the big, heavy gun there was awkward at first. Prudhomme walked up and down in his room, getting used to the feel of it. He stopped before his dresser and looked himself up and down in the mirror. The floppy boonie hat obscured most of his face, and the jungle fatigues, a size too large for him, hid his real figure nicely. He looked just like any of the several thousand off-duty soldiers always crowding the streets of Saigon.

Then for the first time, he felt doubt about what he was going to do. Was it really the right thing? He lifted the bottle of Chivas Regal he kept on the dresser and poured two thick fingers into a drinking glass, closed his eyes, and drank. The Scotch warmed its way quickly down into his stomach and sent its tendrils of soothing fire deep into his innards.

He looked into the mirror again and saw himself there. What was it Chaplain Williams had said? You cannot destroy the devil? And there was something else, something about saving his finite sense of righteousness at the cost of his infinite soul? Well, the chaplain was wrong. Man can destroy evil and man must face evil, and it could only be done by slugging it out, toe to toe. Defeat evil by transcending it? Wrong again, Chaplain. Maybe that was okay if you lived in a cave somewhere, contemplating some hypothetical afterlife, but in the real world, evil consumed you if you did not fight back.

Prudhomme finished the Scotch. Evil serves a purpose all right, he told himself. It's there to prove how strong we are, how right we are. "Thank you, God, for choosing me," he whispered to his image in the mirror.

After crossing the lobby unnoticed, Prudhomme stepped into the dimly lit back corridor. It was deserted. He hesitated for the briefest instant and then began walking slowly toward the storeroom at the opposite end. His footfalls echoed loudly in the empty space. He paused and held his breath, listening. Something was wrong, he could sense it. It was only ten minutes before seven, early for Harry but not too early for the others. Normally, fifteen or more men crowded into that room to play craps, and some of them should be in there now, whooping it up. Not a sound. About twenty feet farther down the corridor, on his left, was the stairway.

A tiny voice inside his head said, Those who watch others are often watched by others, and he knew he had been seen coming into the building. Now he was in a trap.

Three men stepped quickly out of the stairwell and

blocked Prudhomme's way. Instinctively he whirled around, only to discover two others blocking his escape back to the lobby. None of them were carrying firearms, but they were well equipped with an array of lethal clubs and knives.

"Purdom?" one asked, mispronouncing his name.

Prudhomme levered the hammer back on his revolver and braced himself against the wall as they rushed him.

He shot the nearest man between his eyes. The explosion of the gun in the confined space reverberated like a cannon salvo, deafening him to the cries, gasps, heavy breathing, and thudding of feet and bodies that engulfed him. With no time to cock the hammer, he fired on double action, shooting the second rushing man through the heart, but the man's momentum carried him forward, and crashing into Prudhomme, he knocked him to his haunches. Prudhomme fired a third time and missed. Shielding his head with his left arm, he managed to shoot two more through the body, but not before taking a vicious rain of knife cuts and clubs that broke his left arm in two places and slashed and gouged him severely about the head, back, and shoulders.

Surrounded by the bodies of four assailants, he managed to stagger upright and face the remaining attacker.

They stared at each other. Prudhomme was covered with blood, his breath gasping and wheezing; the assailant was covered with sweat, his eyes staring wildly at the muzzle of the magnum. Prudhomme pulled the trigger, and the hammer fell with a fatal click.

A misfire!

The man shouted in wild triumph and swung his lead pipe. It struck Prudhomme's right forearm with such force both bones broke with a sharp crack. The revolver flew into the air and fell to the floor right between the man's legs, where this time the sixth and final round went off directly into his groin.

With both arms smashed to limp uselessness, Prudhomme staggered through the rough semicircle of dead and dying men. He was weak from loss of blood and his broken bones sent white-hot flashes of agony to his brain with every step. A wave of blackness surged up in him, and he fought to retain his consciousness and keep his balance, but it was no use. He fell onto his left side and screamed in agony when his broken arm smacked the floor. He flopped onto his back and could only lay there in his blood, gasping and moaning.

Then the door to the stairwell opened, and a sixth man stepped out into the corridor. Tom Prudhomme knew it was all over. The man was huge and black and from one of his hands dangled a glittering machete. It was the Hawk.

"Mr. Prudhomme, I presume?" His voice rumbled and washed over his victim like an enormous breaking wave. And then the Hawk straddled him. "You would not let my people go." There was mock sadness in the voice. The Hawk shook his head and fingered the machete blade. "But you did well in here." He nodded at the bodies piled in the hallway. "They will put up a plaque to you somewhere, honoring your heroism tonight. These"—he indicated the dead men with a wave of the machete—"are expendable. I can always get more. But the Harry Scheldts are harder to find, and you shall not have him. Good-bye, Mr. Prudhomme."

The Hawk grinned viciously and raised the machete above his head. His perfect white teeth gleamed brilliantly in the ebony of his face.

"Goddamn you!" Prudhomme shouted with all his remaining strength.

And then, the Hawk's face began to disintegrate before Prudhomme's unbelieving eyes. His jaw dropped open and spilled fragments of teeth and blood; his left cheekbone exploded in a ragged pustule of bone and flesh; an eye caved in upon itself in a liquid spray; the bridge of his nose collapsed, and blood gushed out of his gaping mouth; and as he slowly crumpled down out of Prudhomme's vision, the top of his head wrinkled and split like a field under the bite of an invisible plowshare.

Tom Prudhomme gradually regained consciousness. The hallway was full of people. From somewhere shone very bright light. Someone cradled him gently and spoke to him.

"It's okay, it's okay," Bill Washington whispered. "You gonna be okay."

"Bill, I—" Prudhomme coughed and could not continue.

"Shh, shh, relax, ole buddy, relax." Washington shook his head. "Man, you shore got yourself into some bad shit in here!"

"Bill, I saw—I saw—" Prudhomme gasped in pain. His body throbbed from his broken bones and knife wounds.

"Easy, easy. An ambulance is on its way."

An officer, a major wearing an MP armband, stooped into Prudhomme's line of vision. "Chief," he said, shaking his head, "what in the living *hell* happened in here?" He leaned down and squeezed Prudhomme's shoulder gently. "You old bastard. I'm sure glad you're on our side!" Then he was gone.

"The chaplain was wrong!" Prudhomme croaked.

Washington looked at the military policeman standing nearby and silently shook his head.

"Easy, easy," Washington intoned. Prudhomme sighed. "That's better, man. Don't worry, I'll go with you to the hospital, so don't you worry 'bout nothin'. Man, am I *ever* glad I followed this old devil in here tonight," he said to the MP. "Sorry, Tom," he apologized to Prudhomme, "but you been actin' so strange these past few days, I knew somethin' was not right with you. And when I come around that corner back there and saw that big mothafuck' standin' over you with that machete, I opened up." Washington swallowed hard and glanced furtively at the bloody thing stretched quietly and now harmless on the floor nearby. "Five rounds right in the bull's-eye," he marveled. "I ain't *never* shot so good in my life."

"It was glorious," Prudhomme whispered.

"Well, pretty good, even if I do say so myself," Washington responded, thinking he was being complimented for his marksmanship.

"It was frightening," Prudhomme muttered. His eyelids were growing very heavy.

"Bet it was, ole buddy."

"And I got the message." Now the light seemed to be growing dimmer, and Washington's voice sounded far away.

"You *gave* the message, brother, you *gave* it," Washington said.

"Thank God." Prudhomme sighed. His eyelids fluttered closed.

"Amen," Washington said.

After that night, Warrant Officer Tom Prudhomme was a better man than ever.

Today would be a very special day for Warrant Officer Harry Scheldt. Today he was going to the mortuary.

The U.S. Army mortuary facility at Tan Son Nhut Airbase was the key component in Harry Scheldt's plan to link the HJO drug suppliers with his stateside mob distributors. The plan was so simple, so ingenious, so wonderfully foolproof, that Harry could not suppress a delighted chuckle whenever he thought about it. He would use the cadavers of dead American soldiers to smuggle the drugs back into the United States.

Last year the mortuary had shipped over six thousand bodies from Vietnam to the U.S. That was an average of five hundred corpses a month, guaranteed; probably more, if the fighting were to pick up later in the year. Already one month had slipped by in 1968, but there were still eleven more to come, and Harry was optimistic. And now that the Hawk had promised to take care of that snooping, dangerous CID agent, Prudhomme, nobody could interfere with the operation.

Harry estimated that he could safely begin shipping

several kilos of the very best stuff every month. Then, as procedures got ironed out, shipments would increase in frequency and size. How much heroin could you cram into a human body, anyway? This morning he would find out. He was taking a kilo of the stuff out with him for the first trial run.

Precisely how the stuff would be shipped from Vietnam and retrieved at the other end, Harry did not know. His contact, a very canny mortuary specialist, had demanded complete autonomy and revealed few details about his side of the operation. Everyone had agreed to his conditions. Harry supposed they were a form of insurance against the possibility he or the mob might try to deal with some other individual.

Harry whistled his way into the shower. It was only six A.M. Well, he told himself, his contacts would figure out the mortuary guy's angle soon enough; that was not his worry. He was only a middleman, and he had done his part superbly. The Hawk liked him; the mob liked him. Who could ask for more?

Harry turned on the water and adjusted the spray. It felt good. Harry liked to shower as early in the morning as possible because that was the only time lots of hot water was available. As soon as the other officers began using the showers, the hot water quickly ran out. Harry laughed. Fuck the rest of 'em, he thought. I'll just use *all* the hot water this morning; let the bastards boil all they want to!

Harry soaped himself thoroughly. While lathering his crotch, he began to think of the Hawk. His penis stiffened. That great big beautiful Hawk! Harry closed his eyes and daydreamed.

The great lunar New Year offensive of 1968 began as a fiasco for Miss Nguyen Thi Lam and her comrades of the 524th Viet Cong Independent Sapper Company. First, there had been no great uprising among the Saigonese, as she had been assured there would be. Instead, the streets were deserted, and homes and shops were tightly shut-tered. Then, her group had gotten lost several times. Worst of all, Miss Lam had become separated when, at the sound of approaching vehicles, she and her comrades had hastily taken cover along a side street.

It had been her own fault. She had hidden in a door-way by herself, so during the long wait for orders to move on, the excitement and physical exertion of the past hours took their toll, and she fell asleep. When she snapped awake, it was full daylight, and she found her-self completely alone and lost in a hostile city.

With some effort, she controlled her panic and fol-lowed the direction in which she assumed her comrades must have gone, but the longer she walked, the more confused and desperate she became. She had just crossed a major intersection when a roaring jeep engine caused her to dart instinctively into another doorway. She found herself standing in a deserted lobby of some kind. There was a flight of stairs at the back, and without thinking, she ran up to the second-floor landing. To her left was a corridor lined with doors, all closed.

Heavy footsteps echoed below. Miss Lam's heart thumped wildly. Outside, a jeep radio blared static and words in a foreign tongue she recognized instantly as English. She had taken refuge in an American building! On feet made light by fear, she flitted down the corridor and let herself into the first room she found open.

Harry's heart skipped a beat as the shower curtain was brutally thrust aside. He stood there in full view, naked, erect, slick with soapsuds, his few strands of hair dangling wetly into his face. He blinked water out of his eyes and squinted in utter disbelief at the diminutive fig-ure standing there with an AK-47 assault rifle leveled at his belly. She was wearing black pajamas and sandals made of old rubber tires. Ammunition pouches criss-crossed her small chest. Under a floppy hat she was wearing her black hair drawn into a severe bun gathered at the nape of her neck. The girl's face was round and smooth and pretty, in a childlike way.

Harry stared at the intruder. He thought he recognized her. Yes, she *was* familiar. But it couldn't be her. That girl was dead. Harry smiled uncertainly at her, but she only stared back at him impassively. This has *got* to be a joke, Harry told himself. Someone had bribed one of the maids to get herself up like this in order to give him a scare; that had to be it!

And then the Hawk's words echoed in his mind: "Where the currents are swift and deep...who will know? Who will care?"

Warrant Officer Harry Scheldt shrieked in terror and tried to stuff himself as far back into the shower stall and as far away from the woman as he could get. His shoulder accidentally bumped the hot-water faucet. It was early, Harry was the first one up in the building, and there was plenty of hot water, too much, really.

Scalding water mixed with clouds of steam boiled down over Harry's head and shoulders. He bellowed in agony and fumbled desperately for the hot-water handle. When he finally managed to ignore the searing pain long enough to get a grasp on it, the handle came off in his hand. He shrieked again and twisted the cold-water handle desperately. It had absolutely no effect.

Harry staggered forward but stopped abruptly before the unwavering gun barrel sticking out of the rapidly gathering fog of steam. The woman's figure was growing indistinct, and to Harry, her face seemed bloated and distorted. As scalding water cascaded over his buttocks and thighs, he closed his eyes and screamed in an agony of fear and pain.

The drain had clogged, and burning liquid sloshed around his ankles. As he hopped wildly up and down to relieve the hell-fire sucking at his feet, one foot hit the bar of soap he had dropped, and he fell with a sickening crunch onto his back. Burning water washed into his armpits while shivering streams of white-hot agony laved his belly and crotch, causing him to utter a mindless, ululating wail of pure agony.

He must have broken something in the fall, because try as he would, he simply could not get back to his feet. It was as if he were floating in a lake of liquid brimstone, the shower head spitting molten torments over his front, the rising water on the floor boiling him in back.

Young Nguyen Thi Lam stood rooted to the spot, filled with fear and loathing, all thought of refuge or finding her unit temporarily blotted from her mind as she watched, horrified and fascinated, the fat ugly American twisting and shrieking inside the clouds of steam. Then the shrieking tapered off into a rasping monotone. She had to leave quickly. Someone might have heard all the noise.

She tore her eyes away from the thing in the shower and padded quietly to the door. Her tiny feet left impressions in the moisture that was beginning to condense over all the surfaces in the room. Soundlessly, she eased open the door and peered cautiously into the corridor.

Carrying her rifle at port arms, a finger resting lightly on the trigger guard, Miss Lam tiptoed quietly down the hall. With the AK-47's stock folded, the weapon fit snugly under her left breast, its pistol grip pressing firmly into her ribs. As a member of an armed propaganda team, Miss Lam used her weapon only for psychological effect. She had never shot at a man before, but if she had to now, she would.

Her heart almost popped out of her mouth as a door slammed open behind her and a strong male voice bellowed in English, "No fucking hot water again!" In that instant, she flitted lightly into the stairwell that led down to the ground-floor lobby through which she had entered the building. The lobby was still as empty as when she had come in.

Far behind, in Harry Scheldt's room, the only noise was the gentle hissing of the shower.

The sunlight coming in at the window diffused beautifully through the swirling, ethereal clouds of billowing steam. Miniature rainbows formed and disappeared, vying with brilliant halos and flashing, spinning globes of light in a silent kaleidoscope of glorious optics that would have enchanted the eye and soothed the brain, had there been anyone there to see it.

Bayonet's Contrition

OATES LAY FLAT ON HIS STOMACH WITH JUST ENOUGH
of his head sticking up from behind a gap in the sandbags
to see what the VC were doing. He was very calm. He
had been through this before. Popeye, shoot straight! he
prayed.

Oates stood up, braced himself against an oil drum,
and fired a short burst into the enemy soldier nearest to
him. He swung the barrel to the men on the other side of
the street and emptied the rest of the clip in their direction. As he ducked behind the drums to reload, he saw at
least one of them flopping in the gutter.

The street erupted into a shooting gallery. The firing
was deafening. But the VC were well disciplined and returned the Americans' fire almost at once. Bullets
*whang*ed and spat all around the doorway, but no one
was hit. As Oates was slamming the clip home in his
rifle, someone ran up on the other side of the oil drums.
Before Oates could react, the man with the shotgun
stepped up behind him and gave the Viet Cong soldier a

load of eight .38-caliber soft lead slugs point-blank in the face. Calmly, the shotgunner then stepped back behind the cover of the doorway.

Aspby was the first to see the grenade skittering across the lobby floor. He was too far away to pick it up but too close to run for cover, so he tried to kick it and missed. He lost his balance and fell flat on his rear. The shotgunner reached down and in one fluid motion picked the grenade up and tossed it out into the street, where it bounced harmlessly into the gutter. It was a dud.

The fiasco saved Aspby's life, because if he had been standing at that moment, the RPG round that came whizzing through the open door would have skewered him dead center. Instead, it passed an inch over his head, flew through the lobby, and exploded with a deafening concussion in the elevator shaft at the rear of the building. Everyone's ears rang with the noise. A thick cloud of plaster dust boiled through the lobby and out the front of the building, coating everything with a layer of white.

The gunner was firing through the front door from a shopfront directly across the street from the Houston. The man with the carbine whom Oates had stationed on the opposite corner had seen him. Rifle-range calm, he stood up, took careful aim, and slowly squeezed off ten rounds. The RPG did not fire again.

Two VC broke from cover and dashed for the main street. They were cut down in a hail of gunfire from three directions as all the men in the doorway blazed away at them, including Aspby with his Browning automatic pistol. Oates marveled that in the crossfire none of his own men were hit.

Oates scurried back into the building. Things were getting too hot for him out there. Another hand grenade thwacked into the barrels. This one went off with a sharp bang, knocking over the very barrel Oates had been using for cover.

Everyone lay pressed flat to the floor, panting and wheezing and loading their weapons furiously. Aspby wasn't frightened anymore, just light-headed and wild to start shooting again. His heart thumped against his chest so hard he thought his ribs would break. He had never felt better in his life.

The lobby was a mess, with empty shell casings everywhere and debris and dust in the air and underfoot. Idly, Aspby wondered what the mamasans would think when they came in to clean up in the morning. The firefight had lasted only two minutes.

It had grown quiet in the street. A full minute passed by Oates's watch, and still there was no more shooting. "I'm going up to the roof," Oates announced. "You men lay low and blast anything that moves by that fucking door."

Oates pounded up the stairs. One man lay dead on the third-floor balcony. He had disobeyed orders and looked over the wall; a bullet had hit him smack between the eyes. On the way to the roof, Oates met two men stumbling down to the lobby, both wounded slightly and grinning wildly. "Purple Hearts! We got Purple Hearts!" they exclaimed as they squeezed past Oates on the stairway. Oates shook his head and continued climbing upward. The muscles in his legs screamed for rest, and he was sweating profusely. I am definitely too old for this crap, he told himself.

Out on the roof Gibson ran up. "We waxed 'em good, Sergeant Major!" he shouted triumphantly, pounding Oates on the back. "They're runnin' back down toward the canal, and there's bodies all over the street down there."

"Any casualties up here?" Oates demanded.

"Two guys wounded just a bit."

"How you fixed for ammo?"

"Just about out."

"Shit." Oates considered the situation. The roof position was a key one for their defense, if the VC were to try coming up the street again. Yet if they had been flanked by snipers in the higher buildings surrounding them, it would get very hot up here very quickly. The roof position would then be untenable.

"It'll be light soon. Do you think help's coming?"

"Yeah. But until the cavalry comes riding in, we're going to hold on here as best we can. You've done well up here, very well. Goddamn, you were fantastic!" Oates embraced the young marine in an enormous bear hug.

"Hey, Chief," Popeye croaked from where he rested against the wall. He patted his M-14 affectionately. "This motherfucking motherfucker mother*fucks*!"

"Okay. Gibson, you have your men keep a sharp lookout down the street, but detail some of your men to keep an eye on the taller buildings around here. If there are snipers around anywhere, they can raise hell with us up here. We'll scrounge the street for ammo and weapons, and I'll send you what I can spare."

By the time Oates reached the lobby again, it was getting light. Someone handed him a hot cup of coffee with cream and sugar in it. He sipped gratefully. Aspby came up.

"Jim, I've served with some fine combat soldiers in my time, but you clerks and jerks did well. You stopped Charlie cold. Where'd you get the java?"

"From the stores you had us confiscate, Goats. We set up a small mess back where the mamasans hang out." Aspby laughed nervously. Despite their splendid success so far, Oates knew he had to keep the men busy and vigilant, otherwise next time the VC came, they might just fold up.

"Jim, I'm going to send a detail out into the street, soon's I'm sure Charlie's gone. We could use some weapons, and we're low as hell on ammo for the ones we got. If the VC've cleared out of this area, we'll be okay. Otherwise, we do what we can. Get me the names, service numbers, and units of all the men on the defense force and anybody else you think did well during the fight."

"Sure, Goats. Why?"

"I'm recommending you all for medals." Aspby began to protest, but Oates silenced him with that imperial wave of his hand he was so good at. "Yes, I am. And if I don't make it, promise me you'll do it for me, okay?"

The idea of Oates "not making it" had never occurred to Aspby. "Sure, Goats. But can enlisted men put each other in for medals? I thought only officers could—"

"I can do anything any officer can, and I can do it better. Now cut the administrative horseshit and get moving."

It was quiet and pleasant up on the roof. The sun was just coming up over the horizon, a brilliant orange ball of light. Aspby loved sunrises. Even hung over, after a night of carousing, or disgusted and frightened as he was now, a brilliant sunrise never failed to stir him.

He paused in the doorway at the top of the stairwell and lit a Pall Mall. He sucked the smoke gratefully into his lungs. Jim Aspby had never enjoyed a smoke more than the one he was having now. He promised himself never to give up cigarettes.

From where he was standing, he could see Gibson and his men over against the streetside wall. Some were relaxing under cover, smoking or drowsing; others peered nervously over the wall into the street below, and others scanned the buildings around about. Aspby lingered in the stairwell. He needed a few minutes to collect himself.

He had known Oates many years, and he had known the man was a war hero, but never had he known just how hard Oates really was. Sure, putting the men in for medals was okay, and Aspby even permitted himself a brief daydream about what a small decoration would do for his own self-esteem, but Oates was doing it as a matter of policy; it was just what a good leader did for his men.

Oates could have chosen to lay low when the VC came by. That, Aspby told himself, is what *he* would have done. But Oates never hesitated to open the attack, even though he had to be plain crazy to instantly convert administrative personnel into infantrymen. Aspby knew they had been lucky. No, goddammit, he chided himself, not lucky, well led. Oates had pulled them through. Nobody else but Oates could have done it.

But this was not the same Billy Goats he'd known in the old days. Aspby shuddered. He was more afraid now of Oates than the Viet Cong. He'd never forget how Oates had socked that old master sergeant out there on the roof. Boy, the stories he'd have to tell around the barracks after this was all over!

"We got a few of 'em," Gibson told Aspby as he crouched beside him behind the wall. "The rest retreated back down toward the canal, carrying their dead and wounded, or what they could carry off. I count eight bodies left behind, but we musta got twice that many."

Aspby looked over the roof. It was littered with dozens and dozens of cartridge casings. "How you fixed on ammo?" he asked.

Gibson shrugged. "A few rounds apiece, that's about it. Top said he'd send up some more if he could scrounge any, but if they come back again, we're in deep shit, that's for sure." Gibson paused, as if there were something more he wanted to tell Aspby. "Jesus, Sarge," he began, "I never seen men in combat before today. It was really strange, y'know, lookin' down at all those Charlies in the street there and them firin' straight up at us! Jesus! The other side of this wall looks all chewed to hell. Man, I could see their weapons flashing back and *hear* the rounds cracklin' all around my ears!" Gibson's face was tense, and his eyes were very bright.

"Well, I didn't see much," Aspby said. "I just stuck my head out the door once 'n' emptied a clip at 'em." He patted the Browning in its shoulder holster. "I got thirteen rounds left. I didn't see who it was I was shootin' at." He laughed nervously. "Man, it was that fuckin' rocket launcher or whatever it was that really scared the shit out of us down there!" Aspby laughed. "It went right over my fuckin' head. If I'd been standing up, it would've nailed me right here—" He put a hand on his breastbone.

Gibson expelled air and thought about what it would be like to be hit by a rocket launcher at close range. "Well, it's daylight now," he said, "and pretty soon somebody's gonna come and pull us out of this." In the street below, several men under Oates's direction picked their way along looking for weapons and ammunition.

"Well, I think the worst of it's over now," Aspby said, and stood up.

"Hey, Sarge, be careful—" Gibson cautioned him, but it was too late.

The first bullet hit Aspby high in the left shoulder, breaking his collarbone and spinning him around. The second bullet hit him in the back of the right shoulder, breaking his scapula; both bullets traveled through his body. The next thing Aspby knew, he lay sprawled on the rooftop. There was no pain, just a vague numbness and disorientation. Why did Gibson punch me? was his first thought, but gradually it dawned on him that he had just been shot.

The sniper shots galvanized the men on the roof. Somebody in the street loosed a burst of fire, and Gibson could hear Oates cursing the man for wasting ammunition.

The men in the street scuttled back to the safety of the lobby. Aside from a few loose clips and two hand grenades, nothing of any value had been found out there; the retreating VC had stripped the bodies they couldn't carry of their weapons and ammunition.

"Paul! Get up on the roof and find out if anyone's been hit!" Oates ordered. Buczkowski returned a few minutes later, following two men carrying Aspby between them. He was semiconscious, bleeding profusely, and his face was a deathly ashen color. He was going into shock. The men rushed him to the makeshift first-aid room, where the two medics tried to staunch the bleeding with sheets and pillowcases.

Oates knelt beside Aspby. "Jim, can you hear me?

Don't pass out, Jim. Stay awake, you hear me?" Aspby mumbled something, and Oates leaned closer.

"I didn't get it," Aspby whispered.

"Get what, Jim?"

"The list of names you asked for, Goats."

All the years Oates had known Aspby, he had figured him for a candy-ass—a pleasant drinking companion and a good garrison trooper, but forever a rear-echelon type. This night, however, Aspby had done his duty. "I'm not gonna let you die, Jim."

Aspby's eyelids fluttered closed, and Oates looked up at the medic who was taking his pulse.

"Weak, but still with us," the medic informed Oates.

"I gotta talk to you." He nodded toward the door.

"Listen," the medic began once they were outside, "we've got to get help soon, or this guy's gonna die. We can't do *shit* for him here. We've got to get him to a real medical facility, and quick. If I had a combat medic's kit, I could keep him goin'"—the man shrugged—"but hell, we wasn't prepared for anything like *this*."

Oates was silent, thinking. The medic misunderstood his silence. "Goddammit, *you* got us into this fucking mess! Now you gotta get us the hell outta it!"

"Help's on the way. Besides, it's our job to hold on for as long as we can."

"Says fucking who? Goddammit, I'll go for help myself if you can't spare anyone from your fucking 'defense' force! Jesus Christ, man, you've had it! You were just lucky the first time, but if Charlie comes back, he'll roll right over us, and you know it. We need real help, and if you sit on yer ass fiddling with your popguns for another hour, we're gonna lose your buddy in there, too." The medic's tension was showing. Some of the men in the lobby had heard him, and heads were turned in their direction.

"Now you listen to me," Oates said carefully, evenly, in a voice loud enough to carry, "I don't tell you how to practice medicine, and you sure as hell don't tell me how to fight this war, understand? We stopped Charlie cold

because the men on this defense force got guts, and they
did what I told them to do. If in the unlikely event—and
I consider it very unlikely—Charlie comes back, we'll
stop him again, okay?"

The medic shrank back into himself. Oates put a hand
on his shoulder. "Just keep Aspby alive for a little while
longer, will you, Doc? The Koreans are right up the
street from here. I'll send someone up there for help
right away."

Out in the front of the lobby, the shotgunner and
Buczkowski were watching the street. Oates patted the
young airman affectionately on the shoulder and then
loped across the street to the two men crouching in the
doorway. They grinned when they saw Oates coming.
"We gave 'em hell, right, Top?" one exclaimed.

"You sure did. Now I've got another job for you two,
the most important anyone's had since all this started.
We need help. Know the Korean compound, up where
MACV Two, used to be?" The men nodded. "Okay.
Move on up there, but pronto. Keep your eyes peeled.
There are still snipers around here. And don't let some
nervous ROK waste you. Make sure they know you're
Americans. Plenty of 'em speak good English. Tell 'em
we need help down here. We need it bad. We have to
evacuate this place, and we need them to give us cover.
And we need medical assistance. Make that clear."

He watched as the two skirted the still burning jeep
and picked their way up Tran Hung Dao along the opposite side of the street. The body of the MP who had been
killed earlier still smoldered, burned black, its arms and
legs flexed grotesquely from the intense heat that had
consumed it.

Suddenly a burst of automatic weapons fire came
from the direction in which the two men had just gone. It
was an AK-47, and there was no answering fire from the
two Americans. Oates's insides seemed to lurch down-
ward with the terrible certainty that his men had just
been ambushed. He peered up the boulevard in the direction they had gone, but could not see any movement.

Oates ran back into the Houston. "Paul, run up to the roof. Tell Gibson he's in charge here now and have him come down. Here." He handed the AK-47 and two full clips to the shotgunner. Oates showed him how to operate the weapon. "Where *you* goin'?" the man asked nervously.

"To get help," Oates answered shortly.

"I can go, Chief" Popeye volunteered.

"No. I'll do it myself," Oates replied. "Think you can shoot this fucker now?"

The shotgunner nodded and hefted the weapon appreciatively. Gibson came up.

"Sarge, you're in charge. I'd keep her buttoned up, bring all your guns down here and on the first floor, in case they try to get back at us. If Charlie does come back again, lay low this time. I'll be back in no time with help. But frankly, Gyrene"—Oates smiled—"the way you bloodied his nose the first time, I don't think he's coming back for seconds."

The men stood looking at Oates, dread and apprehension written on all their faces. "Fellas," Oates said softly, "you're a good bunch. You'll be okay, I know you will. Keep an eye out for snipers, that's all." The men kept looking at him, and Oates hesitated. He'd taken Aspby's Browning, and he began strapping it on as he walked among his men, patting one on the shoulder here, squeezing another's elbow, encouraging them in a low, earnest voice.

"Once I'm gone, shut these doors behind me and don't open up again until you hear English spoken or smell kimchi on some Korean's breath," Oates told Gibson.

"Okay, Top, and don't worry, we'll hang on here," Gibson answered.

"You ain't shittin'," Popeye exclaimed.

"Least I won't be runnin' my ass off for you anymore," Buczkowski quipped.

Oates checked Aspby's automatic, loaded it, and put the safety on. He knew it would not be much use against an AK or any of the heavy weapons the VC had, but he had to travel light.

Oates stepped through the door and crouched behind the barrels. As the metal shutters began to slide closed behind him, he turned and gave Gibson the thumbs-up signal.

It was very quiet out there. Oates told himself again that he was getting too old for such heroics. If I make it through this one, he promised himself, it's the last war for me.

Nothing was moving along Tran Hung Dao in either direction. Oates had the eerie sensation that he was out on an island in the middle of nowhere. After taking a deep breath and then letting it out slowly, he started his run.

He passed the torso of the jeep driver, lying in the gutter beside the still burning jeep. He crouched behind a tamarind tree and surveyed the way ahead. A quarter mile beyond he could see the Korean compound, festooned with barbed wire. Nothing was moving up there, either. Across the street and a little farther up, he could see his two men sprawled on the sidewalk. Obviously dead. In the next block was the Hotel Victoria, on the same side as the John Houston. The place was an infamous whorehouse. There were probably some Americans holed up in there, in from field units, most likely, and enjoying a spree in the big city. They would be armed.

As Oates stepped out from behind his tree, a VC hiding on the second floor of a building just ahead leaned out a window and fired a burst at him. Oates ran under the overhang of the building and squeezed himself flat against the wall. The enemy soldier was just above him. He leaned farther out and fired another burst. The bullets spattered off the sidewalk, and fragments of concrete stung Oates along one side of his face. He took one of the fragmentation grenades out of a pocket, pulled the pin, stepped out slightly, and lobbed it smoothly into the open window above him.

The grenade failed to explode, but the sniper, scrambling madly to get away from it, managed to break one of his arms. Disgusted, Oates fished the second grenade out of his pocket as he ran and tossed it into the gutter, where it clattered harmlessly.

He continued to run down the street, keeping close to the buildings along his right. A figure suddenly stepped out of a doorway, and he shot him reflexively, right between his eyes. He did not stop to see if the man was an enemy soldier or just a stupid civilian. More sniper shots followed him from behind, but they were coming from the rooftops, and the trees blocked them.

At last he leaped over the barrels in front of the Victoria and threw himself inside the doorway.

"Go, man, go!" shouted a black man with an M-16 rifle cradled in his arms. Oates lay panting and bleeding on the lobby floor. He was staring up at two Americans. The white one, a short, stocky redhead with belts of ammunition wrapped around his chest, toted an M-60 machine gun. He swayed drunkenly, chewing the stub of a cigar. A gold Star of David medal hung around his neck. "Whoooee! I am the meanest Yid this side of the Dead Sea, 'n' Moshe Dayan ain't half the bad man I is!"

"We's AWOL, see," the black man shouted gleefully. "We been in town a week, ole Ernie 'n' me, livin' it up and screwin' ourselfs silly. We goin' back up to the outfit this mornin,' until Charlie came to town. We's from th' Dollar Ninety-nine. That's th' Hundred Ninety-ninth Light Infantry Brigade. Fuck this fuckin' 'Nam, anyway." The black man was wearing a gaily flowered Filipino shirt over swimming trunks, his feet stuck into rubber shower shoes a size too small for him.

"We been livin' here a fuckin' *week*, man!" the machine gunner chortled. "God-fucking-*dam*, we had us a time! I been dingin' gooks all mornin'. Must be eight zillion of the little motherfucks out there!"

"Listen, fellas," Oates panted, "I got me some badly wounded men in a BEQ just down the street from here.

Will you give me cover so I can run up to the Koreans and get some help?"

"Run up that street, man?" the black soldier asked, incredulously.

"Yeah. Give me cover?"

"Does the pope shit in the woods?" the machine gunner shouted. "You show me where they are, and I'll waste the little fuckers."

Oates ran out the door, leaped the barrels, and sprinted across the street. The machine gunner leaned out the doorway and fired a long burst back down the street toward the John Houston. It was answered immediately by several weapons, but the machine gunner stepped back inside the Victoria, and the bullets whacked harmlessly into the façade. Then the snipers saw Oates scrambling along the street, and they began to take him under fire. Bullets smacked and whined all around him. He abandoned all pretense at seeking cover and ran full tilt down the sidewalk. Bullets plucked at his clothing and split the air around his head, but he knew none were meant for him, not that morning. He dropped the Browning so he could run faster. The Korean compound was now only half a block away. His arms and legs pumped furiously. Oates threw his head back and opened his mouth wide and sucked the air into his lungs.

A Viet Cong soldier, unaware what was going on, stepped suddenly from inside a doorway, an RPG anti-tank weapon over one shoulder. Running full tilt, Oates's 215 pounds collided solidly with the smaller man, putting him effectively out of the war for the rest of that day.

Both men sprawled and rolled in the gutter. Oates lay there stunned, his head spinning and full of bright spots of light. His nose, broken in the fall, gushed blood. He had also lost two of his front teeth in the collision. Groggily, he managed to get to his feet. He had already forgotten about the enemy soldier, but for a dreadful moment he couldn't remember which way he had been running! Then his vision cleared, and he glimpsed the whitewashed walls of the ROK compound just ahead.

Slowly, painfully, he limped along in a grotesque kind of jog.

Oates was in a nightmare. All the hounds of hell were hot after him with safety only a few yards away, but he felt weighted down, unable to save himself. Each forward step seemed to take an eternity to complete. And then, at last, he stood before the main gate of the Korean compound. It was tightly shut. Rolls of concertina wire were pulled in front of the huge iron doors. Oates flung himself down and began crawling madly through the wire. His mind screamed, Go easy, be careful! but his body would not listen. He chased his way wildly through the merciless strands. Their razor-sharp barbs slashed and cut his clothing and flesh, but he felt no pain.

"Don't shoot! Don't shoot! I'm an American! Megook! Megook!" he shouted, praying he was using the right Korean word for "American."

A small door popped open beside the gates and several Koreans boiled out. They grabbed Oates and pulled him inside. Coils of concertina wire trailed in after him, stuck in his clothing.

Oates lay on the ground inside the wall, wheezing and coughing. His hands and face flowed with blood from lacerations. His trousers had been completely shredded by the wire.

"I'm an American," he gasped. "You speakee English?"

"Sure, Sergeant Major," one of the Korean soldiers answered in fluent English. "You ever been to Fort Benning?"

May 2, 1968, and time at last for Sergeant Major Billy George Oates to go home.

The action at the John Houston had earned him another Purple Heart and a Silver Star, and despite the promise he had made that morning as he ran for his life down Tran Hung Dao, he had managed to get wounded two more times since, running around fire-support bases at night, as if what had happened at FSB Charlie the year before hadn't been lesson enough.

Most of the gashes he'd gotten that morning in Saigon, crawling through the barbed wire, had healed well; a few would stay with him, but they were honorable wounds. Aspby had made it, thanks to the Koreans. The last Oates had heard, he'd been recuperating at Walter Reed Hospital, badly maimed and facing painful months of recovery, but alive with his future still before him. Oates had recommended him for a Bronze Star for valor.

Now the sergeant major stood rigidly inside General Foster's trailer as the division chief of staff read the lengthy citation for his Legion of Merit, the award he was receiving to mark the end of his tour with the division. It went on and on about how he did this so well and that so good, and after a few moments Oates stopped paying attention altogether.

General Foster held the medal to Oates's breast pocket. "Well, Goats, if we were back stateside, I'd have the whole division drawn up on the parade field to witness this, 'cause givin' this medal to you is one of the most thoroughly enjoyable duties I've ever had to perform. 'Course, over here, we don't want big crowds, do we, in case Charlie drops a few in on us." He chuckled. The general was having some difficulty getting the pin to go through the fabric of Oates's pocket flap. "Goddamn thing won't—ah! *there* we go!" The men present, mostly staff officers and commanders from the Second Brigade, laughed and applauded as the general finished.

General Foster shook hands with Oates, and flash bulbs popped. More pictures were snapped as the general handed him the medal citation, bound in an attractive cover, holding it so the photographer could capture the fancy lettering with his camera.

The general and Oates stood together for one last photo, General Foster's arm draped casually over his sergeant major's shoulders. "I have never known a finer soldier," the general said.

"Speech, speech!" shouted the assistant division commander, a brigadier general. Oates had known him since he was a lieutenant, and he knew the brigadier to be an incurable ham.

"Gentlemen," General Foster said, "it is customary on these occasions that the person presenting the award give a summary of the recipient's history and accomplishments. I do not need to do that for Sergeant Major Oates, because we all know him too well for any of that. I will simply repeat myself and say again that he is the finest soldier I have ever known. We will miss you, Sergeant Major. Godspeed you home." The general's voice actually quavered on the last word.

There was a pleasantly embarrassing silence for a moment or two after the general spoke, and then Oates said, clearing his throat, "I hope you realize, gents that I get *another* Purple Heart this morning: the general ran that goddammed pin right through my chest when he was pinning that medal on me." Everyone laughed.

"That's 'assault with a friendly weapon,' Sergeant Major," joked a colonel, the commander of the Second Brigade. He and Oates had served together as enlisted men shortly after World War II.

"Gentlemen, I'll be brief," Oates began. Someone muttered, "Thank God!" in a stage whisper, and everyone laughed again. "I have a chopper to catch in a few minutes and, as a very fine officer once said, 'miles to go before I sleep and promises to keep.' You all know him, Lieutenant Colonel Dickerson, Fourth of the Tenth."

"Hear, hear!" shouted the others.

"It's men like Colonel Dickerson, Sergeant Major Pat Ryan, and young Jones over there who've made this division what it is, not guys like me. By the time you've been around as long as I have, you do things without thinking. But you young whippersnappers, you think about what you do, and that means every step you take out there in the jungles, everything your men do—and I don't care if they're medics or truck drivers or mechanics—*everything* they do is a small act of valor, and it's you, it's *them* who deserve the medals, not old farts like me."

Oates paused. "Thank you for letting me serve with you," he said softly.

There was a short round of handshaking and backslapping, and then, because he really did have a flight to catch, Oates shook hands with General Foster one last time and walked quickly to the door.

It was said later that a thousand men were waiting silently for their sergeant major outside the general's trailer. All Oates knew at the time, as he stepped out into the glaring sun, was that a sea of faces stretched before him. He froze on the top step, staring speechless at all those faces. General Foster and his staff crowded to the door behind him. "You knew about this, didn't you?" Oates whispered over his shoulder at the general. Foster only shrugged.

A young private from one of the infantry companies stepped forward. "Sergeant Major Oates, the enlisted men of the Eighteenth United States Infantry Division want you to have this as a token of our esteem," he announced in a powerful voice. He handed up a leather gun case. Oates took it and held it. "Open it!" someone shouted, and then others joined in; soon they were all chanting, "Open it! Open it!"

Oates unzipped the case and took out an AK-47 assault rifle. The wooden stock had been beautifully finished and the metal parts freshly blued. The weapon had been fixed so that it couldn't fire, otherwise Oates would not be permitted to take it home with him. The papers needed to get it through customs had been sealed into an envelope inside the case. He hefted the weapon in one hand. It felt very familiar.

Oates read the small brass plaque screwed into the stock: "Presented to Sergeant Major Billy George Oates by the men of the 18th U.S. Infantry Division. He won this the hard way. Bu Lon, Vietnam, 2 May 1968." And then, in spite of the refinished stock, the blueing job, the freshly cleaned and lubricated parts, Oates recognized the weapon. It was the one he had taken from the man he had killed at the John Houston.

After the fight, someone had retrieved the rifle and sent it back up to the division. A very strange feeling came over Sergeant Major Oates and for an instant it seemed the weapon was more than just wood and metal, somehow part of all these men now standing before him, with whom he was one, and the man who had tried to kill him with it, with whom he now shared a terrible intimacy.

Oates held the weapon high, so everyone could see it. The sun glinted off its polished and oiled surfaces. It was a simple gesture, but sublime and powerful, and it awakened in all those men something that months of war and hardship had managed to keep submerged—a wild and primitive joy, an ecstasy for life. Oates was going home, and so, by God, would they! All his years as a soldier, all his instincts, convinced him this was true.

"May you all get home safely!" he bellowed in an enormous voice that carried to the farthest reaches of the crowd. "And God bless you, you miserable bastards, every goddammed one of you!"

Wiping tears from his cheeks, he stepped down among the men.

To Purer Reveille

THE HANDSOMELY ENGRAVED INVITATIONS READ:

The Chief of Staff of the United States Army
requests the pleasure of your company at the retirement
review for
GEORGE D. GRACEHART
Sergeant Major of the Army
and the appointment of
BILLY GEORGE OATES
as Sergeant Major of the Army
Friday, the 25th of April
at four o'clock
Summerall Field, Ft. Myer, Virginia
Reception follows
Ft. Myer Main NCO club

It can be very hot in the Washington, D.C., area in
April, and this year was certainly no exception.

Sergeant Major of the Army (Designate) Oates, wear-

ing his army green uniform, sat perspiring on the review-
ing platform with his wife next to outgoing Sergeant
Major of the Army Gracehart and his wife. Oates had
been astonished when the Chief of Staff had picked him
out of a field of twenty nominees to be next SMA, the
top enlisted job in the army. But once he thought about
it, Oates couldn't think of anyone better qualified to be
the chief's personal adviser on enlisted affairs than himself.

Out on Summerall Field the U.S. Army Band (Persh-
ing's Own) was playing Sousa's "El Capitan." Sergeant
Major Oates fanned himself with his program, proving to
his satisfaction that it was good for something. He
wished the review were over, the swearing-in done with,
and himself on the job, free of all this pomp and circumstance. Always before he had enjoyed reviews like this
one, but today the ceremonies seemed inappropriate,
jarring, mindless revelry when the occasion really called
for mourning.

Vietnam was on his mind. Strange he thought, even
after World War II and Korea, he'd really enjoyed Vietnam in spite of the close action he'd seen there. Yet,
since he had come home in 1968, he had not been able to
get the place out of his mind. And now, almost any day,
the country would fall to the Communists. Who would
ever have thought it?

The band was playing "Colossus of Columbia."

Oates brushed at a rivulet of perspiration creeping
down the left side of his face. His sleeve passed over the
rows of ribbons on his left chest, the visible and public
testimonials to his accomplishments as a soldier.

The band was playing "Stars and Stripes Forever" as
the U.S. Third Infantry (the Old Guard) marched onto
the parade field. They were in splendid array, as always,
and Oates's spirits soared.

He thought of Aspby. Aspby, at last word, was still
recovering from his wounds but back on duty, working
somewhere in the D.C. area. Oates promised himself he
would look him up.

The Old Guard Fife and Drum Corps was playing "Jefferson and Liberty." Oates was feeling much better now.

We only serve the policymakers, he reflected, his mind back on Vietnam again. During the coming years, as the Sergeant Major of the Army, the Chief of Staff's personal enlisted adviser, he would make sure nobody ever forgot how splendidly the American soldier had fought in Vietnam. Nobody, in his presence, anyway, he promised himself, would ever put the blame for that debacle on the men who fought the war.

The retreat ceremony started. Everyone stood.

The band was playing "The Star-Spangled Banner."

Old Glory, Oates thought, how often have I fought beneath you, for you, how I love to see you! These ribbons on my chest, they mean nothing. Military glory is really not medals. Glory comes from being good enough, brave enough, and strong enough to represent your people in dirty and dangerous places; true military glory comes from putting yourself between the innocent and the horror of war. Sergeant Major Oates had been doing that all his life, doing it so well that despite the best efforts of her enemies, America was still free and would remain so. For that service, Oates and all those like him, believed they owned a piece of that flag, forever theirs, even after, someday, draped in that same flag, they would be laid in the earth.

If nothing else, he told himself, we earned for the Vietnamese people twenty years of freedom they wouldn't have had otherwise.

"Honey, lookit this." Jack handed Ana a letter postmarked Saigon. She took the envelope and inspected it. After more than four years in the States, she still found reading English difficult, although she could speak it fluently now. "It's from General Ton!" she exclaimed.

Thomas Chang, their two-year-old, implored his father to pick him up from the floor. "What does he say?" Ana asked.

"Fer chrissakes, *read* it, Ana." Jack hefted Thomas and swung him around in the air, making chuffing noises like a helicopter. "Pop-pop-pop!" The boy screamed delightedly, trying to imitate his father's sound effects.

"Daddy, Daddy! Me too!" screamed Daniel Ng, their four-year-old. The boys had "gotten into" helicopters in a big way since the family had come to Fort Bragg, North Carolina, a place that abounded with them.

"Jack, General Ton wants you to come *work* for him?" Ana exclaimed after scanning the letter.

"Yeah." Jack swung Daniel around. The boys screamed and shouted and importuned until their mother silenced them with a scowl and a warning shake of her finger.

"Jack, how is that possible? Has he retired from the army? What about your own career?"

"Aw, fuck this goddamned army. Who wants to go on living in this place, with all these crazy paratroopers jumping out of perfectly good airplanes?"

"Fuckin' army," Daniel echoed.

"You see how he picks up your filthy language, Jack!" Ana protested.

"Yes, the gen-gen's retired," Jack said, ignoring the admonishment. "He's operating an export-import business with offices in Bangkok, Saigon, and Taipei. Taipei, Ana! Bangkok! He wants me to be his private secretary!"

"What does he 'import-export,' Jack?"

"Who cares? He's offered me, uh, thirty thousand a year, to start."

"Thirty—! Holy shit!" Ana gasped.

"Daniel," Jack warned his son sternly, "you keep your ears shut when your mother uses such filthy language." Daniel grinned up at his father. He sensed something very important and wonderful was going on.

Ana's face reddened. "Jack," she said suspiciously, "none of that is in this letter," and she shook the envelope under his nose.

"Aha," Jack remarked to his sons, "she *can* read English, after all!"

"But how do you know this about your salary?"

"'Cause General Ton called me on the telephone a while back and told me."

"All the way from *Saigon*?"

"No, Bangkok. He was there on business. Besides, he's rich. Also, he's serious. Also, I want the job."

"But what about the army?"

"I got my twenty in. I can retire."

In fact, Jack had submitted his retirement papers the day General Ton called him.

"It might be a big mistake, going back there now," Ana mused.

"Go back, go back!" Daniel shouted. His parents smiled at him.

Jack took Ana gently by the shoulders. Motherhood had been good for her. Always a self-reliant person, these last years with Jack and the children had increased her self-confidence and made her even more assertive. She had adapted to American life rapidly, studied English intensively, learned to drive a car and, as the wife of an American serviceman, applied for and received her U.S. citizenship ahead of schedule.

Jack had changed, too. Outwardly, he was still the brash and outspoken Jack Kelley of old, but he was no longer a wheeler-dealer, and he spent his free time these days at home with his family. But he was restless. The army was no longer interesting to him. The job offer from General Ton meant freedom from routine and a chance for a kind of adventure different from any he had ever known before.

Jack kissed Ana. They had so much in common and knew each other so well by now that sometimes words were unnecessary between them. It was not just the children or their love for each other that had grown. It was the bond they had forged that dreadful night in Saigon. Like a frontier couple, they had stood side by side and fought a common enemy. It was a bond few can ever understand.

"I don't know," she whispered. Until she had met General Ton and his family, Ana had never much liked or trusted Vietnamese people. As a Chinese, she had good reason not to. But General Ton was different; he was truly a man who belonged to the entire world. "When do we leave?"

"Friday."

It was June 1973, and Graham Martin had just been sworn in as U.S. Ambassador to the Republic of Vietnam.

On April 1, 1975, April Fool's Day, it was hot and humid in Saigon.

Jim Aspby hailed a cab outside the passenger terminal at Tan Son Nhut Airport.

"How much to Saigon?" he asked the driver.

The cabbie looked his passengers over. A big American with long hair and a beard and a South Vietnamese army major? They could pay. "One thousand pee," he answered in English. Take it or leave it, he indicated with a shrug. Aspby suppressed a flash of anger. It's all over, he thought. The Republic of South Vietnam lay in ruins and he would be leaving in a few days, but this man would have to stay and face life under the Communists. Why not a thousand piasters? He had ten thousand dollars in traveler's checks in his pocket and nearly that much more in a bank back home.

"Okay." He winced as he pulled the door open. He was still not fully recovered from the two bullets he had taken in his shoulders back at Tet 1968. When he was tired, like now, the old wounds still bothered him. Those long, agonizing months recovering in the hospital and the almost endless therapy afterward had aged and hardened him, had put lines in his face and gray in his hair.

Aspby had flown out from San Francisco on World Airways. The plane had been full of South Vietnamese army officers going home to—what? To be with their families at the end, to get them out somehow. The North Vietnamese juggernaut was relentlessly crushing South Vietnam out of existence. Hue had fallen on the twenty-sixth of March, Da Nang on the twenty-ninth; the fate of Nha Trang was in the balance. Saigon's turn could only be days away. It was a somber homecoming for these Vietnamese officers.

The major had boarded the flight at Honolulu and asked if he could sit beside Aspby. Aspby had been delighted, but the major had not said very much at first. Aspby respected his silence. He had enough to brood about himself. He was determined to find that little drop of blood he had left in Saigon with Lien.

After a while the major had begun to talk. His English was excellent.

"My American friends told me not to go home. They say, 'Stay with us, Major Song! We will get your family out through people we know in Saigon.'" He sighed. "They are good friends, but sometimes you Americans promise things you cannot do. I *have* to go home, to be with my family at the—at the end. What kind of man would I be to run away?"

"Major," Aspby said, "I hate to say this, but we Americans are like the man who promised his friend he'd stick by him to the end, but when his friend got sick, he ran off and left him."

"My family living now in Saigon. But I was born in Can Tho, and I served there, in the Twenty-first Infantry Division—do you know it?—before I got job in the Joint General Staff, in Saigon."

"What will you do, once you're back with your people?"

"I don't know." Major Song stared at the back of the seat in front of him. "I have friends in government, but they will be thinking only of themselves now."

"Are you a staff officer?"

"Now I am. Before, I commanded an infantry company for many years. It became—too much for me. But I know people. I, uh, arranged a transfer to Saigon, andthen my government sent me to your Command and General Staff College at Fort Leavenworth."

"We've never met before, have we, Major Song?" The major shook his head. Aspby shrugged. "For a minute there, I could swear I knew you from someplace. It was the strangest feeling."

"Not possible." Major Song shook his head firmly. "We never meet before today."

Aspby made up his mind. "Major, if you help me, I'll help you. I want to find someone back in Saigon, and if you help me, whether I find him or not, I'll see that you get your family out. I know people, too. I promise you that, Major, not as an American, but as a man."

Major Song regarded Aspby silently, thinking the proposition over.

"You can trust me," Aspby said.

"Very well," Major Song agreed. They shook hands and afterward told each other all about themselves.

"James, *how* you get us all out?" Major Song asked as he stepped by Aspby into the backseat of the cab.

"I will, Major. I just will." He had not the slightest idea how he would do it, but he knew he would, somehow. He knew that Jack Kelley and Ana were back in town, and Jack was working for General Ton now. He would start there. Greg Pappas, also retired and married now to a pretty secretary working for the U.S. Agency for International Development, was a minor official at the U.S. embassy, and he would help. Jack would find Mrs. Ba, and she would help, too. And now he had Major Song's help as well. With all these allies, he could not fail.

Aspby leaned across the roof of the cab for a moment. The sun was very hot and bright and reminded him of the first day he had ever come to this land, March 23, 1962. Thirteen years. So much had happened since. The streets were bustling now, just as they had been that first pristine day of an experience that would last him the rest of his life.

"Dear God, how I love this place," he whispered. "I always have, I always will."

He cleared his throat and got into the cab.

About the Author

Dan Cragg is a retired sergeant major who now holds a civilian job at the Pentagon and lives in Springfield, Virginia with his wife, Sun, and his son, Tam.

The confusion...
the horror...
the truth

VIETNAM

one of the most controversial periods of U.S. history